THE BOOK OF EARTH

THE AZIMAR ARCHIVES BOOK FOUR

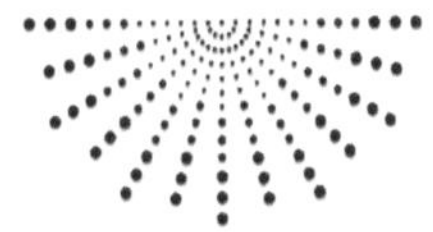

JACKLYN HENNION

Dedicated to Aaron, Diego, Rosemary, and Seamus. Thank you for your support!
And, as always, for Chase. You're the best.

PRONUNCIATION GUIDE

Alastor: Al-uhs-ter
Areanath: AIR-ee-uh-nath (*nath* sounds like *bath*)
Azimar: AS-ee-mar
Dars: DARZ
Doldural: dol-DURE-all (*dure* sounds like *lure*)
Eilonwy: eye-LON-way
Mothlenor: MOTH-len-or
Nevina: nuh-VEEN-uh
Nunor: NEW-nor
Rushavi: Roo-SHAW-vee
Silvana: sil-VAWN-uh (*vawn* sounds like *yawn*)
Suvusa: Soo-VOOS-uh
Tathiel: TATH-ee-el (*tath* sounds like *bath*)
Tiryn: TEER-in
Vyris: VEER-is

AUTHOR'S NOTE

This novel would not have been completed without the help of my Kickstarter backers. Your support got *The Book of Earth* produced when I wasn't sure I had it in me to finish this novel.

I would like to especially thank:

My sister, Josie, and my brother, Steven

Robert and Leslie

Dilly

Doug

Gerald

James

Jonathan

Ron

Ryan

And all of my backers that pledged to receive the entire paperback collection!

A NOTE ON NAMES, THE ART OF NAMING, AND THE MAGIC OF CHARACTERS

I have never been great at creating names.

If you asked my husband, he would tell you that half of the characters of *The Azimar Archives* have terrible, even stupid, names.

Mothlenor doesn't have the same evilness to it that Galbatorix does, even though he was modeled after the antagonist from Paolini's *Inheritance Cycle*. To be fair, I created that name when I was all of twelve and never had the heart to change it.

I *did* change Melonya's name. She was originally Alecto - named after one of the three Greek Furies. Alecto means "unceasing in anger", and Alecto was often seen as a goddesses of vengeance. Or so my scant memory of college Greek and Roman history and my high school Latin classes lead me to recall.

If you Google Alecto right now, you'll find helpful hints on how to defeat her and her sisters as boss fights in a couple of video games and some references to the Carrow family from the *Harry Potter* franchise. The entire vibe the name gives off is not of the loving, doting, always-giving-advice-even-when-she's-not-asked dragon that we've come to adore.

So I changed it. Using a name generator.

As I said. I'm not good at creating names.

In fact, the only *good* name I think I've come up with for this series is Halcia. For the linguistically adept (or those who read dictionaries for fun), you may think Halcia is derived from the word Halcyon. And you would be correct!

But what does a bitter and often rude dragon have to do with a word meant to describe times that were peaceful, calm, even idyllic?

Beats me. It just sounded really cool.

Halcyon can also be used to describe a prosperous or golden time. And Halcia is, after all, a gold dragon. But that may be a stretch.

So, how did I come up with the names I *did* use?

To answer that question, I need to admit that I started working on *The Azimar Archives* in the early 2000s. Like, the very early 2000s.

At the time, I wasn't entirely convinced that boys *didn't* have cooties, cell phones were uncommon for teens and pre-teens, and my family did not have a computer. I did, however, have the QWERTY keyboard memorized.

So I did what any desperate and questionably sane child with ambitions of becoming a best-selling author before the age of 20 would do - I drew out a keyboard on a piece of loose leaf paper and used a pencil as a dart to pick letters at random. Then I played anagrams until I found something that resembled a name.

It was an art.

I'm also not good at art.

I did change some names. As I got older and the internet got more sophisticated (and I bought a laptop), I used name generators and adjusted where I thought necessary.

Other names I kept, but changed the characters.

Nunor was originally one half of a pair of human sorcerers. But I like my grumpy dwarf far more. Alastor was always Alastor, but Alastor used to be the secondary antagonist. Ferrand took his place. And we all love to hate Ferrand.

I guess the entire point to this diatribe is that writing is not a straight and narrow path. There are weird forks in the road, hidden valleys, and perilous cliffs to traverse. And the path from beginning to end is full of danger. Or, if not danger, at least some trips to a bookmarked name generator website.

And that's the fun of it.

TRISSA

"*Mother, please answer.*"

Trissa waited, but no response came.

The king's tower was cold and drafty, especially as the broken window in his study had not been fixed. Trissa wiped snot from her nose with the back of her hand and buried herself deeper into the covers of the small bed her father had brought up for her. She wasn't sure her father wanted to repair the window. Trissa had often seen him standing in front of it, staring out into the grey clouds and over the dirty city.

The bed was too small for the room it had been arranged in, but it was large enough to make Trissa feel very small and alone. She wanted her mother's warm weight beside her, or Auntie Illa's reassuring arm curled around her shoulder as she fell asleep. In her father's tower, there was no warmth or comfort. Even the covers, though they were thick and clean and smelled nice, were not enough to put her at ease.

Trissa tried calling for her mother again, sending out her plea with a steady stream of arcane energy. Her mother had taught her how to reach out her mind to those who could hear it. It wasn't all that different from shouting in the baths, listening as her voice echoed off the walls and wondering if someone might hear her.

Only this time, her Auntie Illa was not in the next room to rush to her aid.

Trissa couldn't tell if it was working, though it had always worked when she wanted to speak to her cousin Arella.

"Please, if you can hear me, answer."

The voice that came back to her was not the one she hoped to hear.

"I can hear you fine, Trissa. But your mother cannot." Her father's voice was calm and cool, and the sound of it sent a chill down her spine. *"Please come here."*

Trissa slid off the bed, leaving behind the heat of the small cocoon she had made for herself, and walked slowly out to the study. Her father was there, watching the doorway to the bedroom. He normally sat in a very tall chair behind a big wooden desk, but now he stood in the middle of the room like he was waiting for her. It made Trissa uncomfortable to see him standing so patiently for her.

He had tidied the study after moving Trissa up to his tower, and there was much more room for maneuvering without worrying about toppling over a pile of books or notes. He had even retrieved several toys from her bedroom and stored them in a decorative chest that she could access whenever the desire arose. Trissa had been too scared to point out that nearly every one of the toys in the chest had not been played with since she was very little. Telling her father, who had nearly killed her mother right in front of her very eyes, that these toys were for babies seemed silly and foolish.

"There you are, my darling." Mothlenor held out a hand for her. It was thinner and frailer than she remembered when she took it. Everything about her father seemed thin and frail, though he had never seemed so before. "I should have told you that I have sealed the queen's quarters. Your words can't reach her, and she can't reach out to you."

"Oh." Trissa wiped her nose again. It had hardly stopped running with clear phlegm in the days since she had moved into the tower. The sleeves of her dress had begun to crust with dried excretions from her nose, and she desperately wanted a bath and a fresh set of clothes.

Mothlenor frowned. "Are you cold?"

Trissa nodded.

"I suppose it does take time to grow accustomed to the chill here." Mothlenor sighed, then pointed at the empty fireplace set into the wall opposite the window. "Would you like to try lighting it?"

Trissa stared at the fireplace blankly for a second. "There's no wood. And I haven't a light."

Mothlenor smiled. "With magic, darling."

Trissa shook her head fervently. "No, Mother says I am still too young to learn magic."

Mothlenor's smile froze. "But you're with me. And I think you're old enough to begin learning." He knelt to one knee, positioning Trissa so that she stood in front of him, facing the fireplace. "Don't you want to give it a try?"

Trissa bit her lip, fighting the sudden urge to cry. "What if I can't?"

"Oh, I bet you can. Your mother and I are both very powerful, after all." He lifted her arm, extending it so that the palm faced outwards. "Let's give it a try, shall we?"

Trissa nodded hesitantly.

"Alright, keep your arm up. Don't lock your elbow. Just like that." Mothlenor adjusted her arm slightly, putting a small bend in her elbow. His fingers were long, she noted, though the nails were trim and very clean.

"Like this?" Her hand was shaking slightly, Trissa noted.

"Perfect, darling." Mothlenor put his own hand over hers. His skin was a shade paler than hers. Trissa wondered how that could be, when she never got any sun and was the palest child in all of Etritia, according to Auntie Ishta.

"Concentrate, Trissa." Her father's voice pulled her thoughts away from her Auntie Ishta and back to the fireplace. "Concentrate, and think of the warmth you want from the fireplace. Think of the redness of the flames. Imagine the brightness of the fire." He paused, watching her. "Got it?"

"I think so." In truth, Trissa had no idea what to think about. She had never given a fireplace more than a cursory thought.

"Alright, then let's light it!"

There was a surge of energy and a feeling like a burning and tingling sensation from her hand, followed quickly by a loud popping. Trissa instinctively shrieked and leapt back into her father's arms. Mothlenor was laughing, apparently amused by her startled response.

And in the fireplace there danced a large flame.

"Very good, Trissa," Mothlenor said. "I am very impressed."

"I did it," Trissa breathed.

"You did, yes." Mothlenor stood, still holding one of her hands in his. "I need your help, Trissa. But is there anything you would like to do before we begin working?"

Trissa frowned, staring at the fireplace. "I would like to see Mother." She did not look up into her father's face, afraid of the anger she would see there.

There was a long pause.

"Alright."

Mothlenor was smiling when Trissa dared to look.

"Really?"

"Of course." Mothlenor stood with a bit of effort and a low groan. "Come, I'll show you."

Trissa followed as her father led her to the great desk. He picked her up and sat her on the edge, her feet dangling several inches above the ground.

"Are we not going to go downstairs?"

Mothlenor shook his head. "No. But we can see her from up here."

Trissa frowned. She desperately wanted to hold her mother, to feel her protective and calming embrace. But she did not want to press her wants further.

Any method of seeing her mother would do better than none.

Mothlenor pulled a small box from within his robes. A half twist of the lid unsealed it to reveal a small and chipped stone about as large as her father's thumb. Her father set the stone in her palm, but did not release it right away.

"Be very, very careful with this. It took many years to find this, and if it was to be damaged further, it might be rendered useless."

Trissa nodded solemnly, and her father let her take the stone. Trissa stared at it. "What is it?"

"It is a dragon's eye. You can use them to see people that are far away." He leaned against the desk. "You can use it to see your mother."

Trissa wrinkled her nose at the stone. "How?"

"You need only think of her, and the stone will show you an image." He crossed his arms in front of him, the long sleeves of his robe rustling together. "You can see what she's doing right now, but she won't see you or know you're able to see her."

Like a spy.

"Can I try it?" Trissa asked, holding the stone up and looking from it to her father.

Mothlenor nodded. "Of course, darling."

Trissa frowned, staring at the stone. It was so small. How could it show her anything? She concentrated, thinking of her mother. She missed the way her mother held her when she was afraid. Trissa never had to even tell her when she needed those embraces the most. Her mother always knew.

The stone changed colors abruptly. It had been a cloudy white with hints of yellow, but as Trissa recalled the way her mother always smelled of flowers, the white darkened into grey and the yellow was joined with reds and oranges.

And there was a little image within the stone.

Trissa held it up closer to one eye, shutting the other tight.

It was her mother. The queen sat in a chair in front of the fireplace in their quarters. Trissa could see the way the fire-light danced over her face. Her eyes were red and puffy, and she looked like she had not slept in several days. She held one of Trissa's toys against her chest. Trissa couldn't be sure which one it was, since they all looked mostly the same, but her mother had it pressed against her sternum. There was a vacant, almost dead look in the queen's eyes.

"Are you satisfied?" Mothlenor asked.

"She looks so sad."

"She will be fine."

"She misses me, I think." Trissa squinted harder. Her mother's lips were moving slightly, as if she were speaking.

"You will be with her again soon. We just have to complete our work here in the tower first."

"How long with it take?"

Mothlenor held out a hand. "That will depend on you, my dear."

Trissa returned the dragon's eye, though she did not want to part with it. "Me?" She frowned, staring at the small stone held between her father's long fingers. "You need my Gift."

Mothlenor nodded, focusing on the stone himself. Trissa could see colors swirling again. "I need you to tell me all you can about this man."

Trissa squinted, peering into the little stone her father held out. From its depths, she could see the tiny figure of a man with red hair.

"That's Commander Ajax." Trissa would recognize him

anywhere. She had Seen him many times and had heard a great deal about him from Nevina.

Mothlenor palmed the stone. "He is *not* commander. Ferrand is."

"Sorry," Trissa said quickly. "I didn't mean it."

Mothlenor took a breath, his eyes closing briefly. Trissa thought to ask why such a little mistake could make him so angry, but decided against it.

"It's alright, Trissa. Just try to remember that titles and names are important. I made Ferrand my commander. He answers to me. Ajax, or Roland as he's been calling himself, is a murderer and traitor wanted by the Etritian Empire."

Trissa didn't know what treasonist meant, but she knew her father was wrong about the man she had seen in the stone. Or worse, lying.

"I need you to tell me all you can See about him, Trissa." Mothlenor held the stone out again, but Trissa did not bother to look into it again. "For the good of our empire."

"For the good of the empire," Trissa agreed.

2

ROLAND

Roland sat up, propping himself on one forearm and blinking sleep from his eyes. The road to Layle's cottage had been long, and his sleep had been short and fitful even at the best of times. And this was not the best of times, though he did have a roof over his head.

Ishta and Roland shared the kitchen and the small entryway as their sleeping quarters. Ishta slept with her cloak wrapped around her in front of the fireplace, which was no longer lit but still warm. Roland had taken a spot closer to the door and slept with his hand on the hilt of a knife. He used no blanket or cloak to warm him. Not when he slept indoors. They got in the way when a weapon was needed.

Roland did not expect anyone to attempt an intrusion. He and Ishta had not been followed from the little tavern where they had met. And the people of the nearby town seemed to care for their witch on the hill.

But it had become a habit to sleep lightly and with a blade in hand.

And something had woken him.

He looked first at the large white stone that sat atop the

mantle. Had it moved again, and had he heard the gentle rocking?

The dragon's egg was still at the moment, though the creature within often stirred at irregular intervals during the daylight hours.

Roland listened. There was no sound within the house. The women slept. Outside, a cricket chirped steadily.

"Ajax, I'm here."

Roland relaxed, dropping back down to the floor and rolling over onto his other side.

Nevina lay beside him, her head resting in the palm of one hand.

She seemed thinner, somehow. Less substantial.

"Nevina." Roland ran a hand over her cheek, but his fingers met no resistance.

"Forgive me," she said, smiling thinly. "I can't stay long. No more than a moment."

"Is something wrong?" Roland tried to touch her again, this time brushing his thumb across her lips. Her eyes closed blissfully, but he could not feel her soft skin beneath the pad of his finger.

"There's no time to explain." Nevina cast a quick look around. "Is this her house?"

"Yes." He didn't need to ask who "she" was.

"Layle's done well for herself."

"She's well loved here."

Nevina's eyes settled on the dragon's egg on the mantle. "And there it is. The fourth egg."

Roland sighed. "And much good finding it has done for us so far. Arella is keeping the dragon within from hatching for reasons she can't or won't explain."

Nevina nodded. "It's not time yet."

"And how will you know when it *is* time?"

"Oh, I won't know." Nevina laughed. "Arella will. And Trissa. They are the Gifted ones, after all."

"You're also Gifted."

Nevina's nose wrinkled. "I'm dead, Ajax. My Gift died with me."

Roland sighed again, letting the matter go.

"And what else has happened?"

"We found the Amulet of Fire."

Nevina's brow lifted, and Roland took the questioning expression as an invitation to continue.

"Mothlenor summoned some sort of beast. Alastor swears it was a dragon made of smoke. Like a wraith."

This time, Nevina's brows furrowed. "A dragon wraith?"

"It was destroyed. Brought down by a fire spirit."

"Are you sure? A wraith can never truly be destroyed as long as—"

"—the soul it was made with is still in the summoner's possession," Roland finished. He shrugged a shoulder. "We haven't seen it since. Perhaps the wraith's soul was freed."

"Or perhaps the wraith is recovering."

"Perhaps." But Roland did not want to consider that possibility.

If it took a spirit of fire to stop the wraith last time, what will it take to do so again?

Nevina shuddered suddenly, her form losing opacity and nearly vanishing completely.

"Are you alright?" Roland reached for her, cursing when his hand went right through where her shoulder should have been.

"I've stayed too long. But I had to see you. Had to see this place."

"Had to see Layle?" Roland asked.

Nevina shook her head. "There's no time. I wish …" Nevina sighed. "But perhaps there will be a day when I will be free to look on her and tell her all that I should have told her years ago."

Roland reached for her again, forgetting already that she

was not substantial enough for him to hold. "We will stop Mothlenor. Maybe Tiryn can find a way for you to be with me again."

"Don't hold on to that hope too long, Ajax. It's impossible."

Nevina was fading again. He could make out her bright blue eyes and the features of her face, though they were nearly gone.

"I'll find a way to be with you again, Nevina."

"Roland?"

Roland rolled over, knife in his hand. The room was dark, but he could make out the small child that stood several feet away. She was barefoot and wearing a rough-spun gown.

"Arella. What are you doing awake?" Roland cast a look over his shoulder, but Nevina was gone. If she had ever truly been there, and not a conjuring of his imagination.

"Nevina was here, wasn't she?"

Roland sat up, crossing his legs beneath him and setting the blade aside. "She was. How did you know?"

"I could See her. I knew she would come."

Roland nodded. Ishta stirred, and Roland put a finger to his lips and motioned Arella closer.

The girl obediently came to sit beside him. "What did she say?"

"Not much," Roland whispered. "She couldn't stay long."

Arella nodded. "She's sick, but not sure why."

"Sick?"

The girl nodded again. "Something is happening at the castle. Nevina is sick, and Trissa won't talk to me."

"Is Trissa mad at you?"

"No, she's sad." Arella yawned. "Sad and scared. She wants to be with the queen, but the king won't let her go."

Roland pondered her words for a moment. Arella rubbed her eyes and yawned again. "You should go back to sleep. It's very late."

"I only wanted to see Nevina." Arella stood again, her feet unsteady. Roland gave her a steadying hand as she stretched. "I hoped to ask a favor."

"What favor? If I see Nevina again, I can ask for you."

Arella turned a pair of very tired eyes on him and pouted sleepily. "Can you?"

He nodded. "Of course."

"Can you ask her to help Trissa and the queen? And Trisha's Auntie Illa. They are very alone in the castle. And Trissa said everyone is frightened."

Roland forced a smile. "I'm sure Nevina will do her best."

We're all doing our best. I just hope it's enough.

"Are you afraid, too?" Arella asked. Her eyes were glossing over in exhaustion.

Roland hesitated, then nodded once. "I am."

"Of what?"

Roland stood, putting a hand gently on Arella's shoulder and guiding her to the closed door of the bedroom she shared with Layle. "I am afraid of a great many things. Large flying insects. Heights. Even the dark, a little."

Arella giggled. "Everyone is afraid of the dark. I meant —"

"I know what you meant, Arella. But it is much too late, and you are much too tired for us to have this conversation. Maybe another time."

The door opened before he could touch the handle, and Layle stood on the opposite side of the threshold. She was also barefoot, wearing a nightgown very similar to Arella's, though the sleeves were shorter. Heavy metal bangles stood out on her pale forearms, and Roland thought he could see white marks around her wrists that might have been old scars.

"Arella, what are you doing out of bed?"

"I wanted to ask Nevina a favor. She was here to talk to Roland."

Layle fixed Roland with an angry glare, but he could only shrug.

"She was only out here for a few moments. And she didn't get to speak to Nevina."

"Maybe next time," Arella managed around a yawn. She stepped around Layle and disappeared into the darkness of the bedroom.

"Goodnight, Arella." Roland met Layle's hard stare. "Goodnight, Layle."

In answer, Layle retreated into the bedroom and made to shut the door.

"Layle, wait."

She did, holding the door open only a few inches.

"I'm sorry. For showing up like this."

"So you've said, many times."

"I never intended to come back into your life again."

Layle sighed. "It would have been nice to see a friendly face every once in a while, but I can understand your choice."

Roland was surprised. "You *wanted* me near?"

Layle scoffed. "You found me shelter. Helped me leave Etritia. And my mother trusted you." She shrugged. "But I was young and foolish, and many years have passed. I've done well enough without you."

"I'm sorry."

Nevina, Silvana, Layle. How many of the women in my life have I disappointed now?

"You can make it up to me by leaving. Soon."

"I can't do that. Not until the Amulet of Air is found."

Layle nodded. "I know."

"I can send word to my nephew. He can help us."

She frowned, scrutinizing him. "Silvana's son?" When Roland nodded, she continued. "Would it be faster if I contacted him?"

Roland raised an eyebrow. "Perhaps."

"Then we will do so in the morning."

She shut the door, not waiting for his answer.

Morning came slowly. Roland did not sleep more than a few minutes at a time. Every time he shut his eyes, he thought he could feel Nevina's breath on his neck and hear her voice in his ear. But when he awoke again, she was not there.

So he would stare at the empty fireplace, thinking of Nevina and wondering why she had felt so thin and insubstantial, until he dozed again. Every once in a while, he thought he saw the dragon's egg on the mantle give a reluctant twitch. But never while he was staring directly at it.

He was sitting up and staring at nothing, listening for Nevina's voice, when Layle left her bedroom again. She was dressed, her hair plaited and draped over one shoulder. She didn't acknowledge Roland at first, and instead made her way directly to Ishta.

Layle prodded the former servant girl awake. "Can you take Arella to town for a few things? Roland and I have work to do, and I don't want my granddaughter to see it."

Ishta wiped her face and sat up. "Yeah, alright."

"Arella has the coin, and the shopkeepers know her well. Just keep an eye on her."

Ishta stretched as she stood. "Of course."

Layle stopped Ishta as she bent to grab her boots. "And don't let her buy any sweets."

Ishta chuckled. "Not even one?"

Roland suppressed a smile. "Who buys just one sweet?"

Layle raised an eyebrow, glancing first at Roland and then giving Ishta a hard look. "Arella certainly doesn't. She'd eat my purse empty if given the chance."

Ishta nodded solemnly. "No sweets. Not even one."

Arella emerged from the bedroom. Her hair was done

much the same way as Layle's, though the light strands had a little more brown in them than her grandmother's. "Auntie Ishta, you're going to be my market companion today. Are you ready?"

"Just about." Ishta hopped from one foot to the other, slipping her boots on quickly. She stood tall, doing a small spin for Arella. "How do I look?"

Arella wrinkled her nose. "Like a boy. And like you need a bath."

Ishta shrugged. "One of those was intentional."

"Go on. Those coins aren't going to spend themselves." Layle pointed towards the door. "Stick to the list. And don't cause trouble with that spoiled little baker's son again."

Arella narrowed her eyes. "I won't cause trouble with him so long as he keeps his hands to himself."

"I mean it, Arella," Layle snapped. "His parents refused to sell to us for a week the last time you hit him. How long can you go without bread, hm? Or those little cakes you like so much?"

Arella rolled her eyes and left the cabin, Ishta close behind her.

The sound of the door closing behind them was the last sound within the cabin for several seconds.

Roland and Layle both watched from the front window as the two young ladies followed the worn path down the hill. Roland waited until the top of Arella's head disappeared from sight before breaking the silence.

"So, she likes to hit other children?" Roland asked.

"Only the ones that push girls half their size into mud and throw dirty straw on them while they cry."

Roland raised an eyebrow. "He did that to her?"

"No, to another little girl in town. Arella punched the boy right in the nose. His mother swears she broke it, but I'm inclined to think his nose was always that ugly."

Roland snorted. "Sounds like he deserved it."

Layle glared at Roland. "From another child. Not from Arella. Not when her grandmother is known to be a witch."

There was another moment of silence when both continued to stare out of the window, though Arella was long gone.

"What do you need from me?" Roland asked.

Layle did not look away from the window. "A picture of Alastor, if you still have the artistic skills my mother told me about."

Roland was surprised. He hadn't drawn in years. Not since he and Alastor took to the road together. "She told you about that?"

Layle was rummaging in a cupboard. "She did. She loved that little drawing you did of her. Do you still have it?"

Roland shook his head. "No, it was left behind when we left the castle."

"Shame. I would have liked to see it someday." Layle pulled out a small stack of scrap parchment and a few sticks of pressed charcoal. "Arella likes to draw, too. So I have a few supplies on hand." She set them on the table and nodded for Roland to sit. "Probably not the quality you were used to having in Etritia, but ..."

"They'll do just fine." Roland sat and began working.

"We haven't much time. It doesn't need to be perfect. Just a decent likeness is enough."

The table was slightly uneven, and there were several small knots where he had chosen to sit, but they didn't impact his work much.

While he sketched, Layle was busy in the kitchen. She put a kettle of water on to boil and disappeared for a moment. When she returned, she carried a small hand mirror and a sheet of crisp linen. The linen she tore into thin strips, each about three fingers in width. The rest of the linen she folded neatly and set on the mantle, next to the white dragon's egg. The egg wobbled slightly at her presence.

From another cupboard in the kitchen, Layle retrieved an amber bottle with a stoppered lid and a clay pot with a wooden spoon sticking out from the top. "How is it going?"

"Just a few more minutes."

From the fireplace, the kettle began to whistle. Layle removed it from the fire and set it and a small washbasin on the table. "I'm ready when you are."

Roland spent another moment on Alastor's eyes. He tried to capture the roguish look Alastor had recently developed. Once satisfied, he passed the sketch over to Layle.

She made an approving sound. "He looks quite a lot like his father, doesn't he?" She tilted her head, examined the art further. "Bit of a troublemaker, if I had to guess. You can see it in that little smirk he's got. And in his eyes." Layle set the parchment down. "It's an excellent drawing."

"Will it help?"

"Only one way to tell." Layle cleared her throat and reached for Roland's hand. "Do me a favor and hold the mirror steady for me."

Roland did as he was directed, letting Layle position his hand and angle the mirror as she needed it.

"We don't have to do this. I can still send a letter."

"Shut up, Roland. This will be faster, and it will only hurt for a little while." Layle closed her eyes, concentrating.

Roland could sense energy moving in the surrounding air. It felt different from how it did when Alastor or Tiryn used their arcane skills. Muted, somehow. Or stifled.

"I have to store the energy for the spell in my arms, then direct it quickly past the bracelets and into the mirror," Layle explained. "It can take time to build the energy up, since the arms are not as good at channeling energy as the palms."

"Take the time you need."

Layle winced, her eyes squeezing shut even more for the span of a heartbeat. "When I say so, I need you to think of your nephew, and imagine his face in the surface of the mirror."

"Alright." Roland nodded.

Another moment passed. "Ready?"

"I am."

Layle's eyes opened. "Now."

Roland concentrated on the mirror, thinking of his nephew. He imagined Alastor's cocky grin, his dark hair that too often fell into his eyes, and his impish attitude.

The surface of the mirror shimmered like water for a moment, then Alastor's face appeared. He was asleep, his chin resting against a head of dark brown hair.

"It's all yours, Roland," Layle whispered. She leaned back in her chair, closing her eyes and clutching one of her wrists.

"Wake up, Alastor."

Alastor did not need to be told twice. He sat up, searching the room. "Roland? Is that you?"

The woman in bed beside him stirred. She spoke in a thick Vyrisian accent. "My love, keep sleeping. It is early yet."

Roland sighed. "I see you've made friends."

"Where the hell are you, Roland?"

"To your left. No, your other left, you idiot."

Alastor approached, tilting his head. "Ah, in the pitcher of sweet water, are you? Nice trick."

"Be quick, you two. It's not easy to hold this spell."

"Who is that with you?" Alastor asked.

"Layle. I've found her."

"Already?"

"And another dragon's egg."

"Very nice. All we found was the Amulet of Fire."

"Roland," Layle warned. Blood was dripping from her wrists.

"I need your help. Can you meet me?" Roland told his nephew where Layle's cottage could be found.

Alastor frowned. "That's close to Etritia."

"I know."

"I'll be there as soon as I can."

Without warning, the image on the mirror disappeared.

"I'm sorry," Layle said. "I could not hold it any longer."

"You're fine. The important parts were said. The rest can wait." Roland grabbed a strip of linen, intent on helping Layle clean her wounds.

"Water first. To wash the wounds." She placed both arms into the empty water basin up to her elbows.

"It's still hot," Roland protested.

"I'll be fine."

Roland poured water from the kettle over Layle's wrists. Her hands slowly turned red from the heat of the liquid, but it washed the blood on her wrists away.

"Now, the serum from the amber bottle."

Roland unstoppered the bottle and splashed a little onto each of Layle's wrists, and she massaged the serum into her skin carefully, getting what she could under the arcane bangles that had cut her.

"This one next?" Roland asked, holding up the clay pot. It smelled sweet. "Is this … honey?"

"Mixed with a few herbs, yes. I keep it on hand for cuts and scrapes. But honey is rare in these parts, so use it sparingly."

Roland drizzled the dark and thick liquid while Layle turned her wrists. Her fingers and palms were slick with blood and serum.

"That's enough. Now the bandages."

"Over or under the bracelets?"

Layle snorted. "Over. You can get hardly anything under them."

Roland wrapped each wrist, tightening or loosening as Layle instructed, and knotted it off by her forearm.

"Not the knot I would have used. But it will work." Layle rinsed her hands quickly in the water basin.

"I've used that knot on bandages for years and never had an issue with it."

"Because it's one you learned for bandages you have to put on your own body. It's simple and will hold, but there are better ones to use when you are bandaging someone else." Layle tugged the sleeves of her dress down. They covered the wrappings on her wrist very well, but Roland could still see the small bulge where his knots were. "And you have this issue." Layle gave Roland a critical look.

"Oh. It'll be fine. Are you worried about Arella noticing?"

"Yes, actually." Layle began tidying the kitchen up. "I don't want her to know that I was doing anything other than cleaning the house and waiting for her to return."

"Why?"

Layle sighed. "I told her that I lost my arcane abilities." She handed the honey and the amber bottle of serum to Roland, pointing out the cupboard where they belonged. "And if she knew I could still do a few spells when the need arose, she would demand that I teach her."

Roland placed the clay pot and the amber bottle in their respective places. "And you don't want her to know how to control arcane energy?"

"No. The world is not kind to those who can do such things." Layle opened the front door and dumped the bloody water out into the grass. "They are returning." Layle grabbed the linen from the mantle and the hand mirror. "I still have a few things to put away. Could you distract her for a moment?"

Roland nodded. "Of course."

Arella and Ishta entered the cabin not even a minute later.

"Auntie Ishta bought me a sweet!" There was honey and a few crumbs smeared across Arella's lips.

Ishta immediately shushed her, dropping a basket of goods onto the table. "Did we not agree that we wouldn't let your grandmother know?"

Roland spun Arella around until she was facing the door again. "Why don't you get started on caring for the chickens and pigs, hm? Maybe take a moment to wash your face a bit, too, or you'll ruin Ishta's chances of ever getting to take you to market again."

Arella groaned but left the cabin again.

"It smells like blood in here, Roland," Ishta said.

"Nothing to be concerned about."

"Anything I should know?"

Roland nodded. "My nephew is coming."

3

TIRYN

Tiryn sat in the shaded interior of the Elori tent, knees pressing divots into the thin blanket that separated him from the scorching sand beneath. It was hot, even he could feel it, and when he wiped his brow, there was sweat on Tiryn's hand.

Suvusa, her hands nimble and quick, had braided and twisted his long hair into an artful design that sat tightly against the back of his head and off his neck. It felt strange to not feel his hair brushing against his ears, but she had insisted that he would be more comfortable with it up.

"And when will I ever have the chance to touch such fine and pale hair again?" Suvusa had asked, running her fingers through it. "I do worry that your skin will brown, though. I don't know that the methods the Elori use to protect the sun from burning us will work for you and the master dwarf."

"I will be fine, Suvusa. Elves do well in heat and sunlight."

But Tiryn had underestimated how hot the desert could get. Though they spent much of their time under the shade of the tent, Tiryn and Nunor both began to darken under the harsh sun. Nunor, his hair done up in a style much like Hiruscu's, had burned patches of skin on the back of his neck and across his nose. His chest and arms, bared after removing his tunic to wrap about his head, were a bright and angry red. Hiruscu and Suvusa had finally urged him to slather some of the red paste they used onto much of his exposed flesh, but Nunor complained of the stickiness and how it dried and tugged at the dark hairs on his torso and forearms.

"It's just ochre mixed with cactus jelly," Tiryn explained, examining the concoction.

"It's slimy and stinks," Nunor complained.

"Use it. It will keep you from burning too much."

"And you plan to use it as well?"

Tiryn had returned the heavy clay vase Suvusa kept the sun protection in. "No. I will burn slower, and I will heal faster. And this will have to last us all until Rushavi and Suvusa can travel and find the rest of the Elori."

Nunor had grumbled quietly in dwarfish and applied the sticky substance without further argument.

That conversation had been several days ago, and Nunor's red and burned skin began to heal almost immediately.

"You look Elori," Hiruscu commented, nodding approvingly. "Like clay, though. Not dark enough."

Hiruscu's grasp of the Azimarian language was not as strong as his wife's, and the couple refused to speak their native tongue in the presence of their guests. Tiryn heard them whisper to each other sometimes, mesmerized by the melodic sound of their conversations, but he had no idea what they said to one another.

It would have been rude of him to ask what they spoke about in the privacy of their few moments alone together. So Tiryn ignored their conversations as best he could and tried not to be too entranced by the mystical-sounding language Suvusa and Hiruscu used.

Nunor, on the other hand, was so enamored with the

Elori couple that he began to act the part of their servant. Whatever need Suvusa may have had, Nunor thought to anticipate it. He was not always right, but Suvusa seemed to find Nunor's strange devotion endearing. She and Hiruscu both began to refer to Nunor as Little Brother.

Tiryn couldn't be sure if it was because of Nunor's stature or if it was because he was sometimes annoying and underfoot. Or a bit of both.

"Little Brother," Nunor remarked, beaming. "Did you hear that?"

"I did," Tiryn said.

"Never mind I've got more'n a decade on them." He puffed out his chest. "I am their Little Brother."

"Will you help with the baby, Little Brother?" Tiryn asked.

Nunor grimaced and shook his head. "Never have liked babies. Too fragile."

Between the moments of quiet whispers in the Elori tongue and Nunor's new moniker, Tiryn felt loneliness for the first time in many years. He had been alone a number of times, but he had rarely felt lonely.

In fact, the last time he could recall feeling true, deep loneliness was the first night after Thessaly had been destroyed.

Tiryn shook away the brooding thoughts of losing his friends and father and concentrated again. He sighed, wiping more sweat from his brow. He had perspired more in the last two weeks than he had ever done in his life.

He returned coalstick to parchment and considered his text again. At the moment, it read only two words.

My friends—

What next?

My friends, I have no idea what I should be doing or where I should be going. I have been ill with sunstroke and arcane sickness for several days and am only now able to stand on my feet for more than an hour without support.

No, better not to mention my own failings.

The flap of the tent slapped open and shut again.

"Ah, I was just coming to check on you," Nunor said. "Suvusa says you've been getting stronger every day."

"I have, but I am ashamed that it has taken this long."

"You were incredibly dehydrated, Tiryn. Did you even drink any water after we reached the desert?"

Tiryn didn't answer. Instead he began writing again, slowly and with concentrated effort.

"Sending a message to Alastor?"

"Yes, it's been too long since the last one."

"Do you think he'll come?" Nunor asked.

"Someone will surely come. And it would be nice to know how progress is on the rest of the amulets."

"Oh," Nunor said, quickly following it with a curse. "Alastor sent one of his damned little birds. Ugly little thing, that one. They were on their way to collect the Amulet of Fire."

Tiryn lifted a brow, staring at the dwarf. "And you've only just remembered to tell me?"

Nunor shrugged. "The message arrived while you were ill. I was more concerned about making sure you survived and keeping an eye on the dragon Suvusa keeps with the babe than remembering to tell you something you may never recall hearing."

Tiryn nodded. "That's fair." He sighed, flipping through the pages of the notebook he held. "Then there are only two left."

"You have the poem for the earth amulet, right?"

Tiryn stopped on the appropriate page. "I would hardly call what is written on these last few pages poems, but I have them."

"And what does it say?"

Tiryn cleared his throat. It was parched and itchy.

"Golden sands keep more than bones,

But secrets lost to ancient times.
The beast as hued as desert eyes
Shall be the one to find earth's missing stone.
Ageless, and aging, and both at once.
Whispers and legends guide the seeker
To what is sought."

Nunor waited, staring at Tiryn expectantly. "Is that it?"

"That is it," Tiryn confirmed.

"Fuck." Nunor put his hands on his hips, wrinkling his nose. "It's useless."

"Not entirely. We knew to search the desert. We found the dragon, as hued as desert eyes."

"What desert eyes?" Nunor asked, scoffing loudly.

"The eyes of every creature that lives in the desert, I imagine." Tiryn flipped carefully through the pages of the book again. "The dragon looked to be brown when I first saw it, but if you looked closely, I suspect it would have greens and yellows in its scales as well."

"And the common creatures of the desert—birds, reptiles, the Elori—would all have eyes of those colors," Nunor said.

"Exactly."

"And the secrets lost to ancient times?" Nunor asked.

"Perhaps the same as the legends that guide the seeker," Tiryn said.

Nunor made a face. "It's a shit poem."

Tiryn nodded. "I suspect Areanath realized he was running out of time." He began writing again, finishing off his short missive with care. His body still felt weak.

"What do you think they are?"

"What?"

"The secrets?" Nunor said gruffly. "The legends that will guide us?"

Tiryn turned towards the entrance to the tent when he heard footsteps outside. "Perhaps Suvusa knows."

Suvusa entered, cradling the head of the baby that was

cocooned in a sling to her chest. "I know many things, but I do not know the thing you want to hear."

Nunor bowed, his braided hair swaying ever so slightly with his head. "Do you know any legends of the Amulet of Earth?"

Suvusa nodded. "There are some."

"Any that include dragons?" Tiryn added.

Suvusa's head tilted. "Yes."

Tiryn closed the book he held and sat in the pile of bedding he had spent so many hours in over the last week. "Can you tell us one?"

Suvusa nodded, then sat as well. She leaned against a heavy trunk and propped her dark feet atop some pillows. The baby fussed, and Suvusa pulled him from his sling and laid him against her chest. Rushavi was naked, and he lay quite still against her. "Rushavi will sleep until Hiruscu brings dinner, so there is time for a story."

"Which one will you tell?" Tiryn asked.

Suvusa smiled. "The first one."

4

SUVUSA

Suvusa cradled Rushavi close to her breast, cupping his tiny rear with her hand. She risked him urinating on her as he slept, but it was not the first time and would not be the last.

She kissed the top of his head, where thick black curls already crept across his bald head.

The love of a mother can withstand a little piss and shit, Rushavi. Have no fear.

Rushavi's dragon seemed to sense her thoughts and moved slightly. She felt the sliding of its scales over her covered breast and a claw against her rib. And then the creature fastened itself to her and began to suckle.

If the dwarf and elf noticed, neither said anything. Not that Suvusa was bothered by it. She was a mother, after all. And mothers cared for their children. She happened to have a child born from an egg in addition to one born from her own womb.

"I will start from the beginning, and perhaps you will find the answers you search for in my telling."

Suvusa settled deeper in the sand, leaning back further against the heavy trunk. All the things their Elori family had

29

left them for the baby and their journey onward were inside. When their supplies dwindled enough, their tent and belongings would be packed away inside and they would begin the walk across the sands to find their people again.

But that will not be for some time.

"Once, there was a god," Suvusa began. "He was the first of all the gods, and it was through his hands that the world was built. He called upon the heavens, and the land came at his command. He whistled for the winds, and the clouds answered. He sang, and the waters of the sea heard him and gathered at his feet.

"After his work, he grew tired, and decided to create night. For the stars, he scattered sand from the desert into the air. The moon was a smooth pebble he plucked from the river and set into the sky. And when he grew cold, he made a fire and fell asleep with its warmth beside him.

"Of course, it was still dark when he awoke, so from the ashes of his sleeping fire he took a warm ember and set it high into the heavens to chase the night away. This ember he named the sun, and with its light he toiled to create all manner of creatures."

"I know this story," Tiryn interrupted. "My mother told it to me once. It is the story of how the first elven gods came to be."

"If that is how you know the story to end, then you do not know it," Suvusa said.

Tiryn dipped his head apologetically and was quiet.

"The god had all the world for his enjoyment, yet he was still lonely," Suvusa continued. "One night, instead of immediately falling to sleep when night fell and his fire was warm, the god screamed in despair to the heavens, cursing that he could not make himself a wife. In his agony, he beat his chest until the skin broke, letting two drops fall from the wound. The first fell into the sand and disappeared. The second fell into the fire and was burned. Seeing himself bleed, he wept.

The first tear was carried away on the wind, and his second tear fell into the sea.

"It was only then that the god fell asleep, not knowing that he would awaken to a miracle.

"Where the first blood drop fell, the earth began to shake. From the depths of the sands, a new god emerged. He was tall and wise with a thoughtful face. He claimed for himself the name Farnir, and Farnir sat beside his father and waited.

"From the fire where the second drop of blood fell, another god was born. He was sturdy and strong, and his voice could shake the very mountains. He named himself Ilir, though the humans of the world came to call him Elir. He also sat beside his father and waited.

"The next god was created by the tear blown away by the wind, and she was willowy and quiet. She claimed the name Vyris and joined her brothers."

"Vyris?" Nunor asked. "Like the elven lands?"

"You are getting ahead of my story, master dwarf. All will be understood in time."

"My apologies, Suvusa." Nunor bowed his head. "Please, continue."

"The final god crawled from the sea, where her father's second tear had fallen. She was beautiful and kind, and when she could not find a name for herself, her brother Ilir asked to call her Ymis, for it was as lovely a name as she was a god. She accepted, and to the humans that eventually worshipped her, she was Imis. She was the last to join her father's side and wait for him to wake.

"When the first god arose from his slumber and saw what had been done, he rejoiced. He hugged each of his children in turn and bade each of them take a portion of the world as they saw fit. They would care for their land and bring peace to the world.

"Farnir wanted the desert from which he was born, and he was given it and the mountains that bordered it. Ymis returned to the sea where she came from, though she loved her siblings and visited each regularly. The elves and humans of the world grew to revere her very much, and Farnir asked her for guidance every year in caring for the people.

"Ilir and Vyris both wanted the land opposite Farnir's desert. Ilir had no birthplace to return to because he had crawled from their sleeping father's fire. And Vyris wanted the land because its mountains were the closest to the heavens, where she said the winds that birthed her blew from.

"In the end, their father granted the land to Ilir. He named the land after his sister, to ease her anger. But it was not enough, and she went north and spent much time punishing the land with her cold fury and the howling winds she controlled. Ymis was able to calm her, and Vyris eventually reconciled with her brother and father. But by then her lands were covered in ice and snow. Vyris accepted her mistake and cared for the few creatures that lived with her.

"One day, their father called the four siblings together. They met at the place where their father had slept on the night of their births and sat silently together until night fell. When their father arrived, he wept.

"'Children!' he cried. 'I have created the world and all that live in it. I have created you, and from you have been given countless grandchildren and great-grandchildren and generations more. But I have still not created the one thing my heart desires most—a mate.'

"The four gods, seeing their father weeping so, wept with him. And where their tears gathered, they were turned into glittering stones.

"Their father, seeing the latest miracle of his children, gathered the four stones and bade his children follow him. In the sand he dug a hole in the rough shape of his image. Then he arranged the four stones within. Where the head would be, he placed the golden brown stone created by Farnir, so that his wife would be as intelligent and wise as the first son.

In her chest, he placed the pale white stone Vyris made, so that her soul would be as light and free as the winds that bore the oldest daughter. In her womb, he placed the red stone of Ilir, so that her body would be as strong as the second son's, and she could birth him many children. And the blue stone of Ymis he split into two and placed each where her hands would be, so that his wife would be as kind and generous as the youngest daughter.

"And from his own body, he plucked one of his own eyes from his head and placed it where one of his wife's eyes would be, so that she would always see the world as he did."

Suvusa stopped for a moment, letting her tongue rest. At some point in her story, Hiruscu had entered the tent, but he sat just inside the entrance, watching through the narrow gap he held in the tent's opening.

"All of these things the first god buried in more sand, which he shaped into the form of a wife. When it was done, he fell asleep. His children also slept, hoping for a mother when the sun rose again."

Rushavi stirred, and all present shook themselves from the trance the story had created.

"Dinner must be ready," Suvusa said.

"It is," Hiruscu said.

"What about the rest of the story?" Nunor asked. "What happened to the god's mate?" He paused, then snorted loudly. "And where were the dragons?"

Suvusa laughed. "When they awoke, the gods were delighted to see that their third miracle had come to be, and there was a wife for the father waiting to embrace them all."

"And the dragons?" Tiryn asked.

"I had hoped that you would understand that much, Tiryn." Suvusa stood, taking her husband's supporting hand. "The gods were all dragons."

Tiryn shook his head. "Ymis and Ilir were elves."

Suvusa laughed again. "And if you ask the humans, I'm

sure they would swear Imis and Elir were human. But you are both wrong. They were dragons."

"And the stones used to create the mother?" Nunor asked.

"The amulets, clearly," Tiryn said.

Suvusa nodded. "So, that is the first tale concerning the gods and the amulets."

"Are there more legends concerning both dragons and the amulets?"

Suvusa nodded. "There are more. I must confess that I do not know them all. But I can tell you the ones I do know. But not tonight." Suvusa sighed. She was weary, and her body begged for rest. "Tonight, I will eat and drink and sleep."

"Who does know them all, Suvusa?"

Suvusa frowned. "Our family shares the burden of knowing all the legends that have passed. If there is a story I do not know, there will be some in the family that do."

"So …" Nunor looked to Tiryn. "If the legend that will guide us is one that only the Elori family can tell us, we will have to wait until the child and Suvusa can travel."

Tiryn nodded. "I suppose that is a possibility."

Hiruscu gave Suvusa a worried look. He likely understood less than she did of the talk between the elf and the dwarf. She shrugged, and he returned it.

She kissed the top of her son's head before tucking him into his sling again.

There is nothing to be done about anything until you are big enough to take traveling, Rushavi.

5

NIEVE

Nieve's village was crowded for several days after their return from finding the Amulet of Fire. Her father welcomed both her and Syrani home with wide arms. Verelyn leapt into Alastor's embrace and spoke sweet nothings into his ear in blended Azimarian and Vyrisian. Her voice carried well enough for the entire company to hear, and Jaimes's ears went red while Eilonwy quirked a suggestive eyebrow at him.

Nieve tried to ignore Verelyn's affections, though they irritated her, and focused instead on Syrani and Halcia. They would stay, Syrani had promised, at least as long as it took to build a suitable home for the dragon. And then they would do their part to continue searching for the remaining amulets.

She had assumed it would take months for such accommodations to be built, but Nieve was both surprised and disheartened to find that it only took a handful of days. With the help of the Vyrisian twins and Alastor, the village was able to expand the barrier that protected them and raise a sturdy but simple framed building to serve as small protection from the weather. It was more than wide enough for

Halcia, and long enough for both dragons to lie snout to snout, which they did for two nights.

On the third morning after the building was complete, Nieve's father hosted a wedding.

The ceremony was a simplified version of Vyrisian and Azimarian customs. Hands were bound, a drink was shared, and Jaimes and Eilonwy were declared husband and wife. Jaimes looked handsome but slightly underweight in a borrowed robe, and Eilonwy looked stunning and graceful in an old Vyrisian dress from Nieve's mother's things. The dress had not seen daylight in decades, but the silver-haired elf looked like it had been made for her for that exact occasion.

Even Syrani and Alastor had both dressed for the occasion. Syrani had borrowed one of Nieve's own dresses, and though the neckline was loose on Syrani's slightly smaller chest, it looked beautiful. Nieve had to routinely chastise her for tugging at the skirts.

"It's uncomfortable, Nieve," Syrani whispered to her over a glass of sweet water. "I can't move properly."

"But it's lovely, and everyone will notice if you keep hiking the skirts up to your knees." Nieve took Syrani's arm, forcing her friend to drop the bundled skirts she carried as they walked. "Just relax and leave it be for a few more hours, and then you can change."

Alastor wore a robe much like his brother's, though he actually filled the fabric out better with his broader shoulders and thicker arms. Alastor had also washed his hair, and Verelyn couldn't keep her hands from playing with his dark curls. Nieve caught Alastor's eye during one of Verelyn's extensive playful fits to give him an exaggerated gag. He replied with a rude hand gesture.

The ceremony itself was very short, and rounds of sweet water were passed around for the guests. Eilonwy joined many of the other elves in a traditional Vyrisian wedding dance, though Nieve noticed that Jaimes did not participate.

"Alastor told me he has an old injury to his leg," Syrani said when Nieve asked. She stood with her hands behind her back and had refused all invitations to dance. "It's gotten better, but Jaimes is still careful with it."

"It's a shame, to not dance with your wife on your wedding day."

Syrani shrugged.

Jaimes and Eilonwy left for Larten not two hours later, once more in their dirty riding clothes atop Melonya.

"We'll be going, too," Syrani said. She had also returned to her usual attire and seemed far more comfortable.

"Today?" Nieve asked.

Syrani shook her head. "Tomorrow, I think."

"I'll go with you, Syrani."

"No, go with Alastor. He is heading for a town close to Etritia. The final dragon egg has been found."

Nieve scoffed. "Alastor doesn't need my help. And if I don't go with you, who will?"

"Tathiel will go with me." Syrani frowned. "And Alastor asked for you."

Nieve was silent. Syrani continued.

"Tathiel and I will be going to the desert, to help their companions there. Their last message said they had found the next dragon, so Tathiel thought it would be best if we both go with Halcia, and Melonya will join us there."

Nieve sighed. "Two dragons are probably easier to hide in the desert, if they can be hidden anywhere."

"Tathiel's thoughts as well. It's the best we can do right now, but we can't neglect the final amulet."

"Which is where Alastor and I will go," Nieve muttered.

Syrani put a hand on her shoulder. "I know you don't want to go anywhere without me. But this is necessary."

"I know." Nieve rolled her eyes. "I just worry that you'll

forget that there are people in the world that care about you, and you and Halcia will fly off and never return."

Syrani smirked. It was small, but it was genuine. Nieve had never seen anything like it from her before. "I could never forget how much you care for me. Or your father. Or …" She shrugged, motioning over her shoulder to indicate the village as a whole. "Or anyone here." The smirk disappeared. "And I will be back."

They embraced. "Just promise you'll reach out if you want me by your side out there," Nieve said. She spoke into Syrani's shoulder, and the words came out muffled.

"And promise me you'll try to get along with Alastor. His father was my chosen brother, after all."

Nieve groaned. "The arcanist will be fine with me. Even his singing no longer irritates me as it once did."

Syrani, Halcia, and Tathiel set out for their journey the next morning. Their departure was seen by the entire village. As she watched the crowd gather to wish Syrani off, Nieve could only think of how much her friend had changed since they had last left the village only weeks ago.

Syrani had always wanted to remain a stranger to those around her. And now the other inhabitants of Nieve's village were waving farewells and shouting well wishes as she and Tathiel fastened an elegant double saddle to Halcia.

The change was a bittersweet one, in Nieve's opinion.

Nieve's father gave the three of them a traditional Vyrisian farewell, placing a palm atop their heads and blessing them. Halcia had to bend down low for him to reach the crown of her head.

The words were just that—only words. There was no power to them, though once there might have been. But the rest of the villagers, especially young Eysa, cheered when he finished and wished them off.

Tathiel stepped into Halcia's new double saddle first, taking the seat in the rear. He nodded once to both Nieve and Alastor, who stood to either side of the Elder. "I'll let you know when we reach the desert and find Tiryn and Nunor."

Syrani lingered for a moment, then surprised all three by embracing each one in turn. She addressed the Elder. "It is difficult for me to say this, but ..."

The Elder raised an eyebrow, waiting for her to continue. Nieve masked a snort as an emotional sniff.

Syrani set her jaw, her chin lifting slightly. "I am very grateful and humbled by the generosity you and your daughter have shown me over the years, and I am happy to call this place home."

The Elder patted her on the shoulder. "I don't think that was difficult at all." He motioned to Halcia. "Go, Syrani. And when you return, perhaps we can discuss sharing your knowledge with our people once more?"

Syrani chuckled. "Of course, Elder." She touched three fingers of each hand to the opposite collarbone and bowed. Nieve's father returned the gesture.

As Syrani passed Nieve, they clasped hands for a brief moment. No words were exchanged, and only the barest of looks were shared. But there was enough affection in that small touch to convey the words Nieve wanted to say aloud.

Be careful, Syrani.

Syrani did not answer, not in any traditional sense, but Nieve knew what her friend was thinking all the same.

Keep that damned arcanist out of trouble.

The entire village watched as Halcia took two lumbering steps towards the barrier around the village and leapt into the sky. The downbeat of her wings tousled hair and billowed dresses. Poor Eysa was knocked to the ground, but the look of awe on her face was endearing.

They all watched as the great dragon disappeared from sight far beyond the barrier.

Alastor approached, putting an arm around her waist and staring up at the spot where their companions had disappeared. "She'll be fine, Nieve. She's strong, and Tathiel is a great fighter."

"Alastor?" Nieve sniffed, wiping at her eyes.

"Hm?"

"Get your hand off of my hip before I cut it off."

"Of course."

But Alastor wasn't wrong. Syrani *was* strong, and there was no doubt in Nieve's mind that her friend would be fine without her.

And her departure hurts all the more, knowing that.

Not that traveling with Alastor would be exactly safe, she reminded herself.

"So." Nieve turned to him. "Where are we going? Syrani said somewhere close to Etritia?"

Alastor nodded. "It's a little town on the western edge of the Felgar Woods. My uncle is already there."

"And when do we leave?"

He shrugged. "Today, tomorrow? We'll have to gather supplies and make sure the horses are ready for another journey."

"I will defer to your judgment," Nieve said. "You know the human lands far better than I do."

"Then we leave tomorrow," Alastor said with finality. "We should consider what to do about a disguise for you."

Nieve wrinkled her nose, already suspecting what the arcanist would suggest. Tathiel had told them how he and Eilonwy had blended in with the humans of Larten without raising alarms.

"How do you feel about pretending to be my sister?"

Nieve relaxed her shoulders slightly.

It could have been worse, she supposed. *He could have said wife.*

6

FERRAND

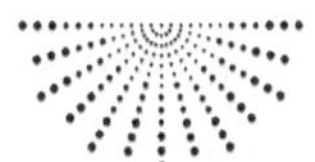

The wine was watered down, but Ferrand drank anyway. Even the king could no longer reliably procure suitable drink, it seemed. What should have been a slightly sweet and earthy red was instead nearly indistinguishable from the more common and cheaper varieties of ruby elixirs the rest of his men suckled.

And if the King's Guard were forced to drink such poor libations, then what of the filth of the city? Clean water was a rare resource outside of the castle. The ale they imbibed was surely similar in many ways to their own piss.

Ferrand finished his wine and poured more.

Any man too consumed by fear to rise above his own station deserves the misfortunes of hunger and thirst.

After all, Ferrand himself was proof that it could be done.

"Ferrand the Whore."

The memory of Jorvun's voice made his stomach twist.

"Commander?"

Ferrand suppressed his surprised jump and turned. A young knight stood in the open doorway of the barracks. His surcoat was too large on his slim shoulders, and the end of the belt around his hips trailed down below his knees.

"What?"

Is this the sort of man we're now accepting into our numbers? Has he ever even been with a woman?

"The king has sent for you. He asks that you come right away."

Ferrand sighed and took another sip of his drink.

"Sir?"

"I heard you, boy." Ferrand glanced over his shoulder at him. "Who confirmed your appointment, knight?"

"Knight S-Sorrenson, sir," the knight stammered. "Only just last week."

"And where is Sorrenson?" Ferrand asked. It was hard enough to put a face to the name.

The child knight didn't reply right away, so Ferrand turned to face him.

"Well?"

The boy fidgeted with his belt. "No one has seen him for a few days, Commander. He seems to be missing."

Missing ...

There was a time when missing meant that a knight had likely fled the city. They were sometimes hunted down and killed for their desertion. Some, those who planned and properly prepared for their flight from Etritia, were never found. But as the number of missing knights continued to grow, it became clear that something far worse than desertion was at hand.

A plague had spread across Etritia over the last few years. This plague did not kill slowly, and it focused entirely on King's Guards. Their bodies were found in alleyways and abandoned homes, with throats cut or necks broken. One had even been found hanging from the gallows days, perhaps a week, after he had been strung up. The knight's face was unrecognizable, and it was only from the tattoo on his hand that they were able to identify him. He had been hung between two thieving Etritian citizens, but removing the black bag over his head had revealed that he had been stabbed in the throat.

The only thing they shared in common was a missing sigil from their surcoats.

"Commander?" the boy said. "The king is waiting."

"I heard you."

Ferrand finished his drink before standing. "Find Sorrenson. I'm sure he's somewhere in the city. Let me know where his body was left."

"Yes, sir."

It was not a far walk from the barracks to the kitchen entrance of the castle. That particular entrance was not the closest to Mothlenor's tower, but he did not mind meandering through the quiet and still halls of the castle.

When he had first navigated them, while Mothlenor's brother still held the throne, they had been bright and busy and filled with laughter and chatter. Now, aside from the occasional King's Guard, he usually only ever met one other person in the desolate halls.

Illa was in the kitchen, as he suspected she would be. Why she still bothered to cook meals when there was hardly anyone to enjoy them escaped him, but it afforded Ferrand the opportunity to enjoy her company whenever he desired. And her meals, though they had grown paltry over the years, were delicious.

"Illa, my darling, what has the queen requested for her dinner today?" Ferrand asked. She did not jump or twitch at the sound of his voice. No, she was a strong one, and she did not show her fear so easily.

"You know as well as I do that the queen has not been eating as of late, Commander," Illa answered. She was cutting vegetables, each stroke of her knife quick and calculated. "But I am preparing a vegetable soup in the hope that I can coax her into taking a few bites tonight. And Trissa loves carrots."

Ferrand eyed the pathetic collection of vegetables on the counter. There were a small number of fingerling potatoes, which had been washed and likely deemed too small for cutting. There was a head of leafy greens. Cabbage, if Ferrand had to guess. It was rusted, but still edible. And finally …

"I only see one carrot, love."

"They have been difficult to procure. But Trissa will forgive me, I have no doubt."

Ferrand pressed his body against her and placed a hand over each of hers. He pushed hard on her fingers until she released the knife she had been clutching tightly enough for her knuckles to turn white. "You do realize that you are speaking to one of the few men in Etritia who could bring you all the carrots your little princess desires, do you not?"

"I do," Illa answered stiffly.

"But you do not ask?" Ferrand gripped Illa's wrists, small and bony enough to belong to a child.

"It would be inappropriate of me to ask it of you, Commander." Her voice still did not quiver. "You have more important things to concern yourself with."

"You are very brave, Illa, to assume to know what I find important." Both of her wrists fit nicely in one hand, and it was easy to hold her arms in place on the table. With his other, he pulled her hips back slightly, then pressed the side of her face into her vegetable cuttings.

The knife and several potatoes clattered and thumped to the floor.

"While I have you in this rather delicate position, there is something that has been weighing on my mind that I hope you could perhaps help me understand."

"Of course, Commander," Illa said. Her breathing was labored under the pressure of her chest against the table. Still, her voice did not betray the fear he could smell on her.

"Someone has been murdering my King's Guards. Would you happen to know anything about it?"

Illa hesitated for the briefest of seconds before answering. "Murdering King's Guards? I'm not sure anyone is capable of such a monstrous thing."

"You seem rather adept with that knife. Could you perhaps be the one?"

"Never, Commander." She winced. "I apologize, but I believe there is a carrot poking me in my rib."

Ferrand smirked. He found the offending carrot and tossed it across the room. "Better, darling?"

"Much."

"I ask again. Do you know who could be killing my King's Guards?"

"If I did, I would have reported it when last we met, Commander."

"I thought so. But it is never poor thinking to ask."

He didn't believe her for a second. "I rather enjoy your company, Illa." He lifted the skirts of her dress, exposing nothing but bare buttocks beneath. "I think I require another few moments of your time."

"Of course, Commander. However, may I make one request?"

Ferrand smirked again. "You may request, but I may not oblige."

"Would you consider not leaving your seed in me?"

It was a simple enough request.

And it would be a shame if she were to die in childbirth like so many other women I have favored over the years.

"I will consider it, yes."

"Thank you, Commander."

When the time came, he spent himself on her inner thigh, and she once again thanked him for doing so.

"It was nothing. I have enough bastards running through the streets of Etritia, I think. I do not need another."

Illa straightened her dress, covering herself once more.

Ferrand tied his breeches with quick gestures. "Tell your princess that she will have carrots enough to make her sick this time next week. I will see to it, darling."

"You are generous and thoughtful, Commander," Illa said.

She bent to retrieve her knife, but Ferrand grabbed it first. They straightened together, staring at each other. Her voice and words may have never held fear, but her eyes did.

"And if I find that you know who has been killing my men, you will join them on the gallows. Do you understand?"

"I understand, Commander."

He flipped the blade over, handing it to her hilt first. "Good."

Illa turned and resumed cutting vegetables, though most were now scattered along the floor at her feet.

Ferrand left her, headed for Mothlenor's tower.

He may receive a scolding for delaying his king, but there was little concern for anything more severe than a few harsh words. And if Mothlenor knew there was a killer in the city . . .

No, best not to tell him. I don't need him questioning my ability to keep the city under control. Not now, when we could very well turn the hunt for the amulets in our favor.

The stairs to Mothlenor's tower were warm. They had never been warm in the past. Gone was the usual icy chill of arcane energy oozing from the very stone. There was no eerie sensation of being watched as he took the steps, no flickering shadow just outside the periphery of his only remaining eye.

It was no wonder that Mothlenor had sent someone for him, rather than Calling on Ferrand himself. Ferrand was accustomed to being roused at all hours of the day by his king's voice. He had spoken to Mothlenor through wine glasses, dozens of mirrors, pitchers of water and ale, even puddles of horse piss.

He must still be too weak from controlling the dragon wraith.

It was the only explanation Ferrand could think of.

As he reached the final steps of the tower's long staircase, he picked up the sound of a child crying.

Trissa.

The princess had not stopped her wailing for more than a few hours at a time since she had been whisked away from her mother's arms. Mothlenor always seemed annoyed by her tears, but Ferrand had not heard him raise his voice at the girl even once. Nor had he struck her or berated her since she had taken up residence in his tower.

Ferrand disapproved of the king's coddling of his daughter, but did not dare to say so.

He knocked on the door, unsurprised when it opened slowly with the slightest touch.

"My lord?" Ferrand asked as he entered. "You sent for me."

Mothlenor stood in front of the window, staring out across the city. The window, broken during the wrangling of his dragon wraith, had not been repaired. Debris, stray leaves and dust, littered the floor of his study. The room was colder than the stairs, likely due to the window and not Mothlenor's returning arcane energy.

Trissa was nowhere to be seen, but she could still be heard, sniffling and sobbing in the bedroom beyond the tower's main room.

"How goes the task of growing my army?"

Ferrand barely managed to change his sigh to a throat-clearing cough before it finished passing his lips. "I have recruited every able-bodied man in Etritia and in the surrounding cities, save for those that are needed for the mines and hard labor."

"Have the women do the labor. Take those men as well."

"Yes, my lord."

"And how far will that get us?"

Ferrand knew the answer, but hesitated.

"Commander." Mothlenor turned, facing Ferrand. "How far will that get us?"

Mothlenor's face had changed drastically since his encounter with the dragon wraith. There were deep wrinkles around his eyes and frown lines around his mouth and on his brow. Even his hair had greyed significantly. There were rumors among the King's Guard that Mothlenor kept his body young through arcane means, and Ferrand knew he had changed little in the years since they had met.

But the sudden alteration was alarming.

"It will not be enough, my lord," Ferrand finally answered.

"Have you sent men south?"

"South?"

"To the Free Cities." Mothlenor raised an eyebrow. "There are men there, are there not?"

Ferrand scoffed. "The Free Cities are *free*. We have no right to call their men to war."

"I am the king." Mothlenor's face contorted. "I have every right!"

Ferrand sighed. "Very well. I will send men south."

"Good." Mothlenor turned to face the window again.

Ferrand cleared his throat again, unsure if he wanted to broach the next topic. "And what of the rumors that the Free Cities have been plagued by those who sympathize with the non-human heathens?"

"Your men can investigate. And dole out due punishments."

"Very well, my lord." Ferrand turned, ready to leave the dismal tower behind him.

"Commander," Mothlenor said. His voice was quiet, but there was still more than a hint of the dangerous power he still possessed carried in that single word. "Take the princess back to her mother. Her cries tire me, and I can return her to me as the need arises."

Ferrand raised his only remaining eyebrow. "Of course, my lord. But would it be perhaps better to keep her in a room close to the tower, but still separate from her mother? The queen will undoubtedly resist you removing the child once she is able to hold her again."

Mothlenor scoffed. "You think too much like a northerner, Ferrand. Anna will resist, yes. But she knows she does not have the strength to truly fight against me. She will relent and do as I say. Especially if she knows that Trissa will be returned to her periodically if they both behave themselves."

Ferrand was not so sure that he agreed with Mothlenor. Anna may not be physically strong or exceptionally gifted in the arcane. But if Mothlenor's power did not return to him quickly …

"Did you have another issue with my request, Ferrand?" Mothlenor turned a steely gaze on him, and a sudden chill brushed against Ferrand's arms and face.

"Of course not, my lord."

"Then take the child from my sight."

Mothlenor called for his daughter, and she emerged slowly from the adjacent room. Her face was red and tear streaked, and she wiped at her nose more than once as she crossed to stand beside Ferrand.

Trissa's tears slowed and eventually stopped as they left Mothlenor's tower.

Her father had not wished her a farewell, and the princess had not offered him one.

Only when they left the curved staircase behind did Trissa finally speak. "I don't like it there."

"And why not?" Ferrand asked. He held the small child's hand, much to his disgust. But she had insisted, and he did not want to refuse such a small request while in Mothlenor's presence.

"People have died there."

"People have died everywhere, princess," Ferrand answered. "If you cried every time you came to a place where someone spent the last moments of their life, you would never stop shedding tears."

"But they died *badly* there. It frightens me."

Ferrand rolled his eye. He did not question the princess on her meaning of *badly*, despite his curiosity. He knew Nevina, the Coven witch, had been killed there. He had been one of the first to see her body and had overseen the disposal of it himself. But if there were others like her, he did not know.

It wouldn't surprise him, though.

They turned a corner, leaving the more formal parts of the castle behind them and entering the long row of bedrooms.

Once, these had all been filled with family and trusted servants of the king.

Now, all but one was empty.

"Your mother will be happy to see us, I think."

"She won't be happy to see you."

Ferrand could have slapped the little shit. Instead he glared down at her, but she was unfazed.

Damned brat.

"And do you know why that is, princess?"

Trissa's chin lifted slightly. "She says you are a cruel and mean northerner. And that you hurt people."

"Your mother is quite correct. So, if I were in your position, I would refrain from making remarks that might upset cruel and mean northerners."

"I am not afraid."

Ferrand couldn't help the annoyed sneer that curled his lips. The scarred flesh of the burnt half of his face tugged unpleasantly. *You should be, princess.*

"You are afraid of ghosts, but not of the man that raped and murdered nearly all of your kin? You are very foolish, little girl."

Trissa finally released his hand, but it was not the frightened jerk he had hoped for. She dropped her hand from his and reached instead for the ornate handle of a door undistinguishable from the ones on either side of it.

"I have seen your end, Ferrand Whoreson, and I can promise you that it will be a fitting one."

The door opened with a light push from the child. Ferrand knew the room had previously been sealed off, but Mothlenor had released the locking spell only a day or two after casting it. Or, Ferrand assumed, it had become too difficult for Mothlenor to maintain in his weakened state and he had simply let the spell dissolve.

The room beyond the threshold was bathed in the warm red glow of firelight. Anna was curled at the foot of a plush chair, her head leaning against the seat as if it were a pillow. Illa, the kitchen wench he had only recently fucked like a filthy whore, sat in the chair and caressed her queen's head.

Both women looked up as Trissa proudly announced her return. The door swung shut before Ferrand had the chance to question the princess on her words.

He stood, listening to the murmuring on the opposite side of the door.

Whoreson.

The word had come from Trissa's mouth without the slightest hint of uncertainty.

Ferrand spat on the door. "Little Coven bitch."

The princess's words hounded him all through his return to the barracks.

He ordered all his best men, the ones more likely to be murdered in the streets of Etritia, to march south. He didn't have many left, and only one that he truly trusted.

Dirk may have been murdered only a few weeks before, and Brynne may have died with the *Kingfisher* years ago, but he still had Clay to see to the tasks he commanded. Clay would bring him men to recruit and elves to kill.

And Clay had a penchant for violence that only Ferrand himself could surpass.

All the while, Trissa's childish voice echoed in the back of his mind.

Perhaps ... he thought.

Perhaps, when this is all over. When Azimar has been conquered and the north subdued, Mothlenor will grant me one small request.

His men did not question the orders they were given. And Ferrand was not in the mood to repeat his orders or explain his reasoning.

Perhaps, when this is all over, Mothlenor will let me murder his daughter.

7

EILONWY

Eilonwy watched the first streaks of orange and red break over the horizon. Those morning moments were always the most peaceful, and she took solace in the fact that, while the rest of Larten was changing, the sunrise was always perfect.

She could hear Mathius moving about downstairs. Mathius was always an early riser, same as she was. He was shuffling about his room, but he was quiet enough that his movements were unlikely to wake others. He would be preparing breakfast soon, and he would need her help to serve the guests in residence. They had been unusually full for some days now, and some of the longest boarders were King's Guards straight from Etritia. It made her skin crawl to even see their surcoats emblazoned with the Etritian crest, but Mathius kept the only inn in Larten. And she had insisted on staying in Larten as the innkeeper's niece.

The King's Guard would leave, eventually. They always had before.

Eilonwy turned in bed and woke Jaimes with a kiss to the temple. His arm slid over her naked waist and wrapped around her until his hand brushed the small of her back. His eyes did not open, but a slow smile pulled at the corners of his mouth.

"I love the way you wake me. It tells me right away that I'm not living in some sort of dream, and that you are really here with me."

She brushed a lock of sandy brown hair from his face and kissed his temple again. "I feel the same." Eilonwy rolled out of bed, leaving the bedding behind for Jaimes. "Mathius is already up. He'll need me downstairs shortly."

"Mathius can wait. The bed is cold without you." Jaimes sat up, patting the empty space she had left behind.

She gave him a wink. "The bed can wait to be warmed again." There was an empty table against the opposite wall. It had once held a variety of equipment and more candles than could be counted at a glance. Now it only held a basket of wilting flowers and a single wooden jar of cream. There were still a few spots of wax on the table's surface, but hours of scrubbing had pulled most of them away. Eilonwy grabbed the jar and pulled the lid off. It was nearly empty.

"And what about me? Should I also be made to wait to be warmed again?"

Eilonwy snorted in reply. She turned and motioned for Jaimes. He obediently tossed the covers aside and slid to the edge of the bed. "What are your plans today, Jaimes? More time in the garden?"

"As always." He reached for the jar, but Eilonwy knelt and administered the cream herself, starting at his calf. "Should I bring some flowers for you, my lady?"

She nodded, giving him a smile. "You know the ones I like, of course?" The cream was absorbed into Jaimes's skin quickly, and he flexed his calf a few times as she worked her way up his thigh. "Anything else you plan to do?"

"Take a walk, I think," Jaimes said slowly.

She knew what that meant. His walks were always a trip to the graveyard at the top of the hill just outside Larten. His parents had been buried there, including a mother he had never known and the woman who had nursed and raised him as her own. There was also a certain glass jar hanging from a high branch in the tree that grew there. It was empty, as it had been for the month or so since they had returned to Larten with it.

Eilonwy smacked Jaimes's thigh. "There you are. All done for today. I'm surprised how long this batch lasted. You don't seem to need to reapply quite so often lately."

"It's your ministrations, Eilonwy, clearly." Jaimes kissed her hand, his lips pressing against the small metal ring she wore.

Eilonwy stood and touched the amulet resting on a leather tie against the hollow of her neck. She couldn't feel the changes that coursed over her body, but she could see the way Jaimes's eyes brushed over her body. "Can I come and find you if there's time for us to share a meal together?"

Jaimes pulled her closer, kissing a spot several inches above her navel. "I don't know how my wife would feel if she knew I was taking meals with the innkeeper's niece."

Eilonwy snorted and rolled her eyes. "I'm sure your wife would be fine with it, seeing as they are one and the same."

Jaimes was kissing a delicate trail down her abdomen and it sent gooseflesh across her skin. "Are you sure you cannot stay?"

"Jaimes …" He slid off the edge of the bed, coming to his knees in front of her. His kissing did not stop, and she could feel his warm breath and the wetness of his tongue. "I am needed downstairs." But she did not step away or do anything to make his kissing stop.

He spoke into the flesh of her inner thigh, and the warmth of his words made her knees soften. "I only need a few moments."

She looked down at him, raising an eyebrow. "You think you can finish what you've started in only a few minutes?"

His grip on her thighs tightened slightly. "Get on the bed, and we'll see."

She lay on the bed, letting him position her legs as he wished. "If you make me late, I will not forgive—Oh!" It came out as a moan, and all thoughts of breakfast and gardens and glass jars quickly left her. "Jaimes …"

Her hand found the top of his head. His hair was thick and soft and curled, and it was long enough for her to bury her hand in it as she pressed his mouth more firmly to her. Her other hand swept across the bedding until she found his, and their fingers intertwined.

<hr>

Mathius was in the kitchen kneading dough when she made it downstairs. He was whistling low and softly as he worked, and Eilonwy donned an apron as she entered.

"Rolls and sausage today, Mathius?"

He looked up, and she noted a smear of flour on his cheek. "There you are! I thought you may have slept in." He turned back to his kneading. "Rolls and sausages today, yes. The first batch for the early birds should be ready to come out now, if you don't mind."

Eilonwy could smell the bread baking. It had a lovely, yeasty scent to it. She used her apron to pull the baking stone out and carried it over to the counter adjacent to the one Mathius was working at. "Sorry, Mathius. Jaimes was insistent I remain a little longer with him this morning. I won't be late tomorrow."

Mathius shook his head. "No need to worry. Jaimes has had a rough time of things lately. Some extra affections from his wife might do him a world of good." He covered the balled dough with a large linen square and turned to her. "Beer and butter, or sausage?"

Eilonwy tilted her head. She heard footsteps on the stairs,

heading for the dining room. "Beer and butter. You do the sausage. We've got one of those early birds now."

Mathius nodded, then stuck his head out of the kitchen door and gave a cheery greeting to the guest descending from their room. When he turned back to Eilonwy, there was a questioning look to his face. "The bird's a guard. You want me to handle him?"

Eilonwy shook her head. She already had a plate with a pair of rolls and a pat of butter in one hand and a mug of beer in the other. "No, I can handle myself, Mathius. You know better than that."

Mathius shrugged. "Sausage it is."

Eilonwy gave Mathius a small curtsey. "How do I look?"

"Like my lovely little Eilen."

Mathius held the door open for her, and she gave him a quick peck on the cheek as she passed. "You've got flour on your face, Uncle."

The King's Guard who had come down for breakfast was sitting in the back corner of the dining hall. Eilonwy recognized him. He had been the first one down for breakfast each morning for the last two days, and he always sat in the same seat at the same table. It wasn't unusual for customers to find a particular spot that they gravitated to for meals, but not many chose to sit with their backs pressed into a wall and their eyes constantly roving over all other guests.

He watched her approach. Eilonwy was used to stares from men. Some stared at her chest, others at her legs or her rear, and still others at the scar that ran over one eyebrow and back into her hair above her temple. But this King's Guard stared at all of her in a calculating way.

It made Eilonwy uncomfortable.

"Good morning, sir. We've just put some sausages on, so they'll be out fresh for you in just a few moments." She set the plate and mug down, then pointed at the rolls. "Those only just came out, so they're nice and hot." She wiped her hands on her apron. "Anything else I can get for you?"

"Your name."

Eilonwy arched an eyebrow. "Sorry?"

He blinked very slowly at her. "I know you are not an idiot, girl. I said your name."

"Eilen, sir."

"Then, Eilen, perhaps you can ask the owner of this swine pen when I might expect a breakfast that doesn't consist of something so paltry as rolls and sausage?"

Eilonwy paused, biting her tongue before she said something that might cause Mathius trouble. She cleared her throat. "What would you find more palatable, sir?"

"Lamb. And wine. Or perhaps mead."

Eilonwy nodded. "I believe we are preparing a lamb roast for lunch today. I can see about holding something back for you to enjoy tomorrow morning. And I can bring you a fresh drink right away. Might I suggest the mead? It was only brought in from Hythe late last week, and I believe they received it from Cusch."

"That is much better, thank you."

"May I ask how long you will be staying, sir?" Eilonwy retrieved the mug of beer. It hadn't even been looked at. Any of their usual guests from Hythe or Emery would have paid dearly for a mug that this King's Guard hadn't even acknowledged.

The King's Guard gave her another assessing look. "Until my work in Larten is done."

Eilonwy returned to the kitchen without a backward glance.

"First few sausages will be finishing up in a moment." Mathius had his back to her and was leaning slightly over the top of the oven, where several links of sausage were browning on the hot surface.

"I hope you're still planning on lamb for lunch, Mathius."

He turned. "What's wrong, did he say something?"

Eilonwy rolled her eyes. "He wants *lamb*. For *breakfast*."

Mathius grimaced. "Definitely a King's Guard from Etritia then." He shook his head. "Lamb for breakfast. When we're lucky to be getting any at all."

"Oh, and wine and mead."

Mathius's grimace deepened. "The man will ruin me if he stays long."

Eilonwy stabbed a sausage link and plated it. "Don't worry, he'll be gone 'when his work in Larten is done,' whenever that will be."

"Lovely," Mathius said flatly.

Eilonwy brushed a bit of flour from Mathius's hair. "You've still got a bit of white here, Mathius." She laughed, tugging a hair from his head and holding it up for him to see. "And a bit of grey."

"Hey now, you'll make more come in!"

"You're getting old, my dear," Eilonwy teased.

"It'll happen to all of us at some point. Even you."

Eilonwy inspected the grey hair pinched firmly between her fingers. "I will never go grey." She turned her nose up. "My beauty will last until the day I die."

"Spoken like a true elf," Mathius muttered in a low voice. "Go on then, you ageless beauty, and take that poor King's Guard his drink and sausage, then come back and start on the beer and butter for the other early birds. I'm sure more will be coming down soon."

Eilonwy filled a second mug with mead from a cask in the larder and took them to the King's Guard. He was still alone, and he still sat quietly in the back corner of the dining room where he could see all who entered.

She dropped the food and drink off without a word and turned to the kitchen again, but the King's Guard grabbed her wrist. His grip was a little too tight and painful, and she had to fight her instinct to break his hold and shout at him.

"If I were you, Eilen, I would be very careful around these parts."

"Why is that, sir?"

"Elves, Eilen. Elves have been spotted on this side of the border, not far from Larten. And if someone in Larten were known to be aiding those filthy creatures …" He released her wrist and plucked the mead from the table. "Well, they would be dealt with harshly. And I would hate for someone as pretty and intelligent as you are to be caught up in that nonsense."

Eilonwy rubbed at her wrist. "I find it hard to believe that anyone in Larten would aid an elf, sir."

The King's Guard lifted an eyebrow and watched her over the rim of his mug. "Have you ever seen an elf?"

Eilonwy shook her head. "No."

"I have. They are devious, conniving little monsters." He took a sip of his mead and set it down again. "They can be very charismatic and very charming. They have a way of bewitching those that are too feeble-minded to withstand their tricks."

"Sounds dangerous," Eilonwy said. She tried to keep her voice and face neutral, but she felt a strangely cold anger creeping over her.

"Very dangerous. Can you imagine the damage that could be done if even a single resident of such a small town were to become poisoned by their words?"

Eilonwy only nodded. She didn't trust herself to answer his question aloud.

The King's Guard speared and sliced through a sausage with one savage cut. "I hope you understand my concern, then, Eilen."

"I do, sir." Eilonwy bowed. "Have a good meal, sir, and I will see you later."

"If you wish to see me sooner, rather than later, I am sure you can figure out which room is mine." He brought the slice of meat to his mouth but hesitated before eating it. "I would be happy to continue your education on the banal fiends of Azimar over a private dinner in my quarters."

Eilonwy stared at him flatly for the briefest of moments. "I apologize, but I'm married."

The King's Guard sighed. "Shame." His attention immediately left her and focused instead on the food in front of him.

Mathius was rolling dough when she entered the kitchen again, but he stopped at the sight of her. "What did he say this time?"

Eilonwy went to the adjacent counter. Mathius had plated the remaining sausages, and she began dropping pairs of rolls beside the browned links. "What makes you think he said anything else?"

"Because you look ready to murder someone."

She slammed a roll onto a plate, smashing the pillowy dough. "He's here to hunt down anyone helping elves." She spoke in a low whisper, and Mathius had to step closer to hear her as she continued. "He called us devious monsters."

Mathius sighed. "You know how Etritians are. And most of the southerners. Elves are evil creatures and should be exterminated."

"You don't seem concerned. What if they find out you're helping elves?"

Mathius shrugged. "What elves? I'm not helping elves. They could search the whole inn, and what would they find? My niece, her husband, and a bunch of travelers on their way to or from Hythe." Mathius replaced the smashed roll with an unblemished one. "And their own men, of course." He handed the roll Eilonwy damaged to her. "Relax. Eat something. Stop worrying. We'll keep an eye on him, right?"

Eilonwy nodded. "Right."

"Come on now, the beer and butter aren't going to prep themselves."

Eilonwy nodded again, then started slapping dollops of butter onto plates.

Mathius's insistence that he wasn't concerned only proved to Eilonwy that he was quite worried.

If he thinks I haven't learned that about him after the last few years, then he's a fool.

And if Mathius was worried, then Jaimes would surely panic.

Eilonwy bit her lip. Jaimes would insist she leave town is he learned that the King's Guards in Larten were there to hunt down elf sympathizers.

But that would only raise more suspicion. And I couldn't leave him and Mathius behind to face scrutiny without me.

The only solution was to make sure Jaimes didn't learn about it at all.

8

SYRANI

The desert was incredibly warm, even from the back of a dragon. Syrani could feel small beads of sweat forming on her forehead. The desert stretched out endlessly, the dunes undulating like frozen waves of sand. From the sky, Syrani could see a shimmer of heat radiating off the golden surface.

"How could anyone survive in a place like this?" Tathiel asked her.

They both leaned slightly in Halcia's saddle, searching the desert floor for any sign of a camp or shelter where Tathiel's companions might be.

He had told Silvana much about them, and she was eager to meet Tiryn. The dwarf, however, she was less enthusiastic about. Not because he was a dwarf, she had told Tathiel. But because he seemed far too callous and rough.

"It gets considerably cooler at night when the sand loses its heat. And there are ways to find food and water, if you know how."

"I forget, you traveled over the desert when you left Vyris, didn't you?"

"Yes," Silvana said. *"But only for a few days."*

They had been some of the worst few days of her life, not just because of the heat and the sun.

"So, are there permanent shelters? Buildings where they could be?"

Silvana shook her head. *"Nothing in the desert is permanent. The sand shifts constantly. There are no buildings. Only tents raised by bands of Elori."*

"Do you think they might have found shelter with an Elori family?" Tathiel asked.

"We should hope so. Not even an elf could survive as long as they have without assistance."

"I think I sense something," Halcia said, interrupting them. She shifted slightly, adjusting her course. *"People, far in that direction."*

"Only humans?" Tathiel asked.

"I can't be sure," Halcia answered.

Silvana was about to ask Tathiel if he had any suggestions when a bright beam of light shot up into the sky. It originated from the point Halcia was heading for and pulsed with golden light. It lasted for only a second or two before fading.

"Whoever it was just sent up a giant beacon," Silvana said, turning to look at Tathiel.

He had seen it, and he squinted in the direction, leaning to see where the light had shone from between the beats of Halcia's wings. *"That was Tiryn, I'm sure of it."*

It took several more minutes before they were close enough to the source of the light for Halcia to determine that there were indeed an elf and a dwarf present. And another few minutes later, Tathiel and Syrani could see what seemed to be a small tent.

"Is it Elori?" Tathiel asked.

Syrani squinted, searching for signs of life. Even with her keen eyesight, the desert sands made it difficult to tell. *"I believe so, though I am not certain."*

"Only one way to decide for sure, I suppose."

Halcia went in for a landing, opening her wings and letting them slow her descent. Figures emerged from the tent as they neared the ground. One was obviously a dwarf. He appeared to be naked from the waist up. Of the other two, one was a dark-skinned Elori male, meaning the other was surely—

"Tiryn," Tathiel said.

Halcia landed with a spray of sand and some staggered steps. Tathiel immediately left the saddle, hurrying to greet his companions.

Syrani approached more slowly, taking in their surroundings. The landscape was barren save for resilient desert plants that grew twisted and gnarled. All around them was brown and gold with hints of red and yellow. A reptile of some kind spotted her and burrowed into the hot earth, its yellow-brown scales blending in nicely with the ground it had warmed itself on.

"Tathiel, we've only just received word from Alastor that you would be joining us." The other elf hugged Tathiel in greeting.

"Yes, I asked Alastor to send a messenger ahead of us. I'd hoped it would arrive well ahead of us."

"It came with enough warning for me to figure out how to signal our location to you."

"The beacon of light?" Tathiel asked. "Very smart."

"And simple enough to conjure every twenty minutes or so until we spotted you." Tiryn motioned towards Halcia. "I was expecting Melonya. This must be the great dragon Halcia that Alastor mentioned."

Halcia dipped her head. *"Indeed."*

"And you must be her companion." Tiryn held a hand out for Syrani, and she shook it.

"Syrani, yes."

Tiryn motioned towards the dwarf. "Nunor, I'm sure

you've been told about. He's not nearly as rude as he thinks he is."

Nunor did not extend a hand in greeting, but he did give Tiryn a glare and Syrani a nod.

"This is our host, the Elori Hiruscu." Tiryn introduced the dark-skinned human last.

Hiruscu was dressed in a sleeveless and low-cut shirt that flattered him well and accented the muscles of his arms. No Azimarian outside of the Southern Cities would ever wear such a garment, but Syrani was sure the desert heat made it necessary.

The Elori pulled his gaze away from Halcia long enough to bow in greeting to Syrani and Tathiel. Then he nodded towards Halcia. "This is a dragon?" He shook his head. "It is very big."

Excuse me? Halcia bared her teeth in a snarl.

"Ah, forgive him." Tiryn put a hand on Hiruscu's dark arm. "His Azimarian is not the best. I think what he means to say is that he didn't expect you to be quite so grand, Halcia."

"Tiryn, we should take this gathering inside. They aren't here to meet us, after all." Nunor spoke in a low grumble that Syrani found oddly soothing.

Syrani nodded. "He's correct. We came to offer our assistance to the third dragon and its rider." Syrani paused, sensing the air. She could feel no other presence reaching out to meet her. "Is the dragon here?"

Tiryn sighed. "It is, but …" He motioned to the tent behind them. "Perhaps you should see for yourself."

Tathiel and Tiryn both followed Hiruscu, who turned and held the flap of the tent open for them. Nunor did not move, and she realized he was waiting for her.

"Go on, master dwarf. I just need a moment alone with Halcia."

Nunor bowed his head and entered the tent, and the flap closed with a soft slap of heavy fabric behind him.

"Do you sense the dragon here?" Syrani asked Halcia. "I don't."

"I do," Halcia answered. *"But it seems very protective of its rider. I would be careful what you say and do."*

"What of the Amulet of Earth? Can you sense it?" Syrani touched her own amulet. It had been buzzing uncomfortably ever since she and Tathiel had entered the desert. There was *something* in these sands, but where and what it was, she could not tell.

"I feel none of what you are sensing," Halcia said. *"But I do not carry an amulet. Perhaps that is the difference."*

Syrani made no reply. Perhaps Tathiel could explain what she was feeling. She touched a hand to Halcia's neck. The dragon's scales were almost hot to the touch. "Will you be alright out here?"

In response, Halcia stretched and settled into the sand. *"I will be fine. I enjoy the warmth."*

Syrani petted Halcia's head. "I will be back to check on you."

She shuffled her way through the hot sand, already feeling the fine grit in her boots, and entered the tent.

The interior of the tent was dark and noticeably cooler. Rugs and pillows were arranged in no real pattern across the floor. Elori seating, it seemed, was not much different from Vyrisian seating. The only other furniture within was a single small table and a wooden chest.

"This poses a problem," Tathiel was saying.

"I thought so as well," Tiryn added.

"What does?" Syrani asked.

The company was gathered in a semicircle, and at Syrani's question, they turned to her. Tiryn stepped aside, letting Syrani take his place.

Lying on a bundle of blankets, as if she had been sleeping until a moment ago, was an Elori woman. Her long skirt had been pulled up to mid-thigh, and Syrani noted that her dress, much like her husband's shirt, was sleeveless. In her arms, still sleeping soundly, was a tiny baby. And lying across the baby's chest, his short tail draped over the mother's forearm, was a small green and brown lizard with small, leathery wings.

Syrani sighed.

"The child is only a handful of weeks old. The dragon hatched when he was born."

"The dragon should be much larger," Tathiel said. "Melonya was the size of a large dog after six weeks."

"Dragons move at their own pace, Tathiel." Syrani knelt beside the woman. "I would have thought you knew that."

"Look, Rushavi. More friends." The woman's voice was thick with sleep, but she met Syrani's eyes and gave her a smile.

"All of you, get out." Syrani turned to glare at the men. "You standing around and staring isn't going to make the dragon grow any faster."

"Syrani—" Tathiel began.

Syrani pointed at the entrance to the tent. "Out."

"Suvusa?" Nunor asked, directing the question at the Elori woman.

The woman nodded. "I will be fine, Nunor. Let the women talk. We may yet find a solution to this problem of yours."

The men left. Syrani sighed again.

"Have they been treating you alright?" Syrani asked the woman.

She nodded slowly. "My husband handles most of their needs. But when Rushavi was born, I was not expecting to host three elves, a dwarf, and a dragon in addition to a baby."

Syrani smirked. "Men do not think of things like that." She pointed to a small carafe of clear liquid. "Water?"

Suvusa nodded. "Please."

Once Suvusa had drunk her fill and the carafe had been

replaced, Syrani helped her to sit up. The baby stirred gently but did not wake.

"He sleeps heavily," Syrani noted.

Suvusa nodded. "It is the heat. He is not adapting well to it. We will have to begin traveling soon."

"Won't being in the sun all day make him worse?" Syrani asked.

"We will have to risk it. If we can reach the rest of our Elori family, they will have better supplies to treat him."

Syrani thought for a moment, then touched the infant's head gently. The baby stirred again, then was still. The light flush to his cheeks, which Syrani had not noticed until then, began to fade.

"What have you done?" There was no accusatory tone to Suvusa's voice, only one of interest.

"A kind of cooling spell, I think. It will draw heat from the boy and siphon it into this." Syrani touched the amulet on her chest. "But it will only work if I am near."

"You are very kind."

Syrani shook her head. "I didn't know it would work. The idea just came to me."

The small dragon moved, likely in response to the arcane energy, and lifted its head.

Syrani reached out a hand, slowly, and waited for it to touch her.

It did not. Instead, it opened its small mouth and hissed at her.

"Come now, little one," Suvusa chided. She shrugged weakly at Syrani. "Don't take offense, it does that to everyone."

"May I try something?"

Suvusa nodded.

Syrani closed her eyes and reached out her mind to connect with the young dragon's. It was more difficult than she had anticipated. She could sense the creature's mind, but he seemed intent on avoiding her own. It was like chasing down a squirming child. Just when she thought she had a grasp on the young one, it slipped away.

Syrani sat back on her heels. "Fine, then. Be a stubborn child. But Halcia will be disappointed in you."

Her words elicited no response from the dragon. It only curled tighter around Suvusa's arm and shifted its chin slightly where it lay on Rushavi's chest.

"Your friend Tiryn tried to speak with it as well, and had as much success," Suvusa said. The Elori woman motioned for the carafe of water again, and Syrani retrieved it. Suvusa drank deeply, nearly finishing the lukewarm liquid in only a few seconds.

"I brought a second tent. It is not as large and lavish as this one is, but if the men give you trouble …" Syrani shrugged. "And I could stay close, for Rushavi's sake."

Suvusa raised an eyebrow. "I am a stranger to you." Her cheeks were also flushed, though it was again hard to see against such dark skin. But Tiryn should have noticed the signs of illness in her.

Unless he was too blinded by concern for the amulet's location to see the obvious.

"Are you concerned?" Syrani said.

Suvusa shook her head. "No, I am not concerned. We Elori are taught that all creatures of this world are inherently good."

"Trustworthy until they prove otherwise?" Syrani suggested.

"Something like that." Suvusa laughed.

"Then I will have the tent prepared, and we will move you and the children when night begins to fall." Syrani stood and bowed to the woman. "Until then, sleep. I will ensure you are not bothered."

She left before Suvusa replied, but she heard the woman settle down once more against her pillows. The tent blocked out a great deal of light, and Syrani had to blink several times as she exited. The sun was high and incredibly bright. It would be hours before it began to set.

"Well?"

Tiryn was waiting for her. They all were, circled around the entrance to the tent.

"I assume you tried to speak to the dragon?" Tiryn asked. "Did it connect with you?"

"No, it did not."

"He proves stubbornly silent." Halcia had moved, and now lay in the shade offered by the side of the tent that Suvusa and Rushavi slept in.

"Even to you?" Tiryn asked.

"I can continue reaching out to him, if you think he might eventually acknowledge me."

Syrani nodded, wiping a few drops of sweat from her brow. "I would appreciate you trying, Halcia."

The great dragon laid her head down once more and closed her red-gold eyes. *"I will do what I can."*

She turned to Tathiel. "Can you set up the tent we brought with us? Suvusa will be spending her nights with me for some time."

Tathiel nodded and grabbed one of the bags that had already been pulled from Halcia's back. The large two-person saddle had also been removed and lay on its side in the sand.

"Why?" Nunor asked. He and the male Elori were both staring at her, though Hiruscu did so with concern and confusion, while Nunor glared at her with distrust.

"I suppose you also realized Suvusa is ill?"

Syrani nodded. "So you did know."

"Suvusa is ill?" Hiruscu asked. "She did not tell me."

"I think she is more concerned about her son's well-being than her own," Tiryn answered. "It will pass, but I have nothing at hand that can help her."

"I think I can, which is exactly why I would like her and the child close."

"She said nothing about an illness with her or the child," Nunor protested. "Why did you not say anything sooner, Tiryn?"

"When I brought her illness to her attention, I was asked to ignore it."

"It can be ignored no longer," Syrani said. "The Elori mother wants to begin traveling again, so we must give her all the assistance we can."

Tathiel had the tent set up in little time. Tiryn assisted him, and when they were done, Syrani asked a question that had bothered her since watching Suvusa drinking so greedily to quell her thirst.

"How much water do we have among us?"

"Including what you and Tathiel brought? Not enough," Nunor answered gruffly.

Tiryn confirmed Nunor's assessment with a nod. "Our water supply concerns also force us to leave for the rest of the Elori before Suvusa has healed sufficiently. Nunor and I were prepared to wait another month if needed, but …"

"But we have no way to find water in this place," Syrani answered.

"That's not true." Tathiel touched the amulet he bore, the small lump hardly concealed beneath his thin tunic. "There is water hidden in these sands."

"Can you find it?" Syrani asked. When he nodded, she added, "Take Tiryn, if he is willing."

The two elves left in search of water, and Hiruscu followed behind to check the traps he had set that afternoon.

Nunor eyed Syrani with distrust, one hand on the head of his axe. "And what would you ask of me, your humble servant?" There was a sarcastic lilt to the end of his question, and Syrani noted the smirk that hid beneath his heavy facial hair.

"Sit with me, Nunor, and tell me all you have learned of the amulet from our Elori friends." She motioned towards the newly erected tent. "Alastor said you enjoy a good drink, and I have something far better than water with me."

Nunor chuckled, raising an eyebrow. "And here I thought you were one of those stuck-up and snotty sorts of elves."

THE DRAGON

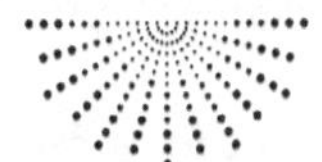

When night began to fall, the tiny dragon was stirred once more from his blissful slumber. He had been dreaming of nothing. His young companion continued to sleep, the heat of sickness making his rest deeper and harder to break. But while the babe slept, the dragon waited, eyes closed and senses roused, as they were both lifted from their bed and carried away. The mother, whose milk had nourished him as much as it had his companion, also suffered from the same sun sickness that made the infant ill. But there was nothing he could do for her. It took all his strength to keep Rushavi well.

"Will you finally answer me, then, little brother?"

The voice, so annoying and insistent, called to him again. Could she not understand that he had more pressing concerns? That Rushavi could have died without him?

"The child will be fine now, I swear it. He is in good company, and my companion can care for both mother and son."

The dragon paused in thought. The voice had mentioned a companion. Did she, like him, have one to whom she had committed her life? Her very soul?

"Yes, little brother. And I am here with you."

The dragon opened his eyes.

Several feet away, lying in the sand as a silent sentinel, was a beast as large as he was stunted. She was beautiful, with scales of red and gold and every fiery shade between. Her size was equally intimidating and inspiring. He had not thought for a moment that he could ever be quite so grand.

"Hello, little brother. I am Halcia. Have you decided on a name for yourself?"

The tiny dragon thought for a moment as he and his companion were carried into a different, smaller tent. It was cooler in here, and there was water enough for days. He lapped from a small bowl that was offered to him, to the delight of those present.

"Ardu. I choose the name Ardu."

JAIMES

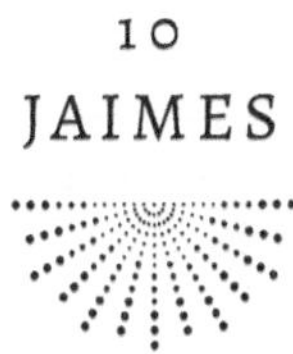

There were precisely two places in all of Larten where Jaimes felt most at peace. Three, if he were to include his bed with Eilonwy beside him. The others were his mother's garden and the grave hill outside Larten proper. The garden was old and well manicured, and it had a calming atmosphere that helped to restore Jaimes's spirits. His father, Harlan, had died in the garden some years ago, but that did not change the way he felt about the quiet solace of the space. He had removed the sweet tansy that had caused his father's death, but Jaimes replanted it not even a year later.

While the garden had the peaceful feel of life and rebirth and green things, the grave hill had the silence of death and the finality of all things around it, and that filled Jaimes with a different kind of peace. The peace of inevitability, rather than the sensation of soulful renewal.

Jaimes started most of his days in the garden. And when he could, he finished them on the grave hill. He took lunch in the garden on a small bench that sat beside a hortensia hedge. It was usually Eilonwy who brought a plate out for him, and they would spend a few moments exchanging chaste kisses before she left him to his musings and plant pruning.

This morning, however, it was Mathius who brought lunch.

"Keeping my darling wife too busy to even spare a moment for me, Mathius?" Jaimes chuckled and dropped a pair of heavy iron pruning shears in the dirt as he stood. He rubbed at his knee out of old habit, but it was actually pain free.

"She's busy, yes. Another pair of King's Guards showed up last night. The whole lot of them are drinking and carrying on in the dining room."

"I hope you don't plan to leave her alone in there too long," Jaimes said. He hadn't meant for his words to sound hard and annoyed, but they did all the same.

Mathius raised a calming hand. "Her being here is exactly what I want to talk to you about, Jaimes."

Jaimes sat on the bench, and Mathius joined him. "Has something happened?"

Mathius leaned in conspiratorially. "Yeah, the whole damned town is filled with King's Guards. Or have you not noticed?"

Jaimes nodded. "I've noticed. Do you know why they're here? We have King's Guards come through often enough. Is there something different about these?"

"Eilon—" Mathius caught himself before he could finish uttering the name. "*Eilen* says they're here to hunt down sympathizers."

"Aren't they always?" Jaimes mashed the inside of a baked potato with the back of his spoon. Eilonwy had dropped extra butter on it, just how he liked it. There was even a drizzle of cream in the center, and the whole thing smelled wonderful. "You've yet to say anything to surprise me, Mathius."

"You don't understand, boy. They aren't here just for a

quick look-see before trotting back to Etritia. They *know* something is afoot in Larten."

That stopped him. He chewed slowly, giving himself a moment to think. "What did you say to Eilen?"

Mathius shrugged. "Not to worry. That we could keep an eye out, and things would be fine."

Jaimes grimaced. "So you basically let on that you're terrified."

"I did not!" Mathius scoffed.

"You did." Jaimes dropped his spoon, his appetite gone. "You always try to brush things off when you're upset about them. You've done it ever since the *Kingfisher*."

"No, I don't."

"Yes, you do." Jaimes gave Mathius a hard look, staring at the man for a moment. "You are worried, aren't you?"

Mathius sighed. "I am."

"And what do you want to do?"

"I want you to convince Eilen to leave. She needs to go back to her mother for a few weeks. Send her home until Larten is safe again."

It was a good plan. He didn't like the idea of Eilonwy being in Larten any more than Mathius did, not if there were serious concerns her identity might be discovered.

He shook his head. "She wouldn't go. Not without you."

"Not without *you*, I think you meant," Mathius said.

Jaimes said nothing for a moment.

I can't leave this place. Not again.

"Let her come to bed early tonight, would you?" Jaime asked. "I'll try to talk to her."

Eilonwy was waiting in bed for him that evening when he returned from the grave hill. She lay back on the covers of their bed, her arms tucked behind her head. The glamour that maintained her disguise as Eilen vanished as soon as Jaimes shut the door behind him.

"You asked Mathius to give me the evening off?" Eilonwy

asked, sitting up. She smiled at him, her head tilting slightly. "Did you miss me at lunch?"

"Of course I did. Mathius is rubbish at exchanging sweet kisses." Jaimes scrunched his nose. "I think it's the beard. Too itchy."

That got a laugh from her. It was a rich, pleasant sound. *Great Ones, I will miss that sound while she's away.*

"What have you brought me?" Eilonwy asked, motioning towards the small basket Jaimes held.

Jaimes set it on the bed for her to examine. "More flowers. I was going to ask you to make a little stock of that cream. I would do it myself but …" Jaimes shrugged. "You won't tell me what you did to change the original recipe."

"Of course I won't." Eilonwy sniffed the flowers and touched a few petals with delicate fingers. "If I did, what would you need me for?"

Jaimes sat on the bed beside her, wrapping his arms around her waist and pulling her close to his chest. "Of course I would need you."

"I just made a fresh batch the other day. Why do you need more?"

Jaimes hesitated before answering.

Eilonwy looked over her shoulder at him. "Jaimes?"

"I think it would be a good idea if you went home for a few weeks. And maybe told your brother to avoid Larten for a while."

Eilonwy huffed and pushed him away. "Mathius told you about the King's Guards and why they're here, didn't he?" She balled her fist and beat it into the mattress. "I *knew* he was more concerned than he let on."

"He thinks it would be the safer choice if you went away until they were gone," Jaimes said. He put a hand on her upper arm. Her skin was soft and warm, and he could feel the muscles flex beneath his fingers as she inspected the basket of garden clippings irritably. "And I agree."

Eilonwy shook her head. "No. I'm not leaving Mathius here by himself. If it's not safe for me to be here, then it's not safe for anyone close to me to be here, either."

"Mathius wouldn't be alone. I would be here with him."

Eilonwy rounded on him. "You most certainly would not." Her face was twisted into a furious glare. "Do you think I would leave not only my dear friend behind to face the scrutiny of King's Guards, but also my own husband? And do you not think it would be suspicious? A young woman leaving town suddenly and without escort?"

Jaimes could see the logic, but he pressed on.

"We can figure out the details. We can say it was an emergency, and that you left with a departing merchant. Just say you'll go, Eilonwy!"

She crossed her arms. "No. I'm not going. Especially if you won't go with me."

"I can't leave Larten again," Jaimes said. He a hand on her arm again, craving the warmth and comfort it gave him.

"What do you mean, you can't leave Larten?" Eilonwy jerked her arm from his hand. "No one is trapping you here."

Jaimes sighed. "It's not that, I just …"

"Just what, Jaimes?"

"I don't want to leave Larten because every time I do, someone I care about gets hurt."

There was a heavy moment of silence. Eilonwy took his hand in both of hers and squeezed it very gently. "Jaimes. I know you think Vash's disappearance is your fault. But we've talked about this. She *chose* to make that leap. If she had not been there, we would have all died." She kissed his knuckles. "And you know what I keep saying about fire spirits. They—"

"They don't ever really die," Jaimes finished for her.

"Well, it's the truth. Water spirits may eventually die if their source dries up. An earth spirit may die if something happens to their land. But wind and fire spirits never die.

They just vanish for a time and reappear when magic is used
to summon them."

"But do you know what it's like to stop existing, Eilonwy?" Jaimes asked. "She told me once. And it's not something
I want her or anyone else to ever experience."

"But it's not your fault," Eilonwy insisted.

"And what about you?" Jaimes touched the scar that ran
over her temple. The skin was white and raised under his
fingertips. "You were hurt the first time I left Larten."

Eilonwy's head tilted, pressing slightly into his fingers,
and she smiled. "Jaimes, I would have died without you. Or
worse. This scar is a reminder that I will always have you to
thank for saving my life."

"But how would things have turned out differently if I
had remained in Larten instead of joining my brother on the
Kingfisher?"

Eilonwy shrugged. "I would have been on that ship,
regardless. As would the men that captured me. And Brynne,
he would have been there too."

"Brynne," Jaimes said. It came out as something like a
growl. "How many more men like him do you think Mothlenor has? Spies sent to befriend and betray innocents?"

"However many he may have, Brynne is no longer among
them." Eilonwy leaned forward, kissing him on the cheek.
Her lips were warm, and he could smell honey and baked
bread when she drew close. "I do know one thing that would
be different if you had not left Larten then. We wouldn't be
here together. And I'm happier with the path we've walked
so far than any possibilities we may have missed."

Jaimes sighed, touching his forehead to hers. "I love you,
Eilonwy."

"I love you too, Jaimes. And the only way I will leave
Larten is if you and Mathius come with me. You cannot
convince me otherwise."

Jaimes nodded. "Alright. I won't try to convince you. We'll

stay and monitor the King's Guards. If something happens, all three of us will decide to leave or stay together."

"Thank you." Eilonwy slipped from the bed, taking the basket of flowers to the table on the opposite wall. "I'll send word to Tathiel, though. And the others. It would be smarter to minimize any further contact until Larten is clear of King's Guards." She touched a few petals from the basket. "And tomorrow, I'll have to feign a sickness for a few hours to ensure some peace and quiet to make another batch of cream for you. I do think it would be prudent to have extra on hand, just in case we have to make a quick departure in the near future."

"You could still tell me what you do differently," Jaimes teased.

Eilonwy smirked. "A woman never shares her secrets, Jaimes. Not even to her husband." She stripped down to her underclothes in a few seconds, and Jaimes made room for her beside him and tucked the covers around her.

He lay against her, one hand around her waist and her back to his chest. But he did not close his eyes right away. He stared at Eilonwy, and the way her shoulder lifted slightly with each breath. At the way the point of her ear stuck out from her silver hair. And the way he could feel her heartbeat. It was slow, noticeably slower than his, and he counted the beats, afraid that at any moment it might suddenly stop.

"Stop worrying about me, Jaimes. Get some sleep."

"I'm sorry. I didn't mean for you to sense that."

"I know," Eilonwy muttered. "But it will become harder to hide thoughts like that the longer we are together. There's nothing to be afraid of. Not tonight."

11

ALASTOR

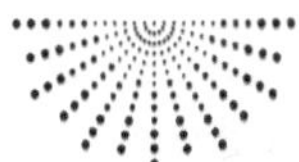

Nieve was consulting the map she had received from her father for perhaps the hundredth time since she and Alastor had left her village.

Alastor sighed, watching from between their horses as she turned the map this way and that and spun in a slow circle.

"I've already told you, I know exactly where we are and where we're going," Alastor said.

One of the horses whinnied, and he petted it and whispered calming words imbued with arcane energy. The horse flicked his ears and returned to the patch of grass it had been eating from.

"And I have already told *you* that I don't trust your judgment." Nieve glared over the map at him. "Humans don't have the same sense of direction that elves do."

"And yet you're the one who's lost."

Nieve balled her fists around the map she held, slapping the spread parchment across the tops of her thighs and looking remarkably like a petulant child. "I am not lost. I just can't find where we are on this map."

"Ah, yes. I see the distinction." Alastor jerked his chin at the offending paper. "How old is that thing, anyway?"

"My father drew it from memory before we left." Nieve rotated the map again, then squinted up at the sun.

"And how long ago was he in this area?"

"I don't know." Nieve shrugged. "A century ago, maybe more?"

Fucking elves.

"You mean your father drew a map of a place he had not seen in over a century?"

Nieve gave him an irritated scowl. "What of it?"

"Nieve, I can't remember what I had for breakfast a week ago. I would certainly not be able to draw a map of a place I had seen only once years ago."

Nieve squinted at the sun again, then made a quarter turn. "You had poached eggs and fruit juice for breakfast this day last week."

Alastor snorted. "I'm flattered and a little unnerved that you've been tracking my eating habits."

She glared at him. "You eat loudly. It's difficult not to notice."

Alastor nodded. "Right. I eat loudly." He cocked his head. "Fruit juice, really? Not wine or sweet water?"

"If I'm remembering correctly, and I'm sure I am, you complained loudly to your brother about your inability to shit since you'd started eating Vyrisian food."

"Ah, yes." Alastor chuckled, remembering the morning in question. "Thank goodness that cleared up quickly, hm?"

"You're disgusting."

"And you're lost."

"I'm not lost!" Nieve did another small turn. "My father's map is just useless."

"Don't blame him. Roads and landmarks might have changed a bit in the last hundred years." He approached Nieve, leaning over her shoulder to investigate for himself.

There were parts of the map that looked familiar, but much of it was foreign to him.

"Right, so we are right …" Alastor licked the tip of one finger, then carefully touched a spot on the map. A large black X appeared where he indicated. "Here. Roughly speaking, anyway." He motioned to the depiction of trees on the thick parchment Nieve held. "And these woods are mostly gone." Alastor waved an arm about them. "Clearly."

"Alright," Nieve muttered. "And the place we're going is right here." She touched another spot on the map.

Alastor nudged her hand until her finger sat two inches to the left.

"Here?"

Alastor nodded.

"Okay. There's a road that will take us close." Nieve traced the path with her fingertip. "It should take us no more than a few days."

Alastor shook his head. "No, that's not how we'll be getting here." He took one edge of the map from Nieve and traced a second path. A dotted line marked the progress of his finger. "We'll take this route. The roads are less traveled and safer, and we'll avoid the larger villages this way."

"I don't see a road there."

"That's because your father is older than the farmlands we'll be riding through." Alastor gestured at the map. "There is a road there, trust me."

Nieve snorted. "That will take twice as long, at least! The other road is shorter."

"The other road is the most densely traveled in this part of Azimar, and runs right through three—no, four—different towns. There are sure to be King's Guards swarming over every inch of it."

Nieve frowned.

"We'll take the longer path, and we'll get to our destination in one piece."

Nieve did not argue. Alastor wasn't sure if he had upset her by deciding their route for them. Or perhaps by knowing their location better than she had, despite her more highly developed senses.

Or maybe he stank too much of the road.

He surreptitiously sniffed at an underarm while climbing back into his horse's saddle.

No, that wasn't it.

But the other points were still valid.

"I'm sorry, Nieve. I didn't intend to insult your intelligence or belittle your contributions. I just want to make sure we don't run into any trouble."

Nieve shrugged. "I understand. No insult taken."

Alastor narrowed his eyes at her, sure she was lying. "Are you certain?"

Nieve sighed. "Until a few weeks ago, I had never left the woodlands of my home. You're one misfortune away from being a vagabond."

Alastor winced, but couldn't disagree.

"I will defer to your leadership for our travels."

Alastor cleared his throat and lifted his chin slightly. "I solemnly accept the responsibility."

Internally, he was chortling.

Oh, the trouble I could give her ...

Nieve rolled her eyes and nudged her horse into a trot.

Alastor followed after her. "Hey, wait now. I'm the leader! I'm supposed to be leading us!"

"Great Ones save me from you."

***

It took them a few hours to reach the next road on their route. Alastor had intentionally chosen ones that he and Roland had traveled several times because there were a few locations where they had cached extra supplies. And they knew the lie of the land and were familiar with some of the farmers that lived close to the roads.

Rain had passed through recently, and the gravel was still wet and pocked with muddy holes. A wagon would have had some difficulty passing through, but their horses were hardly bothered by the damp.

Alastor was also unbothered. He had spent far too many hours riding during storms or sleeping under trees dripping with rainwater to care about the mud that splashed onto his trousers and boots. Nieve, however, seemed unhappy with their traveling conditions.

"Are the roads always so filthy? And so ..." Nieve's nose wrinkled. "Smelly?"

"That stench is the stink of wet horse droppings. You should be grateful. It's far worse in the height of summer." Alastor swatted a fly away from his face. "I thought you would be accustomed to the smell of horse manure. Or do your horses shit honey?"

Nieve rolled her eyes at him. "There is something beneath the smell of manure. Something deeper and more vile."

Alastor sniffed at the air, but he smelled nothing. He shrugged. "I'm sure you'll grow accustomed to it soon enough. Everything stops smelling bad after a few days on the road."

They traveled in silence for a few more minutes. The horses plodded along without complaint, their hooves occasionally catching in the mud.

Alastor yawned, already bored, and stretched in the saddle. "It's too quiet. Roland and I could talk about nothing for hours while riding." Alastor paused, recalling his most recent travels with his uncle. "I guess it's more appropriate to say *I* could talk for hours, and Roland knew exactly when to make polite little remarks."

Alastor gave Nieve a moment to say something, anything. But she did not.

"How about a game then? Would you prefer the question game, or a couple rounds of 'I've Spotted'?"

"Quiet, Alastor."

Alastor rolled his eyes. "I'm sorry, the silence may be appealing to you, but it drives me mad. Just humor me for—"

"Quiet, Alastor," Nieve repeated, more forcefully. "There are men behind us." She pulled her hood up over her head, covering her long and pointed ears.

"You didn't expect us to have the entire route to ourselves, did you?" But Alastor spoke softly, listening for horses on the road.

"They're coming up behind us, on foot. Three, I think." Nieve tilted her head. "And two more are ahead of us, waiting."

"Ah, a good old ambush, then. It's been a while since I've been in one of those." Alastor waived another fly away from his face.

"And that stench is getting worse." Nieve scanned the road. It was wide enough for three horses to stand abreast, and to either side was thorny underbrush and tall weeds. "Should we go off the trail?"

"Nah. If they're heading our way, then they already know we're here. Must have been watching the road."

Nieve pulled her hood down farther. "Lovely."

They did not change their pace. Nieve remained silent, likely listening for the approaching men. Alastor whistled, creating some nonsense tune that sounded upbeat and cheery. But he was nervous. How well could Nieve handle herself in a fight?

She was good with spell work, sure. Nieve had proved that much when they were trying to excavate the Amulet of Fire from the massive ice pit it was buried in. But Alastor had never seen her handle a weapon or engage in close combat.

It's fine. As long as she doesn't get in the way, I can handle them myself.

He continued whistling. With each inhale, Alastor tried to see if he could smell the stench Nieve complained of. He had a thought as to what it might be, but he didn't want to alarm Nieve further if she had not already realized what it was.

There was a small bend in the path that navigated around a large and knobby oak. The tree was large, almost as large as the ones Alastor had seen in Vyris, and there were old scars at about waist height where some foolish woodcutters had thought to cut the ancient thing down.

Alastor knew the tree well. He and Roland often used it to store supplies because the raised roots kept goods dry and away from most scavengers. It was empty now, Alastor remembered. But there was a farm only a few miles up the road that sold milk, meat, and assorted foods to those who had the coin for it.

Just around the bend in the road, beyond the shade of the oak, stood two men on horseback.

"If you can do a little chicanery, now would be the time to cast it," Alastor whispered to Nieve.

One of the men raised a hand, indicating for them to stop.

"Hello, there!" Alastor called, pulling his horse to a slow trot. "Is there some trouble on the road?"

"Yeah, there is," one of the men called back. "The trouble being that you've got a couple of nice horses, and we'll be needing them."

Alastor laughed. "I see that you've got a couple of nice horses yourselves. What could you possibly need with ours?"

"Who you traveling with there, good sir?"

"My sister," Alastor said quickly. "She's ..." Alastor cast a glance beside him towards Nieve, surprised to see a large and burly man sitting in the saddle of Nieve's horse. He hadn't even sensed the arcane energy she'd spent to cast the glamour spell. "She's very ugly, as you can see. And a half-wit. Not even good for field work, if I'm honest."

Nieve glared at him from under the hood of her cloak.

"Take her, if you'd like," Alastor continued. "You'd be doing me a favor."

"I don't want your sister."

"Ah, women not your favored gender? She's got a twin brother. Only a little uglier than her. And a fair bit smarter."

The man grimaced. "Shut it, already! I don't want your damned sister, nor her brother." He pointed at Alastor's feet. "I want your fucking horse, your gold, and those nice boots of yours."

"A couple of common thugs, are we?"

"More'n a couple." The other man finally spoke, nodding to indicate the trail behind them. "So I'd do as we ask, if I were you."

Alastor turned in his saddle. Behind them, rounding the bend of the oak, were three more men. They were on foot, just as Nieve had said they would be. There was a hungry, almost feral look to their eyes.

At least Nieve had the number right.

"My apologies. You've got yourself a whole group of common thugs."

The first man pulled a short sword from his belt. He held it clumsily, like he wasn't truly accustomed to holding anything longer than a knife. "Would a common thug have this?"

"No, I suppose not," Alastor said, shrugging.

"We're King's Guards. And we're under orders from the king to confiscate all the horses we find."

"And demand my gold and boots?" Alastor asked, raising an eyebrow.

"Taxes," the second man said. He was shorter and balder than his counterpart.

"Taxes?"

The balder man spat over his horse's shoulder. It was thick and yellowy, and Alastor gagged at the sight of it. "Yeah, taxes."

"Fair enough. A kingdom must make money somehow, right?"

The first man reached for the reins of Alastor's horse. "Then hand over the horses and any gold you've got. And don't be forgetting them boots, either."

Alastor leaned forward in his saddle, resting an arm across the horn. He slapped the man's hand away. "Oh, but I know that you're not really King's Guards."

Behind him, Alastor heard the three other men's feet squish slightly into the wet and muddy earth as they stomped closer.

"You're making some poor mistakes, good sir," the first man said.

The other one in front of him asked, "How can you be sure we ain't who we says we is?"

"Because I've traveled quite a lot, and you don't get around Azimar as much as I have without knowing how to tell the difference between a King's Guard and a thug."

"King's Guard or not, we still outnumber you. So I'll be taking your horses." The first man reached for the reins of Alastor's horse again.

"Oh, I see you've also made a poor mistake."

The man squinted up at him, hoisting the short sword threateningly. "Come again?"

"You see, my sister and I are not common travelers."

That was all the signal Nieve needed. She released the energy Alastor had felt her collecting. She aimed for the three men behind them, and Alastor wasted no time turning to see what damage she was inflicting.

He shot a blast of pure energy into the first man's abdomen, making his and both the strangers' horses scream and buck. Alastor calmed his horse to a standstill with a firm tug on the reins, but the thug was tossed from his horse's saddle and knocked to the ground.

There was a series of sickening crunches as the hooves of two scared horses descended onto the man's head and torso.

The shorter, balder man was knocked from his horse, but he was quick enough to roll out of the way before he was trampled like his companion. Both frightened horses fled into the roadside thickets, screaming as the thorns cut into their hides.

Alastor frowned. "Oops."

The balding thug scrambled to his feet. He was covered in mud and small pebbles and flecked with his partner's blood. He took one look at Alastor and fled after the horses. The thicket was more difficult for him to climb through, and he struggled and cursed as he fought through it.

It wasn't until a thick, thorny vine wrapped itself around the man's neck that Alastor looked to Nieve. Her hands twisted and curled about each other, the fingers bent unnaturally. She had abandoned the glamour spell, and her long and thin fingers looked eerie and grotesque as she bound the man in ropes of overgrowth.

"Nieve, don't let him suffer." He put a hand on her shoulder. "It's not humane."

"Humane?" Nieve asked.

The thorns twisted and tightened, and the man was flipped onto his back.

Nieve twisted her hands more. "Humane, like the way my kind has been treated by yours over the years?"

"Please, for my sake. Make it quick."

The thug gasped for air, his mouth opening wide. A long vine shot down his throat, and he instantly stilled. When the vine retreated, it was more red than green and brown.

Alastor shuddered.

"For your sake, Alastor. Not for his." Nieve stepped down

from her saddle. "Help me find the horses you scared off. I want to treat their wounds."

Alastor did not need to be asked a second time. And he did not look behind him to see how Nieve had killed the other three thugs.

Alastor used the short sword that the first thug had dropped to cut a small path through the brush. "I didn't mean to scare them off like that. I swear it."

"You don't think before acting. That's your biggest flaw." Nieve grabbed Alastor's wrist as he brought the sword down onto the thicket. Her grip was strong enough to stop the swing of the blade. With her other hand, Nieve waved in a side-to-side motion. The thorns and thicket parted for them.

Alastor sighed. "Yeah, I'm starting to realize that."

"Good. The realization is the first step."

They got through the worst of the thicket. Nieve pointed, and Alastor followed her direction. "You said that this road was safe."

Alastor snorted. "I said this road was *safer*. Not that it was safe. I also said that there would be fewer King's Guards. And those were obviously not King's Guards." Behind them, the thicket remained split apart.

Nieve gave him a conceding shrug. "That is fair."

Alastor could hear the snorting and whinnying of frightened horses further ahead. The horses had not gone far, either because they did not feel the urge to travel too far from the road or because they had gotten caught among the trees and thickets. "You're much more adept at magic than I had thought."

Nieve stepped over a large tree root that had stuck out of the earth. "My father is Vyrisian, remember? He prides himself on passing on the knowledge of our people."

"Hence his badgering Syrani about instructing the others in your village."

"Exactly." Nieve pointed ahead. "They're just beyond those trees there. See them?"

Alastor could see the two horses. One was lying down, a good indication that it had injured itself while running away. "What do we plan on doing with them?"

"We'll take them on the road with us. I'm sure those men stole them from some farmer somewhere. A family nearby may know where they came from."

They approached the horses slowly, keeping themselves in their sight as much as possible. The injured one slowly stood, but did not put much weight on one of its front legs.

"Are you any good with healing magic?" Nieve asked.

"No, actually." Alastor winced and retreated a step as the horses both whinnied and stamped at his approach. "I'm more of the fireball-flinging arcanist. I'm not so good at the finer arts."

"I'm not surprised at all." Nieve grabbed one horse by the reins, shushing it with calming whispers. "They seemed frightened of you, anyway."

"How about I just go back to the road and keep an eye on the two horses that *don't* think I'm trying to kill them?"

Nieve rolled her eyes. "You do that. I'll return momentarily."

Alastor could not avert his eyes from the dead man that was strung in the thorns and vines like a fly in a spider's web. The other three men that Nieve had killed had only slightly less horrifying deaths. Alastor's horse was standing off to one side of the road, his eyes wide and nostrils flaring. Nieve's horse seemed unbothered.

Alastor patted his horse on the neck. "I know, buddy. She's a bit more aggressive than we're used to, isn't she?"

His horse snorted in reply.

"Shall I do something about this mess, hm?"

The horse made no answer to his question.

Alastor sighed. "Alright, I can at least get them off the

road. Someone will surely ride by soon enough, and we don't want to cause ourselves trouble, do we?"

His horse still did not answer.

Alastor cursed. He knew he was only delaying himself. The sight of three men impaled on stakes made of compacted earth made him ill, but they didn't need to be left there for someone else to find.

"Fuck, she's good. Used the water in the mud to freeze it into shape." Alastor sent a few small and carefully aimed pulses of arcane energy at the stakes, breaking them. The men crumbled to the ground. "Madwoman. Don't cross that one, Alastor."

His horse snorted again.

By the time Nieve returned with the horses, Alastor had dragged the four bodies off into the thicket. The final one he left right where it was. It was easy enough to miss if any passersby kept their focus on the road.

"There's still blood on the path," Nieve said.

"I think there will be a lot more blood on the road if we keep riding this way."

Nieve nodded. "I think so, too. That smell is hard to disguise. And I can hear the flies from here."

"Shall we continue, then? See how bad things are?"

"We haven't much choice now, do we? The next fork in the route isn't for another ten miles or so, right?"

"Beyond the next few farms, yes."

Nieve tied one of the spare horses to Alastor's saddle. "This one will be a little groggy for some time. So hopefully she doesn't remember that she's afraid of you."

"How is her leg?"

Nieve shrugged. "It was broken. It's fine now."

It was another few minutes before Alastor could smell the stink of carrion and blood and hear the buzzing of flies. He covered his nose and mouth with the sleeve of his tunic as they drew near the farm he and Roland frequented on their trips through this area. The horses they led seemed familiar with the place; they walked through the open farm gate and stopped several feet inside the yard.

There were several bodies laid out in a rough line, with drag marks and blood trails marking where they had been moved from.

"Great Ones, they killed everyone here," Alastor said through his mouth covering. "There was a whole family."

"Are they all here?" Nieve asked. She did not have her face covered, though her nose was wrinkled in disgust.

Alastor dismounted and walked the line of dead. "Yes, they're all here. Even the boy." The blood trail from the youngest family member, a child of no more than ten, led to the stable. The stable doors were open, and the stalls within were empty. "I think we can safely guess where the horses came from."

Nieve did not dismount from her horse. "Do you still think those men did not deserve to die as they did?"

"We didn't know they were murderers. Only that they were thieves."

"They stank of death, Alastor. *I* knew they were murderers."

Alastor sighed. "Next time we run into a band of killers on the road, please let me know." He climbed back into the saddle and urged his horse onward.

"You don't want to stay and bury them properly?"

Alastor shook his head. "No, they should be buried by friends, not by strangers. We'll ride on and let their neighbors know what has happened to them. And that their killers have been dealt with."

"And if the next farm has been treated similarly?"

"We ride for the next one, and so on, and put these deaths behind us. There is no time to waste for grieving."

Nieve brought her horse up next to his. "There is a little time, arcanist."

Alastor shook his head. "I can't bury anyone again. Not yet."

Nieve was silent for a moment. She did not ask who he had buried, though Alastor would have told her if she had. When they were once more on the road, Nieve nudged her horse until it was a step ahead of Alastor's. "The next farm, then. How far is it?"

"Not far. Another mile."

"Perhaps they are in need of a pair of good workhorses."

If they are alive, Alastor thought.

1 2

ARDU

The tent was cool and shaded, and for the first time in several days, Rushavi was crying relentlessly. Even Ardu's presence was not enough to calm his companion, nor was his mother's touch or her soothing voice. His wails were high-pitched, and each one sent a tingle down Ardu's scales. Rushavi's plump cheeks were flushed, and salty tears ran down them and into the cloth that swaddled him. Ardu watched, distressed, as his companion's chest rose and fell sharply with each hitched breath.

"What is happening? Why does he cry?" Ardu asked his sister, the great dragon Halcia.

There was a note of irritation to her voice when she answered. *"There are those present that are better able to answer than I. Perhaps you should ask Syrani. She is the one caring for him."*

Ardu hesitated. He did not want to talk to the elf or the mother. Not yet. But both women had grown increasingly annoyed with Ardu's insistence on staying in physical contact with his companion at all times. The elf had even scolded him on several occasions when Ardu hissed at her.

"I have asked you, sister. Can't you answer?"

"I could, Ardu, but I am rather preoccupied at the moment. And this constant back and forth as your messenger for the Elori and my friends grows tiresome. It is time you learned to speak to our allies on your own."

Ardu hesitated, but Rushavi continued to cry. The mother and Halcia's companion both sat nearby but did nothing to calm him.

"Why do they do nothing for him? Do they not see that he is in distress?" Ardu lifted his head as Syrani moved, but it was only to turn a page in the book she held.

"Ask for yourself, little brother."

Finally, Ardu left Rushavi's side, inching closer to the elf woman. He stopped, looking at her, until she looked away from the book she held and down at him.

"Have you finally decided to acknowledge my presence, little one?" she asked him, using the mundane speech of the humans so the Elori mother could understand.

Ardu inclined his head.

"Well, then." The elf set her book aside and came to her knees beside Ardu. "I will once again try to connect my mind to yours, so you may communicate with me. You have to let me in, understand?"

He inclined his head again.

There was an uncomfortable pressure in his head, and Ardu's first instinct was to shrink away.

"Stop fighting it. The sensation is temporary," the elf woman said.

Ardu stopped fighting. The pressure instantly lessened, and when it faded, there was an odd sort of buzzing in his mind.

"Ardu?"

"Yes." It did not feel entirely the same to talk to the elf woman as it did to speak with his sister, but the difference was not unpleasant enough to be unbearable.

"My name is Syrani. Not elf woman."

Ardu puffed his little chest in annoyance. *"Why do you let Rushavi cry? Why do you not comfort him?"*

Syrani laughed, and the Elori woman raised an eyebrow.

"He is upset that we let Rushavi cry," she explained to the mother.

The mother snickered, then turned to Ardu. "It is good he cries. He will have good lungs and a good voice."

"He is in no danger, Ardu. He is not hungry, nor dirty, nor in need of anything we can give him."

"Then why does he cry?"

"Because he is healthy and has the energy to do so. He will tire and sleep soon."

"He never cried so before. Not since his first days of birth."

"He was ill, Ardu. I'm sure you knew that."

Ardu had known. He had known before anyone else and had done more than any other to help his companion.

"If you are concerned, you can speak to him as you do me. Give him comfort that way, if you wish."

"He does not understand me when I speak to him. He matures too slowly."

Syrani sat deeper into the sand, crossing her legs in front of her. *"Is that the reason you have slowed your own growth? Because Rushavi is only an infant himself?"*

"I did slow my own growth, yes. But it will start again soon. Thanks to your persistence in connecting with me."

"But why? Why stop your natural growth?"

Ardu did not answer right away. He returned to Rushavi, curling around his little bundled body. Rushavi still cried, though with less intensity. He would indeed fall asleep soon. *"Because he is my companion. I wanted to grow with him."*

Syrani shook her head. *"It will take him years to grow into adulthood. And there is no way to know how your choice to stop your own growth will affect him. You are connected, after all. Deeper than any mental connection could be."*

"Connected?"

"You are companions. Meant to be by each other's side."

Images came to him from Syrani. They were memories of Syrani and Halcia over the years. First, a tiny red and gold dragon emerging from a golden egg, then glimpses of Halcia as she grew.

"Halcia and I missed much of the time we had together as she grew up. I regret that I did not spend every moment with her as she matured. It ... damaged our bond."

Ardu nestled himself closer to Rushavi. *"We are ... bound together,"* Ardu said slowly.

"Yes. And that bond will grow stronger as time passes and you both grow." Syrani returned to her seat, picking up her book once more. *"Do not make the same mistake I made. Do not leave Rushavi's side when he needs your comfort and affection most."*

Syrani's presence disappeared from his mind, leaving a small hole where her mind had occupied his. It felt strange to be without it, though he had been so hesitant to speak with her at all only moments before.

Ardu turned his attention to Rushavi. The infant had stopped crying, and now slept lightly. He hiccupped once, his little chest rising sharply before settling into gentle motions as his breathing returned to normal. Ardu pressed his snout against Rushavi's temple, feeling the pulse of the tiny heart from that tender spot.

"Rushavi," Ardu said, speaking softly to the oldest connection his mind held. *"Everything is alright. I am here with you."*

13

EILONWY

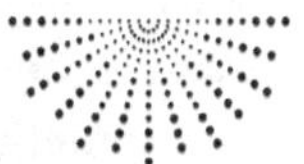

Most days, it was easy for Eilonwy to find a spare hour away from the kitchen and the bustle of the inn to work privately. There was one room in the inn that, at Jaimes's insistence, Mathius never rented out. It had belonged to his mother, Silvana. It was musty, and some of the dresses and aprons that hung in the wardrobe were riddled with moth holes, but Jaimes, and to some extent Alastor as well, refused to allow it to be cleaned out and repurposed.

Eilonwy had repurposed it anyway.

She'd changed nothing, of course. Silvana's books were still neatly piled away in a plain little chest at the foot of the bed. Her clothes still waited in the wardrobe, though Eilonwy had mended the holes and spelled the furniture to repel additional pests. The dust was wiped away and the pillow fluffed, but the bed was never slept in and the wash-basin never used.

But a small table had been added to one wall. It was not even half the size of the table Jaimes had used for crafting and testing his tinctures and medicines, but Eilonwy did not need much space to formulate the cream Jaimes used. She

105

just needed the privacy the mostly abandoned room afforded her.

And, of course, she needed time. It was the time that had recently proven most difficult to procure, not the space nor the privacy. With nearly a dozen King's Guards patrolling Larten and all of them spending their nights and mealtimes in the inn, it had become difficult to get away without arousing suspicion. There was always some guest in Etritian uniform that needed something from her, often-times requests disguised as a sexual come-on. Or a room that needed airing and cleaning. Or any of the other count-less little things men could not seem to handle appropri-ately on their own when a woman was around to do it for them.

Mathius tried to shoulder much of the extra labor, espe-cially when he realized many of the King's Guards were quite forceful in their advances. But he was only one man, and there were ten additional guests to cater to. The inn was full to bursting.

It was a little more than an hour after lunch had been cleared away when Eilonwy finally got her chance to slip upstairs to Silvana's room. She whispered a few words to Mathius, telling him where she would be and why if he abso-lutely needed to disturb her.

"But don't you dare come and get me, Mathius. Or I will be very, very angry."

Mathius put a hand over his chest solemnly. "I will man the inn solely until your return, or go down with her."

Eilonwy removed her shoes as she hurried up the stairs. It had taken so long for her to find the appropriate walking and running speeds to mimic a human. They moved so slowly that she wondered how they managed to get anything done in a timely fashion. Even dwarfs moved a little faster, though their short legs and small paces made it difficult to tell. But Eilonwy, as Eilen, moved gracefully and with perfectly normal speed up the stairs and shut the door to the inn's only unoccupied room behind her.

Eilonwy sighed, releasing the glamour spell that hid her elven features. She would never admit it to Jaimes or Mathius, but it was uncomfortable to hold on to a spell like that for so long. There was no doubt in her mind that she would have fallen ill to arcane sickness after a few short days if not for the Amulet of Water around her neck. It held more power than Eilonwy ever could, and she relied on it to keep her glamour spell active during the day.

It was worth the discomfort of maintaining the spell to stay close to Jaimes.

And she worried for Mathius, too. The grey hair she had spotted had not been the first sign of his aging. Mathius had developed faint lines in the corner of his eyes, and he sometimes complained of pains in his body.

Eilonwy had been able to watch Jaimes and Alastor grow up, but Mathius was the first human companion she had been forced to see grow old. Roland, though he was older than Mathius by several years, had not visibly aged at all in the years she had known him. She suspected the strange healing ability that Tiryn called a curse and that Roland simply took for granted was to thank for his lack of wrinkles and his pristinely ginger hair.

Eilonwy lifted her arms over her head, stretching the muscles in her shoulders and upper back with gentle twists.

Even I am beginning to feel the effects of life in Larten on my body. Or perhaps it's just the lack of strenuous activity getting to me.

There would be time for trips outside Larten and opportunities to free herself from her human disguise once the King's Guards left the inn. But until then, she would have to remain as inconspicuous as possible.

Eilonwy's attention went to the small table in Silvana's room, where the flowers Jaimes had been collecting from the garden lay in carefully arranged bundles. One pile of drying flowers was larger than the rest. This was the pile that he had collected for her enjoyment, and not for any medicinal properties they possessed. The flowers filled the room with a delicate floral scent, and Eilonwy often let the pile grow until it took up half the small space she had before clearing them away.

The others she used for Jaimes's tincture, though she never needed as much as Jaimes brought for her. She had simplified his recipe into something that could be made quickly and without too much knowledge of alchemy or herbs and plants. There was one ingredient she had added to increase the potency of Jaimes's cream, and she had yet to tell him what it was.

Eilonwy had infused his creation with arcane energy.

She had to fight the disgust at her dishonesty every time she finished producing a jar of his ointment with a small burst of concentrated effort and willpower. But her adjustment to his formulation had done wonders for Jaimes. His pain was nearly nonexistent ever since she had given him that very first jar of cream. There was no turning back, even though she knew he would be furious with her for tainting his formula with arcane energy.

Eilonwy selected some of the driest leaves, nettles, and petals from her collection of plants for the tedious task of transforming them into a medicated balm. She began by grinding the plant matter with a small mortar and pestle until it was a suitable size for tea brewing. The tea itself was simple to make. A small arcane flame heated water quicker than any mundane flame.

"Vash? Are you there?" Eilonwy asked the small flame.

There was no answer. There never was.

The tea always took time to brew. It needed to be strong. It would be further concentrated when she boiled off most of the excess water, but the stronger the initial brew, the better. It hid the scent of arcane energy well.

While the tea was steeping, she heard a commotion outside. There were raised voices, male by the sound of it. Quarrels in the streets of Larten were not unheard of, especially since the cost of goods had been on a steady incline for longer than she had resided at the inn. Men would argue over the cost of everything they could think of, and the arguments only ever ended in a few different ways. A handshake or curses. Perhaps even a brief exchange of blows, if the argument went too sour.

But Eilonwy's attention was captured when she heard the sharp shriek of a woman in pain. She rose and went to the window, opening it only wide enough to see the street below. Two King's Guards were dragging a woman from a building across the street from the inn. The woman dug her heels into the ground and struggled, but she was no match for the combined strength of the knights.

Eilonwy cursed and stormed for the door. She was nearly to the stairs before she remembered to activate her glamour spell. The stairs were empty and the inn was quiet.

Mathius was on his way to the exit as well, and Eilonwy caught up to him as he reached the foyer. "Did you hear it too?"

"I heard it. Do you know what's going on?"

"They're dragging the seamstress from across the way out of her shop."

"Demelda?" Mathius scrunched his face as he pulled the door open. The bell over the door gave a loud and jangling rattle. "What do they want with her?"

Eilonwy lifted the skirt of her dress and brushed past him. "I intend to find out."

The head King's Guard was exiting the seamstress's shop, stooping to avoid the low entrance. Eilonwy stomped onto the cobbled street, calling to him. "Just what do you think you're doing?"

The King's Guard gave her a cursory glance. "Performing my duties to the king."

"Eilen!" Mathius was following behind. She could hear the puffing of his breath.

"By pulling a woman from her home and dragging her through the street?" Eilonwy asked. She stopped in the center of the road, unsure whether to continue arguing or to follow the other two guards.

"By arresting a suspected elf sympathizer while a proper search is performed." The King's Guard stepped away from the shop's entrance, and a short and balding man stepped meekly from the building. "We've been notified that the woman residing here may be housing and assisting elves. We are merely investigating those claims." He gave Eilen another look. "It does not concern you. Unless you have evidence against this woman?"

Eilonwy shook her head, staring after the woman Mathius had called Demelda. She had been dragged to the center of Larten, some two hundred feet from her shop, and had been forced to kneel and watch from afar as her home was searched.

"Is this true, Artur?" Mathius asked the man standing outside the shop. Eilonwy recognized him but had never met him. She thought he might be the seamstress's husband.

"I-I hear her whisperin' in the night, sometimes. Down in her shop." He gave Mathius a pleading look and shrugged. "She don' never tell me what she does those times."

A crowd had begun to gather as Demelda's continued screams and shouts of protest drew bystanders from their homes.

A knight stepped from the shop long enough to drop three or four bolts of fabric onto the ground. The King's Guard overseeing the search looked from the fabric to

Eilonwy. "Go back to the inn, Eilen. This does not concern you."

Mathius put a hand on her shoulder. "Let's just do as he says."

Eilonwy shrugged his hand off. She lifted her chin and raised her voice loud enough for all to hear. "Are we not in the Free Cities? Is Larten not under our own governance?"

She had expected at least a few whispers to follow her questions, but the street was silent. Only Mathius made any noise, and it was a low murmur of warning not to draw attention to herself.

The knight's expression did not change. There was no anger or confusion in his voice, either. "Larten is only free to govern herself in issues that fall far below matters of the kingdom's safety. Threats of invasion by elves or dwarfs are handled by Etritian knights, not southern peasants." Another collection of fabric bolts were tossed into the street, and the knight kicked them aside to clear the entrance to the shop. He held out an arm, indicating the open doorway. "But if you would like to assist in the search, I am sure it would not go unrewarded if you were to discover signs of elven presence within."

Eilonwy didn't even get a chance to answer. A man's voice called from inside the shop, and the knight stepped through the entrance and out of view.

"What are you thinking?" Mathius asked. He kept his voice low, putting his hand on her shoulder once more. "You shouldn't argue with them. It'll only cause you trouble."

Eilonwy shook her head. "This is madness, Mathius. If they can search a home, destroy someone's livelihood over whispers in the night ..." She turned to face him. "What will come next?"

A shriek of pain came from within the seamstress's home, followed quickly by several manly laughs. The next thing to be tossed through the entrance of the shop and into the dirty street was no bolt of cloth. It was a person.

His ears had been cut short, a sight Eilonwy was now all too accustomed to seeing. The scars were old and healed, as were many of the white lines that crisscrossed his bare back. He was barefoot, and when he staggered to his feet and tried to run, it was with a noticeable limp. Eilonwy couldn't tell if his sharp features were from Vyrisian heritage or because he was half starved.

Eilonwy moved to let him run past her, and their eyes met for a brief moment. His were full of fear.

Before he had even gone more than a few stumbling steps, a loop of rope dropped around his neck and tightened, pulling him back with a choking gasp.

Mathius's grip on her shoulder tightened, but it wasn't enough to hold her in place. It was Jaimes's sudden arm around her waist that stopped Eilonwy from rushing to the elf's aid.

He struggled with the rope around his neck. He was weak, his arms thin and bony. A rope like the one that held him would have taken Eilonwy no time at all to rip. But the elf struggled, the dark metal cuffs on his wrists clanging together as he strained against the pull of the rope. Finally, he lost his footing and fell backwards onto the road. Two guards immediately descended on him, kicking him over onto his stomach and binding his hands together behind his back.

Demelda was screaming for them to let him go, but the elf himself said nothing.

"It seems your assistance was not needed after all, Eilen." The knight exited the shop, stooping again to avoid the low crossbeam.

Eilonwy watched the second pair of King's Guards drag the limp elf to join his human conspirator. "I suppose I should be grateful that you were here," she said. "To protect us from such dangerous creatures."

"Eilen," Jaimes warned in a low voice. "Let's leave them to finish their business and return to the inn."

"Do as your husband says," the King's Guard said. "The punishment for the crime of harboring an elf is a public whipping. It is not a sight for women to witness."

"I would witness it, if it's all the same."

"Eilen—"

Eilonwy directed her words at Jaimes but kept her eyes on the King's Guard. "You may return if you wish, but I would like to remain here."

The King's Guard said nothing, but only turned his back on Eilonwy and the gathered crowd to follow the men that carried the elf away.

Only two lesser King's Guards remained to stand guard at the entrance to the seamstress's shop. The husband, Artur, stood meekly just inside the entrance, wringing his hands and glancing from the goods strewn through the street and the interior of his home, which Eilonwy assumed was in equal disarray. He did not watch as his wife was hauled towards the center of Larten.

Jaimes pulled on her elbow, and she followed him out of the street and out of earshot of those around them. "Just what do you think you're doing?"

"I am about to watch a woman who aided an elf be whipped." Eilonwy kept her tone flippant, but heat was rising up her neck and in her cheeks.

"Go home, Eilen." Jaimes nodded up to the inn, now the building closest to them. "Don't stay out here."

"Let her go, Jaimes," Mathius said. He had joined them, but he kept his voice low and watched those around them as they either returned to their homes or made their way to Larten's small square.

"Thank you, Mathius."

"Oh, you misunderstand." Mathius paused as a pair of

young men passed close by on their way down the street. "I'm not suggesting it out of a desire to let you do as you wish. But if you see what happens to that woman, perhaps you'll take our concerns more seriously."

Eilonwy smiled, but her teeth ground together. "I will not be driven away."

Mathius nodded once, curtly. "Let her go. We'll see if she changes her mind."

Jaimes sighed. "At least let me join you."

"No, I'll be joining her. Don't torture yourself, Jaimes."

Jaimes made a face. "Mathius …"

"We'll be fine. It's not the first whipping I've seen. And your wife is stubborn."

"Alright." Jaimes sighed again. "Just don't make a scene."

He left, but not before giving Eilonwy a quick kiss on the temple.

Mathius matched Eilonwy's hurried pace with long strides. "What are you planning?"

"I don't need to be watched like a child, Mathius."

"I'm only here to make sure whatever your intentions are, they don't come back to bite us all in the ass."

Eilonwy frowned. "I don't know what I'm planning."

"He's got you that upset, has he?"

"Who, Jaimes? Or that King's Guard?"

"Either," Mathius said. "Or both," he added with a short laugh.

Eilonwy glanced around them before answering. She slowed her pace, letting the small crowd that was making its way to the center of town precede her. Ahead of them, the seamstress and the battered elf both waited on their knees in the cobbled street surrounded by King's Guards. "There are far more dangerous creatures in this world than that elf up there, Mathius."

"I know it."

"Jaimes has good intentions, but he is more concerned with those closest to him than he is with the world at large."

"And you aren't?"

Eilonwy thought for a moment, watching as Demelda was pulled to her feet and brought to a heavy wooden post that stood in Larten's little square. Eilonwy had passed the post countless times while running errands for Mathius or Jaimes. She had always known in the back of her mind that it was meant for cruelty. But she had never seen it in use before.

"How could I not be concerned for all, when this is the future?"

Demelda's hands were bound to the post above a crossbeam some six feet off the ground. A single length of heavily corded rope knotted around each wrist and looped around the post was enough to secure her.

It took Eilonwy a moment to understand the purpose of the crossbeam. But when Demelda slumped against the post, crying loudly, she understood. The crossbeam would hold Demelda up even if she could no longer support herself. If the seamstress fainted or collapsed, she would remain upright enough for the rest of her sentence to be carried out.

"So, what madness are you considering? Killing the guards? Raining fire down on Larten?" Mathius crossed his arms, looking at her with a very sad and very serious expression. "Nothing you do to try to stop this will go unnoticed, and it will put you in danger. And Jaimes. And myself. And any other southerner here foolish enough to be housing an elf as Demelda did."

Eilonwy nodded. "I know."

The first crack of the whip was deafening in the stillness of the air.

"I won't do anything to stop this."

The sentence was carried out swiftly, though not silently. Demelda screamed with every strike, and the crossbeam held her weight from the fourth one on.

There were ten in total, and the sharp tang of blood was in the air when the lead King's Guard dropped the whip and ordered her to be removed.

Eilonwy prepared herself to watch one of her kin as he was whipped. How many lashes would he receive? Twenty? More? Would they whip him until he bled to death?

But the elf was not whipped.

It was announced instead that he would be taken to Etritia and executed in the presence of the king. Then both seamstress and elf were bound with their backs to the whipping post, where it was decided they would remain until the King's Guards had concluded their business in Larten and were prepared to return to Etritia.

"What do you think will happen to Demelda?" Eilonwy asked. "Her punishment is over once she's released, right?"

Mathius shook his head. "Her punishment will never be over." He nodded over at the seamstress, who sat with her sliced back pressing into the rough wood of the beam. Spit landed on her face and head as the crowd began to disperse. "She will be a pariah in Larten. And in all the Free Cities. She could leave, and maybe find a place to start a business again. But she will never be able to find another husband or lover. The scars on her back will always be there." Mathius sighed. "Anyone that sees them will know she's done something evil to deserve them."

Something evil.

Eilonwy said nothing.

Many of the King's Guards had already returned to the inn by the time Eilonwy stepped through the door once more. There was loud and happy chatter, and the dining room was full of men calling for celebratory drinks. Jaimes was in the kitchen, filling mugs with ale and looking sick with worry.

He hugged her when she entered, giving her another kiss on the temple and not saying a single word. She took a platter of filled mugs and dispersed them, making cheerful talk and smiling at jokes about killing elves and carving their ears.

Mathius announced a free round to the King's Guards for their hard work in tracking down another fiend. It was received with cheers.

When she entered with her third tray of drinks, the head of the King's Guard held up a glass of mead to her. "To Eilen, for trusting in my men and I."

Those in the room laughed and drank.

Eilonwy smiled. "I couldn't bring myself to believe that anyone in Larten would be foolish enough to hide an elf. And you proved me wrong." She bowed her head. "I apologize for doubting you."

"Ask her for a song!" Someone piped. General acknowl-edgment followed the suggestion.

"Ah, I'd heard you've got a talented singing voice," the King's Guard said. "Do you have a song for an occasion such as this?"

Eilonwy shook her head. "I only know a handful of old love ballads and a few drinking songs. Nothing good enough for this crowd."

"I insist." The King's Guard spoke loudly enough to draw both Jaimes and Mathius from the kitchen. "Surely you know *something* appropriate enough."

"I really shouldn't," Eilonwy protested again. She set the platter down on a nearby table, and the remaining drinks were quickly snatched up. "I've just remembered I left something unattended upstairs. I should get back to it."

The King's Guard glowered and opened his mouth to speak, but Mathius interrupted. "I know one that will keep the spirits up!" He started on a local favorite, and the regular patrons in attendance joined in quickly.

Eilonwy left the room quickly, giving Jaimes a reassuring

smile and a touch on the arm before taking the stairs to the second floor.

———

Eilonwy did not rest that night. She waited until Jaimes was sleeping deeply and the noises of the inn had quieted, and then she slipped from the bed and dressed in the dark. There were still a few hours until sunrise, and it was that short time in the middle of the night when it was both too late and too early to be out and about. Eilonwy didn't take the stairs down to the first floor. It would only slow her down.

Instead, she dropped gracefully from the window ledge to the ground outside with hardly a sound and set off without a second's hesitation. There was no one out in the street. She had expected one, perhaps two King's Guards patrolling the streets. But there was no one.

She waited in the shadows under the inn to watch and listen, doubting herself for a moment.

Could it be so easy? Or is it a trap?

Eilonwy continued, moving swiftly from shadow to shadow.

The debris littering the street in front of the seamstress's shop had been removed. Whether Artur had collected it and returned it to the house or whether it had been pilfered by passersby, Eilonwy couldn't guess. But the shop itself was dark and silent.

She reached the whipping pole without seeing a single King's Guard. The elf stirred when she knelt beside him and took out a knife.

"Have you come to kill me?" he asked. His head hung low, his chin nearly resting on his chest, and his eyes were shut as if he had been sleeping.

"No," Eilonwy answered in Vyrisian. "I am here to free you, kinsman."

The elf looked up at her. "Thank the Great Ones."

"Are you well enough to travel?" She handed him a waterskin. It was old now, and Jaimes had not used it since their days on the *Kingfisher*. It would not be missed.

He nodded. "Demelda was mending my wounds. I would already be gone from this place if we had not been caught." He drank deeply, wiping his mouth with the back of his hand.

"Can you take the woman with you?"

"We were going to leave together, Demelda and I." He looked over his shoulder at the woman sleeping behind him. "She did not think there was anyone in the Southern Cities that believed as she does."

Eilonwy nodded. "Nor did we. It seems we were all wrong."

"How long have you been here?"

Eilonwy cut the ropes holding Demelda with quick, sharp movements. "Long enough to want to save this place, if possible."

Demelda stirred, wincing as she shifted. "Artur, is that you?"

"No, it's not." Eilonwy moved to kneel before her. "Are your wounds alright?"

Demelda reached for her, blinking rapidly. "I had hoped …"

"Don't hope. Not for him," the elf said. "It is too late for hope."

"Are your wounds alright?" Eilonwy repeated, coming closer to the seamstress so she could see her better.

"They hurt, of course. But they haven't killed me." Demelda blinked again, then squinted. "You're that girl from the inn, aren't you?"

Eilonwy snorted. "I am no girl. I'm old enough to be your grandmother's mother."

"Another elf? In Larten?" Demelda took the waterskin Eilonwy offered with clumsy hands. "How?"

"It has not been easy. And I have been lucky. But your luck has run out, and it's time for you to leave."

Eilonwy and the elf helped Demelda to her feet. She swayed slightly, but steadied herself with a hand on the whipping post. "I wanted one last night with my husband."

"Your husband is the reason you're out here instead of at home and in bed," Eilonwy countered. "There is nothing left for you here. Not anything worth risking your life."

Demelda nodded. "You're right."

Eilonwy passed a bag to the elf. "Food, water, it's all there. No coin, but I don't expect you'll need Azimarian gold in Vyris. There's a jar of cream for her back, too. Freshly made."

I'll have to explain the missing batch to Jaimes somehow.

Eilonwy held a knife out for him, hilt first. "And take this."

"Thank you."

Eilonwy jerked her head over her shoulder. "Go. Before the town starts to wake up."

The two hurried off, the elf guiding Demelda through the dark.

Eilonwy followed more carefully, retracing her steps until she was once more under the window to the room she and Jaimes shared. A simple leap was enough to give her a hand-hold, and once inside their room again, she breathed freely.

Jaimes sensed her weight as she returned to bed, and he reached a hand for her in his sleep. She took it and slept soundly.

NUNOR

It was two days before they had mastered how to quickly break down the Elori camp and get moving across the sandy desert. Suvusa did what she could, carrying Rushavi as she did, but the bulk of the work fell to Nunor and Hiruscu. Tathiel and Tiryn were often gone, either scouting out the endless sea of golden sands around them or searching for scarce caches of water and wild game. Tathiel seemed to have better luck finding water than Nunor and Tiryn had before his arrival, but Nunor did not quite understand how.

Even Tathiel seemed only slightly capable of explaining how he routinely lucked upon small buried pools or the water-rich shrubs that grew sparsely in an otherwise bone-dry land. These plants were precious and carefully harvested. The liquid they contained was oddly thick and a little cloudy, but it tasted clean and cooled their throats. And the meat of the fat leaves could be sliced and cooked. Some even grew rounded fruits unlike any Nunor had seen. But these they saved for Suvusa. Tiryn said their nutrients would be best for feeding both mother and child.

So Nunor and Hiruscu broke camp every morning while Syrani packed what they tore down onto the back of a large and beautiful dragon. Nunor had yet to speak to the gold and red creature. She seemed fiercer and quicker to anger than Melonya. The only time he had heard her speak was when she complained of being used as a pack animal. Her teeth were bared as she spoke, and they were very large and very sharp. Nunor made the decision at that moment to not bother her until she addressed him.

He sometimes found himself wondering how often she was able to eat while they remained in the desert, and how long it might take for his small stature to make him an easy target for a hungry dragon.

Hiruscu sat on a small pile of blankets, watching Syrani check the load that Halcia carried. Nunor stood beside him, refusing rest for the moment. They would be moving soon, and he preferred to keep his muscles awake and ready until the day was done.

"How far away do you think the rest of your family is, Hiruscu?" Nunor asked.

Hiruscu shrugged. "We are closer each night."

Halcia spread her wings, and Syrani ducked and turned away as the dragon took off. Sand sprayed with each down beat of Halcia's wings, and Syrani kept her face covered with one arm until the dust settled.

Nunor squinted against the billowing grit, which was continually stuck in his beard, his clothes, and nearly everywhere else on him.

It will take years to wash the sand from my skin.

"And how far do you think we'll walk today, Hiruscu?"

Hiruscu stood with a sigh, grabbing a blanket and draping it over his head and shoulders to protect them from the sun. "As far as we can until it is time to stop."

Nunor nodded, grabbing his own scarf and twisting it about his head. "Right."

Halcia would fly ahead, dropping her cargo wherever Tathiel and Tiryn had deemed suitable for the night, and by the time the two Elori, Nunor, and Syrani arrived, every-thing would already be set up and waiting for them. Last night there had even been a meal and water waiting for them. Nunor hoped the same would be true tonight.

They began the long journey. Nunor always took the rear of their small group. He naturally fell behind as they traveled, and he walked with the comforting touch of his axe under his fingers. Hiruscu often took the lead, though he did not carry a proper weapon. He kept a knife on his belt, but he used it to hunt and clean game. It would be a poor weapon if a serious fight came to them.

But they had yet to meet anyone in the desert, and Suvusa said they likely would not.

Syrani and Suvusa walked side by side, and when the mother lost balance on the unsteady ground or her covering slipped from the crown of her head, Syrani was there to offer assistance.

They walked for several hours, taking small breaks when needed. There was a copse of tall cacti, and they sat in the shade they offered for nearly an hour at about midday. Syrani, under Suvusa's careful instruction, harvested the fruits that grew along their branches. Hiruscu used his knife to scrape the long needles from a few, then dug a deep hollow where the tough skin was now bare. Water wept from the wounds, and he refilled their skins before they pressed on.

"Won't that damage them permanently?" Nunor asked the Elori man.

Hiruscu shook his head. "No. They will heal. And next year, we will drink from them again."

"You pass through this area every year?"

"It is how the Elori are. Always moving, always searching for the next stop along the path." He motioned for Nunor, pointing at a spot on a tall and thick cactus. "See, the family has already been here."

Nunor inspected the spot Hiruscu indicated. There was a hole similar to the one Hiruscu had made, but the wound seemed to be healing. The edges were lightly browned and wrinkled, and tiny hairs were growing where the skin of the plant had been shaved clean.

"How long ago would you say they were here?"

Hiruscu frowned. "Not long."

Nunor waited for more, but Hiruscu only shrugged and turned away.

"Of course." Nunor growled, adjusting the wrap about his head. "Not long."

They traveled southwest, following a trail only Hiruscu and Suvusa could see. The sun beat down on them, burning Nunor's back as they walked. It was exhausting, the constant marching over shifting sands, but it was all that could be done until they reached the rest of the Elori tribe.

At long last, as the sun began to lower in front of them, they spotted the tent off in the distance.

They came upon Tathiel soon after. He waited for them with skins of fresh water, which he passed to each.

"It's not far now, and Tiryn has dinner finished and waiting for you." Tathiel took Rushavi in his arms so Suvusa could drink her fill. The young dragon quickly crawled from the mother's shoulders to Tathiel's, burrowing under the thin blanket the elf wore to protect his head from the sun.

"It's not cactus again, is it?" Nunor asked between gulps of water. The liquid was cool and perfect. "If I have to keep eating grilled leaves, I will eventually lose my sanity." He polished off the water Tathiel had given him, leaving only dregs to splash over his neck and across his face. "Dwarfs need meat."

Tathiel smiled. "Perhaps Halcia can be persuaded to part with some of the iguana she found. But I would hurry, Nunor. It was very small, and she is much larger than you."

"Never mind," Nunor grumbled quietly. "Better to wait than stir the ire of such a beast."

Tathiel smirked. "Come on, then. The camp is ready and waiting, and I'm sure you're tired."

It took another hour to reach the tents. They settled into the sand around the fire Tiryn had built with groans and sighs. Nunor did not accept the meal offered to him at first, but some harsh words from Syrani changed his mind. They all needed their strength, and all the pouting he could muster would not change the fact that there was no meat to be had.

"Besides," she added, "if we found a bit of desert game, it should go first to Suvusa and Ardu."

Nunor ate the cactus, which had been cut and grilled on small skewers, and said nothing more.

"Any news?" Syrani asked, turning to Tiryn.

Tiryn shook his head. "No. Many of the Elori's tracks have been wiped away by the desert. The few that I have found are old. I've seen no sign that we are gaining on them."

"I have."

Nunor turned to Halcia. She licked at an elongated skull that looked absurdly small between her forepaws. "And when, pray tell, were you planning on telling us about it?"

"Just now, master dwarf." Halcia locked eyes with him, licking her chops. The skull split with a sickening crack after a small flex of one clawed foot.

Nunor barely suppressed the shudder that threatened his spine. *You are small, and she is hungry.*

"What did you see, Halcia?" Syrani asked.

Halcia turned to her rider. *"I saw the dust kicked up by many travelers. A thousand, perhaps. Coming from the east."*

Suvusa and Hiruscu exchanged a look.

"The east?" Nunor asked. "You mean, we have been going the wrong way this whole time?"

"Impossible," Hiruscu said simply.

"I know what I saw. It was a large group, traveling quickly. Perhaps on horseback."

Suvusa shook her head. "Then you did not see the Elori. We are not so many, and we are not so fast."

"The Elori will be in Cai Myrh, our place of long rest. It is south and west of here."

"What else could it have been?"

Sourness filled Nunor's stomach. "It could be the dwarfs."

Tiryn's head went up sharply. "Darlyth called for Doldural's gates to be shut."

"And Darmon took issue with that. I could see my cousin going against his father's wishes."

"Will they cause us harm?" Syrani asked.

"I don't think so," Nunor answered. "Especially when they see two dragons and a pair of Elori."

"They will not harm Rushavi or Ardu?" Suvusa asked. Even now, infant and dragon alike clung to her.

Nunor shook his head. "No."

"Why do they come this way?"

"It's likely that they seek the Elori tribe, same as we do." Nunor stood, brushing sand from his rear. "They will catch up to us soon enough. We can ask them then."

It was another two days before the dwarfs came within sight of their camp. The sand their steeds kicked up created a billowing cloud that stretched across much of the eastern horizon.

Tathiel did not meet the group outside the camp, as he usually did. They found him at their campfire instead, a bare blade over his knees.

"Tiryn went to meet the dwarfs," he said by way of greeting.

Nunor collapsed into the sand, catching the water skin

Tathiel tossed his way. "I thought he might. If Darmon is leading them, then at least Tiryn is a familiar face to him."

"I told him it was a stupid idea. One elf against a small army?"

"They won't hurt him." Nunor wiped sweat from his arms and chest. "Doldural still has a functioning treaty with the elves, after all."

"But the way you talk about this Darmon …" Tathiel's knee jigged, making the blade bounce slightly. "He doesn't sound like someone to follow treaties well."

"You would normally be correct, but Tiryn will be fine."

As night fell, countless flares of bright red firelight spread across the dark mass of the dwarf encampment. Nunor watched them, trying to imagine the faces that would be gathered around those flames.

Which one did Darmon sit at? Would Grinor be with him?

And what of the woman from the Obsidian Order? Alain? Did she follow her king's decree, or did she join Darmon?

"You're worried."

Nunor jumped. It was the first time Halcia had ever spoken to him and him alone. He looked over at her. She was curled into a lazy ball, her tail draped over the rear legs. Her head rested in the sand between her forepaws, and though both of her eyes seemed closed at first glance, the right one was open ever so slightly. The reptilian pupil beneath was fixed on Nunor.

"I am," he answered.

There was no one else nearby to hear him. Suvusa and Syrani had taken to bed early, and the interior of their small women's tent was dark. Tathiel still sat at the fire, his blade still sitting across his knees, but his attention was far from Nunor and Halcia. Hiruscu had wandered the edge of the firelight for several minutes before retreating to the larger tent for the night.

"Do you worry that you spoke poorly? That your friend is in trouble?"

Nunor shook his head. "No, it's not that."

"Then what?"

Nunor thought for a moment. Something had been eating at him since the first mention of the approaching dwarfs. It was hard to articulate.

"Hm, I can't say for sure."

Halcia sighed through her nostrils, the warm air billowing the sand. *"Shall I eat them and be done with it? It will take but a moment, I am sure."*

Nunor snorted. "I'm sure it would take you no time at all, but I ask that you refrain. They are still my people."

"If you insist."

Nunor was silent, watching the fires. They were close, only a few miles away. He could smell the smoke that drifted on the wind.

"Great Ones be damned, they have pork." Nunor could smell it, sweet and smoky and surely delicious.

"I know." Halcia's nostrils flared as she breathed in deeply. *"They taunt us."*

Nunor's stomach rumbled. "Perhaps they will share their feasts with us after the sunrise."

From the dwarf camp, a brilliant column of gold light went up. It illuminated the night sky for a brief second, then was gone.

"Tiryn." Nunor stood. "He's sent a signal."

"That was the same light we saw while searching the desert for you." Halcia was also up again, but only far enough to sit on her haunches. *"What does it mean?"*

Nunor relayed the question to Tathiel, who had sheathed his weapon once the light had faded.

"It means he is safe and will return in the morning." Tathiel's shoulders were relaxed. "We are safe tonight." He headed for the tent, his damnably long legs crossing the distance in only a few steps.

"I could have told you that, Tathiel," Nunor protested. "There was no concern."

Tathiel paused to give him a hard look, one hand clutching the heavy cloth of the tent flap. "Then why are you awake and watching them, when every other night you have been asleep by this hour?"

Nunor didn't have an answer.

He stayed awake, despite Tathiel's snide remark. And as the lone figure of someone far too tall to be a dwarf approached in the early hours of the morning, Nunor began his daily task of breaking the camp as if it were any other morning.

* * *

"Did you really think I would not realize what my father was planning?"

The interior of Darmon's tent was grotesquely opulent, in Nunor's opinion. There were boar furs draped across the sand, and a damned bed, frame and all, covered in satin pillows. Everything was red and gold, and Darmon himself was no different.

"I'm not sure to what you're referring," Nunor said. He took the gilded goblet of wine that Grinor offered him, but did not drink.

Wine, in the desert?

"It seems our dear king has neglected to tell his own son of his failing health." Darmon sat in an oversized and over-stuffed chaise, his short legs stretched out as he propped himself up on one elbow. A large warhammer leaned against the short side of the chaise, the leather-wrapped handle within easy reach of Darmon.

"What Darlyth has cared to share with you is not my

concern." Nunor scrutinized the interior of the tent once more. "What is all this, Darmon? This isn't you."

"This will be me, once I am made king."

Nunor shook his head. "If you know about your father's illness, then you know he doesn't want you to take the throne after him."

Darmon smiled. "So, you admit that you have intentions for the crown?"

Nunor slammed his wine goblet on a nearby table. "If it means keeping you from it, then yes."

"So what was the deal you tricked my father into making?" Darmon smirked. "Find the Amulet of Earth and you get the crown?"

"There was no such deal," Nunor said. "If I find the amulet, I will earn a new name. What is done after is Darlyth's business. He is free to name whomever he wishes to the crown."

"Whatever lies you might say will not change the truth—I will be the one to reclaim the amulet and return it to my father."

"We could work together," Grinor said in his soft voice. "It need not be a competition. Doldural does not need to war with itself."

Nunor sighed. "Grinor is right." He gritted his teeth, surprised he was about to ask Darmon for assistance. "We could use your help. With food and supplies, perhaps a few steeds—"

"And, in exchange, we go with you to find the Elori tribe and hunt for the amulet, and play the diligent son while you claim my birthright?" Darmon shook his head. "No."

"Darmon, you cannot keep this pace up for long. I saw your men." Nunor gestured towards the tent's exit. "They are tired. You push them too hard. And this—" he waved his hand around them "—*fine* arrangement you have surely doesn't help." Nunor recalled the number of firelights he had seen in the night, and the number of wearied faces he had seen as Tiryn led them through the camp to Darmon. "How many of Doldural's knights did you take with you?"

It was Grinor who answered. "All of them."

Nunor stared for a moment. "You took *all* of the knights from Doldural?"

Darmon shifted uneasily.

"Who would protect your people if Doldural was attacked? You would have nothing to rule over, you …" Nunor gritted his teeth again, but it did not help the spew of curses that left his mouth. "You fucking daft piece of dog shit, you mud-eating piss puddle. If I didn't know your parents, I would swear you were conceived by an ass and birthed by an over-bred bitch."

"Is that any way to speak to your future king?"

"You are not, and never will be, my king!"

The silence that followed Nunor's shout was absolute. Even Grinor's whistling breath seemed to stop.

Nunor took a deep breath and let it out slowly. "Go home, Darmon. You will eventually come to slow us down. An army of this size cannot keep the pace you've set. If you want to see the amulet in Doldural once more, then provide my company with supplies and steeds, and we will be on our way."

Darmon was silent for a moment. Then he stood, passing his wine to Grinor. "Alain, please come in."

The tent opened briefly. Nunor spotted Tiryn waiting outside before the gap closed again and Alain stood inside with them.

"Yes, sir?"

"Select thirty knights of high proficiency and send our best knights and the rest back home. Have them take anything nonessential with them." Darmon nodded to Grinor. "You will go with them. I will have no need of a diplomat, and I'm aware you're only here to keep an eye on me and report back to my father everything you see."

Grinor stammered a reply, but Darmon cut him off with a wave of his hand and curse.

"Sir?" Alain asked. "What is your plan?"

"We will travel light when we join my cousin on his search for the amulet."

"Darmon—" Nunor started.

"I will be the one to retrieve the amulet, Nunor." Darmon glared, his hand on the hilt of the large knife he wore on his belt. "Doldural deserves someone without a cursed name as their king."

15

MOTHLENOR

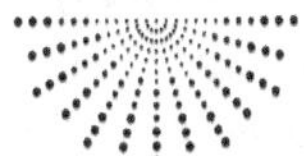

Even with his daughter gone, Mothlenor still found it difficult to concentrate for more than a few moments at a time. Controlling Nevina's soul had brought on a bout of arcane sickness that lingered even after days of rest and little exertion. Mothlenor felt his age, even if his body did not truly betray it. And even that little trick was troublesome to maintain.

Trissa's constant crying had played havoc with his ears and his mind, but it had kept him from falling into a tired stupor for hours on end.

His tired body ached for the comforts of his bed, but he continued to sit behind his desk. There were reports to read and analyze, and he could not trust anyone else to do it for him.

Anna was no longer on his council, not since he had made her his queen and her pregnancy had been revealed. And Ferrand …

He has the mind for ruthless killing, but not for careful plan-ning and thoughtful decision making.

Mothlenor rubbed at his face, realizing with mild disgust that unshaven stubble was blending harmoniously with his unkempt beard. "How am I to gather the remaining amulets if I cannot find the strength for a shave?"

The report he was reading folded on itself as soon as he set it aside. It had not even been open long enough to lose the creases in its pages. Worse still, Mothlenor couldn't remember a word of it.

He stood, the fatigue in his body fighting against him, and went to the door of his study.

A meal, a bath, and a walk about the halls, and I will be a new man.

The castle was quiet, and the halls were empty. Mothlenor could count on a single hand how many people now walked the castle on a recurring basis. Himself, Anna and Trissa, the servant girl that was now solely responsible for the castle's upkeep and care, and Ferrand. There were guards, of course, but they only came when summoned and did not stay longer than necessary.

By fortunate chance, he found Illa not far from the bath, and sent her ahead to prepare it for him. Even she seemed startled to see him about. Or perhaps she was surprised by his appearance.

A shave. Then I will look and feel more like a man.

The bathing room was one of the few rooms of the castle that was still used routinely. It was clean and well cared for, though Mothlenor noted a few chipped tiles in the stone floor that needed mending or replacing. He made a note to send for a stone mason from Cardyn. It would not do well if Trissa tripped and injured herself.

The water of the bath was cooler than he ever recalled it being. He bathed quickly, and though he asked Illa to have the water warmed, there was no discernible change by the time he finished. He shaved, standing naked and cold on the stone floor, using mundane tools. He would have normally magicked a blade and mirror into his hands, but there was little reason to exhaust himself unnecessarily.

He nicked himself only once, which he attributed with a curse to the faint tremble in his hands. The blood welled into a fat drop and rolled into his beard. It seemed darker than it ought to have been.

The meal was almost just as disappointing. The kitchen was empty, and it took him a moment to remember that Cookie, the old wench that once cared for the hungry stomachs of the castle, had died a few years ago. Illa had disappeared while he was bathing, and Mothlenor wondered if she was perhaps with Anna and Trissa.

The kitchen seemed larger than he remembered. Or perhaps it was just the emptiness that made it seem so. The table, once filled with assortments of fruits and cheeses and baked goods, was bare. The counters were similarly empty.

Mothlenor found a partial loaf of bread and some fruit, which he washed down with a glass of wine. The wine he conjured from his study because none of the drinks in the larder looked to be of particularly good quality.

Is this what has become of the castle? Of Etritia? Left to starve and suffer thirst while trapped within our own walls?

It was his doing, but he had not made the decision to close Etritia's gates all those years before without careful consideration. And it had not been for naught. Elves had been vanquished within a week's journey of Etritia. Even across the King's Bridge and into Vyris their numbers had dwindled.

The dwarfs had proven more stubborn, but even they could not hold out for much longer.

And when Doldural finally fell, wherever it was hidden beneath the mountains of its namesake, the Etritians would finally be free to return to their farmlands safely.

We will be prosperous once more.

Mothlenor left the kitchen, remarking on the dullness of the rugs and tapestries that lined the floors and walls. How long had it been since they had been properly cleaned? Or

seen by a weaver? There were threadbare spots where countless feet had worn through the wool since Mothlenor's
coronation.

*But we cannot be truly great and magnificent until all the
known world is ours.*

And that would not happen unless he could summon the
Great Soul.

Mothlenor kept walking.

The library, once a place of warmth and light and rich
with the scent of leather-bound books, was dark and chilly. It
smelled musty, though he could see no discernible sign of
dust or decay. It merely seemed … forgotten. The fireplace
had no soot, and the few books he pulled and opened felt
stiff in his hands. Like the chill had sapped the life from the
leather and stiffened the binding.

Mothlenor mused for a few moments, pulling books he
had read years ago from their shelves and flipping absently
through the pages. He was tempted to carry some away to his
tower, but there would be no time for pleasurable reading.

He left the library with one book under his arm. It was a
children's book, the spine worn and cracked. He had faint
memories of his mother reading it to him when he was a
child.

Perhaps Trissa would not cry for her mother so much if
there were books in the tower. He would even get her more
toys, if she could behave herself.

Mothlenor's steps faltered. Was Trissa even literate?
Surely Anna had not abandoned their child's education, even
if there were no tutors to be had in Etritia.

*Perhaps a tutor is in order. From Cusch, or another of the
eastern cities.*

His next stop was, of all places, Areanath's old chambers.
They had been thoroughly cleaned out. No sign of his elder
brother remained. Not even the bed was left. It had likely
been moved off to another bedroom in the castle some-

where. The rooms were completely empty, save for a spiderweb in a corner of the ceiling.

But still, somehow, the stench of tobacco smoke hung in the air. He could almost hear Areanath's voice, asking him to reconsider. Telling him it was not too late to turn away from his quest. Repent, pay reparations, and pass the throne to Anna.

"Don't be ridiculous."

Mothlenor left, but not before flicking a small flame at the web and watching it burn away.

Those small tricks left him weary, but he had vowed one more stop to himself.

One more stop, then he would return to his tower. There was still much to be done, though his arcane sickness kept him exhausted. Reports were still waiting for him. And he had a new dragon's eye to keep watch with.

A short rest would not delay us much, however ...

The idea was tempting.

Once, right after Areanath's death, Mothlenor had gone to the treasury in search of the Amulet of Air. It was then that he had discovered Areanath's last betrayal. Not a day had gone by when he did not curse his brother for such a selfish act. But Mothlenor had never returned to the royal treasury.

He'd ordered it cleaned, and had burned or buried the dwarfen and elvish art, weapons, and books. He'd had objects sent down there for storage over the years as well. Books, mostly, though he had cut and preserved two locks of hair. The first had belonged to Nevina, taken just before Ferrand's men had removed her body from his tower. The second he had cut from Anna's head before she went to birth their child.

But he had not set foot in the room since the day before his coronation. There had been little reason to.

There was still little reason to do so, other than for the

sense of nostalgia it might give him. But that was enough. Mothlenor took the hallways slowly, musing over small nothings as he walked. It felt like he was returning to a place that summoned only bad memories.

And why wouldn't it feel so? It is where the search for the amulets began, after all.

There were no guards on the doors. Another artifact from his brother's time that he had dispensed with. The lock was undone with a small twist of Mothlenor's hand and arcane energy that took a shamefully long time to summon. The doors he opened himself, but only enough for him to step inside. There was no light in the room beyond what spilled through the doorway.

Thankfully, there was a long lamp hook leaning against a nearby alcove, and Mothlenor was able to lift a lantern from its hook in the same recess.

How the mighty have fallen. Mothlenor snorted. *I've forgotten how irritating even the most mundane tasks become without the use of magic.*

The treasury was nearly empty. Directly across from the door was a long table that took up most of the far wall. There were assortments of gems across its top, but Mothlenor was certain they had been there long before he had taken the throne. The shelf of books was still there, though it was quite empty. Atop the bare bookshelf was a familiar small box. Mothlenor opened it, recalling the fury he had felt when he had last opened the locked latch and peered inside.

There was no depression left in the velvet interior from the Amulet of Air, and the acrid tang of spent arcane energy had long dissipated. But the site of the empty box still lit a flame in Mothlenor's chest.

It was not completely empty, however. Inside were two small locks of hair. One pale, the other dark. Each was fastened with a small length of twine, and he brushed each one gently with the tip of a shaking finger. Nevina was gone.

It was my hand that did the deed, but her actions killed her.

There was still hope for Anna. There had been a few times over their years together when Mothlenor had thought of killing his wife. But she had always found a way to redeem herself.

There was still hope for her, yet.

He continued exploring what little was in the room. The gems he passed over. They would be difficult to sell for some time, and their worth therefore was of little interest to him.

Mothlenor opened a chest that sat on the floor against one wall. In his brother's time, it might have been filled with gifts from the Vyrisian or dwarfen kings. But it was now perhaps half filled with Etritian gold. The two chests beside it were already opened and empty.

Mothlenor ground his teeth. *This is the extent of our wealth?*

Where had the riches of the past gone? To finance an endless war against the elves and dwarfs?

Ferrand had surely used his fair share on countless trips to the untamed northern lands, but those trips were now at an end. Mothlenor had a new dragon's eye, and it waited up in his tower for him.

Mothlenor slammed the lid of the chest shut, making the coins within jingle.

Etritia was far worse than he had ever planned for. He had been warned about the food shortages, though he had increased trips to the eastern cities of Cusch and Cardyn. Their lands were untainted by the stain of elven or dwarfen influence, especially after the fall of Thessala. Their farmlands were safe for their citizens to cultivate and care for, and food was bountiful. But the difference had not been great enough, apparently.

How long had it been since he had walked the streets of the capital? Did he dare to do so now, in such a weakened state?

The unfortunate answer was no, he could not bring himself to traverse more than the distance from the kitchens to his brother's former garden. Not until he had recovered from his arcane sickness.

And what would he find outside the castle walls? Anna had told him stories of abuse and murder at the hand of the King's Guards, and Mothlenor knew many of Ferrand's men —and Ferrand himself—were capable of such atrocities.

But it was only the deserving that hung from the gallows. And surely Anna's retelling of the conditions Etritians faced outside the castle walls was colored by her womanly weaknesses. Compassion and kindness, coupled with her inability to see the greater good the sacrifices of a few could bring, surely distorted her interpretation of reality.

Regardless, Etritia was far poorer in wealth and spirit than he had ever wanted or intended.

And who besides his brother was entirely to blame?

"Ajax and his band of thieves and killers."

If Ajax had not stolen the golden dragon's egg, then he could have used the beast to raze Vyris to the ground. He could have used it to smoke the dwarfs out of the gilded halls and into the waiting arms of Etritia's best knights.

Mothlenor left the pathetic and empty treasury. He didn't bother locking the door behind him. Ferrand would come across the unlocked door sooner or later, and that was fine enough for Mothlenor.

He had grown lax and lazy since the birth of his daughter, Mothlenor could see it now. There was no time for fatigue and exhaustion. Arcane illness or no, there were still amulets to be found and a Great Soul summoning to prepare for. A dragon's eye waited for him, and there was a former commander to be hunted and captured.

"Reports be damned," he murmured to himself as he hurried down the nearest hall that would lead him to his tower's entrance. "Etritia will not survive long at this rate."

16
SUVUSA

Suvusa was grateful to the dwarfs for their food, and even more grateful to have a steed to ride on across the desert. It was a beast unlike anything she had ever seen before. Its short, coarse hair was pleasantly soft, and though the animal was smaller than a horse, it carried her and Rushavi well. Riding was uncomfortable, but she did not have the strength to walk such great distances each day. And she could focus on feeding Rushavi, who seemed to be hungry more and more often as his heat sickness lifted.

"What are these beasts called again?" she asked the dwarf Nunor.

"Mules. A crossbreed of the donkeys you are familiar with and the horses of much of Azimar." Nunor walked on foot beside her, sometimes holding the reins of the beast that carried her.

"Why mules? Why not donkeys?"

Nunor smiled. "It seems my cousin intended to present himself as garishly as possible to the Elori. Doldural mules are highly regarded for their strength and sturdiness, but we usually use donkeys for travel." He patted the mule's neck, and it nickered affectionately. "They're better suited to our size than the mules."

"Your cousin seems to be very eager to meet my family," Suvusa noted. She could see Darmon at the lead of their party, her husband beside him. The female dwarf walked on his other side, acting as his guard, but she did not join in on the talk and laughter that Darmon and Hiruscu made together. Of all of Damon's closest companions, the one Nunor called Grinor seemed the least suspicious. The old dwarf walked behind Darmon, keeping his head low and only speaking on a few rare occasions.

"I heard you arguing with your cousin about the old dwarf."

"Grinor, you mean?" Nunor asked. "Darmon wanted to send him away with the rest of the dwarfs, but I insisted he stay. Darmon was furious."

"You fought?"

"Of course we fought," Nunor answered. He made a sort of snorting guffaw that Suvusa noticed he frequently made when annoyed. "He's my cousin. What good is he for if not to constantly antagonize me?"

Suvusa laughed, startling the mule enough for the creature to fold its ears back and bray. Hiruscu turned at the sound and gave her a broad smile.

"I see Grinor is still here, so you must have had the better argument."

"No," Nunor sighed. "Tathiel told us both to shut up and ask Grinor what he wanted. And Grinor asked to stay."

"And Darmon? He accepted this?" Suvusa asked.

"He doesn't really care." Nunor spat in the sand. "He's only eager to find the amulet and return home in a parade of glory." Nunor glared at his cousin's back, and his words had a dark edge to them. "He expects to be king soon."

"I have heard. There were several things said about your family to me. Not all about Darmon." She wrinkled her nose, looking to the sky to track the sun's progress. "Did you know that the Elori do not carry the names of our fathers? We do not believe that …" She paused for a moment, trying to find the words to explain what she meant.

Nunor sighed. "You don't have to continue, Suvusa. I understand."

"Then you know my thoughts of you have not changed? Not because of your name, Little Brother."

Nunor smiled. It was hard to see through the thickness of his beard. "You are too kind to let a thing like that bother you."

Suvusa leaned over slightly to look Nunor in the face. His skin was growing wrinkled from the sun, like an aged fruit. "But you still worry?"

He shrugged. "Not about the Elori. But about my own people."

"Yes?"

Nunor squinted up at her. "Aren't you supposed to tell more of that story about the Great Ones?"

Suvusa smiled. "Answer my question, and I will tell you."

Nunor huffed and was quiet. Suvusa thought he might not answer.

"I am concerned," he began, "that even if I were to lose my cursed name, I wouldn't be accepted as a dwarf leader."

"You want to be the king?"

Nunor shook his head. "No." He cursed, the word a short and guttural one that Suvusa thought sounded quite filthy. "But I have done so much for Doldural. And I could do more, if given the chance."

"Tiryn told me that you are a master blacksmith." Suvusa shifted on her mule. Her rear was killing her. Her tailbone would be sore, and she would be very surprised if her inner thighs were not red and burning from constant chafing.

"It's a respectable trade, especially for someone with a cursed name." Nunor stopped the mule, holding the beast steady as Suvusa stood in the saddle to adjust her clothing. "But I have no order to call my own. No honor to claim."

"Because of your name?"

Nunor nodded.

Suvusa sat in the saddle once more, and the mule continued walking. "You just want to be seen for the things you have done."

"And to be given the opportunity to do more for my people, yes."

Suvusa considered his answer for a moment.

"What about that story, hm?"

Suvusa laughed. "Very well, then. Here is the next part that I know."

<hr>

"When the first god and his four children awoke, they found a mate for their father waiting for them. She was exactly as they had wished her to be—kind, generous, intelligent, and strong. For many, many years, the gods were happy. They cared for the land as a family and brought peace to all the peoples.

"But the elves, dwarfs, and humans did not always share the peace their gods did. Wars became common. And, over time, many began to neglect the gods. Worshippers became murderers, and the gods became hunted.

"Once again, the first god called his children to him, and when night fell and all were together, he wept. 'Our world now turns against us. How do we stop this bloodshed?' he asked his children.

"Ilir, who was once revered as a god of war and battle, stood first. 'We should kill those who would kill us and remind them who their gods are!'

"Vyris, who was less known to the people of the world, stood second. 'We should go into hiding and leave the world to these peoples. They will eventually stop their bickering and learn to live together.'

"Ymis, who had been worshipped as a goddess of mercy, stood next. 'Let us not completely abandon them. Surely there is something we can do to restore peace.'

"Then all three turned to their oldest brother, who was both wise and clever, as Farnir stood. 'Perhaps,' he said, 'we should let every god choose for him or herself how to deal with the people of the world. Those who wish to fight should be free to do so. Perhaps they can teach the people fear. Those who wish to hide can do so, and maybe they can teach wistfulness. Those who wish to continue their guidance can do so, and the people of this world may learn compassion.'

"The first god and his mate said nothing."

Suvusa stopped to adjust Rushavi's weight against her chest. He had gotten a little foot stuck in the fabric sling that carefully wrapped around her waist and shoulders and kept him close to her.

"He seems healthier," Nunor noted. "Squirms a lot more."

"He will be running after Ardu in no time, I am sure of it."

Nunor glanced up at Darmon and Hiruscu. "Does my cousin know of Ardu yet?"

Suvusa shook her head. "No. They will learn of him when we can no longer keep him a secret."

Nunor nodded.

"Shall I continue?" Rushavi sat easier against her chest, but Suvusa felt fatigue settling into her.

"Please." Nunor bowed his head slightly, touching the mule's neck.

Suvusa continued.

"The first god gave no direction, for he was too saddened by all that had passed to come to a decision of his own. His wife, though she was intelligent in her own right, had not lived the long life of the other gods, and was not sure what course of action to take. So, in the end, it was Farnir's suggestion that was used.

"Ilir fought against the elves, dwarfs, and humans. He was bitter and angry, and his spirit was fiery. He was gravely wounded in many battles, and eventually succumbed to his injuries and was lost. He was mourned by his family, and his spirit journeyed to the great open sky.

"Vyris went into hiding far to the north, where the ice and snow might keep any who sought her away. But she was eventually found, and though she pleaded for her life, she was also killed. And so her spirit joined her brother's.

"Ymis tried to help the people of the world, but they grew spiteful and angry and attacked her. She, like her brother Ilir, eventually died from her injuries. Her spirit joined those of her siblings, and her children retreated to the eternal depths that had birthed her. They were never seen again.

"Though his siblings asked him many times what course of action he would take, Farnir could not decide. He did not want to fight, for he had watched the people in his care grow. He did not want to hide, for it was not in his nature to retreat from hardship. But when he tried to continue as his sister Ymis had, he too was attacked and wounded. So Farnir devised a fourth plan and returned to the desert he arose from to carry it out. He was never seen by his family again.

"And so the first miracle of the gods came to an end.

"When she saw that all four of their children had failed in their respective attempts to end the wars between the people of the world, the sixth and final god turned to the first and said to him: 'Husband, something must be done. I will go down to the world and try to bring peace myself. But I will not go as a god, I will go as one of them.'

"So the wife lay down in the same spot where she had come into being and instructed her husband to build her a new body. One that was not the body of a god, but that would allow her to pass among the people as one of their own. Then she closed her eyes and went into a deep sleep.

"As she slept, the first god did as his wife instructed. He removed the glittering stones that his children had created from their own tears, and shaped for his wife a new form. When he was done, he lay beside the fire to wait for her to awaken again.

"And so the second and third miracles of the gods also came to an end.

"When she awoke, the wife went to her husband. But she had slept so long, and her husband had been so weary, that his spirit had joined those of his children. The wife wept for many days. She tried to use the glittering stones of her children to make for her husband a new body. She even removed her own heart and placed beside her husband's, but while hers continued to beat, his did not. She was no longer a god, and nothing she tried worked.

"She took the stones with her when she went to the world. A Great War was going on, one that had waged for years. The mother, who still possessed her husband's eye and could see things no normal mortal could see, was able to see an end to the war. But many died, including many of her children's children, such that she became the last of the gods.

"She gave the glittering stones to the people of the world, making them promise to never cause such destruction again, or their oldest god, their creator, would return. And he would destroy them."

It took Nunor a moment to realize she was done speaking.

"So, that's it?"

"That is all I know of the dragons and the amulets, yes," Suvusa answered.

Nunor huffed. "But that tells us nothing of where the earth amulet could be."

"What of the story of Farnir?"

Nunor jumped, cursing as he realized Tiryn had been walking only a few paces behind him.

Suvusa laughed, but Nunor was less pleased.

"Dammit, don't sneak up on me like that, Tiryn. You're going to get stabbed one of these days. And you won't see me crying."

"Master Nunor, he has been walking with us for many steps. Since I first began my tale," Suvusa said.

"What of Farnir's plan?" Tiryn asked. "Do you know it?"

Suvusa shook her head. "That is not a story I can tell."

Nunor groaned, waving a hand dismissively. "Ah, you don't need to tell it so nicely. Just say what happened."

She shook her head again. "I have never even heard the tale."

"Who could tell us this story?"

Suvusa thought for a moment.

There are not so many who know all the old tales ... "Our mother would know. She knows all the stories."

Tiryn sighed. "So we must wait until we reach the rest of the Elori."

"It will be soon. Hiruscu has seen many signs of their passing."

"Then we must wait," Tiryn said. "And trust that the Elori have our answers."

Camp took longer to set up that night than on previous evenings. There was hushed argument between Darmon, Nunor, and the elf Syrani. Suvusa ignored it, though Hiruscu kept his eye on the trio as Rushavi and Ardu both ate their fill.

"I grow weary of this constant bickering," she said to her husband in the Elori tongue.

"As do I, but there is nothing to be done about it."

Suvusa thought of the story she had recounted, remembering the sixth and final god. "We could refuse to help them find their missing amulet until a truce is made among our friends." But even as she said it, Suvusa knew it was unlikely to be done.

"I don't know if I am ready to call Darmon a friend. He is greedy and spiteful."

"Yet you laugh with him?"

Hiruscu shrugged. "For the moment, they are many, and we are few. And I worry for the children."

The children. He includes not just Rushavi, but Ardu as well.

Suvusa closed her hand around her husband's.

When it came time to bed down, Suvusa learned the source of the disagreement she had witnessed. The woman's tent she and Syrani had shared along the road to the Elori would now have a third member. The young dwarf, Alain, made herself as small as possible in the already cramped quarters, and did not speak to Syrani at all.

"We are all women, after all. There is no need to be uncomfortable around each other," Suvusa said, trying to ease the tension. "Let the men stink up their sleeping quarters with belches and bodily odors. We can have this space for our own peace."

Alain smiled nervously, but still said nothing.

The uneasy silence was broken by the sound of men shouting and weapons being drawn. Beneath the urgent sounds of panic immediately outside the tent, Suvusa heard the familiar beat of large wings.

The three women left the tent together, Rushavi in Suvusa's arms and Ardu still concealed beneath her clothing. Halcia descended and landed in the camp with wings spread wide and teeth bared.

"Stop, Ilir damn you!" Darmon shouted, one hand raised at his men. "Can't you see that this is no lowly beast to wander into our camp?" He bowed to Halcia. "Forgive my men, great dragon. They are foolish."

"And what does that say about the dwarf that leads them, if they are stupid enough to draw weapons on a dragon."

Suvusa heard Syrani's drawn-out sigh at Halcia's words.

"Forgive my sister," another voice said. *"We should not have risked startling you."*

From the darkness, a second dragon emerged. This one was covered in scales of shimmering blues, and there were not nearly so many spikes along her neck and spine. At her approach, Ardu stirred in his slumber.

Darmon cleared his throat. "Melonya and Halcia, I presume? I was not told you would both be here tonight."

Melonya dipped her long neck, the triangular shape of her head and snout nearly touching the sand. *"I had a favorable wind on my return, and am here earlier than expected."*

Darmon laughed. "Two dragons and a company of dwarfs. What a sight we must make."

Suvusa shifted her weight, concealing Ardu's small serpentine body deeper within her clothing.

"I am not here for you, dwarf. I am here for my companion, Syrani. If she were to decide to leave you, I would go with her."

"I must agree with Halcia, Master Dwarf. I understand that there is some disagreement between you and your companions and mine. If it came to it, I would protect my family against your men."

Darmon shook his head. "There will be no need, I swear it. We are allies here, all of us!"

"Then you do not mind if my sister and I remain here in the camp for the night?" Melonya asked.

If Darmon were uneasy at the idea of two very large dragons passing the night so close to him and his men, he hid it well.

He stretched out an arm, indicating the large bonfire that had been made in the center of the ring of tents. "Share our warmth with us and be at ease."

Syrani snorted and entered the tent once more. Alain immediately followed, and Suvusa watched as Halcia and Melonya settled themselves before following the other women.

Alain was already lying down, her boots and weapons close at hand. Syrani sat atop her own covers, her legs crossed and eyes closed, meditating. It was her nightly ritual, and Suvusa should have known that the addition of a third person in their tent would not change her habits.

Suvusa laid Rushavi down into the carefully folded bundle of blankets that served as his sleeping cot, then settled beside him. Ardu instantly slithered from around her waist and out from the sleeve of her dress. His little green and brown body curled up against Rushavi and was still.

Two more nights passed similarly, and when they began preparations for the third evening, Hiruscu found her.

"Did you see the road ahead?" he asked in the Elori tongue.

Suvusa shook her head. "I have barely had the strength to keep my head upright. Rushavi feeds constantly, and it is tiresome."

Hiruscu took her into his arms. They were thick and warm and heavily muscled. She had not felt the intimate touch of her husband's arms in weeks, and her face and neck flushed as he held her. "You will be able to rest among family soon. We are nearly rejoined with them."

"Already?"

Hiruscu laughed. "The dwarfs travel fast, despite their small steps."

"It will be nice to be among other Elori. And to sleep once more next to my husband."

"I thought you enjoyed the company of other women?"

"I do, but they can't hold me the way you can, my beloved."

Hiruscu made a sound somewhere between a scoff and a pleased snort and pulled her closer.

"And when Rushavi cries in the night, I can't kick them awake to care for him while I continue to rest," she added. Her words were muffled by the dark flesh of his upper arm, which she buried her face in. He was sweating and stank, but it was a familiar smell that made her belly warm and her throat close with the threat of tears. "I am so tired, Hiruscu."

"Go, sleep. I will take Rushavi and Ardu and care for them."

Suvusa shook her head. "No, I can endure a few more nights. Then we will be alone together, and you can be on mother duty for a few days."

Hiruscu kissed her forehead. "Anything for you, Suvusa. We will be home soon, and we will bathe with our child in the sands of Farnir's birthplace, and he will be an Elori."

Suvusa endured two more nights, though each day was harder than the last. Nunor spoke to her often, keeping one hand on her mule. She could not often follow his thoughts as he shared them, but he did not seem to mind the lack of conversation. She slept in the saddle some, but was often awoken by Rushavi's cries as he needed her.

"He certainly feeds a lot," Nunor commented more than once. "And he grows quickly."

"Yes, he will be strong," Suvusa said softly as she rearranged Rushavi's sling once again. "Like his father, and his father's father."

They were welcomed late in the second evening by a dozen Elori. Suvusa did not listen to their cries of joy at seeing a party of dwarfs and so many strangers. Rushavi was heavy on her chest, and Ardu slithered irritably about her waist as she descended the mule and found her husband.

"Hiruscu, please. I will greet our family in the morning. For now, I need sleep."

"I'll take her somewhere to rest," the elf, Syrani, said. "You haven't looked well, Suvusa."

"No," Suvusa argued. "Stay, and ask for the story of Farnir. It is the one you have been waiting to hear."

Hiruscu murmured a few words in the Azimarian tongue to Syrani and then led Suvusa away.

"I will settle you in, my beloved, and then tell the rest of the family that you needed rest more than food and drink. They will understand."

"You are too good for me, Hiruscu."

"If the children wake, I will be there shortly to care for them. You are too tired."

With her husband's help, Suvusa stripped down to nothing for the first time in several days. There were shallow cuts where Ardu's claws had torn her skin, but nothing serious. Her skin was covered in grime and sweat from their travels, and she laughed sleepily at the state of her clothing. Hiruscu held Rushavi as Suvusa settled deep into the soft covers and perfumed pillows of the bed their family had prepared for them.

"Rest, Suvusa," Hiruscu urged her. "I will prepare the children for sleep."

Suvusa took a deep inhale and was asleep before the exhale.

NUNOR

Nunor watched as Hiruscu led Suvusa away to rest. The growing fatigue Nunor had noticed in her was worrisome. She had spent the entire day alternating between nodding off in her saddle and feeding Rushavi. And Rushavi was an entirely different concern. There was something off in the way the babe looked, but Nunor couldn't determine what it was.

Perhaps Hiruscu will know better what ails his wife and how to care for his son.

The company of dwarfs were welcomed by the Elori with joyous cries, and Darmon was careful to position himself right in the center of the commotion. Nunor spat in the sand as Darmon spoke eloquently of his wish to reunite the dwarfs and the Elori as old allies. The woman, Alain, stood silently at his side as his guard, quietly surveilling the crowd.

It wasn't until Hiruscu returned and brought Nunor and the three elves to their attention that the Elori greeted them. Tiryn, Tathiel, and Syrani had been noticed long before, but the Elori as a whole appeared to be more standoffish towards the elves than Suvusa and Hiruscu had been.

"These are friends," Hiruscu said in his slightly broken

Azimarian to the gathered Elori. "They want stories of the Old Gods."

There was a murmur through the crowd as his words were translated into the Elori tongue and circulated.

Hiruscu held both arms outstretched and smiled broadly. "Welcome to Cai Myrh."

An elderly woman approached Hiruscu. Her face was heavily creased with wrinkles and her dark skin freckled with age spots, and her grey hair had been braided into tightly woven strands that hung over her shoulders. She spoke to Hiruscu in the Elori tongue, one eyebrow sharply raised as they conversed. Those Elori around them were silent or spoke softly amongst themselves as the woman addressed Hiruscu. Nunor thought he caught mention of Suvusa's name, but the context was lost entirely in the fast Elori speech.

Hiruscu's answer was long, though the words were rapid. The woman's lips pursed as Hiruscu continued. Finally, she raised a hand, and Hiruscu stopped speaking. She asked a question in the Elori language, and Hiruscu interpreted it for them.

"She asks if you have heard the first tales from Suvusa already."

Nunor nodded, and the woman asked another question through Hiruscu.

When Hiruscu translated, his brown was furrowed, as though he himself was curious what the answer may be. "Then why do you request more of our tales? Were hers not enough?"

Darmon cleared his throat, addressing Hiruscu. "It is only a passing interest. We search for the Amulet of Earth, and seek your guidance."

Hiruscu began to repeat Darmon's words, but the woman shook her head.

This time she spoke, and her Azimarian was even more broken than Hiruscu's.

"No amulet here."

Nunor stepped forward. He did not speak to Hiruscu, but to the woman directly. "We believe the amulet's location is mentioned in the tales of the Old Gods. These lands were once cared for by Farnir, and it is possible that stories of Farnir may reveal where the Amulet of Earth is hidden."

"Like Farnir's temple?" Hiruscu asked.

"What is Farnir's temple?" Tiryn asked.

Hiruscu shrugged. "It is not real. Only in stories."

"You mean a myth," Tiryn said.

The woman glared at Hiruscu and smacked him on the arm. He began to quickly translate what had been said.

Darmon rounded on Nunor. "You said nothing about needing to hear old wives' tales before."

Nunor smiled. If it looked to Darmon like more of a sneer, Nunor didn't much care. "You didn't ask."

"I thought you already knew where the amulet was? Why have we traveled so far with the Elori couple if they were not leading us to the amulet?"

Nunor snorted and did not answer.

"The secret to the location of the Amulet of Earth is likely to be discovered in one of the tales of the Old Gods the Elori have passed down," Tiryn answered. "Suvusa did not know all of the stories, though she did tell the ones she is familiar with."

Darmon was interrupted from speaking again by the elderly woman, who addressed Nunor when she spoke. "Sleep now. Speak tomorrow."

"She wants Suvusa to speak for her," Hiruscu added. "And Suvusa needs rest."

Nunor bowed, and Tiryn was quick to follow his example. "We are honored."

Many of the Elori parted ways with the old woman, but

several remained behind to greet the company of dwarfs and to shake hands with the elves. Hiruscu explained that, for many, it was their first encounter with a dwarf. And for many more it was the first time they had met an elf.

Hiruscu led them around Cai Myrh in a slow and meandering path, following no discernible trail or street. Nunor wasn't concerned about getting lost or disoriented. Tiryn would know exactly how to lead them back to where they had met the elder Elori woman.

The Elori camp was half tent and half permanent structures. The tents were both the enclosed styles that Nunor was accustomed to seeing and a strange, open-air type that he had never seen before. The latter were little more than posts buried deep in the sand with long and sheer fabrics tied to drape between them. He could see Elori eating together in groups, talking and laughing.

Within one such tent, the old Elori woman sat with a group of young ladies at her feet. She spoke to them calmly and steadily, and the women listening focused entirely on her words. The elderly woman, however, turned as Hiruscu led them past. Nunor could feel her watching him as they passed.

Nunor spotted men and women working side by side in a variety of tasks. One couple worked a large loom together. Another pair, this one a father and daughter judging by the age difference, sat beside each other at a low table and were cleaning game. Nunor paused long enough to see what kind of meat he could expect to eat with the Elori, but was disappointed to see that it was mostly lizards and two thin and haggard hares.

A woman with incredible arm muscles wearing a sleeveless vest and bright orange bottoms worked over an anvil. Nunor couldn't get close enough to see what the blacksmith was shaping, but the sound of her hammer hitting metal was pleasant to his ears.

"Come on, Nunor," Tiryn said with a smirk. "You can chat blacksmithing with the Elori woman later."

Nunor grumbled, but followed the rest of the party Hiruscu led. "I just wanted to see what quality of ore can be found here."

"Did the dwarfs and Elori not trade amongst each other not long ago? I would suspect they got their ore from Doldural."

"What makes you think their ore is Dolduran?" But Nunor realized the answer as soon as the question was asked.

"Where in a desert would they find metal, Nunor?" Tiryn asked with a laugh.

There were not only tents, but proper buildings as well. The more permanent structures were built from reddish brown stones, and Nunor noted with surprise that their foundation was also a dense red-brown rock. All around was golden brown sand, and the solid earth stood out starkly against it.

Hiruscu noticed him staring, and before Nunor could properly form a question, the Elori was already speaking.

"This is Cai Myrh, where Farnir was born. His first breath melted the sand, and his fire stained it red. This is home for us."

"I thought the Elori were a wandering people?" Syrani asked. She stood on a flat section of stony ground, examining the Elori craftsmanship of their permanent housing.

"We are. But we rest here. And the Elori that cannot travel stay here. Suvusa and I will stay here until Rushavi is grown enough to walk the sands."

"Is this where your family was headed when Rushavi was born?" Tiryn asked.

Hiruscu nodded. "We hoped Rushavi would come later, and Suvusa would be here. But the Old Gods had other thoughts."

"And the rest of your family went ahead without you?" Tiryn asked.

Hiruscu shrugged. "It happens. They prepared a place for us, and the journey is not a hard one."

Nunor scoffed. "It seemed hard on Suvusa."

A worried expression crossed Hiruscu's face briefly. "Yes, it was."

Hiruscu continued the tour of the Elori home. They shook many hands. After some time, the faces Nunor saw and the names he heard began to blend together. He was not accustomed to meeting so many people all at once, and he usually had a difficult enough time matching names to even half-familiar faces.

Finally, and to his great relief, Hiruscu declared their walk through the camp complete. Nunor recognized a nearby tent as the one Suvusa slept in. He wasn't surprised they had circled back all the way to where they had started without him realizing it.

"Thank you, Hiruscu, for your hospitality," Tiryn said. "I look forward to speaking with your brother again tomorrow. He promised to show me how to use the Elori double blade."

Hiruscu shook his head. "My brother speaks to you better, but I use the blade better. You want to learn, I teach you." He thumbed himself in the chest, then gestured to a tent that looked nearly identical to all the ones that surrounded it. "We have three this size. They are good for tonight?"

Sleeping arrangements were quickly made. Nunor would stay with the elves and Grinor, Darmon would sleep with his knights, and Alain, Syrani and the few other female dwarfs would share the third tent.

Nunor overhead Tathiel muttering to Syrani. "Don't cause trouble. We've got a delicate situation, and we need to remain friends."

"I haven't done anything to warrant that tone," Syrani said. "Everything will be fine."

Nunor stripped off his boots as soon as they were inside their tent. "So, Grinor. Care to explain how we've come to find ourselves in this fucking mess?"

The old dwarf muttered to himself for a moment as he removed his own outer layers.

"I didn't quite catch that." Nunor pulled his axe from the loop in his belt and slammed the head into the sand, leaving it buried deep enough to stand upright.

Grinor sighed. "I said Darlyth all but told him outright that he planned to name you king." Grinor shook his head. "Your little violent threats may fool your companions, but they do not fool me. Stop with that nonsense."

Tathiel snorted. "It never really fooled us, either."

"Hey." Nunor jabbed a finger in Tathiel's direction. "I'd mind that tongue. I'm not in the mood for it, boy."

"What does Darmon plan to do, Grinor?" Tiryn asked. "He knows less than we do of the amulet's whereabouts."

Grinor got to his hands and knees with a groan. The Elori had arranged several thin rugs across the sand with a pile of plain pillows and thick covers in one large bed. Grinor dropped his boots along one side. "I doubt he really has any plan at all. If he does, he's kept it to himself."

"So, what? He's going to just swoop in at the last moment, snatch the amulet and run home with it? Claim he was the one that found it?" Tathiel asked.

"I expect so." Grinor grabbed several of the pillows, then looked up at Tathiel and Tiryn. "You don't mind, do you? I'm not the young dwarf I once was, and I was never made for sleeping on the ground."

Tathiel shrugged and Tiryn waved his permission.

Grinor began arranging the pillows into one large pile. "Darmon knows that I do not care much for his notions of war, but the knights will do as he orders. He is the future king of Doldural in their eyes, after all. So whatever it is you plan to do, I would make sure Darmon is kept well away."

Nunor did not fall asleep right away. It wasn't Grinor's snores that kept him awake, nor the perfumed smell of the incense the Elori lit as the sun faded.

It was thoughts of potentially facing his cousin in combat that kept him awake. How would Darmon try to prevent Nunor and his companions from collecting the amulet? What would the dwarfs present in Cai Myrh do if they were ordered to attack their allies?

How can I keep Darmon from claiming the amulet when he has thirty knights at his command?

Nunor awoke to screaming some time later. It was still dark out, and Tiryn and Tathiel were up and out of the tent before he had registered his surroundings. He grumbled as he climbed over the disarray of bedding and grabbed his axe.

Elori rushed from their tents and into the night air. They spoke rapidly amongst themselves, searching for the source of the scream. They seemed just as confused as Nunor, and more than a few of them carried small weapons.

Suvusa screamed again, emerging from her nearby tent naked but for a thin patterned shawl that she had tied around her waist. She carried something in her arms, and Nunor's heart seized for a moment when he spotted chubby legs and an outstretched hand.

Rushavi.

Tiryn was already at Suvusa's side, easing her to the ground before she fell and dropped the child.

"He is fine, Suvusa."

Nunor found his breath again and rushed forward, barefoot on the night-chilled sand.

"He is not fine, look at him!" Suvusa laid the babe out for all to see. More Elori rushed from their tents, stopping with hushed whispers and gasps as they saw the infant.

Rushavi, who was only born some weeks ago, was far larger than he had any right to be. Nunor had never spent much time around very young human children, but even he could tell that the child was older than he should have been. The chubby cheeks Nunor had pinched and commented on only days ago were thinning out, and his face was now slimmer and his eyes bright and curious.

Rushavi rolled from his back onto his hands and knees, then pushed himself onto his feet. He was wobbly and unsure, and when he tried to take a step he fell.

Suvusa reached out to catch him, but it was Tathiel's quick elven reflexes that caught the boy instead. Tathiel picked him up, holding him aloft and examining him.

"What has happened to him?" Suvusa asked.

Hiruscu emerged from the tent, carrying clothing for his wife. "Suvusa," he began. The rest of his words were in rapid Elori.

"What do you mean you noticed this last night?" Suvusa asked.

"When I put you to bed, he was already …" Hiruscu waved at Rushavi, searching for the Azimarian words he wanted. "Big."

"You did not tell me?"

Hiruscu shrugged. "I thought you knew. I thought it was normal. He was eating well, I thought he had grown."

Suvusa spat something in Elori. If Nunor had to guess at its meaning, he would have suggested she'd called her husband a fucking idiot.

"I noticed it too. Yesterday." Suvusa's attention shifted to him, and Nunor's face reddened. "I thought something looked a little off about the boy, but he was not as grown as this. He looked a little oversized, but nothing this severe."

"What caused this?" Suvusa asked.

Hiruscu held out the bundle of clothing. "His brother has also grown." Hiruscu set the bundle on the ground, and it immediately began to wriggle and writhe.

Ardu's head finally worked out from under the pile, and he looked up and hissed at Hiruscu before extricating himself fully from the mess and approaching Tathiel. Several of the Elori screamed at his appearance. One frightened woman tried to back away, but only managed to stumble into the man behind her. Both tumbled to the ground, bringing some others down with them.

Nunor could understand their reaction. Ardu was much larger than he had been when Nunor had last seen him. He was now roughly the size of a house cat, excluding his tail, which was short and clubbed at the end.

"What is going on?" Syrani squeezed between two Elori, fighting her way to the center of the onlookers. Alain, also barefoot and with a warhammer in her hand, was right behind the she-elf.

Tathiel sat Rushavi on the sand, and Ardu curled around him, baring teeth.

Several Elori yelped and leapt back, but Hiruscu calmed them in the Elori language.

"Oh." Syrani looked from child to mother. "How did this happen?"

"I had thoughts to ask the same of you, Syrani." Suvusa glared at the elf. "What did you do to them?"

"Me?" Syrani raised an eyebrow. "How could I have done this?"

"You are the arcanist among your company, aren't you?"

Syrani snorted. "I am no better an arcanist than Tathiel and Tiryn are."

Suvusa looked to Tiryn, who still held her gingerly.

He nodded. "She's telling the truth."

"So, who has done this to my son? Who has stolen months of my motherhood away from me?"

Suvusa was looking to Tiryn, but it was Tathiel who answered.

"I think it was Ardu."

"I think you're right, Tathiel," Syrani said.

Tiryn helped Suvusa to her feet, letting Hiruscu take her into his arms and cover her nakedness. "How can you be sure?"

Nunor snorted. "We could just ask the little shit."

Syrani knelt to address Ardu, but no sooner had she reached out to touch him than he lifted his head to hiss at her.

She did not recoil, but she did not reach further. "Ardu. Did you do this?"

Ardu hissed again.

"Well?" Nunor grumbled. His toes were beginning to chill. Alain looked equally uncomfortable, and Nunor noticed a shiver in her shoulders.

Syrani stood, giving Ardu a blank stare. "He doesn't seem ready to speak again just yet."

Tiryn sighed. "I think it best to return to our beds for the evening and address this issue again in the morning."

Hiruscu waved the Elori away, speaking rapidly to them. They left slowly, whispering amongst themselves as they went.

Suvusa picked Rushavi up, holding him to her chest. "How could I have not noticed before now?"

Nunor gave her a touch on the elbow. "You were so tired. He had been eating constantly. It wore you out."

Is this perhaps why the babe was suddenly so voracious? Because this was going to happen?

"But I am his mother," Suvusa argued. "I should have known sooner."

Suvusa walked away, heading back for the tent she and

Hiruscu shared. Ardu followed behind, his heavy tail leaving drag marks in the sand behind him.

"Ardu," Syrani said.

The mottled brown and green dragon paused and turned, hissing again at Syrani.

"If you are doing this, you need to stop. Let your growth happen as it should. And let Rushavi be the child he should be."

Ardu continued walking. If he said anything, it was to Syrani alone. And Syrani did not repeat his words, if any.

"You didn't tell your cousin that there was a third dragon, Master Halfhelm."

Nunor seethed at Alain's words. "Once again, my cousin did not ask. He has been told many times of the finding of the Amulet of Water and the vital role Melonya played in it. He knew there would be a dragon for each amulet. But he did not ask about the dragon meant to retrieve the Amulet of Earth." Nunor shrugged. "I will tell him nothing freely that could bring our people to ruin."

Alain made no reply. Her face was unreadable, though Nunor caught a slight twitch in the corner of one eye. She simply turned on her heel and walked away.

18

ANNA

Anna could not sleep. Sleep had been difficult for her to come by regularly since Trissa's sudden return. Only a few days had passed, and she knew that Mothlenor would come to retrieve their daughter soon enough. There was little doubt in Anna's mind that Trissa would be gone in another few days.

And will I rest then? Knowing my daughter is in the king's tower, afraid and unable to sleep herself?

Doubtful.

But Anna did not leave her daughter's side.

Instead, she sat in a chair in Trissa's room, watching the young girl as she slept. Trissa's light brown hair was matted slightly, despite Anna having spent the better part of half an hour brushing the tangles free before Trissa went to bed. The poor girl just tossed and turned so frequently that it never remained neat. And Trissa hated sleeping with her hair in braids or a silk bonnet.

Anna watched Trissa turn in her fitful sleep once more, resigning herself to the fact that her daughter's fine and fragile hair would be unruly come morning. How long had it taken to comb her hair after Ferrand had dropped her off at their doorway without a word of explanation? Hours?

And that look in Ferrand's eye ...

Anna had seen it briefly before the door closed and separated the commander from them. It had been ruthless and furious, and ...

Hungry.

"Anna?" Illa whispered from the doorway. "You should try to rest."

Anna glanced over in Illa's direction. Illa was still wearing her black servant's dress, but her feet were bare and her hair covered. A small witch light bobbled at Illa's feet, charmed to illuminate her path. Anna had conjured it hours ago, and yet it still glowed.

She must have left it on while she slept. Even Illa cannot stand the dark any longer.

"So should you," Anna replied.

"I've slept enough for tonight." Illa stretched, and there was an audible crack from her back or shoulder. "I would be happy to watch over her."

"So I can toss and turn in the next room, fretting that she will be taken from me again?" Anna shook her head. "No, thank you."

"Then lie down beside her and sleep, my queen." Illa was frustrated, but she softened her tone. "Please. I worry for you."

Before Anna could answer, there was a heavy-handed knock at the door. Illa jumped, but Anna only sucked in a sharp breath.

"Do you think it is the king?"

Anna shook her head. "Why would he knock when he can appear right at the foot of our daughter's bed?"

"Ferrand, then?"

Anna rose to her feet. "There's only one way to know for sure."

They went to the door, Illa several steps behind Anna. Anna collected arcane energy in her palm, ready to protect the three of them if Ferrand had decided to harass them at such a late hour.

Her arcane energy dissipated as soon as she opened the door.

"My lord," Anna managed.

"I am sorry if I have woken you, Anna."

Mothlenor looked exhausted, like he had not slept in as many days as she. His skin was pale, and there were grey hairs about his face that she knew he would normally conceal.

Anna opened the door wider, though she was afraid she knew the reason for his visit.

"Illa, please check on Trissa."

"Yes, An— My queen."

If Mothlenor noticed the accidental use of Anna's name instead of her title, he did not betray it.

"Thank you for admitting me," Mothlenor said, shutting the door behind him.

"It would be foolish for me not to, when you can find your way into my quarters with little effort."

A queer smirk crossed Mothlenor's lips briefly, and she noticed a small cut on his chin that had not healed yet. "I have stretched myself too thin, my queen. A knock was all I could manage today."

Anna said nothing. Even at his weakest, she had no doubt that he was stronger than her. He was powerful enough to chill the very air they breathed without trying. He could still kill her if he wished it.

"I'm sure you understand why I am here." Mothlenor crossed the room to the fireplace, which was unlit and cold. He motioned towards the lone chair. "Please, sit."

More witch lights lit with a wave of Anna's hand, and she obediently sat. The seat was still warm from Illa sleeping there. "You're going to take Trissa away from me again." Anna could feel tears stinging her eyes. "I can't let you take her."

Mothlenor knelt beside her, putting a hand over hers. His palm was cold and clammy against the back of her hand. "Anna, my darling." His voice was a rich croon that sent gooseflesh over her skin. "You don't have a choice." He was close enough that she could smell the wine on his breath.

Anna choked on a sob.

"However, I have come with a proposal that I think will work for us both." Mothlenor stood, bracing his weight against the arm of the chair. "I have strayed from my goals, Anna. And I place the blame entirely on myself." He circled around to the back of the chair, and Anna stiffened as he brushed a hand through her hair. "I need you, Anna. Come back to my council, assist me with my work again, and I will allow Trissa to remain in your care."

Anna blinked, releasing tears. "What?"

"I spent some time in rumination this afternoon, and I have discovered a few truths that I am not proud of." Mothlenor still stood behind her, but moved to linger over her shoulder. He smelled of fresh soaps, and her shoulders instinctively raised as he leaned to speak closer to her ear. "Despite my power and knowledge, I *need* you, Anna. You are the star that guides my thoughts and lights my path. And I have done poorly since you left my council."

She stared over her shoulder at him. "But I …" Anna shook her head and began again. "My lord, you dismissed me."

Mothlenor nodded. "I did. And I realize now that it was a mistake."

Anna still didn't understand. *Why would I return to his council? So he won't take Trissa from me?*

"Let me make myself a little clearer," Mothlenor said. He straightened, immediately taking on the cold exterior Anna was accustomed to seeing. "I will move you and Trissa to quarters that are closer to my tower. You will both meet with me in the mornings, and you will have the freedom to return to your rooms when you are dismissed or when evening falls. In return, I will use Trissa's Gift and your skills as a fellow arcanist to find the remaining amulets or break my brother's curse. You will sit on council meetings again and assist me on other duties as I see fit."

Anna considered for a moment.

If I agree, he will abuse Trissa's Gift. And no good will come from it. If I refuse, he will take her anyway.

She and Ishta had been so close to getting Trissa out of the castle. Now her only hope was to keep her daughter safe however she could.

"Trissa stays with me?"

Mothlenor nodded. "And she will be within your eyesight most every day."

"Can I make an additional request?"

He tilted his head, and she took it as an invitation to continue.

"I would like Illa to move into our quarters as well. As our handmaid."

"Done." Mothlenor blinked once, his stony exterior as calm as ever. "Though, if I find that the two of you are as fond of each other as you were of her sister, she will be shown the same mercy as your previous lover."

"It will not come to that, I swear it."

"I have an additional request myself."

Anna raised an eyebrow, relaxing in her chair slightly. If Mothlenor was making requests of *her*, then there was truly nothing to fear tonight. "Of course, my lord."

"Trissa needs a tutor."

"I have educated her so far." Anna frowned. "She can read simple texts and knows her letters. Her writing improves slowly, but she is still young. Why—"

"Because you will be busy assisting me, remember?"

"Then I would like to help choose the tutor," Anna said quickly. "I know her abilities, and I know how she learns best. I would like to make sure she has a tutor that understands her as I do."

"Done." Mothlenor extended a hand. "Then we are agreed?"

Anna took it, though a not so small part of her mind argued that she was making a terrible mistake. "We are agreed."

"Excellent." Mothlenor pulled her to her feet, and Anna obediently went to him. "I am very pleased to have you working by my side again, Anna." He pressed his palm to her cheek, his thumb rubbing where her tears had already dried. "Do not disappoint me again, my love."

Anna's skin tingled where his fingers touched.

"I have grown very fond of you, and it would bring me no joy if I had to kill you."

He kissed her, pulled her close enough to wrap his arms around her.

She did not fight him. And when their lips parted, she stood on tiptoes to whisper in his ear.

"Yes, my king."

The fire in his eyes when he looked at her frightened her more than any other look from him ever had before.

Her knees were shaking when he left.

"Anna?" Illa touched her lightly on her back. "Are you alright?"

"I have just made a deal with a demon."

ARELLA

Arella was chasing after a little boy. He was half her age, less maybe. And his skin was darker than any she had seen before. It was pretty, too, and painted with some sort of red mud that flaked and peeled on his shoulders and bare chest.

Arella wanted to shout after him. She had never played with a boy before. The only boys in her village were older, and their idea of play was getting the girls to do handstands or roll about on the grass so they might get a glimpse of female undergarments.

But this boy seemed innocent enough to enjoy simpler games. Or making castles from the sand he ran across.

Arella could not call out to him, however. Her voice did not work, her mouth did not form the words of greeting she so desperately wanted to say. She could only watch as the boy ran from her and into a strange building. The building was tall, and Arella's first impression was that it was on fire. It was so bright with orange and reds that it had to be engulfed in flames.

But it was not.

It simply reflected the sunlight so brightly, so fiercely, that it seemed to be aflame.

And then the boy was gone.

Not just the boy, but the building, and the sand, and the sense of danger and fear that had gripped her heart at the sight of the young boy running away from her.

Sand was replaced with snow. The reds and oranges of sunlight became whites and greys. There was no boy.

But there was blood.

Arella almost stepped in it as she ran over the thick snow. She raised her arm, much too large to be her own, and shielded her eyes as a blast of wind blew sleet into her eyes. Snowflakes settled in her lashes and under her eyes, but it wasn't enough to obscure the splashes of red against the white ground.

There was so much blood. It was the brightest thing she could see, and it steamed on the cold earth. Arella followed the trail until she found a body.

Arella fell to her knees, a scream burbling in her throat.

She awoke before the scream escaped her lips.

It was still dark, and her grandmother still held her close to her chest. Arella could hear the snores in her grandmother's exhales, could feel the weight of her arms and of the covers they shared.

This is not the dream. This is real.

The *other* had been the dream. Or perhaps she had Seen something.

But Arella had not felt the heat of the sand or the chill of the snow, and that was how she knew it had not been real.

Not to her, at least.

She settled back into her grandmother's arms and returned to sleep.

———

W hen she finally awoke for the day, she could hear voices in the next room. The memories of her visions were still with her, still sharp and clear.

Real, then, she thought. *Visions of the future? Or of the past?* There was no way to tell.

"Arella?" There was a knock at the door, and Ishta opened the door just wide enough to lean into the room. "Your grandmother has tasked us with another run to town. For a delivery this time. I thought you might like to visit the baker while we're there. See if he's got some milk buns?"

Arella nodded, forcing a smile. "Yes! I'll be ready in a moment."

And she was. Arella did not waste time brushing her hair or dressing very carefully, not when milk buns and the grass and the outdoor breeze waited. And not when she would have to feed pigs and collect eggs when she returned home.

Ishta was a better companion than Roland, who brooded and watched and did not let them linger. Ishta stared long-ingly at meats and cheeses and breads like many of the women in town stared at silks and dresses. And Ishta could be easily convinced to part with a bit of coin in exchange for snacks. Roland was more frugal, though he had bought her honey cakes on their first outing, proclaiming it a tradition whenever he visited a new town and had money to spare.

"Do you want to race to the bottom of the hill? I bet you can't beat me again." Ishta gave her a sly smile, but Arella only shook her head.

"Not today. Today, I think walking would be better."

"Are you alright?"

"I had a bad dream last night." Arella set the pace as they started down the hill and towards the neighboring farmhouses.

Ishta fell into step beside her. "Do you want to talk about it?"

Arella shook her head again. "I don't think it's the kind of dream you would understand."

"Ah." Ishta nodded knowingly. "Like the kind of dreams Trissa has."

"Probably."

"You know, it was usually my sister who talked to Trissa when she had a dream like that. But I've heard about a few of them. You can tell me about it, if it would make you feel better."

Ishta passed the small package she carried from one hand to the other and held her free hand out for Arella to take. It was warm and calloused, much like her grandmother's, and there was an odd sort of comfort in the familiarity.

Arella sighed. "A milk bun would make me feel better."

Ishta snorted, lifting an eyebrow. "Just one?"

"Two," Arella decided. "With fig jam."

Ishta eyes widened. "You have fig jam here? I haven't had fig jam in years."

"The baker doesn't always have it, but she always keeps a little for me when she does."

"Oh, Great Ones preserve me, I am not in Etritia anymore." Ishta lifted her hands to the sky and laughed. "Fig jam. Wait until I tell Illa. She'll be livid."

"Do you miss Etritia?"

Ishta didn't answer right away. "No. No, I don't miss Etritia. She's not the same as she used to be. But I miss my sister and Trissa. And the queen." Ishta cleared her throat. "But I'm here now. With you and your grandmother. So tell me what you dreamt about last night."

Arella shook her head. "I'll be alright."

"You certain?"

"Yes," Arella lied. "Milk buns with fig jam are all I need."

In truth, as they continued their walk into town, Arella considered who she might discuss her dreams with. Her grandmother would worry if she shared them with her.

And why had she not considered that Trissa might have the same sort of dreams and visions?

"*Trissa?*"

Silence.

Arella focused harder, thinking of the cousin she had never met.

"*Trissa? Please answer. I want to talk to you.*"

This time, Trissa did answer.

"*No, stop. You can't talk to me any more.*"

Trissa sounded frightened.

"*Why? I want to talk to you. I keep Seeing things, and—*"

"*No! Stop talking! We'll be heard.*"

"*Heard?*"

"*Don't talk to me again. Leave me alone.*"

And with that, Arella was pushed away, and Trissa said no more.

"Arella? Did you hear me?" Ishta pointed, using the hand that held the linen-wrapped bundle, and Arella followed her gaze. "Is this the place we're meant to bring this to?"

Arella was surprised to see that they were already on the outer limits of town, where there were a few farmers that raised animals for milk and slaughter. The dirt path they had been following had widened, and there were ruts where wagon wheels had gone along the road numerous times.

Ishta was pointing towards the first of the farms, which sat closest to her grandmother's house. It was a small house, nearly as small as Arella's own home, and the thatched roof was in need of cleaning. Smoke drifted from the chimney, and Arella could smell something sweet and smoky in the air. Arella shook her head. "No, not that one. The next one."

"What are we bringing to this woman, anyway?"

Arella shrugged. "I think it's something for the barn."

"Something for the barn?"

"Yes. I heard her talking to grandmother." Arella lifted her chin. "She wanted something that would make her husband's wood hard again."

Ishta laughed hard enough to bring tears to her eyes, but refused to tell Arella what she found so funny about a soft barn.

2 0

SYRANI

"*It is too late to stop it.*"

Syrani did not share Ardu's parting words with her companions before returning to bed. He had chosen to share them with her and only her, and she could not bring herself to admit aloud that she was responsible for Ardu's actions.

The dwarfs, for their part, said nothing amongst themselves of Rushavi and the young dragon. Alain had ordered them to remain quiet, and that the child was a concern for his mother and not a curiosity to be stared at and gossiped about. Syrani did nothing to show her surprise and approval before bedding down, but when Alain wished her a good night, Syrani returned the sentiment.

It was the first time the two women had spoken directly to each other, despite the fact that they had been sharing a tent for several days.

Syrani spent the night listening to Elori whisper amongst themselves in nearby tents. She could not understand the Elori language, but she could guess at the topic of their conversation.

By the next morning, it was clear that news of Rushavi's

unexpected growth spurt and Ardu's appearance had spread throughout the Elori camp.

When she rose from her bedding and returned to Suvusa's tent, a crowd of Elori had gathered around it. Rushavi was even more aged than he had been only hours before. He was now standing upright, holding his mother's hand in his own. He walked, though on the unsteady legs of a young child, and he had dark, wild hair that stuck out about his head in all directions.

Syrani embraced the mother, though she was stiff and unyielding in her arms. "Suvusa, I am sorry this has happened."

Suvusa's face was pale, with sagging and puffy spots under her eyes. "Is there a way to reverse it?"

Syrani shook her head. "I don't know."

Suvusa's deep inhale had a slight hitch in it, as if she had only just stopped crying. "Then we should continue on. The Great Ones have chosen this path for Rushavi for a reason."

They were followed through the camp by several Elori, who whispered in their native tongue as Suvusa walked with Rushavi's hand in hers. Ardu was nowhere to be seen at first, and Syrani wondered if the dragon had perhaps decided to remain behind.

No sooner had the thought crossed her mind than a small shadow passed overhead. Seconds later, Ardu landed on the path ahead, gripping a small lizard in his narrow jaws.

"Ardu," Syrani said in greeting, bowing to the dragon.

He hissed in return, the sound rolling out around his meal.

"I see you've learned to hunt. Did Halcia teach you?"

The lizard disappeared down Ardu's throat with a few quick snaps of his jaws.

Syrani stepped aside, leaving a gap between her and Rushavi. "Please, join us."

Ardu took his place beside his young companion without a word.

The whispering behind them only grew worse as they continued. Suvusa held her head high, but her face was even paler than it had been moments before.

Alain joined them, falling into step beside Syrani, who slowed to make it easier for the petite dwarf to keep up. She did not wear her usual armor today, instead opting for something lighter. She still wore her heavy boots, but the metal shin guards had been dispensed with. Her chest plate had been removed, making Alain much slimmer than she normally seemed. Instead, she wore a black tunic and leather bracers on each forearm. Her large warhammer was gone, but Syrani noted the row of daggers on her left hip.

"Prince Darmon and Master Halfhelm are waiting for us. Darmon has been informed of the events of last night." Alain eyed Ardu warily, likely noticing that he was easily half again the size he had been only hours before.

"Was it you that told him? How long did you wait after I left before rushing to him this morning?"

Alain didn't even bat an eyelid at the accusatory tone in Syrani's voice. "I did not rush to him. And it was Master Halfhelm that told Darmon of the dragon."

"Some of my companions might take offense if you continue to refer to Nunor by only his cursed name."

"But not you?"

Syrani shrugged. "A name is a name." Up ahead, the large and ornate tent Hiruscu had carefully navigated their party around the night before was plainly visible. Nunor and Darmon waited outside, Tiryn and Grinor standing between them.

"What will happen?" Alain asked in a low voice.

"We will hear a story." Syrani gave the dwarf a critical look. Alain was younger than she appeared at first. "After that, who can say?"

They entered the tent together. Hiruscu was already within, seated on the sand with one elbow propped up on a large pillow. He waved them over, and they approached as a group. Suvusa did not follow.

Syrani touched the Elori woman's elbow lightly. "Are you alright?"

Suvusa nodded. "I will be the Azimarian voice for today's tale." She nodded towards the head of the open-air tent, where a large chair and more pillows waited. "Rushavi and I will sit there."

Syrani sat with the others, watching Suvusa. The mother held her child's hand tightly, keeping him close, though Rushavi wandered as far as her hold on him would allow. He was a curious child, his eyes wide and staring.

Syrani wondered if the boy had spoken yet.

More Elori entered, and several smiled at Suvusa as they saw her. Their smiles faded into looks of bewilderment as they spotted the boy who should be an infant. Suvusa said nothing.

Eventually, there was no room for more Elori to be seated within the tent. It did not stop the dark-skinned folk from packing themselves in and around the tent. Some carried small fans to cool themselves with. Still others were caked in the slimy cactus jelly mixture that kept their skin from blistering under the sun.

There was laughter and much discussion in the fast Elori tongue. Syrani did not understand the words, but there was a lighthearted feel to them, like there were no deep and serious conversations. There was no time for them, it seemed. There was something more important happening. Something they were waiting for.

Suvusa remained standing, though Rushavi had slipped from her grip. He was playing with two other children roughly his size, and all three mothers watched the odd child with apprehension. One of the other children had brought a ball made from fabric and twine, and the three took turns kicking it back and forth. Rushavi didn't have the same coordination as his peers, and each kick of the ball threatened his balance. Ardu circled around all three of the little ones, his head tilted so he could always keep one eye on Rushavi.

The elder Elori woman that they had seen the day before entered the tent. Her dress was fancier than it had been yesterday, and her wrists and neck were adorned in clay beads that had been painted yellow and brown. Her grey hair, still braided as it had been before, was now dusted with colored powders, giving her head patches of bright red and green. She made for the chair at the head of the tent. Instead of sitting in it, however, she sat at the foot of it, where the pillows were deepest. The chattering in the tent continued, though it was softer and quieter.

Suvusa sat at the woman's feet, crossing her ankles and settling comfortably. She exchanged a few words with the older woman, then turned to face Syrani and her companions.

"Where is Tathiel?" Syrani asked Tiryn, who was seated closest to her.

"With Melonya and Halcia," Tiryn whispered back. "When he was told how long this could last, he decided he would rather wait for the condensed version."

Syrani rolled her eyes.

The impatience of youth.

Still, she should be grateful someone was with Halcia and Melonya.

The tent fell silent when the elder woman raised a hand. Syrani thought she was signaling for quiet, but instead her hand landed to rest on the chair behind her. The opposite hand went to Suvusa's shoulder, and Suvusa covered it with one of her own.

Then, the women began to speak.

Their voices were nearly simultaneous, the rich

Azimarian words Suvusa spoke blending and weaving with the strong Elori words of the elder woman. Syrani was momentarily entranced, and nearly missed the beginning of their story.

"So we meet again, guided by the will of the Great Ones to this sacred place of peace, to hear a tale from the mouth of the Speaker. We, Ashana and Suvusa, will act as her voices, so that her words may be heard and understood by all present."

There was a pause, heavy in the desert heat, and Syrani leaned forward slightly.

The Speaker? Who is that?

"We begin."

Suvusa was looking towards her husband and the rest who sat clustered around him, but Syrani realized that she was staring blankly. There was distance in her gaze that suggested her eyes saw nothing.

"This tale is one of the last tales of our Great Ones, and is of Farnir and his return to his birthplace, and tells of his actions once reaching that blessed earth.

"After conversing with his siblings on the actions they should take against the peoples of Azimar and Vyris, Farnir was silent for many, many days. His siblings each went to him, in turn, and asked him what path he would take. Would he take the path of the warrior and fight those who had once worshipped him? Would he take the path of the hermit and seclude himself away? Or would he take the path of the lover and show compassion to those who would harm him?

"Finally, after many moons, he went to his father to ask for his advice."

Syrani tilted her head, intrigued.

"The oldest god, father to all other gods, could not answer his son's request. He was sickly and had refused sustenance for some time. Seeing the world and the way his children's children were being slaughtered had broken him, he would not speak.

"Farnir next went to his mother. Though she had not birthed him, he still cared for her. Onia was intelligent and wise, and Farnir knew that if his father could not help him find a better solution, his mother could."

Out of the corner of her eye, Syrani saw Tiryn and Nunor exchange a look.

"Onia listened to Farnir's concerns. She sent him away, but not before making a promise. 'Return after the moon has cycled once, and I will have a solution for you.'

"Farnir did as he was told and returned to the desert of Azimar. After one month, during which his last sibling was lost, he returned to Onia.

"She greeted him, but she was not happy to see him. 'I have found a solution, but it is not a good one. It will require great sacrifice from you, my son.'

"Farnir puffed out his chest and held his head high. 'I am not afraid. Tell me what I must do.'

"So Onia told Farnir of the solution she had found. 'You must build a sacred temple, and store within it all that us gods hold precious. Only those of virtuous faith may enter the temple, and it must be hidden from all others. And, when the time comes, you must lock yourself within the temple to await the day when it can be opened once more.'"

Syrani was watching Rushavi. The young boy had endless energy. While his two Elori companions had given up and returned to their mother's laps to rest, Rushavi ran around on his chubby little legs, chasing after Ardu. The brown and green dragon ran and kicked up small clouds of sand, letting Rushavi get almost close enough to grab his tail before darting away again.

"Farnir accepted his mother's instructions. He returned to the desert, seeking out the place where he had first emerged from the earth. Once there, Farnir began work on his temple. It was constructed entirely by the Great One himself. He magicked the walls of the temple so that it would be shielded from all who would enter with ill intent. Once completed, he gathered the treasures of the Great Ones and placed them inside.

"Finally, he returned to Onia. 'Mother, I have completed the task you have given me. But how will I know when it is time for the temple to be reopened?'

"Onia did not answer.

"Farnir returned to the temple, and with one final look at his birthplace, shut the door."

Syrani sensed an end to the story, but the two Elori women were not quite done.

"And that is the last tale of Farnir, who has never been seen since."

The elder Elori woman removed her hand from the chair and patted Suvusa on the head. Suvusa blinked rapidly, then stood. She helped the elder woman to her feet, and the two left the tent. Suvusa grabbed Rushavi by the hand again, and the two waited out in the sun as Elori streamed out.

"That was it?" Nunor grumbled. "It didn't answer anything, did it?"

"It did," Syrani said. "I think we should find Farnir's temple."

"Farnir's *lost* temple, you mean," Grinor said. "It hasn't been seen since the doors were shut, if I am to understand that rather austere ending to the tale." He narrowed his eyes, looking at Syrani. "Young lady, are you saying you believe the Amulet of Earth has somehow ended up in the temple?"

"That old bat did say the temple was full of treasure." Darmon dusted sand from his clothing.

"It could not have been stored there originally, no." Syrani crossed her arms, her eyes once more on Suvusa. "After all, the last tale we heard told of how the mother reclaimed the amulets after all the children had been lost. Including Farnir."

"Onia, the mother of all the Great Ones," Nunor muttered.

"But when the amulets were lost again, it could have been hidden in the temple for those 'of virtuous faith' to find." Syrani sighed, watching the way the Elori carefully avoided Suvusa and her son. "Perhaps it is finally time for the temple to be opened once more."

"It is good the Elori know where the temple is, then." Hiruscu surprised Syrani by patting her on the shoulder. "Come, I tell you."

"You know where Farnir's temple is?"

Hiruscu shrugged. "Where it should be." He gave Syrani a critical look. "But it *is* lost. No Elori have ever seen it."

Outside the tent, Syrani watched as Ardu hissed at an Elori that stepped too close to Rushavi and Suvusa.

"Maybe we will."

MATHIUS

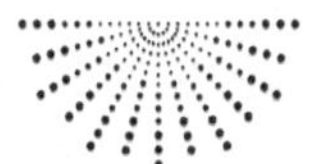

Mathius had been blessed with the ability to rise at the slightest hint of morning light ever since he was a child. His father had spent many early mornings training him in combat, and as the captain of first the *Seahawk* and later the *Kingfisher*, Mathius prided himself on being up and working with his crew when the first streaks of light would hit the decks.

As the owner of the only inn in Larten, his ability to rise from sleep so early no matter the amount of ale he had drunk or served the previous night served him equally well.

Mathius awoke as he usually did, dressed in the silence of the inn, and left his room to head for the kitchen. His kitchen was not empty when he entered, and the face that greeted him was not the kind and caring face of Eilonwy.

"Good morning, Mathius."

"Captain," Mathius said.

The King's Guard leaned against one long prep table with a metal mug of dark brown liquid in one hand. "Ah, so you are a military man. I wondered."

"What makes you say that?" Mathius surveyed the kitchen, noting the mortar and pestle that had been used to grind some of the rare coffee beans he kept tucked away in the back of the pantry. The bag of beans still sat next to the mortar and pestle, and there was a lightly steaming kettle nearby.

The man brushed a hand over his surcoat, straightening a stray wrinkle out of the large emblem of a tower and a pair of crossed blades. "You called me captain."

Mathius nodded, then poured the remnants of the ground powder sitting in the bottom of the mortar into a second mug. "It's obvious you're leading the rest of the King's Guards here. But I doubt the commander would trouble himself to come all the way down to Larten." Mathius poured hot water over the ground coffee and swirled the mixture. He turned to the captain, indicating the side of his face with a hand. "Plus, I heard he has a rather nasty scar on his face."

The captain laughed. "He does indeed." He nodded towards the bag of coffee beans. "I hope you don't mind. I've been up for some time now, and I didn't want to wake you when I can find my own way around a kitchen."

Mathius shook his head. "It's no trouble." He sipped at the coffee, his eyes on the King's Guard. "Can I ask what has you awake so early?"

The captain stared at Mathius. His gaze was calculating. "Someone has set the elf and his conspirator free."

Mathius choked on a mouthful of coffee but managed it down. "What?"

"My reaction was similar."

Mathius instantly thought of Eilonwy. Had she freed the elf?

Of course she did. Who else?

"Were there no guards to watch them?"

"There was one, but he stepped away from his post to enjoy an hour with a woman he's come to fancy. He has been punished." The knight sipped his own coffee, staring at the middle distance.

"What will you do?"

The knight shrugged. "I doubt we could find the elf and the seamstress, but I have dispatched men to look for them. We shall remain here a little longer, hunting for whoever still remains in Larten that has strayed from the king's cause."

"Could it not be," Mathius began, swirling his mug again, "that the elf and his conspirator somehow freed themselves?"

The captain nodded. "It could be. We searched both for weapons, and the elf was already bound in the king's arcane bracers when he was captured. But if he had found a way to escape once, there is no doubt he could do it again." The knight looked up, and Mathius heard footsteps on the stairs. "Elves are notoriously sneaky bastards, and women can be sly and cunning."

Mathius peered around the doorway to see Eilonwy coming down the stairs.

She had already donned her disguise as Eilen and was dressed primly for a woman of her supposed livelihood. But the fierce scowl on her face told Mathius that her sharp elven ears had picked up the captain's words.

Eilen descended the stairs and entered the kitchen, but not before replacing the angry glower with a cheery grin.

"Good morning, gentlemen. You're up early, sir. Can I get a breakfast started for you?"

The captain nodded. "Please. I believe you have come to know my preferences well, Eilen."

"I sure have. I'll bring something out for you shortly." Eilonwy smiled pleasantly at the knight, who took his mug of coffee and left for the dining room.

Mathius watched the knight as he walked away, one hand on Eilonwy's elbow. When he was sure they would not be overheard, he pulled her further into the kitchen. "You're in big trouble."

Eilonwy quirked an eyebrow. "Will you call me a young lady and go to my father about me?"

"I'm serious, Eilen."

Eilonwy pulled her elbow from his grip and reached over his head to pull cooking pots and utensils down from their hooks. "I did what needed to be done."

"They're going to stay in Larten, looking for another traitor," Mathius said. He set his mug aside, trying to take a deep breath. His chest hurt.

"And they won't find one." Eilonwy put a warm hand on his arm. "I promise, Mathius."

The pain in his chest subsided, and he took a long inhale and held it for a few seconds. When he exhaled, he nodded to Eilonwy. "Alright. I believe you. You've given me no reason to, Elir damn you, but I guess what's done is done." Mathius motioned to the coffee mess still remaining on the prep table. "Can you take care of this? And get started on breakfast. I need a few moments to question my sanity."

He went to the garden, hoping Jaimes would already be out enjoying the cool air of the early morning. But there was no sign of the sandy-haired young man among the leaves and flowers. He waited a few moments, cursing his luck.

No, that's not fair, he thought. *Eilonwy is only doing what she has always done—protect her kin. And, until now, I have helped her. I've told her of elf hunters in Larten, I've warned her of scouts in the land around the Southern Cities. I have encouraged her to fight for her people.*

Mathius scratched at his beard. It was thinner than he remembered it being a few years ago, and he found more silver-grey hairs with each passing month.

But I am too old to protect her here. And Larten is no longer safe.

He entered the inn again, cutting through the dining room to make for the stairs to the second floor. Eilonwy was still in the kitchen, her back to him as she cooked over the oven in the corner. Another King's Guard was coming down the stairs as he began his ascent, and he dipped his head as their eyes met, but said nothing. He didn't want Eilonwy to realize he was headed to the second floor, and he hoped she would assume the footsteps her elven ears picked up were those of another guest.

He knocked softly on the door to the room Jaimes had once used as a shoddy research facility, and where he and Eilonwy now lived together. There was an annoyed groan and the sound of covers being moved about. Jaimes answered the door with a sour expression on his face and a thin blanket concealing his groin and buttocks. The smell of herbs and flowers instantly hit Mathius. He'd have to tell Eilonwy to air the smell of her cream concoction before it spread to the hallway.

"What?" Jaimes's voice was groggy, and his eyes were not entirely open.

"We need to talk," Mathius said, pushing past Jaimes and into the room.

"Can it wait? The sun isn't even up yet."

"The elf and Demelda were freed last night."

Jaimes cursed and shut the door. "Alright, I'm listening."

"Tell her to go home."

"I have!" Jaimes rubbed at his face. "We damn near came to shouts over it."

"What did she say?"

Jaimes sat on the bed with a heavy sigh. There was a hand-stitched quilt that Mathius was sure had once belonged to Jaimes's mother bundled at the foot of the bed. "That she won't leave us here. It's all three of us, or none of us."

Mathius cursed. "She's a nightmare, that one. I love her, but doesn't she realize the danger she's in?"

"That all of us are in," Jaimes countered. "She is well aware. And that is the problem."

"But she can't stay here. Especially not after what happened yesterday."

"What do you propose then?"

"Can you get into contact with your brother?"

Jaimes made a face. "What can Alastor do?"

"I'm not sure." Mathius scratched at his beard again, thinking. "He could contact Tathiel, to start with. Maybe her brother can convince Eilonwy to leave Larten for a bit."

"I have a way of reaching Alastor. Tiryn devised it." Jaime stood, taking the covers with him. "It uses magic, but Tiryn made it simple enough for me to do without having to rely on my underdeveloped skills." He went to the wardrobe he and Eilonwy shared. It was mostly full of neatly folded fabrics that Mathius recognized as some of the skirts and dresses Eilonwy wore. There was also a neat stack of plain trousers. From underneath this stack, Jaimes pulled out a small leather pouch. "He and Roland have been using a similar system for years, but it has some severe limitations."

"Like?" Mathius asked.

"For example, it relies on the others in the circle actually checking the damned thing. Which Roland apparently is not particularly good at doing." From the pouch, Jaimes pulled out a familiar black book and a small coal stick wrapped in cotton.

"*You* have the book now?"

Jaimes shook his head. "I have a replica of the book. Which Tiryn made. Tiryn has one, as do Tathiel and Roland."

Mathius was mildly offended. "And not me?"

"Not from lack of effort on Roland's part, don't worry. But to make the replicas, we had to split the remaining pages from the original book. And if we split them into too many replicas …" He shrugged. "Well, then we start to lose func-tionality."

Mathius squinted at Jaimes. "None of what you've said makes sense."

Jaimes tossed the book and coal stick on the bed. "Let me get dressed, and I'll explain."

Mathius turned to face the door. "Alright, I'm listening.

So, you replicated Roland's black book. With magic, I presume?"

Jaimes was moving about the room behind him, presumably rummaging for clothing. "Yes. We pulled about half of the remaining blank pages from Roland's book and divided them into three piles. Each of those piles, with a bit of ingenious work on Tiryn's part, became a replica of the original, with the pages from each replica remaining connected to the original. In an arcane sense, anyway."

"Impressive. I didn't realize magic could be used like that."

"It took a lot of effort on Tiryn's part. He and Roland used to share two halves of a torn piece of parchment that functioned in much the same way. Whatever one wrote on one half, the other could read on the other. They only used it a few times. Because once a message is written, it can't be removed."

"So, you could run out of pages? Or room for messages?"

"Yes." The wardrobe door closed with a soft snap. "And if they had misplaced the parchment or if it was stolen, then all of their messages could be read just as easily as any old letter."

"Huh. And the book is the same?"

"I did say it had limitations. Come here."

Mathius turned. Jaimes was sitting on the bed, book in hand. "You said you had to rely on someone actually checking the original. Who has it now?"

"Alastor should. He prefers not to use the book himself. He's got his own method of sending messages." Jaimes flipped through the first several pages of the small black book. Pages with short sections of text in several prints flickered by as Jaimes searched for a blank page.

"His creepy little birds," Mathius said with a shiver.

"Creepy?" Jaimes said with a laugh. "I think they're rather charming. Did you know you can ask them to sing for you?"

Mathius grimaced. "Wait until you wake up in the middle

of the night for a piss and find one staring at you from the floor. Damned near wet myself."

Jaimes motioned to the bed beside him. "Here, what should I send to Alastor? It should be short."

Mathius sat with a groan. "How about 'Eilonwy is a git, send rescue.' That short enough?"

Jaimes rolled his eyes. He wrote a few quick lines, then showed the book to Mathius.

Concerned for E. Assistance requested.

Mathius nodded. "When can you expect any sort of reply?"

"Dunno." Jaimes shrugged. "Might get a little bird tomorrow morning, might have Tathiel busting down the door to the inn in a week's time. There's no way of knowing."

"Wonderful." Mathius stood again with a second groan. "Let me know what happens, if you can. I have to get back downstairs before Eilonwy has my head for making her handle breakfast on her own."

"I'll be here, I suppose."

Mathius took his time returning to the kitchen.

No idea when this assistance might come, huh? Not exactly convenient.

Still, Mathius was impressed with the effort Tiryn and the others had put into making sure even those with little or no arcane ability could stay in contact with everyone else.

I guess I never need worry about being unable to cry for help if anything should happen to us here.

Eilonwy was passing out mugs of ale to a dozen or so King's Guards, and Mathius took the opportunity to slip into the kitchen without her realizing he was descending the stairs.

He was pushing a batch of rolls into the oven when she entered the kitchen.

"There you are. I was starting to worry that you had spent

so long clearing your head that you'd cleared it of all respon-
sibilities and wandered off into the desert."

"And leave you to run this inn all on your own? Never."

Eilonwy gave him a close-lipped smile. "Forgive me?"

Mathius nodded, giving her a one-armed hug. "What's
done is done. Just promise me you'll be careful."

"For you, I'll try."

2 2

TATHIEL

Their next steps were planned quickly. Tathiel let Syrani
and Nunor do much of the talking; the former was
naturally adept at planning and the latter was going mad
without a clear goal in mind. Tathiel was surprised by
Syrani's ability to remain calm as Nunor's irritation at his
cousin grew.

Everywhere Nunor went, Darmon was only an arm's
length away. As Syrani set about preparing for another long
travel through the desert, Nunor supplied helpful advice and
suggestions and asked questions. Darmon, however, argued
and countered with his own suggestions. The two dwarfs
bickered constantly. Tathiel never saw Syrani so much as
twitch an eye.

It was impressive.

"It's done." Syrani found Tathiel and Tiryn both in a
lunching tent. Tiryn was feeding small cuts of cactus fruit to
Rushavi while the boy played in the sand with Ardu. "We
have a heading to take, and Hiruscu has mapped out the path
that will be easiest on the mules. If we leave shortly, it will
take us a little less than a week to reach the place where the
temple should be."

"I think we should wait a day. Maybe two." Tiryn handed a thin sliver of bright purple fruit to Rushavi. The boy held it awkwardly in his fat little fingers and began sucking on the food. "Suvusa still needs rest. Rushavi's aging has impacted her too. He took the energy he needed to grow from her. She is dehydrated and weak, and the boy will still need his mother to feed him occasionally for a little longer."

Syrani hesitated, watching the boy as he gummed at his snack. Tathiel wondered if the child had grown teeth yet.

"Alright. I'll tell the others."

Tathiel stood. "I'll come with you."

They walked in silence until Tathiel was sure they were out of Tiryn's earshot.

"You wanted to say something?" Syrani asked.

"Yes. I wanted to apologize for Tiryn and Nunor."

"I can understand you apologizing for Nunor's behaviour, though I have to admit that I find his gruffness refreshing. But Tiryn?"

Tathiel shrugged. "He's a little odd. Even for an elf. A little too careful, and a little too predictable."

"You knew he would want to wait longer before leaving?"

"He's always been one for the cautious approach when it's possible." Tathiel shrugged. "I can't say I blame him on this one, though. We need Suvusa fit for riding."

"I worry that if we wait too long—"

"That Rushavi will be an adult before we reach the amulet? And Suvusa would have spent the best part of her motherhood with him on the back of a mule?" Tathiel asked.

Syrani nodded. "Something like that, yes."

"Tiryn believes the aging process will slow down significantly after the first few days. Rushavi should not age past the size of a ten-year-old boy, if he is correct. Ardu will continue to grow, but he should be much larger than he is, so that's not of great concern." Tathiel could hear Nunor and Darmon arguing somewhere nearby, and he slowed his steps.

"Tiryn is still considering ways to stop Rushavi's aging sooner."

Syrani stopped. "Can I confess something to you?"

"Of course."

She stared off in the direction the angry dwarfed voices were coming from. "I think I'm the one to blame for this. Ardu was intentionally keeping himself from growing so that he and Rushavi could age and mature together. It … took a lot of effort. And when he and I connected, he lost control of it."

Tathiel smirked. "Halcia said you would blame yourself."

Syrani grabbed his arm. She had a good grip. "Ardu said there was no stopping it."

"When?"

"Last night, when we were all outside Suvusa's tent."

"That doesn't mean it's your fault." Tathiel sighed. "If he lost control just by forming a mental connection with someone, then he didn't have much control to begin with.

"But I pushed him to talk to me," Syrani argued. "So it's my—"

"It is *not* your fault," Tathiel said firmly. "Do you remember when Halcia was young? Those months after she hatched?"

Syrani shook her head. "I missed a lot of those early days. I was trying to settle into my new home."

"Well, I remember when Melonya was young. When she hatched, it was like she came out of that egg smarter than many of the elves I've met. The first thing she did was bind herself to Eilonwy and me. She knew exactly what she was doing and how to do it."

The corner of Syrani's mouth curled. "It was the same with Halcia. She even named herself."

"So did Melonya. You think I'm smart enough to come up with a name like that?" Tathiel smirked again. "I had been so worried that she would be feral when she hatched, and she knew exactly how to show me I was wrong. And she learned how to speak so quickly! It was perhaps a couple of days before she was holding entire conversations."

"What are you saying, Tathiel?"

"I'm saying that Ardu knew what he was doing, and he knew that it was risky." He shrugged. "I also understand why he did it, too. Would you want to be bound to a companion that spent the first few years of its life drooling and shitting itself and having to be hand fed? While you're big enough to take down a horse with hardly any effort?"

"I suppose not."

"Ardu feels guilty that he took a risk and it failed. And he's passing that guilt to you."

"Do you think so?" Syrani's brow furrowed.

"I think it's better to support Ardu as this progresses. And Rushavi, when he is old enough to understand."

Syrani sighed. "Which I'm sure will be in only a day or two."

"It's better than drowning in self-pity." Tathiel started walking again. Nunor and Darmon's argument was growing louder, and nearby Elori were staring at the tent the two dwarfs occupied.

"I was not—" Syrani stopped herself, taking a deep breath. "I was only worried that I had damaged another bond between rider and dragon."

"I doubt you did anything close," Tathiel said. "How is Halcia, by the way?"

"I should ask you the same. You saw her only this morning."

Tathiel shook his head. "No, she wasn't with Melonya. I haven't seen her in a few days."

"You oversized cave worm!" Darmon shouted. "You can't speak to me that way."

"I can, you fucking stone-sucking mud eater. You're not king yet, except perhaps the king of bloated, dung-covered

assholes!" Nunor burst through the tent's opening, his axe in
both hands. "I swear to the Great Ones, I should have throt-
tled you in the crib. Doldural would have been better for it!"

Darmon followed after him, his own axe out. "I order you
to get back here and solve this like dwarfs!"

Nunor turned on his heel and spat in the sand. "If you
want to solve this like dwarfs, I'd be happy to. But you'll be
going home with your head in a saddlebag, you daft fuck."

"Gentlemen, perhaps we should discuss this like elves
rather than solving it like dwarfs?"

Nunor turned to glare at Tathiel. His face was an
alarming shade of red. "Shove it, long ears. Get out of my
way before I split you up the middle."

Tathiel stepped aside. "Go on. Find me when you're calm
again."

Nunor stomped off, bellowing curses in Azimarian and
dwarfish.

"Care to help me out with this one?" Tathiel murmured to
Syrani, tilting his chin towards Darmon.

"Actually, I need to go. You can take care of him. He's all
bloat, no bite." Syrani walked away, her pace a little fast and
agitated.

Tathiel sighed. "Alright, Master Darmon. I would be
happy to hear your complaints. But let's do it inside, shall
we?"

Darmon belted his axe. "The she-elf made a fine map for
us to follow."

"Her name is Syrani, and I'm sure she would be happy to
hear you say so."

"But there was no discussion of *tactics*," Darmon said,
ignoring him. "You can't just walk across an empty desert,
with no knowledge of the dangers waiting in the sands, and
not have a plan to combat anything that comes to kill you."

"I agree," Tathiel said, following Darmon into the tent.
There was a low table with bowls of the same cactus fruit

Tiryn had been feeding Rushavi. There were also a few large pieces of animal hide that had been cleaned and stripped and were painted with a series of lines. "Is this our map?"

"This is the *Elori* map." Darmon waved dismissively at it. "I can't make heads or tails of it. The scale is all off. There's no direction. Where is north? Where is south?"

Tathiel looked it over. "Oh, I see. It's all based on landmarks." He pointed at a cluster of green lines. "This must be the grove of desert plants we passed on our way here." He spotted a second cluster. "Or maybe this one is."

"See? Fucking useless." Darmon slammed a fist on the table.

"Not to the Elori."

"So we take an Elori guide. Fine. But that doesn't solve our problem."

"Which is?"

"We need an army to get us through the desert."

Tathiel took a brief moment to stop himself from expressing his serious doubts that they would need an army. "Don't you have several dwarfs at your command?"

"I do." Darmon nodded. He seemed calmer, more confident. "And I will make the same proposal to you as I did my cousin. I would be happy to bring my men on this journey with us, but with one condition."

"And that is?"

"I lead the expedition into the temple, and I return to Doldural with the Amulet of Earth."

Tathiel laughed. "Those are two conditions. And they're both ridiculous."

"The amulet is rightfully mine. I will not have it stolen away from me a second time."

"The amulet belongs first to the Great Ones, or have you not been paying any attention to what the Elori have been saying?" Tathiel sighed, rolling the Elori map up. "They were *gifts* to the humans, elves, and dwarfs."

"Pure fantasy."

"And the Amulet of Earth was *gifted* to the king of the dwarfs. You, contrary to your own inflated notions otherwise, are not the king of the dwarfs."

Darmon's grip on his axe tightened. "Semantics. My father is dying. I am his heir."

"Yes. Your father is dying. And rather than remaining by his side for his last few months and sending someone in your stead to aid your cousin, you are in here trying to blackmail us into letting you ransack a temple for your own petty gain," Tathiel said softly. "What else do you want, besides the amulet? The treasures of the Old Gods? Whatever lies in that temple, be it jewels or artifacts or whatever your mind can think up, it was valued so highly by the Great Ones that they would rather it be lost to time than stolen away by someone undeserving of it. And you think you can trick us into letting you claim it for yourself?"

Darmon was silent.

"You will not get the amulet. And you will not lead anyone anywhere."

"I command the dwarfs." Darmon's voice was low and soft.

Tathiel tucked the Elori map under his arm. "We don't need them."

Darmon balked, stuttering something intelligible.

"We leave in two days. Suvusa needs the time to rest before she goes with us."

Tathiel turned his back on Darmon and left the tent. Nunor was standing only a few feet away.

The dwarf was much calmer than he had been a few moments before. "You said to find you when I was myself again." He nodded towards the tent. "Thought you might need my help with him. Glad to hear I was wrong."

"I didn't spend all those years following you and Tiryn to not learn how to handle an angry dwarf."

Nunor laughed, the sound loud and hearty. Only dwarfs could laugh so richly, in Tathiel's opinion.

He gave Nunor a hand on the shoulder. "Come on, let's see if the Elori have something to drink beside water."

When the Elori learned that their new dwarfen friends would be leaving so soon, they insisted on having a feast. Tents were moved to clear a space large enough for all to eat and dance together. A large bonfire was built, and something that smelled heavenly spent far too long cooking at perhaps half a dozen smaller fires. Tathiel tried to slip close enough to inspect it, but the Elori women tending to the food were quick to slap him away with giggles and shouts in their native tongue.

When it was finally brought out, Tathiel was upset to realize it was grilled cactus. His disappointment only lasted long enough for him to taste the Elori's imitation of meat. It was far more satisfying in taste than it had been in smell. The similar dish that Hiruscu made as they traveled to the Elori camp only days ago was nothing in comparison.

"The Elori do not often have meat in their diet," Suvusa explained. "Especially since our people and the dwarfs have lost our close connection."

Nunor, grimacing, poked at the cactus steak he had been presented with. "My lady Suvusa, I will do everything in my power to make sure Doldural once again honors the Elori."

That brought a smile to Suvusa's face.

Tathiel and Nunor did find a drink stronger than water that the Elori seemed to enjoy very much. It was a cloudy liquid with a sweet bite and a bitter aftertaste. And it was not strong enough for Nunor, who complained endlessly about it whenever there were no Elori in hearing range.

"Honestly, I would be better off just drinking my own

piss. There's likely still more kick to it than this!"

"I like it," Tathiel said, refilling both his and Nunor's glasses. "And for all of your whining, you're still drinking a fair amount of it."

"Ah, can't be disappointing these fine people. And if there's no meat, might as well see if I can drink myself to sleep."

"Have you seen Syrani?" Tathiel asked. He scanned the crowd again, but she was nowhere to be seen. Tiryn was being coaxed into a dance by two Elori women. He mimicked their hand and foot movements half-heartedly, clearly uncomfortable. And Darmon and Alain sat together. Darmon was speaking quietly to Alain, who had her eyes fixed on something in the crowd.

Tathiel followed her gaze to see Hiruscu and Rushavi. Hiruscu held his son's hands and kept him steady as he bounced and jumped in a gleeful and childish dance.

"Not since she left you to deal with my cousin." Nunor gulped down more of the drink. "You think she went out to spend time with Halcia?"

"Perhaps." Tathiel stood. "Here, finish mine, would you? I'm going to see if I can't find our friend."

Nunor took the cup. "Don't stay too long, boy. Tiryn looks like he's just about had enough dancing. And they'll come for me next, I just know it."

Tathiel wandered out of the camp, picking a direction at random. His instincts led him right to Syrani, who was perhaps a quarter of a mile beyond the outermost tents of the Elori camp.

"There you are. Were you concerned about Halcia?"

Syrani's back was to him, her gaze fixed on the setting sun. "Yes. But she's fine. She was exploring, apparently."

Tathiel stood beside her, scanning the sky. "Not really one for staying patiently in place, is she?"

Syrani made an amused sound. "No, not really." She

pointed. "She's over there. See?"

There was a faint black dot against the fading sunlight. "Will she stay out all night?"

Syrani shook her head. "No, she promised to stay close after nightfall."

There was a quiet moment. The sounds of the feast behind him were softer, and there was the gentlest breeze blowing over the sands.

Syrani's hands touched something resting on her chest. "Do you feel it? The pull of the amulet?"

Tathiel closed his eyes, concentrating on his own amulet. He could sense an almost imperceptible tug, drawing him deeper into the desert. He couldn't tell if the sensation was physical or mental. "I do."

"It's out there, somewhere."

Tathiel nodded. "We'll find it. We've found the first two. And we're on the trail."

In the end, they did not wait the two full days Tiryn wished for.

Tathiel awoke early the next day, before the sun had fully risen. His tent mates were gone. Even Grinor, who slept heavily and with thunderous snores, was nowhere to be seen. He slipped on his boots quickly and left, returning to the spot where the Elori had carried on their dancing well into the night.

There were voices on the air. Many of them were Elori as they finally bedded down for sleep or whispered what sounded to Tathiel's ear like sweet, seductive nothings into a lover's ear. The tone alone was enough to pique his interest, even if he could not understand the words. And when he caught Syrani's voice, he followed it.

It was not Syrani he found first, though he could tell she

and most of his companions were close. It was Alain, dressed for sleep and with her long hair down and unbraided, that he spotted first. She stood behind a tent, eavesdropping on the conversation Syrani and the others were having.

"Can you hear anything?" Tathiel asked.

Alain jumped, her hand reaching for a weapon she didn't have on a belt she wasn't wearing. She glared when she realized who it was. "I was just out for a walk. I didn't mean to overhear anything."

Tathiel shrugged. "I don't think they'll mind if you join them. It sounds like it's pertinent to you and your master, anyway."

Her glare deepened. "Darmon is not my master."

"I'm sure he realizes that." Tathiel waved her forward. "Come on. They've seen me dressed in my sleepwear and haven't judged me for it. Let's go."

The only ones surprised to see Tathiel and Alain approaching were the other dwarfs.

"Ah, good. You here, Alain." Grinor offered a spot beside him for her to sit. "It saves these fine fellows from inciting another argument with Darmon. He's more likely to agree to leave sooner if you are the one to tell him it is necessary."

"Why, what's going on?" Alain asked, sitting beside Grinor.

"Rushavi has grown again," Syrani answered.

"I thought he was constantly growing?" Tathiel asked.

"He is," Tiryn said. He was standing, pacing the sand with one hand on the back of his neck. "But every several hours the process seems to progress rapidly for a short time."

"Why didn't you wake me when you left the tent?" Tathiel asked.

Nunor barked out a laugh. "Because most of us haven't been to bed yet." He took a long swig from a familiar cup, then belched.

Tathiel raised an eyebrow. "You finally got drunk?"

"It only took all night," Nunor admitted with a shrug. "Grinor has been with me."

"I was asleep for some time, but I got up to get some meditation in," Syrani said. "And found Suvusa and Hiruscu with Rushavi."

"And why didn't you wake me, Tiryn?"

Tiryn shrugged. "I was wandering around the camp. Syrani found me before making it to our tent."

"Just say you were with a woman and be done with it, you pointy-eared fuck." Nunor refilled his cup again. The decanter dribbled out half a glass and no more.

Tiryn glared at Nunor, but said nothing.

"How bad was this latest growth?" Alain asked. "You said we might need to leave earlier than planned?"

Tiryn sighed, coming to a stop in his pacing. "I had hoped we would have enough time to reach the temple before Rushavi became a young man, but now I am not so sure. I'm not familiar with the specifics of the human aging process, but—"

Tiryn was interrupted by the rustling of a nearby tent flap. Suvusa and Hiruscu emerged, and a young boy stood between them. He was perhaps two feet tall, almost as tall as Nunor, and walked unaided into the odd circle of elves and dwarfs before him.

"I tried to braid his hair, to match his father, but it seemed to grow before my very eyes." Suvusa touched her son's head, where the hair had been shaved clean off. "So we will do this for now, and hope we can make something of it when it grows more slowly."

"Fuck," Tathiel said quietly.

Hiruscu squeezed an arm around Suvusa's shoulders. "I will bare my head like my son, if he wishes to look like me."

Suvusa laughed. "Thank you, my love. But his will grow back much faster than yours. And I like your hair now."

"Rushavi," Syrani said, reaching for his hand, "I don't

know if you remember who I am. But my name is Syrani."

The boy nodded and shook her hand.

They each went around in turn, introducing themselves. Some got a nod, or a wave of the hand and a smile. But none got a word from the young boy.

"He has still not said anything," Suvusa said, kneeling to the ground and looking Rushavi in the eyes. "Have you, my son?"

Rushavi turned into Suvusa, burying his face in her neck.

"He is shy," Hiruscu said. "This is all for tonight. Let him sleep."

Tathiel nodded. "Of course. This must be such a stressful time for him. We will rest a few hours longer before we prepare to leave for the temple."

"Where is Ardu?" Suvusa asked. "I have not seen him, and Rushavi seems to worry for him."

"Hunting," Syrani answered. "I was told that he should be returning soon. Apparently, this process has affected Ardu's need for sustenance. He must eat more often."

"It will be hard for Ardu to find meat on the path to the temple," Suvusa murmured, looking to Hiruscu.

"Halcia will help him, don't worry." Syrani gave the mother a tight-lipped smile. "All will be well for Ardu and Rushavi both, in time."

The three Elori departed. There was a strange silence over the rest of them. Tathiel noted the worry in Syrani's face and the mixture of dismay and concern Tiryn expressed.

"So, we're in agreement, then?" He asked. "We leave today?"

Tiryn nodded.

"I can begin collecting supplies," Syrani said, rising to her feet.

"I'll help," Nunor said.

"Alain, if you could, please speak to Darmon and express the need to adjust our schedule," Tiryn said.

Alain nodded and stood to leave. "If you need further assistance from me, I will be preparing our men for travel."

"Oh, has Darmon decided to bring his army with him, free of charge?" Tathiel asked. There was more annoyance to his voice than he had intended.

To his surprise, Alain smirked. "You have a way with words, elf. I had to hear about your ill manners at great length."

Tathiel shrugged "I won't apologize."

"I understand." Alain nodded first to Tathiel, then to the group as a whole. "Thank you for letting me be privy to this unsettling development. I will ensure Darmon and his knights are ready shortly."

Grinor followed her, wishing them all a good, albeit short, night.

Before long, only Tiryn and Tathiel remained.

Tathiel put a hand on Tiryn's arm. "Are you alright?"

Tiryn sighed. "I'm tired, Tathiel." He sat, taking the spot Nunor had previously occupied. "When I agreed to help Roland with this quest, I didn't realize I would spend more than a decade of my life chasing after lost artifacts."

"For an elf, a decade is nothing …"

"For an elf here in Azimar, or in Vyris, a decade is nothing. But my family … my old friends …"

Tathiel sat beside him. "You mean the elves you lost in Thessala?"

"I have done nothing to search for them. Are they in Vyris somewhere, hidden somewhere we haven't found? Were they lost when the gateway was destroyed?" Tiryn closed his eyes. "I don't know if there will come a day when I will see them again. And if they are trapped somewhere, in some space between gateways, what does a decade feel like to them?"

"What do you want to do?"

Tiryn's eyes remained closed, his head leaned slightly back. "I don't know."

23

TRISSA

Things were different now, and Trissa wasn't yet sure if they were better or worse.

She and her mother had moved to a different part of the castle. It was bigger, but there was now only one bedroom that she and her mother shared. Illa came with them, and she slept in the front room, which was both a sitting area and a study.

Illa planned to sleep in the chair they had brought over from their old rooms, but Trissa's mother insisted on getting her a proper bed. It was not as big and grand as Trissa's own bed, but it was more comfortable to lie in than the chair. Trissa tested it herself to be sure.

Their new rooms were closer to the tower, and Illa explained that they had once belonged to the king.

"My father used to live her?"

Illa shook her head. "Not your father. The king before him. He was your uncle."

Trissa knew who she meant. Nanny Nevina had told her about Areanath. He had been very kind, and very smart. But Nevina had never told Trissa where Areanath had gone.

"What happened to him? Why does he not still live here?"

Illa's face looked very sad. "He died. Many years ago, now. When I was only a little older than you."

Trissa liked their new rooms, even though she now had to share a room with her mother. They were closer to the baths and the kitchens, and they were no longer surrounded by empty quarters that were filled with old memories. Sometimes she could feel those old memories, and some of them were very sad or very angry.

But the memories in her new room were different. There were fewer of them, but they were better. There was more happiness and excitement in the walls of the bedroom. And the study was brimming with so much love that it filled Trissa's heart and made her want to hug her mother and never let go.

But her mother was not happy. She had not been since Auntie Ishta had left, but it was worse now. And after sharing a bowl of bland porridge with her mother, Trissa found out why.

"We have to go to the tower today, Trissa."

"Why?"

"Because I promised your father we would. We have to help him."

Trissa shook her head. "But I don't want to go. It's bad up there."

Her mother nodded. "I know. But I had to make a deal with your father, or he was going to take you away from me again."

Trissa frowned. "What deal?"

"We have to go up there every morning and spend the day helping your father. And in return, we get to stay here together. You, me, and your Auntie Illa. The three of us don't have to worry about being separated again, so long as we keep our end of the deal."

Trissa thought about it for a moment, sucking on the end of her spoon.

She had only spent a few days up in the tower with her father, but she'd hated every moment of it. The nights were the worst. It got unbearably cold, and she couldn't ignore the memories that filled her father's tower once the sun fell.

"We only have to be there during the day?"

Her mother nodded. "You can come home at night, yes. I've asked that you not stay up too late, so you can get your rest."

"And you?" Trissa asked.

Her mother's eyes didn't stray from hers for a moment. "I think there would be some nights when your father needs my company, but you would still have Illa to care for you while I was away."

Trissa tossed her spoon onto the small table they shared and crossed her arms. "What could father need your help with at night? Why can't you just come home with me?"

Their table sat against the wall, and the spoon rolled unevenly until it stopped against the grey stone. Her mother picked it up and set it gently into their empty bowl. "I do not like it either, my darling. But it was part of the bargain we made."

"I don't like this bargain."

Her mother smiled. "Don't fret and pout, Trissa. There are far worse things than a few hours alone in your father's company."

Trissa decided very quickly after arriving in the cold and drafty tower that her mother had been wrong. Mothlenor immediately sent Anna into a separate room to do some important reading, leaving Trissa in the room with him. Mothlenor wasted no time on pleasantries before retrieving the strange stone he had shown her several days before.

"Do you remember what this is, Trissa?"

She nodded. "A dragon's eye. You can use it to see people."

"Correct. And do you remember who we looked for the last time I showed this to you?"

"Mother," Trissa answered. "And Commander Ajax."

"He is *not* a commander, Trissa."

Trissa flinched slightly at the harshness in his words. "I'm sorry."

Her father sighed. "We've discussed this before, my dear. Titles and names are important, Trissa. They have power in them."

"I'm sorry. It won't happen again."

"I hope it doesn't." Mothlenor held out the dragon's eye again. "Ajax—Roland—should be visible in the stone. Do you see him?"

Trissa had to squint, but she could see the faint image of a red-haired male. She nodded. They had already done this once before, and there had been little to show for it. "Do you want me to try to See him?"

Her father put the stone carefully in a shallow dish, which he then set on his desk. "Yes. Here, come stand across from me." He sat in the large chair behind the desk, and Trissa stood opposite him. "Are you ready?"

Trissa nodded.

Her father gently pushed the dish closer until it was nearly under Trissa's nose. "Then I will keep the image of Roland in the stone, and you will tell me what you See."

Trissa stared at the stone, the tiny figure of a man she had never met moving slightly across its surface. He was talking to someone, his lips moving every few seconds. He looked young, maybe even younger than her own mother. But she knew that was impossible.

Nanny Nevina had told her about Roland. About how she had loved him, and how he had tried to save her life. The man in the stone would have to be much older than he appeared to be the same man that Nanny Nevina talked about.

"Why is he not the right age?"

"Come again?" her father asked.

"If this is Co—" Trissa cleared her throat and started again. "If this is Roland, then why is he not the right age? He's too young." She frowned, suddenly doubting herself. "Isn't he?"

Mothlenor smiled at her. Perhaps it was meant to be warm and encouraging, but it was unsettling instead. "It's easy enough to change your appearance, my dear. Age is an easy thing to hide."

"Oh."

"Now, concentrate. And tell me what you See."

Trissa Saw nothing. She stared at the stone, first squinting, then opening her eyes wide enough that they felt they might bulge and fall from her skull. She bent over, propping her elbows on the desk and putting her face close enough to the stone that she could feel her eyelashes brush the surface when she blinked.

Nothing worked. No visions came to her.

The entire time, her father sat and watched her.

"Can I sit?" she asked her father. "My feet hurt."

He gave her his seat without a word, pulling the stone to the opposite side of the desk so it was once more close to her. Much to Trissa's relief, he chose to stand in front of the broken window instead of taking her former place.

More time passed. Trissa thought, if she listened closely enough, she could hear the shuffling of papers as her mother read in the other room.

There were strange marks on the surface of the desk. Trisha ran her fingers over them. They were not terribly deep, and the spacing and shape were curiously like the kind her fingernails might make if she tried to scratch the tough wood. The markings were black, though. As if they had been burned.

"Trissa," her father snapped. "Focus."

Trissa was startled back to attention, staring once more into the dragon's eye.

Roland was sitting, leaning back against a wall. The wall was wood, or maybe brown stone. It was difficult to tell. And he was dozing. Every few moments, his eyes would open briefly, and he would look around. And then he would close his eyes again.

Is that how a man fearing for his life sleeps? Just a few moments at a time?

Trissa tilted her head when Roland awoke again.

His eyes, the way they moved …

He's keeping watch over someone.

After some time, Trissa grew distracted again. Her hands traced over the burned claw marks on the desk. What kind of creature could have made them, she couldn't guess. But whatever it was, her father seemed to keep it around the tower.

Trissa surreptitiously glanced around the room. There was no bird of flame roosting in an unnoticed corner. Besides, the marks could not be that of a bird.

Something more human, Trissa thought.

"Trissa, have you still Seen nothing?"

"No, I haven't." Trissa leaned back into the chair. It was far larger than she was, and she had to stretch her arms to dangle them over the sides. "I'm sorry. But it's hard." Her stomach grumbled. "And I'm hungry."

Her father sighed. "Perhaps a break, then." Even he looked tired, and Trissa felt a pang of guilt at not trying a little harder at her task.

"Can I go to the kitchens and have some lunch?"

He helped her down from the chair. Her legs were numb

from sitting so long. "You may, yes. But come back as soon as you finish, and we will try again."

Trissa nodded and bowed. Once the tower door was shut behind her, however, she ran down the curved stairs and out into the rest of the castle.

She knew the way to the kitchens very well and knew Illa was likely to be there. And if she was not, she knew her way around the larder just as well as she knew the rest of the castle.

Trissa did not notice the strange sounds that came from the kitchen until she was already bursting through the door.

Illa was there, but so was Ferrand. Illa lay on her back on the long table, and the skirt of her dress was pushed up to show her thighs and part of her buttocks. Trissa could see Ferrand's pants and weapons in a pile around his ankles, and he stood between Illa's legs.

"What are you doing to Illa?" Trissa shouted. "Get off her, you're going to hurt her!"

Both adults looked at Trissa, and Ferrand immediately let out a barking laugh that twisted the broken and burned half of his face.

Illa tried to sit up, pushing Ferrand away from her and simultaneously trying to pull her skirts down to cover herself. "Trissa, darling, go back into the hall."

But Ferrand grabbed Illa's face and pushed her once more onto her back. There was a sickening thunk as Illa's head hit the table. "Let her watch. She'll know what's coming for her in a few years."

Trissa was rooted for the spot for a few seconds, long enough for Illa to plead for her to leave again. Only then was Trissa able to turn and flee back the way she had come.

She could not leave entirely. Instead, she ran to the nearest junction, where the hallway to the kitchen split into routes for the Great Hall, the guest suites, and the rest of the castle. Trissa slipped around the corner and hugged the wall.

She sat back on her ankles, keeping one cheek pressed against the cool stone of the wall, and wept.

How long she sat there, she did not know. Would it be foolish to find her mother, to tell her that the commander was harming Illa? What would her father say?

Would Illa be alright?

Was Ferrand going to kill Illa?

Kill Trissa for seeing him hurting Illa?

Who could she tell, if not her mother and father? Arella?

But what could Arella do, when she was so far away? And Trissa had told Arella not to speak with her again, to keep her father from learning about her.

No, Arella was not an option.

Trissa heard heavy footsteps approaching. She froze, unsure if she should run and hide or stay where she was and hope Ferrand passed her by.

"I know you're there, Princess," Ferrand called down the hall. "I can hear your panicked breathing. Like a frightened fox stuck in a snare."

Trissa shook away the image of Ferrand holding a blade over her as she frantically tore at a chain around her ankle.

I did not See that. His words are tricking me.

"You can come out. I won't hurt you. Not yet." Ferrand rounded the corner, stopping to stand over her. "There you are." He patted her head. "Illa is waiting for you in the kitchens."

Ferrand walked away without another word. He whistled as he left, and the savage-looking curved blade on his hip bounced with each step.

Trissa stood and returned to the kitchens. She did not open the door for a long moment.

Illa is dead. I will walk in, and she will be dead on the table. Ferrand has left her there for me to find.

"Illa?" Trissa called softly. "Are you in there?"

"I'm in here, child. You can come in. Everything is fine now."

Trissa opened the door. Illa stood at the end of the table, scrubbing at it with a damp cloth.

Trissa rushed to Illa, wrapping her arms around her. "I thought he was going to kill you. I didn't know what to do."

Illa bent and kissed her head. "I'm fine, Princess."

"What was he doing to you?"

Illa snorted. "The commander does what he wants." Illa pulled Trissa from her and motioned for her to sit. "Let me finish cleaning this, and then I'll make you some lunch, hm? I bet you're hungry."

"But what was he doing to you?"

Illa shook her head. "It's not for me to explain."

"Who else will explain it?" Trissa glared at Illa. "Or should I wait a few years until it happens to me?"

That gave Illa pause. Finally, Illa sat beside her. She did not answer right away, but chewed on her lip and stared thoughtfully at the table.

"Adults—those who love each other anyway—show their love in many, many ways. And some of those ways are more … physical than others."

"Kissing. Like Mother and Auntie Ishta."

Illa nodded. "Like that, but more. You'll understand more when you're older, but there are things beyond kissing. And, I'm sure if they had the chance, your mother and my sister would have done those things, too."

"Because they love each other." Trissa looked down at Illa's hands. The knuckles were white from squeezing the rag so tightly. "But you don't love the commander."

Illa scoffed. "I certainly do not."

"Then why …"

"When adults who love each other do these things, there is always permission beforehand. One asks, the other says yes, and then they know it is safe to continue." Illa turned, looking Trissa directly in the eyes. "The permission is important, you understand? If they love you, and you love them, you will make sure to have permission."

"Did Ferrand ask for your permission?"

Illa shook her head. "Ferrand never asks for anything. He only ever takes."

"So what he did was wrong?"

Illa nodded.

"When will he be punished?"

Illa smiled. "He won't be punished. Because he is the commander, and he can do what he wants. He has power."

Trissa remembered what her father had chastised her for that morning. "Titles have power in them."

"Yes." Illa sighed. "So, even though I did not say yes, I also cannot say no. Or I may be punished instead."

They spoke no more of what had transpired. Illa made Trissa lunch. It was a single potato warmed in the oven's coals with a tiny pad of butter. When Trissa asked for salt, Illa told her there was none to be had. Trissa did not ask for additional butter or a piece of bread.

Illa kissed her on the head before sending her back to the tower.

"Will I see you tonight? In our new home?" Trissa asked.

"Of course, Princess. I will be waiting there for you."

Trissa returned to the tower much more slowly than she had left it. She was not surprised to see that Ferrand was there.

"How was your lunch, Princess?" Ferrand asked her. There was a smirk tugging at his burned lips.

"It was uneventful." She turned to her father. "Illa is out of salt and butter. And she didn't say it, but I think she's running low on many other things, too. Is there anything we can do to bring more food to Etritia?"

Her father nodded. "The commander and I were just

discussing that. He's just returned from an inspection of the castle's larder himself."

"I didn't realize it took the commander himself to inspect a larder," Trissa said.

Ferrand smirked again. "I don't mind, Princess. I take my duties very seriously."

"Are you ready to begin again, Trissa?"

She nodded, taking her seat in her father's chair. The image of Roland was already present in the stone, she could see the blur of his red hair without even needing to pull the dragon's eye closer to her.

Her father pushed the dragon's eye into place. "Tell me everything you See."

"I think I See something already," Trissa lied. Trissa closed her eyes for a second, then snapped them open again. "I Saw Roland. He was holding something." She turned to Ferrand. "You were there, Commander. And there were flames."

Ferrand scowled.

"Is that why your face is so ugly? Did Roland do that to you?"

"Trissa," her father said sharply, "that is the past. I need to know the future."

"She can't control it." Trissa turned in her chair to find her mother standing in the open doorway behind her. She held several papers and books in her arms. "Gifted women cannot control what they See. Sometimes it is the past, sometimes the present, and sometimes the future."

Ferrand snorted. "She can control her tongue, the cheeky little bitch."

Trissa's father nodded. "The commander is right, Trissa. You were not polite just now."

Trissa lifted her chin but did not look away from the dragon's eye. "I apologize."

Trissa's mother deposited the papers onto the desk. "Do you still require my assistance, my king?"

"No, you may leave."

"If it's all the same to you, I would prefer to remain here until Trissa is sent to our quarters."

Trissa's father nodded. "Then remain. It makes no difference." He pointed to the dragon's eye. "Continue, Trissa. And this time, try not to insult the members of my council."

"Of course, Father."

"Remember, we work for the good of Etritia."

Trissa stared at the dragon's eye, watching Roland as he held a large white stone in his hands.

"For the good of Etritia."

24
TIRYN

Tiryn heard of Tathiel's rude remarks to Darmon several hours after their altercation had occurred. While he was not normally one to use veiled threats and clever insults day to day, he had seen time and again how effective they were for Nunor. More recently, when Nunor's words failed him, it was Tathiel who offered his own epithets.

So when Tiryn first overheard from a pair of dwarf knights that Darmon had been infuriated by a cheeky elf, his first instinct was to scowl deeply and consider how best to apologize on Tathiel's behalf.

He did not get his chance to apologize because Syrani soon found him and urgently insisted that he follow her, telling him that Suvusa needed his attention. Tiryn had expected sickness or fever. He did not expect Rushavi to be suddenly aged another few years. He had studied the young boy intently for over an hour a short time ago, and he was sure in his assertion that Rushavi's aging would slow and eventually stop.

In the morning, Rushavi looked little different, thankfully. His shaved head already had a noticeable amount of stubble, and his mother promised to keep his hair cut close so it would not grow unruly and cause him discomfort.

And, miraculously, the entire fleet of dwarf knights were armed and awaiting orders. Darmon himself was standing beside a mule, his axe on his hip and a deep frown on his face.

"What are we waiting for, then? I thought this was a timely problem?"

"We are waiting for Syrani and Tathiel," Tiryn said. "They had a couple of matters to attend to."

Tiryn did not wish to explain that the two elves were conversing privately with Halcia and Melonya before departing. The two great dragons would watch the entire entourage from afar and try their best to remain out of sight until the Elori keep was at least two days behind them.

"They will meet us on the road, if we are ready to depart," Tiryn added.

"Just a moment, Tiryn." Nunor approached, perhaps half a dozen Elori behind him. "If I'm understanding these fellows properly, they want to go with us."

Suvusa raised an eyebrow and spoke rapidly to the men. One answered in the affirmative, giving little elaboration.

"Why?" Tryn asked. "We have Suvusa and Hiruscu to guide us, and we anticipate little danger on the road."

"They do not wish to go to be your guides. They wish to see the temple."

"They aren't the only ones," Nunor said. He nodded towards the exit of the keep. "Seems more are gathering to follow us."

"Elir damn it all!" Darmon cursed. He stepped into his mule's saddle, using an odd kind of rope ladder to bring himself high enough off the ground to reach the pommel. "Just point me in the right direction and I'll start my men off. Follow at your leisure, cousin."

Nunor grumbled something rude and unsavory under his breath and gestured off in a general direction.

Tiryn sighed. *Great Ones, I am tired.*

"Suvusa, can you please explain to the Elori that we cannot guarantee there will be a temple?"

Suvusa shrugged. "There has never been a temple when we have made the journey. But we have never traveled with three dragons in search of a lost amulet of the gods." She shook her head. "They will not care. They only wish to make the journey and see what lies at the end of the path with their own eyes."

In the end, roughly a third of the Elori prepared to leave with them. They were mostly men, though there were many women as well. Tiryn counted no children and no elderly. The only exception was Rushavi.

He had hoped the Elori storyteller would be among the crowd that joined them. She declined to go and watched from afar as the Elori gathered weapons and talked excitedly amongst themselves.

Suvusa said the storyteller had cited her old age as the reason she would not be joining them and confessed it was the same excuse she gave to never leave the old keep again.

"She will never leave this place?" Tiryn asked.

"Never. She will die here." Suvusa shrugged. "All of the best storytellers have. It is an honor to be buried in the stones of the desert keep."

An unsettled feeling settled into Tiryn's stomach. They were standing in a mass grave, and he had not known.

Darmon's men traveled slowly, and even with perhaps forty Elori walking on foot, they caught up before the day came to a close. The Elori were fast travelers, and their dark skin, smeared as it was in red clay, combined with their bright clothing, made them an interesting sight.

They camped much as they had in Cai Myrh, though the tents the Elori and the dwarfs carried were far less elaborate than many set up in the keep. They were smaller and basic and were made of stronger materials to survive the constant tear downs and reassembly.

There was a loud string of shouts, and Tiryn spotted a middle-aged Elori man angrily kicking sand. A half-constructed tent lay at his feet, and a similarly aged woman and four younger men stood nearby speaking with each other in low voices. Tiryn still could not understand their language, but he could tell they were deeply annoyed.

The older man kicked the tent, spewing more Elori phrases that Tiryn took to be profanities.

"Hey, calm down," Tiryn said, touching the man on the shoulder. "What happened?"

The Elori man motioned towards the tent, where Tiryn could see the jagged end of a broken pole poking through a tear in the thin fabric. He began speaking rapidly, gesturing to the pole.

Tiryn waved at him. "I can't understand you, I'm sorry."

The Elori man stopped speaking, letting his words end in a frustrated growl and another kick to the mess of wooden poles and fabric.

"Come on, now." Tiryn touched the man's arm again, pulling him slightly away from the broken pile in the sand. "I can fix it for you."

Tiryn grabbed the pole, fishing around for both halves. The fracture had been jagged, but he fitted the two halves together as best he could. With a little effort, arcane energy flowed from his hands and down to the break. It sealed together, the splinters healing in seconds.

Tiryn passed it to the man. It was slightly warmer than it had been a moment ago, and the spot where the wood had knitted itself together was slightly paler than the darker wood of the pole.

"There you are. No harm done."

The Elori family thanked him profusely. At least Tiryn

thought they were doing so. He left before they made too much of a scene.

That one act of arcane kindness led to many others over the next several days. Broken poles, a wrist fractured in a fall down a sand dune, and countless other small miracles. The other elves were not immune to the requests. Syrani, it seemed, had a talent for barrier magic. She kept the insects from invading their camps at night, though her barriers were strong enough to protect them from much larger creatures.

Tathiel, as he had before, located buried water reserves. He claimed it was not so much an arcane ability as it was him listening to the amulet he carried. The Amulet of Water could apparently sense sources of its element, and Tathiel merely followed the gentle guidance it gave him.

Syrani confirmed that her amulet, too, would pull her towards flames if she allowed it.

The heat of the sands had not changed, and even Tiryn struggled to keep his senses sharp as the days wore on. He and Nunor took little convincing when Suvusa offered the red clay and cactus jelly salve to keep their skin from burning. He willingly slathered the sticky substance all over his face and the exposed sections of his neck and arms. Suvusa once again delighted in braiding his hair, and Tiryn sat in the sand beside Rushavi as she did so.

Syrani and Tathiel, however, were slower to accept the strange and itchy concoction. By the time they did, each had a slight burn across their nose and cheekbones. Tiryn had the decency to not remark on it, but Nunor smugly suggested that their burnt faces could have been prevented if they had only listened to the Elori.

Tiryn refrained from reminding Nunor that the dwarf had been badly burned and similarly adamant in his refusal to smear himself in the protective salve.

Melonya and Halcia were introduced to the Elori with them as soon as the keep was out of sight. There were many shouts, some of fear and many others of excitement. Each evening after, when the dragons settled into the sand for the night, the Elori would take it in turns to approach the pair and offer some small thing to them. Usually it was a grilled cactus steak, which they ate begrudgingly. But there were also cactus flowers and small rodents or lizards that had been caught earlier in the day. There were small stones and bits of iron that had been heated and worked into varying shapes. These inedible trinkets were collected by Syrani and Tathiel and kept.

Halcia, who hated the attention, begged Syrani to return the gifts and keep more from coming. But Suvusa was quick to say that refusing such gifts would disappoint the Elori and lead them to believe they had angered the Great Ones in some way.

Halcia relented.

A few days into their travels, Tiryn received a message from Alastor. The large black bird was nearly shot down by the Elori, but Suvusa relayed Tiryn's wish for it to remain unharmed before any damage was done. And when the bird landed on Tiryn's shoulder and began to speak, the Elori laughed and shouted in wonderment.

"What did Alastor's little pet say?" Tathiel asked him as the bird dissolved into dust and blew away.

"That he will reach his destination soon." Tiryn wiped dust from his shoulder. "And that your sister is having some sort of trouble in Larten."

"Just Eilonwy? Not the others?"

Tiryn shrugged. "That's what he said."

Tathiel rolled his eyes. "Probably causing trouble for Mathius somehow. Melonya will be happy to go."

Halcia's annoyance only grew deeper as she became the primary focus of the Elori's attention after Melonya's departure. At Syrani's insistence, however, she continued to act the part of a pleased god.

Ardu was not left out. His growth, as well as the growth of his companion, finally slowed. It did not stop, but Tiryn noted that there were no more sudden bursts of aging between the two. Ardu was now roughly the size of a donkey, and his clubbed tail was rather intimidating to see. He also received gifts from the Elori, though he snapped and hissed if they drew too near.

Ardu refused to leave Rushavi's side for long, and instead walked alongside his companion. With his wings folded and his short and stubby tail, Ardu almost looked like a very large version of the lizards occasionally spotted in the sands. He even walked and ran the same way those creatures did, with his tail leaving little drag marks behind him. His coloring was the only thing that was truly different, aside from his size. The greens and browns in his scales were somewhat darker, and he did not blend quite so easily with the sand when he stopped to rest.

Rushavi, to Tiryn's surprise, still had not spoken a word to anyone. When they stopped for the evening, Tiryn would often try to pull the boy into conversation. His parents, too, would ask questions of him and speak to him, but he would never answer.

Finally, an idea came to Tiryn.

Several nights into their journey, Suvusa left Rushavi with Tiryn so she could bathe herself in the desert sand. An Elori bath was a simple yet strange affair. A little water mixed with just a touch of cactus jelly and the fine sand of the desert became a thick scouring paste that could be used for cleaning just about anything. Tiryn had tried it once and promised never to do so again unless absolutely needed.

But Rushavi and Tiryn would be relatively alone for a few moments.

He sat across from the boy, who now stood roughly the same height as Nunor and could ride his own mule if the creature was calm and sure-footed. Tiryn focused on

Rushavi's face, concentrating on his dark eyes, which were curious and gentle. Rushavi ignored him, choosing to stare instead at the dried cactus fruit he was slowly eating his way through.

Tiryn held a water skin in his hands. Not close enough for the boy to think it was being offered, but near enough at hand that he could take it if he wanted to.

Rushavi's mind was more complex than Tiryn had expected. There were myriad thoughts, though none were coherent or linear in a way that he could understand. And there was nothing preventing Tiryn from making the simple connection he needed.

"Rushavi, would you like some water?"

Rushavi instantly looked up and nodded, reaching for the skin.

Tiryn passed it over with a smile.

"So, the child understands what we are saying, and chooses to not answer us," Darmon said angrily. "Should his parents not be ashamed?"

Tiryn sighed. "And why would they be? He should still be young enough to be cradled in his parent's arms, and yet he rides a mule and feeds himself."

"He should be swaddled and held against his mother's breast, not answering your incessant pestering questions about how he intends to steal the amulet from you. Don't think I haven't noticed." Nunor spat in the sand, eyeing his cousin. "Ya daft fuck."

Darmon sneered at Nunor, but Alain spoke before he could. "We've asked him nothing about the amulet, I swear it. We have tried to be conversational, but the boy always seems intent on remaining silent."

"The *boy* has a name," Syrani said. "And now we know his preferred method of communication."

"Yes, convenient for you." Darmon nodded. "And not for those of us who can't use said method."

"I can't do it either, Darmon," Nunor grunted. "So it's not like you're the only ones excluded."

"Even his own parents can't speak to him mentally like that. It's a method normally only found in those who are strong in the arcane. Such as elves and some humans," Tathiel said.

And Roland, Tiryn thought. Nunor's quick glance in his direction suggested he had the same thought.

"It still leaves the question of how the dwarfs are to plead for the return of the amulet," Darmon said. "If he will not converse with us—"

"He does not control the fate of the amulet, Darmon," Tiryn interrupted. "He is just a boy. A boy cursed with rapid aging and a dragon for a companion, but a boy nonetheless."

"Do not pretend that you care for him, elf." Darmon's jaw twitched. "You and your kind are only after the amulet as well."

"I care for him a great deal, Darmon," Tiryn said quietly. "I may have come to the desert to find the Amulet of Earth, but it was not for my own gain."

Darmon sneered, resting a hand on his axe.

Tiryn continued, ignoring the small show of power Darmon attempted. "I came here to help your cousin stop a needless war that would cost hundreds of dwarfs their lives, Darmon. I did not expect to find an infant caught between us and your intentions for the crown."

"Darmon …" Alain cleared her throat. "Sir, what if the elf speaks the truth?"

"The elf *does* speak the truth," Tiryn said, lifting an eyebrow at Alain.

Alain gave a slow nod. "Then, perhaps, we should try to

stop this fighting. We are miles from any city or town. We are all following the same path. And we all search for the same thing. Until the temple is found, maybe it would be best to put this animosity behind us."

Everyone was silent for a moment, staring at Darmon. Nunor glared, his lips pursed tight enough that they were all but hidden by his beard. Syrani and Tathiel both seemed calm, almost bored, but there was a faint taste of arcane energy in the air to suggest that at least one of them was prepared for a fight.

Tiryn, for his part, didn't particularly care what Darmon's response was. The dwarf's word was worth very little.

Darmon sighed. "Alright. Until the temple is found."

The dwarfs relaxed, all except for Grinor, who had not spoken and seemed to always be on edge when Nunor and Darmon were within eyesight of each other.

Tiryn bowed to Darmon, and the dwarf snorted lightly in return.

"We must never let the boy out of our sight," Tiryn said. *"Not while Darmon travels with us."*

From the corner of his eye, Tiryn spotted a muscle in Syrani's cheek twitch ever so slightly. Tiryn locked eyes with Tathiel as the two turned to walk away. Tathiel made no indication that he had heard Tiryn's words, but Tiryn knew the younger elf had.

They reached the temple grounds only days later.

Hiruscu and Suvusa, who rode side by side with Rushavi and his mule between them, stopped suddenly in the height of the afternoon heat. The Elori stopped with them, muttering to each other and staring into the sand ahead of them.

Rushavi continued for several steps until his mother called for him to stop.

Tiryn was the first to reach Suvusa. "What's wrong?"

She gestured towards the sand. "This is the place."

"There's nothing here." Tiryn searched again, but there was little more than sand and a few bits of broken rubble. "How can you be sure this is the right area?"

Suvusa sighed, clearly disappointed. "We followed the map. This is where the temple should be."

A mule approached, and Tiryn was not surprised to see Darmon in the saddle. "Then where is it?"

"Still hidden, it would seem," Tathiel answered.

Darmon spat a string of curses in dwarfish, then dismounted from his mule. Behind him, the dwarfs in his command also dismounted. There was a ringing in the air as boots landed in the sand and heavy metal weapons clinked.

Darmon shouted several orders, and the dwarfs began removing helms and chest armor.

Tiryn blinked, unsure he had understood the dwarfish commands Darmon had just given. "What did you just tell them?"

"If this temple is buried somewhere in these sands, then we will find it." Darmon removed his own armor, ripping angrily at the leather ties that held his plate armor to his torso.

The dwarfs replaced axes and swords with shovels. They moved quickly and with no words spoken between them. Tiryn spotted Alain, and there was a grim expression on her face as she hefted a long spade over her shoulder.

"You can't mean to *dig* the temple out from the sands?"

Darmon sneered at him. "It's what we're known for, isn't it? Digging? Finding gems and metals buried in the earth?" He pointed at the spot of empty sand the Elori had led them to with the scooped end of a shovel. "There's a gem buried in there that I must return to my father. And I will not leave without it."

The dwarfs were already moving, forming a large ring and each taking a wide stance and readying their tools.

"You can't be serious," Tiryn said.

The dwarfs had caught the attention of the Elori, who stood and watched as they began to dig in quiet determination. Even Rushavi was interested in the steady movements of the dwarfs.

"Out of the way, elf." Darmon pushed passed Tiryn and took a place in the ring. He fell into the rhythm the other dwarfs kept.

Syrani and Tathiel joined him, watching as the dwarfs worked. Nunor stood off to one side with Grinor beside him. The two wore matching expressions that Tiryn could not quite read.

"This is madness." Tiryn shook his head. "How do we stop them?"

"Why do you want to stop them?" Tathiel asked.

"If the temple is not already here, there's nothing we could do to make it appear," Syrani answered.

"Ah." Tathiel thought for a brief moment, his brows knitting together. "Why stop them? Why not make their jobs easier? Perhaps they will see how fruitless it is."

Tiryn nodded. "Finish their digging for them? Show them there is no way to make the temple appear for us?"

Syrani sighed. "Give me a moment to get ready. Earth is not my strongest arcane element."

Tathiel and Syrani needed little direction. They took up positions around the ring of dwarfs, roughly equidistant from Tiryn himself. Tiryn stood behind and a little to the left of Darmon, who paused digging when he saw Syrani across from him.

"What are you doing?"

"Providing some assistance," Tiryn answered.

Tiryn concentrated on the large spot of sand where the dwarfs had been digging. He felt the arcane energy Tathiel and Syrani were already pouring into the area as it built up.

"We don't need your help," Darmon grumbled loudly. He went back to digging, flinging sand over his shoulder and nearly into Tiryn.

"This requires focus, if you don't mind."

The sand was incredibly heavy. Heavier than it should have been. Like there was something beneath the sands that fought against him.

The three of us won't be enough to do this.

But Tathiel and Syrani surprised him. Both had far more arcane energy than he anticipated, each of them nearly surpassing his own limits.

The ground began to quake, and one of the less sure-footed dwarfs toppled to his knees. Tiryn ignored the confused murmurs of the dwarfs and continued to focus his efforts on lifting the sand before him.

He could sense the sand as more arcane energy was channeled into it. It responded to his efforts by bubbling and churning, but would not budge otherwise.

The dwarfs stopped digging and retreated from the pit they had begun.

"I can't hold this much longer," someone said. Had it been him? Tathiel, maybe? Tiryn couldn't be sure.

"Just a little more. I can feel it giving away."

Tiryn could feel it as well. Whatever force kept the sand from moving was beginning to break. There was more movement in the earth at their feet. It bubbled angrily, almost like water over a hot fire. Small sprays of sand went up at irregular intervals.

Finally, a geyser of red-brown desert shot into the sky as the energy that held it back was overcome. Everyone, Tiryn included, stepped several steps back.

Tiryn instinctively looked up, amazed by the sheer amount of earth that was sent skyward.

As soon as the arcane energy that had been feeding it was cut off, the geyser of sand began to fall back down.

Shouts went up, and Tiryn covered his head with both arms.

Heavy and hot sand rained down on him for a few seconds, then stopped.

Tiryn uncovered his head, brushing sand from his neck and shoulders. Syrani was also brushing sand from her clothes, but Tathiel had not been so quick to cover himself. His hair was coated in fine particulates, and he spat grains from his mouth and brushed them from his eyes.

Darmon and the other dwarfs were less lucky. Many had fallen to the ground and were now digging themselves out of loosely packed earth.

"Are you trying to kill us all?" Darmon shouted. He spat and spluttered, rubbing sand from his mouth with the back of one hand to no avail.

Tiryn offered him a hand up, which he accepted.

"There was an energy holding us back. When it broke ..." Tiryn motioned upward, indicating the shower of sand. "It was not our intention."

"Tiryn," Syrani called. She stood at the opposite rim of the large pit they had formed. "There's something here."

Darmon and Tiryn both approached. The dwarf moved quickly, leaving his knights to collect themselves and their shovels.

There was something visible in the center of the pit, and Tiryn had to stare for a second before he recognized what it was.

"It that ... glass?" Darmon asked.

"Seems to be," Syrani answered.

"Glass what?" Darmon continued.

"I'm not sure. It's pointed. Perhaps the top of the temple? A tower's steeple?"

Darmon shook his head. "That can't be the top. The temple would have to be buried incredibly deep."

Tiryn shrugged. "How deep beneath the mountains is Doldural, Darmon?"

Darmon grunted. "It can't be possible." He sat in the sand, his legs dangling down into the hole Tiryn and his companions had formed. "I'll just go down for a little look-see."

Darmon was sliding down before Tiryn could stop him.

"Idiot," Syrani muttered with a low sigh.

Tiryn wasn't sure anyone but him had heard it.

Darmon brushed a thin layer of sand from the glass object. "It's glass alright. Good quality, too. Toss me down a shovel, will you? I might be able to—"

Darmon's words were cut off by more quaking.

"What are you doing now?" Darmon demanded, glaring up at Tiryn.

"Darmon, get out of there."

Sand was beginning to fill the hole at an alarming rate. It seemed to flow from all directions, guided by what Tiryn assumed was the same unseen force he had already sensed.

"What have you done?" Darmon asked, scrambling up the steep slope of the hole.

"I told you, there's something working to keep the temple concealed!" Tiryn put one foot on the slope, reaching for Darmon. "Come on, I'll pull you up."

Darmon stretched, but he wasn't close enough to grasp Tiryn's hand. "Damn you, I can't reach."

Tiryn inched closer, but the sand moved too quickly for him to find good purchase. A strong pair of hands gripped his opposite arm by the wrist and below the elbow.

"Go on, I've got you," Nunor said. His voice was deep and calm.

Tiryn took another half step down the slope and crouched, reaching for Darmon.

The sand was coming in faster, and Darmon was buried to his knees in it.

"Come on, ya fucking sand-eating shit-sack!" Nunor shouted. "Can't take the crown if you get yourself buried in the middle of the fucking desert."

Darmon growled and leapt. He moved only a few inches more, but it was enough.

Tiryn grabbed him around the wrist and pulled. Darmon's small hand clutched at Tiryn's tunic sleeve until Tiryn had pulled him a little closer and he could get a more comfortable grip.

Nunor and Tiryn did most of the work until Darmon was nearing the top of the rapidly disappearing hole. Once Darmon could find purchase under his feet, it became much easier to help him. The three stood at the edge of the crater and watched as it filled. Within a few more seconds, there was no evidence that there had been a hole at all.

"You're welcome," Nunor grumbled. He turned and left.

Darmon cursed under his breath in dwarfish, glaring at his cousin as Nunor walked away.

"Tiryn."

It was Syrani again, and Tiryn looked up to see her holding something white in her hands.

"What did you find?" He hurried over, passing Tathiel, who was helping a pair of dwarfs to their feet.

Syrani tossed the object to him, and Tiryn instinctively caught it. He had to fight a grimace when he saw what he held.

"I don't know my bones well," Syrani said. "But that looks elven."

Tiryn shook his head. "The weight is wrong. It's human."

"There are more." Syrani pointed into the surrounding sand.

Tiryn scanned the area. There were dozens of bones and bone fragments. Most were larger bones from humans and elves, but there were some smaller ones that perhaps had once belonged to a dwarf. He spotted a small square jaw that was most definitely dwarfen in the sand.

"What is this?" Darmon asked, picking the mandible up and inspecting it. "Some sort of mass grave?"

"That's exactly what it is. The sand must have unearthed it all."

"But where did they come from?"

Tiryn tossed the bone he held back to the ground. "Don't you realize? This is the spot of the Great War."

25

EILONWY

There were still King's Guards in Larten, and they showed no signs of leaving. Their names and faces had become quite known to Eilonwy and too many of the regulars of the inn. Even the fishermen of Hythe and Emery had grown familiar with them during their weekly excursions to Larten.

Eilonwy began to quietly question whether she had made a mistake in freeing the elf and Demelda before the King's Guards had left town. If she had planned better, thought the circumstances through more, she could have waited before acting as she did. She could have trailed the company of knights and sent the elf on his way to Vyris without anyone suspecting a second sympathizer within the Southern Cities.

But then she would hear some joke or story about what happened to captive elves on the long roads to Etritia, and she knew she had taken the proper course. Assaults, abuses, the tales were retold at nearly every meal. Eilonwy, as Eilen, would laugh and smile.

Inside, she was seething.

"More mead, sir knight?" Eilonwy offered a mug to the

one Mathius referred to as the captain, but the King's Guard shook his head.

"I think not, Eilen." He held a few pages of parchment in his hands, and had been reading when she approached him. "I should be heading to my room for the evening soon. Could you have it made up for me?"

"I can have it arranged, yes." She nodded towards the letter. "Anything good today?"

The knight folded the pages back together again and set them aside. "It is too soon to tell. But I feel our time in Larten is coming to an end."

"Shame," Eilonwy said, scooping up his empty plates and balancing them on an open palm. "The inn will miss you, I am sure."

"The inn will miss the king's gold I bring, it would be more fitting to say."

Eilonwy gave him a smile, wrinkling her nose slightly with it. "That isn't the entire truth of it. Your men have made themselves a second home here and we would be happy to have you come again."

She didn't want to believe that they would be leaving soon. Not until the dust had settled behind their horses. There had been a few promises of their departure already, and none had come to pass.

"You are too kind, Eilen. I shall be sure to recommend this inn to any King's Guards who may find themselves in the Southern Cities."

Eilonwy bade the knight farewell and returned to the kitchen, depositing the dirty dishes and mugs she had collected on the far end of Mathius's food prep table.

"Do you need me for the next few moments, Mathius? Some of the King's Guards are ready for their rooms to be turned over for the night."

"Nah, go on your way. See if Jaimes will give you a hand."

Eilonwy scoffed. "Can't bear the thought of me working alone?"

Mathius raised a brow in her direction. His arms were to the elbows in a mixture of ground meat and spices. Lunch for tomorrow, Eilonwy assumed. It always turned her stomach when she thought of how much humans enjoyed meat. Not that she would say no to Mathius's cooking.

"It's more that I can't bear the thought of my niece working alone in a knight's bedroom, *Eilen*," Mathius said stiffly. "It's not proper, after all."

"Alright, fine. I'll see if Jaimes will help me."

Jaimes was more than willing to assist her. Eilonwy knew the game he and Mathius were playing. Lately, one or both of them were always nearby. They offered nothing but smiles and affection and worked tirelessly alongside her. But she knew that they stayed close to keep an eye on her. No amount of promises that she would keep to herself and follow the persona of Eilen as closely as possible would ease them. Not after the captured elf and Demelda had been set free.

Eilonwy and Jaimes started in the downstairs rooms. Many of these larger rooms had been rented by the King's Guards. They changed the bedding in the captain's room together, making quick work of the large linens, then Jaimes set about fluffing pillows and talking amiably about nothing in particular while Eilonwy lit a fire in the small fireplace and dusted ash from the floor.

She made a note to scrub the walls around the fireplace after the King's Guards had left. They were blackening with soot, and it would take time to remove it all.

"Are you alright, Eilen?" Jaimes asked. "I feel like I've been talking to this pillow here."

"Hm?" Eilonwy turned. She shook her head, tossing thoughts of cleaning walls from it. "Sorry, Jaimes. I'm feeling a bit distracted. I think I have a headache coming on."

There was a sort of persistent nagging in the back of her mind that she could not entirely place.

"You? A headache?" Jaimes's brows furrowed. "I didn't realize you *could* have headaches."

She rolled her eyes at him. "They are uncommon, but not impossible. It is just the long day catching up to me. Help me fix these rooms up and let me lie down, and I'll be fine."

They moved on. The remaining rooms downstairs were done quickly enough. Though they were large, they were also simpler. There were two small beds to the captain's large one, and these rooms had no fireplaces to them. It took only a moment or two to strip and reset each one. They even saw to Mathius's room, though he often insisted that it was a wasted effort on him, since he slept so little and was perfectly capable of turning down his own blanket and starting his own fire.

"The laundress must be getting her fair share of Mathius's gold for all this bedding."

"She just airs most of it, actually." Eilonwy bundled an armful of linens and dumped them in the corner of Mathius's room for him to care for. "She only washes the lighter fabrics. And she's been doing it for half price while the King's Guards are here."

"Really?" Jaimes opened the door for her, and they stepped out and made for the stairs. "Why is that?"

"She said it was her way of supporting the king. But I think she might have caught some feelings for Mathius." She rubbed at her temples lightly.

"Are you sure you're alright?"

"We're nearly done. I'll rest after."

They worked quickly and in silence. Eilonwy could sense Jaimes watching her, but he was not overly protective or concerned. Only watchful and helpful, which she accepted with gratitude.

When all was completed, Jaimes offered to light the

lanterns in the halls for her while she took a short rest to ease the growing pain in her head.

She did not lie down, but instead sat to stare out of the window and out to sea. There was something familiar about the nagging sensation in her head, and she puzzled it out while watching the stars as they emerged from behind a few errant clouds in an otherwise clear sky.

"Eilonwy."

She nodded, her question answered. *"I wondered if that was you. Has it been so long that it is a struggle to reconnect our minds, Melonya?"*

"It should not have been so. Your mind was closed, sealed off. I had to fight to get you to acknowledge me," the great dragon said reproachfully. *"Is it because you are trying to hide your annoyance and frustration with Jaimes from him?"*

She sighed. *"You can't even give me a proper hello before starting with your advice and critiques."*

A rumbling laugh rolled over her mind and brought a smile to Eilonwy's face. *"I have missed you."*

"And I have missed you. What brings you here?"

"I've come to check on the companions that remain in Larten. Alastor worries for his brother, and Tathiel for you."

"We are fine, Melonya." Eilonwy hesitated a moment, then added, *"Though there are many King's Guards here now."*

"In Larten?" Melonya sounded concerned, and in her mind's eye, Eilonwy could almost see the dragon's tail swishing in agitation. *"How long have they been there?"*

"Some weeks. Nearly two months, if I've remembered correctly."

"Two months," Melonya repeated. *"Two months with King's Guards living under the same roof, and you haven't found a way to leave the city?"*

"I'm not leaving Larten." Eilonwy's words were perhaps harsher than she had intended. She spoke more softly. *"Larten is my home, and I won't leave Mathius and Jaimes behind."*

"Very well." Melonya paused for a moment. *"Would you consider leaving for a day?"*

Eilonwy hesitated. What point would there be in leaving Larten for a day?

She asked Melonya, and the great dragon answered cautiously. *"We've heard rumors of a sort of elven prison north of the Southern Cities. On the edge of the desert. Tathiel has asked me to look into it, so he and I could destroy it. But if you are with me, there would be no need to wait to free any who are being kept there."*

Eilonwy took little convincing. She sat back in her seat, staring out towards the waters south of Larten. There was no port in Larten, but they were still close enough to get whiffs of salt on the air when the sea breeze blew in strongly enough.

Melonya was out there, hiding in the waters. It had become habit ever since they had first come to the Southern Cities some years ago.

One day, Eilonwy thought, *there might be a time when no one must hide themselves away.*

"So, you'll join me?" Melonya asked. She had heard Eilonwy's thoughts.

"How long will we be away from Jaimes?"

"No more than a day, I think."

"You think?" Eilonwy raised an eyebrow, considering.

"I am in just as much hurry to return to Tathiel as you will be to return to Larten. Tiryn and Nunor believe they are on the path to the earth amulet, and I worry for the younglings that must carry it."

Younglings? And so close to the amulet already?

It had been some time since she had last heard anything from the remainder of their companions.

"I'll go with you. But I need to leave quietly. If Jaimes and Mathius learn that I have left, they will try to convince me not to return until the King's Guards have abandoned Larten."

"I will await you in our usual place, once the night is fully dark."

It was nearly full dark already. Eilonwy changed out of the skirts and ridiculous blouse of Eilen the barmaid and into her old riding pants and boots. She borrowed one of Jaimes's tunics, though it hung long on her. She took a few moments to write him a note, apologizing for leaving without a goodbye but promising to return quickly.

"Take care of the old man," she added, then signed a stylized letter E with a flourish.

Her sword, which she kept hidden in the back of the wardrobe, was easy to hide in the folds of a cloak and carry out of the bedroom. If anyone saw her, it would look like she was simply out on an evening stroll. Which, while unsual, was not entirely out of the question.

She took the stairs quietly, watching for Mathius and Jaimes. They were both in the kitchen, judging by the sounds of cleaning and idle chatter.

She paused on the final steps when she heard her adopted human name.

"Eilen?" Jaimes asked. "She's resting upstairs. Said she was suffering from a headache."

"Suffering from us, more like," Mathius said.

"D'you think she realizes we're keeping an eye on her?"

"She's stubborn, not stupid. Of course she knows."

Eilonwy smiled and made her way across the dining room. It was empty. Out of their recent regulars, only the King's Guards were ones to drink late into the night. And if they were truly to be leaving Larten soon, then perhaps they were resting up for the road ahead.

She took the exit through the garden. It was a little farther from her final destination, but there was no bell over the door to concern herself over. And less chance for Mathius and Jaimes to note her egress.

The night was quiet, and she passed only one other

person on the road. They ignored her, and she said nothing to them. Once out of the town properly, she threw the cloak over her shoulders and released the glamour spell that held the human form of Eilen in check.

It felt like a warm, slightly stifling blanket had just been pulled off her, and she took a deep, relaxing breath of air.

Melonya was already waiting on the burial hill. It was the nearest spot outside Larten that both accommodated her large body and was secluded enough that no one would take notice of her.

There were fresh tears in the earth from Melonya's landing, and Eilonwy made a mental note to return in a few days to fix the damage. The last thing they needed while the King's Guards were present was for a cry to go up about large animals marking the grave hill.

"Are you ready, then?"

"I am. You have an idea of where this prison might be?" Eilonwy lifted herself into the double saddle that sat atop Melonya's back.

"I do."

"Then let's go. And perhaps you can tell me all that has occurred with our other companions."

MELONYA

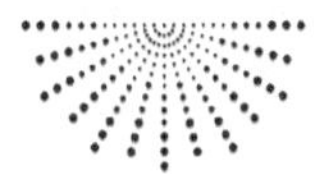

Melonya relayed all that she had learned from her companions. She told Eilonwy of the young dragon hatchling who should no longer be as small as he still was. Of the infant that he was bound to, and of their concerns of retrieving the amulet. Eilonwy was pleased to hear there was a male dragon and made the crude observation that perhaps it meant that dragons could be revived.

"But it's just a child!" Melonya protested. "And all of us are bound in such strange ways that I cannot comprehend."

"It was only a thought, Melonya." Eilonwy's warm hand brushed against the space between Melonya's shoulders. "I worry for you. I don't want you to live a long and lonely life after Tathiel and I are gone."

"Such concerns are centuries away, Eilonwy. There is nothing to worry about for a long time."

"And what of this hatchling? His rider is a human boy. His companionship will end much sooner than that."

"You forget that humans procreate much more easily than elves. The boy will surely have children, and grandchildren. The hatch-ling will not be alone." Melonya hit an updraft, and it lifted her higher into the night sky. *"And he will always have his sisters, as well. And the fourth dragon, when it decides to hatch."*

*"*Oh, yes. The white egg Roland wrote to us about. Has it still not hatched?*"*

*"*No.*"* Melonya snorted, and her breath came out as a plume of vapor. *"It seems the young Coven girl has convinced the hatchling to remain inside its egg until a potential location for the Amulet of Air has been determined."*

"Why?"

"Because having a growing dragon in a human settlement would be a hard thing to hide? Because her Sight told her it would be necessary? Who knows?"

Nothing more of importance passed between them as they journeyed. Eilonwy relayed Jaimes's concerns for her safety and her thoughts on the matter. Melonya knew of those concerns already, but she did not confess to Eilonwy that she had already discussed the matter at some length with Jaimes.

Better for her to find that out later.

"Did you say something?"

"No. Just a passing thought." Melonya lifted her head, sniffing the air. *"I smell horses. And men. We may be close."*

"Let me down," Eilonwy said. *"I'll scout the area and find where the elves are being held."*

Melonya and Eilonwy landed on a scrub-covered swell downwind from the scent of horses. There were several small fires to give the position of the little prison away. Melonya's hearing was not as acute as Eilonwy's, so she remained silent as Eilonwy listened.

"I hear men speaking in Azimarian, and a few murmured words in Vyrisian."

"Then that is the place?"

"Seem to be." Eilonwy rubbed Melonya's neck, watching the firelights in the distance. "From the sounds, I would guess there are perhaps a dozen men?"

"Be careful, Eilonwy. If you are gone for more than a few moments, I will come after you." Melonya bared her teeth. *"And the humans will live very brief and painful lives if they have harmed you."*

Eilonwy nodded. "Fine with me. If I need rescuing, I'll be sure to let you know."

Melonya nudged at her companion's back, pushing her lightly. *"Go."*

Eilonwy did not need encouraging. She set off over the small hill and disappeared over the other side.

Melonya settled down to wait, closing her eyes and concentrating on Eilonwy's mind. Hazy, slightly indistinct images came to her as the moments passed. Torches, a few tents and a single, hastily constructed building made of wood and stones. Eilonwy seemed to be closing in on the Vyrisian speakers, not the Azimarian cajoling that was closer to the cluster of torches.

There was a metal cage, some six feet high and slightly less in width. There were several figures inside, shadowed in darkness. One stood and approached as Eilonwy drew nearer.

Words were exchanged, but Melonya could not focus on both what Eilonwy heard and what she saw. The elf in question, a young male with light hair and the long ears of a Vyrisian, exposed both arms to show her the metal cuffs on each wrist.

It was always the same. Mothlenor's damnable cuffs.

Eilonwy tried the metal of the cage, pulling on two of the bars. But they would not budge.

Melonya stood, opening her eyes. *"Eilonwy."*

"I can't open the cage without magic. And it will alert the humans."

"I'm coming."

She ran over the hill in long, loping strides. The horses heard her approach almost immediately and whinnied in protest. Shouts went up from the men as their horses reared and kicked, and Melonya roared mightily. It shook the ground, and two of the torches collapsed. One rolled into a nearby tent, and Melonya hoped the fire might catch.

"Now, Eilonwy."

There was a metallic crash, and the men of the camp momentarily had their attention split between the huge beast that was descending upon them and the escaping elves. Melonya could see their heads turning this way and that, and hands went to swords.

But they were too late.

Melonya came to a stomping halt just outside the faltering circle of light and roared once more. The remaining torches either fell over or went out. A tent was flaring up, and the gathered men screamed in a mix of terror and fury.

Swords were raised, and perhaps five men in full armor charged at her. She spun, slamming her tail into them and sweeping them out into the dark.

They won't be returning to fight.

"Go, go!" Eilonwy's voice rang out in the dark, and Melonya spotted her guiding the fleeing elves towards the horses. The terrified beasts were mounted easily by the graceful elves, and Eilonwy cut leads with quick precision.

Melonya charged at the lone building, rearing up and letting her weight fall heavily against it. A third of the small structure went crashing down. There was a scream, and Melonya saw a man with one leg crushed under the rubble. She raked her clawed forearms over the roof and damaged walls, and more of the building collapsed. The man's scream was cut short.

Those knights that were not already dead were fleeing on foot. Melonya let them go.

She turned to Eilonwy. *"The captives?"*

"Gone. They took the horses and are headed for Vyris."

"Good."

Eilonwy touched the amulet at her neck, and Melonya felt an odd sensation in the pit of her stomach. "The men that have fled we will allow to live. Perhaps their stories will make others think twice before hunting elves here."

Clouds gathered overhead, very low to the ground, and Melonya smelled rain approaching. *"You are getting better at controlling the power the amulet gives you, I see."*

"Only when it comes to water," Eilonwy said with a smirk. "It seems the Amulet of Water gives me a better affinity for its element."

The rain Eilonwy summoned made short work of the small fire before it could spread too much. Melonya was disappointed that more of the little prison camp had not been destroyed by the flames.

For good measure, she slammed her tail against the metal cage, crumpling it.

"There. That should appear sufficiently destroyed for any who do not believe the story of a great dragon attacking this outpost."

"Morning is coming. We should return to Larten."

Melonya searched the horizon. Far off to the east, the first hints of early grey morning softened the darkness. She huffed, turning back to Eilonwy. *"No, Eilonwy."*

Eilonwy's expression changed several times in the span of only a few seconds. First, confusion, as Melonya's words seemed to register. Then realization, quickly followed by sadness and anger.

"Jaimes."

"Yes."

"How long were you in Larten before contacting me?"

"An hour, no more. Jaimes sent word to Alastor that he was worried for you. I was sent to help, though I did not know the circumstances. Jaimes was waiting, listening for my approach."

"He spoke to you before you could reach out to me." Eilonwy cursed, kicking a torch lying on the ground. It was knocked several feet away and collided with a burnt and collapsing tent. "And you concocted this plan to trick me into leaving Larten."

"His concerns are justified, Eilonwy."

"I never said they weren't!" Eilonwy yelled.

Melonya stepped back, startled. Eilonwy had never yelled at her before.

"Did he tell you that I was willing to leave Larten, if only he and Mathius came as well?" Eilonwy stamped a foot angrily. It would have looked childish if the ground did not shudder slightly with arcane energy. "Did he tell you that I am just as worried for his safety as he is for mine? That if they will not leave with me, I would rather risk my life to make sure I can keep them safe?"

Of course he hadn't. But shouldn't Melonya have known something of the sort?

"Jaimes and Mathius are capable of defending themselves."

"Against pirates and thieves, yes. Against nearly a dozen King's Guards?" Eilonwy's eyebrows raised, waiting for Melonya's answer. When it did not come freely, Eilonwy continued. "Jaimes no longer does magic. You know that. And Mathius, though he is talented with a sword, is getting older."

Melonya laughed. *"Mathius is still younger than Roland by far."*

"Yes, he is younger than Roland. Who has a curse that keeps him young and heals his wounds."

Oh, Melonya thought. *It is easy to forget about the curse.*

"I have seen grey hairs on Mathius's head. I have heard him groan when he rises from his bed in the morning. I have seen him rub at joints and heard him curse his bones." Eilonwy's hands were balled into fists. "If it were just the two of them against the knights in Larten, they might survive. But you and I both know that they would lay down their lives to protect the innocents of Larten if the need arose."

"Have I made a mistake?" Melonya asked.

Eilonwy sighed, her shoulders relaxing. "Take me home, Melonya. Perhaps we can convince them to leave with us."

Melonya did not kneel for Eilonwy to climb onto her back right away. She stood, thinking over the options that were presented to her.

Forcibly take Eilonwy to Vyris, or anywhere safer than Larten, and risk Jaimes and Mathius being left alone to defend themselves in the slim chance the need arose.

Or take Eilonwy back to Larten and risk the lives of all three allies in the far greater likelihood that she was discovered.

"If you do not take me back now, I will walk back of my own accord," Eilonwy threatened.

Melonya kneeled. *"Come along then. It can't be said I didn't try."*

Eilonwy rushed into the saddle. "We must hurry if we are to make it back before my absence is noticed. Mathius can't go more than a few hours without my help."

Melonya waited until Eilonwy was settled and then turned into the wind and took a few loping strides before leaping into the air. There was not much of a breeze to help lift her to the sky, but her wings were sure and her muscles strong. She turned her snout to Larten and began the journey home.

There was a light headwind to slow them down, but it would not increase their time too much. Eilonwy asked of their companions again, but this time requested nothing of the quest they were on. She instead wanted to know about how the others were doing in more personal aspects of their lives.

"The elf, Syrani, is she getting along better with her dragon companion?"

"They seem to be mending their relationship, yes. Halcia is confident that they can grow to be as close as you and I."

"And Alastor had an elf lady?"

Melonya snorted. *"I believe Alastor has had many ladies. The fact that this newest one is an elf makes little difference, I think."*

They continued in that way for some time. Melonya was surprised by Eilonwy's chattiness until she realized that Eilonwy missed their allies. She had been in Larten, away from her family and most of her friends, for months. And, if Jaimes and Mathius chose to stay in Larten, she would remain there beside them for months or years more.

"Eilonwy, when the King's Guard leave, would you like to make a habit of leaving the city with me on occasion? It would be nice to keep ourselves apprised of each other's situations without having to rely so heavily on long-distance communication."

"Are you worried about me, too?" Eilonwy asked with a laugh.

They were nearing the closest spot to Larten that Melonya could land in daytime without being spotted. Larten was still more than a few miles away, but Eilonwy could make the journey on foot easily. *"I am only worried about you being apart from me for so long that you and I might suffer as Halcia and Syrani have."*

Eilonwy rubbed Melonya's shoulder. *"That will never happen."*

"All the same ..." Melonya paused in her thoughts, sniffing deeply at the air. She had caught a slight whiff, but had dismissed it. Now that they were lower, though, the smell was unmistakable.

"What is it, Melonya?"

"I smell smoke." She turned, climbing once more into the air.

"Is it coming from Larten?" Eilonwy stood in the saddle, shielding her eyes to look across the scrublands. *"Melonya, hurry and turn around. I can see the smoke, but not where it is coming from."*

"No, Eilonwy. I am sorry, but I can't take you back there now."

Eilonwy struck her feebly on the shoulder. *"Turn around*

now, Melonya. You were going to take me back to protect Jaimes
and Mathius. They might need me!"

"If there is a fire in Larten, then it is too dangerous for you
right now. And I could not forgive myself if you were injured when
I willingly let you walk into that town again."

"And I will not forgive you if Jaimes is hurt or killed because I
was not there to help him!" Eilonwy began unbuckling the
straps that held her legs in the saddle on Melonya's back.

"What are you doing?"

"I told you before. If you will not take me back, I will return of
my own accord."

"You cannot mean to jump?"

"I will, if you do not turn around right now."

Melonya cursed and turned around, tucking one wing
close to her body and tilting to the same side. "Would you have
me fly right into Larten, teeth bared, as well?"

"Now you understand me."

2 7

HALCIA

Halcia regretted not being present when the elves and dwarfs attempted to unearth Farnir's temple. She could have told them as soon as she laid eyes on the spot that there was no use trying to find it on their own.

Or she could have watched as they struggled while knowing all along that they worked in vain.

Syrani told her of all that happened once Halcia returned from hunting with Ardu.

Though she and Ardu rarely put much effort into hunting. The young dragon mostly got beneath her wings and irritated her with his quiet presence.

He rarely spoke. On the few occasions that he did, it was with ceaseless energy for a rough span of half an hour. And then he fell silent for hours.

She preferred it when he spoke, if she were honest with herself.

Ardu rambled on about everything and nothing at all. The shapes of the clouds they flew through were often brought up. Some of his other favorite topics were how strong Halcia and Melonya must be—which Halcia enjoyed hearing immensely—and how much he wanted to be able to breathe fire. Or maybe ice. Ardu seemed unable to decide which would be the more exciting ability, and it never seemed to occur to him that he could wish for both.

And, of course, he discussed Rushavi more than anything else.

Halcia had never spoken to the boy and was not surprised when she learned that he had not spoken aloud to anyone at all.

But to Ardu, the young rider could do no wrong.

Rushavi was apparently talkative with his companion. The two shared insights into the world that Halcia could not begin to understand or appreciate. The touch of the sand beneath Rushavi's feet was not simply gritty and hot. It was a million shards of molten glass that slowly burned and buried their way into the soles of his feet as he walked. The sun was not high and bright, the wind was not pleasant and cool.

Each mile under the sun was a misery, each breeze a tantalizing breath.

Every sensation was more than it should be, and Rushavi felt each one intensely and unceasingly.

Halcia could only attribute the boy's outlook on the world to his premature aging.

Everything must be new and strange and uncomfortable when you are only just experiencing the first few months of life.

Had it not been the same for her? She couldn't remember.

Ardu shared these small insights into Rushavi's mind regularly, and Halcia used those moments to better understand the child that should only yet be an infant.

She did not, however, pass those insights on to Syrani. It was up to his earthbound companions to learn more of the young child on their own, and for Rushavi to reveal as much as he was comfortable with.

Syrani shared what had transpired while she and Halcia were apart. She spoke of the would-be dwarf king's insistence on unearthing the ancient temple, of the strange energy that kept it hidden, and of the bones that had been buried in the sand.

"It was foolish to make the attempt at uncovering it."

Halcia lay in the sand near where the temple once stood, surveying the desert all around her.

"I agree," Syrani answered. "But it was the only way we could show the dwarfs that they were being foolish as well." Syrani's face was pale, despite the sun and wind-chapped redness to her cheeks.

"You pushed yourself too much. I can tell."

Syrani shrugged. "Not as much as Tiryn did. He is faring much worse than I am."

Halcia had seen Tiryn briefly, and he had indeed looked faintly ill.

"Will you be alright?"

"Yes, I'll be fine. The amulet holds enough energy that I will recover quickly."

Halcia did not ask about Tiryn. He had already recovered once from arcane sickness before they had even joined him in the desert. Tiryn, she knew, was no stranger to the weakness that followed overusing his arcane abilities.

"And the bones? Could they really be from the Great War?" Halcia had difficulty believing something so ridiculous. The Great War had been centuries ago. There should be nothing left of the remains of those lost.

"Tiryn thinks that the energy emanating from the temple kept the bones from completely disintegrating."

"And how did they end up here?" Halcia snorted, startling a nearby Elori into a shriek. Syrani gave the woman an apologetic look, but Halcia made no attempt to share any remorse. *"You can't mean to say that the Great War was here? That it happened right on the spot where Farnir's temple was hidden?"*

Syrani shook her head. "I will say nothing of the sort. I have no answer for you."

An Elori approached, smiling meekly at Syrani and Halcia. He carried a stack of grilled cactus meat a few inches thick.

Halcia groaned, bringing the Elori to a stop.

"I can take no more of this, Syrani."

Syrani gestured the man forward with a reassuring nod. *"Please stop scaring the Elori. We've had this discussion before."*

Halcia rolled her eyes. Behind the first Elori, a small gathering was forming of others as they were led by his example. Halcia spotted more gifts of food and some smaller trinkets. Ardu, of course, had wandered off, leaving her to accept the daily offerings on her own.

"Can we forgo this madness today? I am tired. Can't you tell them that I need extra rest if we are to somehow summon the temple?" To her surprise, she was exhausted. She was always fatigued after flying for hours on end, but this weariness was deeper than that. *"I think the heat is finally beginning to wear on me. Or perhaps I share your arcane illness with you."*

Syrani waited, perhaps thinking, as the first Elori carefully placed the gifted food as close to Halcia's mouth as he dared. She waved someone over, and Halcia was delighted to see Hiruscu approach.

"Hiruscu, I am afraid that Halcia is not feeling terribly well this evening. Would you mind helping me tell the Elori that she won't be well enough to accept their gratuity?"

"And while you're at it, have him tell them where Ardu has gone off to hide, the cheeky little worm. Let him handle the constant barrage of Elori."

Syrani did not repeat her request.

"Yes, I can tell my people to leave for now. That the great dragon needs rest."

Syrani bowed. "Thank you, Hiruscu. You are a great help."

"Perhaps you would like to learn the Elori words sometime?" Hiruscu asked. "When we are not so busy digging temples from the sand, hm?"

Syrani laughed. It was almost a genuine one, but Halcia was better at telling the difference. "I've heard you teaching Tathiel. And I think I will join you some time, yes."

Halcia rolled her eyes again, then closed them. *I'm going to sleep now, Syrani. Wake me when we have some sort of plan on how to deal with the temple.*

She shut out the noise of the Elori as they murmured amongst themselves after hearing the news that their goddess would not be able to accept the treats they brought her.

The sun was high and hot, but the sand under her belly and beneath her claws was soft. When Halcia opened her eyes and stretched her legs, unsheathing her claws, it was short tufts of grass that she dug up. She rose to her haunches, startled, and looked around her.

Gone were the tents of the Elori and the dwarfs's mules. Syrani and Hiruscu, who had been standing so close when she'd fallen asleep, were nowhere to be seen.

"Syrani?" Halcia called, turning in a slow circle. *"Where are you?"*

Halcia felt a presence brush her mind, gently at first. She hissed at the intrusion, sending fat drops of saliva to the ground. It was the first time she had made such a noise since she was a child. But the touch grew stronger, and Halcia instinctively shut her eyes and focused on fending off the invader that sought to read her thoughts.

But he—for it was a male—was too strong.

"You must be very frightened, to hiss at me so." The voice laughed, but it was not an unkind laugh.

"Who are you?" Halcia asked. She hunkered down, eyes still shut tight and her attention on warding off the entity now firmly planted in her mind.

"Open your eyes, and you will see."

Halcia heard a roar in the distance, familiar and yet also strange.

She hesitated, not quite sure if she wanted to obey the stranger who spoke to her.

But the roar was echoed, first once, then twice, then countless times, and Halcia finally chanced a frightened look.

The desert, now filled with hardy plants and clumps and clusters of grasses and trees, was alive with movement.

"Dragons," Halcia said with a sigh.

They were everywhere. Dragons dozed on the grass or ambled over the ground. Small ones, the size of Ardu or even smaller, ran and chased each other between tall palms. Larger ones simply stretched out and watched the young ones play. There was a lake that Halcia had not seen at first, and more dragons leisurely swam in its waters or dried their scales and membranous wings along its banks.

The sound of wings drew Halcia's attention up, and her heart skipped at the sight. The sky, cloudless and blue and beautiful, was full of flying dragons.

"How ..." But Halcia couldn't finish the thought.

"This is only a memory. A recollection of things as they once were."

"Not a dream?"

"It is your dream, yes. But I have given it to you from my own memories."

Halcia froze as a huge dragon walked close by. He was larger than Halcia and her sister Melonya combined, and when he drew near enough, she stretched out her neck to sniff at him.

The other dragon did the same, though he did not slow his gait as he walked by her. Their snouts touched one another's briefly, and Halcia was startled by a gentle shock of arcane energy where their scales met. The larger dragon, unfazed, continued on.

Halcia remembered Melonya's story of her encounter with Neria, the great sea dragon, during the search for the Amulet of Water. *"Who are you, then? Farnean?"*

The voice laughed. *"No, Farnean was my son. And the dragon you just met was his brother, Farlith."*

There was a pause, during which Halcia guessed the stranger's identity.

"I am Farnir, and these were my children and their children, and all those of my line."

Halcia was silent for a moment, watching the dragons all around her. In the waking world—her world—they were all dead. This would be the only time she could see the world as it was meant to be. And she wished to cherish it for a few moments longer.

"You have come here for the Amulet of Earth, which my mother gave to the dwarfs years ago."

"Yes."

"Why have you not taken the amulet yet?"

"My companions haven't found a way into your temple," she answered. *"There is something that bars their way."*

"A simple thing to overcome."

"How?" Halcia asked.

Farnir laughed. *"You need only ask for entrance."*

"Just ask?"

"Just ask," Farnir repeated. *"And the temple will be revealed."*

"Then ..." Halcia hesitated. *"May we enter your temple?"*

The heads of all nearby dragons lifted, and those that ran or walked through the desert oasis halted. A cacophonous roar went up, so loud that Halcia winced against it. The call reverberated in the still air of the oasis, making the trees shake and the water of the lake ripple.

There was no single word of an answer, and yet the tumultuous cry was an answer in itself. And there was immense power in the sound. Halcia felt the energy as it washed over her, sending a shiver across her back. The thin webbing of her wings rippled much like the surface of the lake.

And then there was only silence.

The lull lasted only for a second, perhaps two. Long enough for Halcia to forget the taste of the arcane energy in the air.

A low whistle, like the sound of a thousand distant wing-beats, rolled over the oasis. It was an eerie sound, and Halcia searched for the direction it came from. The oasis was empty, all signs of the dragons that had been there only moments ago now gone. She was alone, save for the quickly approaching howl of wind.

"Farnir?"

There was no reply.

The wind grew stronger, and the acrid tang of arcane energy came with it. There was no single direction to it, and instead it seemed to form a ring around Halcia, penning her. Trees bent and split, even uprooting as they were ripped away by the strange and unseen force that swept through the oasis towards her.

"Farnir!"

She was being shaken. Small, familiar hands pushed on her shoulder, and over the sound of the wind, she could hear her name being called.

Grass struck her, the sharp blades stinging her eyes and burrowing in the space between her scales. Halcia closed her eyes again, fighting off the debris that assailed her.

"Halcia, we need to leave."

Halcia opened her eyes again and regretted it immediately. Sand was whipping through the air, and she could feel the rough grit as it caught in her scales and in the corners of her eyes.

"What is happening?"

"There's a sandstorm. It came out of nowhere." Syrani was tucked behind Halcia's shoulder, using her body as a shield

from the wind and sand. *"The Elori have already found shelter, but many of the dwarfs are struggling."*

"And the temple?" Halcia asked. She took small steps, fighting the wind while trying to keep Syrani covered.

"What?"

"Farnir's temple. Is it open?"

A shadow approached, quickly forming into the entwined figures of Suvusa and Hiruscu.

Suvusa rushed forward at the sight of them, one arm lifted against the wind. "Have you seen Rushavi?" She had to shout to be heard over the roar of the sandstorm.

Hiruscu was calling for the boy, his head lifting only long enough to carry his voice over the wind. Halcia wasn't sure his words traveled far enough to be heard by anyone other than the three immediately beside him.

Halcia lifted a wing, though the wind tore and pulled at it and sharp sand hit it with incredible speed. Syrani beckoned for Suvusa to take shelter close to Halcia, and the two women bowed their heads together.

"Have you seen Rushavi?" Suvusa repeated. "He was right next to me, but I lost him in the wind!"

"Calm down, we will find him. You need to get to shelter." Syrani pointed at an oddly shaped mound in the desert sand, and Halcia had to stare for a second before she realized that several Elori had taken refuge under a tent covering, and one man held a small opening while a pair of dwarfs scrambled to join them.

"Not without Rushavi!"

"Syrani, here!" Tiryn's voice carried well, and Halcia shielded both women as they turned to see Tiryn gesturing deeper into the sandstorm. He stood tall against the wind, his braided hair whipping about his face as he shouted towards them. "Rushavi went towards the temple."

The wind was growing stronger, and even Halcia could not keep her body from shaking with the strain of staying upright. Hiruscu joined his wife under Halcia's protective wing and pulled Suvusa close.

"Go, Syrani. I will take care of her and Hiruscu." Halcia nudged her companion gently with her snout. *"Find the boy. Find the amulet."*

Syrani nodded and staggered towards Tiryn, gradually picking up speed as her legs grew accustomed to fighting the wind.

"Syrani, wait!"

Suvusa made to follow, but Halcia closed her wings around her, forming a protective cocoon. Halcia pulled her own head within the shelter of her wings, keeping the stinging sand from her eyes.

"Move, Halcia. I will find my son!"

Hiruscu grabbed Suvusa by both upper arms and pulled her close. "No, it is too dangerous for us. Syrani will find him. We must stay here."

"No, Hiruscu." Suvusa tried to leave again, pushing against the bony tip of Halcia's wing. But Halcia did not budge, and a low growl stopped Suvusa from trying to leave again.

"Do you trust your companion with your life, great Halcia?" Suvusa asked. She stared into Halcia's eyes, fear and sand and sweat all upon her face.

Halcia stared back and dipped her snout once in a nod.

"Then I must trust her with my son's life."

They could only wait for the sandstorm to subside. It seemed to rage for perhaps an hour, but it was little more than a few moments.

Suvusa and Hiruscu were quickly joined by an Elori woman and a male dwarf. The former half dragged, have carried the latter, despite his protests. Halcia wasn't sure the Elori woman understood what the dwarf was saying.

After a rapid interrogation in the Elori tongue, during

which the dwarf stared at Halcia with both a scowl and frightened eyes, Suvusa addressed Halcia and the dwarf.

"It seems Darmon and his lady knight have entered the temple. Along with Nunor and at least two of the elves."

"Did you see it?" the dwarf asked. The dwarf motioned off to where the sandstorm was still raging at its strongest. "It arose from the sands when the winds came."

"Only in glimpses," Suvusa answered. "Where did it come from?"

Halcia made a scoffing noise, or the closest approximation she could. *"I asked for admittance."*

All eyes went to Halcia, even the Elori woman who had not understood her words.

"You brought this on us?" the dwarf asked. "You've killed us all."

"No one will die today," Halcia said, baring her teeth. *"The storm will subside, and we will gather together and see what has become of our allies."*

The dwarf rolled his eyes and crossed his arms. The three Elori spoke softly to each other, casting glances at both Halcia and the dwarf. And it was very warm inside the little hollow Halcia made with her wings. But it at least kept the sand from her eyes, though it still stung as it hit her back.

"Syrani? Are you alright?"

She got only the barest of acknowledgments in return. No true reply, but at least she knew Syrani was alive.

Gradually, the wind began to calm. The howling grew softer, and the sharpness of the sand against Halcia's back and hindquarters eased.

"The storm is ending." Halcia relaxed, and Suvusa immediately slipped between her wings and ran for the structure that now stood before them.

It was not as lofty as she had imagined it. Halcia had thought it would be grand enough that the highest spires touched the clouds. As it was, the temple was wider than it was tall, though it was still an impressive height.

And the temple was constructed entirely of sand and glass.

The glass was thick and cloudy, and it capped nearly every edge and corner. The rest of the building was entirely sand, and Halcia could see it trickling down the exterior walls. There were no windows, no openings of any kind to view any of the interior of the temple.

Suvusa ran for the entrance, tripping over an Elori as they emerged from beneath their protective covering. She slid to a stop and fell to her knees, even as Halcia noted what had surely brought her to a halt.

"There's no door," the dwarf said. "How did the others get inside?"

"There must have been an entrance," Halcia said. *"And it closed behind them."*

"How will we follow?" Hiruscu asked.

All around them, Elori and dwarfs flung grit-encrusted coverings aside and unburied themselves from inches of sand. There were a few tearful reunions as Elori found companions, and the dwarfs quietly and stoically counted their numbers.

"I don't think we can." Halcia sat back on her haunches, flapping her wings to shake the desert from them. She wished Melonya was here. Her older sister was more adept when it came to dealing with others. *"I think we are meant to remain out here. And wait for their return."*

NUNOR

Nunor was watching Darmon, though he pretended to eat a steak of grilled cactus. Darmon, in turn, was watching the boy Rushavi as he ran and played with the runt dragon. And Alain, as Darmon's trusted knight, was watching Nunor.

What a fucking mess we've found ourselves in.

Nunor's stomach grumbled, and he touched a piece of cactus to his tongue.

"Ugh, will I be glad to get back to some place that has more substantial food."

Tiryn laughed. "Not one for staple meals?"

"Dwarfs need *meat*, Tiryn." He passed his dish over to the elf. "That is not meat."

"I don't know. I seem to recall you complaining quite a lot while we were on the *Kingfisher* about eating too much fish. And fish is meat." Tiryn ate what Nunor had already speared onto his fork without complaint.

Nunor shook his head. "Fish is not real meat. I meant red meat. Fish will only get a dwarf so far. We're not accustomed to eating anything from the sea for too long."

Tiryn smiled, though his head remained bowed over the

remains of Nunor's lunch. "Is it the meat you miss, or the ale?"

Nunor sighed, wishing he had a pint of some amber libation in his hand at that moment. "The ale. I miss the ale the most." Across the distance, Alain made eye contact with him again. Nunor nodded to her, and Alain returned it. "Even Syrani's tea has grown on me. If I drink enough of it, I can almost feel a slight drunkenness coming on."

"Alain is still watching you, hm?"

Nunor sighed. "And I watch Darmon. And Darmon watches Rushavi."

"The poor boy does not need the attention he has been given," Tiryn said. "He deserves to live a normal life."

"He will not have that, Tiryn. It's too late. It was too late the moment Ardu hatched."

A gust of wind blew, kicking up sand and obscuring Nunor's view of Darmon. Nunor's attention shifted to Rushavi while the sand swirled. The young boy and his dragon both stopped in their play, looking off towards the hidden temple.

"Strange," Tiryn mumbled.

"Hm? What is?"

"The wind. There are no clouds, no storm coming in."

"It's wind, Tiryn. No need to get upset about it."

Another gust kicked sand up into Nunor's eyes, and he cursed.

"I think there's a sandstorm coming."

The next moments were a blur of sand and shouting.

Nunor, half blinded by grit, was tugged to his feet by Tiryn as another blast of wind threatened to topple him over. He could see Rushavi being hauled away by the hand, but he couldn't be sure which parent grasped him. He spotted Darmon, or perhaps Alain, in the sudden swirl of sand. Only their stature and broad shoulders made it easy to differentiate them from the Elori and many of the dwarfs.

"Ardu's run off for the temple grounds," Tiryn said.

A small shadow, a child, shuffled past them some ten paces away.

"And there goes Rushavi to follow him," Nunor said.

He could hear Suvusa shouting over the storm, calling for her son.

"Tiryn, we have to follow the boy."

But Tiryn was already turning them around, struggling against the wind. He kept an arm up, shielding his eyes from the sand that whipped around them. "Do you see Darmon?"

Nunor was pressed close to Tiryn, the elf's body acting as a poor windbreak. He looked, searching for a sign of his cousin. Two dwarfen shadows also struggled against the wind, apparently following the boy. "They've spotted Rushavi."

"Shit."

Tiryn called for Syrani, and Nunor did the same. He wasn't sure if the stubborn she-elf would hear them, but she would find a way to reach them if she did.

"The temple has emerged."

"What?" Nunor shouted. "Why now?"

"Hold on, Nunor. We're almost inside."

Nunor tightened his grip on Tiryn's waist and shut his eyes against the grit burying itself into the creases of his eyes. "Why are we going inside?"

"That's where Rushavi and Ardu have gone."

"Fucking shit."

There were a few more seconds of sand whipping around his head and wind whistling past his ears, and then Nunor was no longer standing in the center of a sandstorm. The wind was gone, though he could still hear it very nearby. Tiryn stopped walking, though Nunor could feel the elf shifting in his grip as Tiryn turned.

"We're inside, Nunor." Tiryn put a hand on Nunor's shoulder, gently separating them. "But I don't see Rushavi."

Nunor shook his head, sending golden brown silt cascading off his head and out of his hair. He turned, still remaining close to Tiryn, and examined the door they had come through.

Except it wasn't a proper door. Only a hole in the face of an otherwise blank stone wall. The wall was the same color as the desert, and Nunor had to stare hard to see the sandstorm raging outside against the temple.

"The walls …" Nunor blinked, then scrubbed more grit from his eyelashes and the corners of his eyes. "The walls are moving."

"The entire temple seems to be built from sand." Tiryn was walking in a slow circle around the room they stood in. "No wonder the dwarfs could not unbury it. It's not just in the desert. The temple *is* the desert."

"But there was glass," Nunor said. Shadows were approaching from beyond the temple's entrance, but they were still some distance off. *Darmon and Alain.*

"Probably reinforcement in critical areas. Or decoration." Tiryn had wandered to the opposite side of the room. "There are several doorways here. But no sign of Rushavi."

Nunor turned. He saw no doors, only blank walls. "What doors?"

Tiryn pointed at nothing. "Doorways. Not doors."

Nunor grumbled. "I don't see any damned doorways!"

Tiryn faced him, an eyebrow raised. "It's an illusion. And one dwarfs are too impatient to see past, it seems."

There was a string of swears behind him, and Nunor turned to see Darmon and Alain as they stomped through the curtain of sand that hid the entrance to the temple.

Alain was evidently the rational and quick-thinking one out of the pair of them. She marched in front of Darmon with a shield to protect them from the worst of the wind. The plait in her hair had come undone, and she was crusted from head to foot in sand. She glared at Nunor as she settled the shield against her back and tried to tame the mess her hair had become.

"Damned desert." Darmon shook his head. "And *you*, cousin." Darmon searched the room as he approached Nunor. "Where is the boy? Where is the amulet?"

Nunor sighed. "Darmon, you mud-guzzling half-wit. We've been in the temple for only a moment. Do you think we could have found the amulet and hidden both it and Rushavi away in that time?"

"Then where is he?" Darmon gestured around the empty room.

"If you would stop shouting, I'm trying to listen for him," Tiryn said.

"Why did you follow us?" Nunor hissed in a low voice to his cousin. "You could have been lost in that storm out there."

Alain approached, though she watched Tiryn. "Do you doubt my ability to protect our future king, Halfhelm?"

"In battle?" Nunor snorted. "No. I'm sure your blade is as sharp as your tongue and your hand just as quick to strike." Nunor gestured towards the nearly invisible entrance. "But against an arcane sandstorm?" He shook his head. "My lady, no sword or axe could defend against that."

"Please, stop your arguing," Tiryn called over his shoulder at them.

Alain chanced a look away from Tiryn long enough to glare at Nunor. "A shield did well enough, Halfhelm. And I am not your lady."

Syrani rushed in, sliding to a stop only feet through the threshold. "There you are, Tiryn. Have you found Rushavi?"

Tiryn turned and shook his head. "I can't tell which direction he went."

Syrani approached the same far wall Tiryn stood before. "Ah, illusionary doorways. Interesting."

"Simple deterrent, but effective. And the sand had erased his tracks already," Tiryn said.

"What are you two long-eared fucks muttering about?" Darmon asked. "I don't see any doors."

"Doorways," Nunor corrected.

Darmon and Alain both glared at him. Alain's was more annoyance than anger, but Darmon was clearly furious.

Nunor spat into the sand. "I don't see them either."

Syrani and Tiryn exchanged a look.

"Very effective on dwarfs, it seems," Tiryn said.

Syrani examined the floor of the temple. "Rushavi's prints are gone, but Ardu's are still here. Only barely visible."

"Where did that little monster take the boy?" Darmon asked. He made for Syrani, but Nunor pushed him back.

"I don't think so. Leave the two of them alone."

"You dare put a hand on our future king?" Alain asked.

"I dare smack the snot from my cousin's nose if he stomps through the only trail we have to follow the boy, yes."

Both Darmon and Alain paused.

"Let Syrani track Rushavi. We'll find him and bring him back to his mother."

Darmon sneered. "I don't care about reuniting the boy with his parents. I care about finding the amulet."

"He went this way." Syrani pointed at a section of wall that looked no different from the rest around it. Nunor still couldn't see the doorway Tiryn and Syrani said was present.

Darmon immediately charged forward, but Nunor grabbed his arm and pulled him back once more.

He leaned in close, so that Alain might not hear his words. "Hurt the boy, and you will regret it, cousin. You are outnumbered here."

"Are you threatening me?" Darmon said, loudly. Alain immediately drew her weapon, a heavy warhammer that Nunor recognized as one of his own creations. "You wouldn't."

"I only mean for you to understand that we will protect Rushavi from you if it comes to it, Darmon. I know you care more about the amulet than the child and his dragon companion. But the child is our priority."

"The child will not come to harm from us, Halfhelm." Alain returned her hammer to its place. "But do not threaten Darmon again."

Nunor did not answer. Darmon only glared as he shouldered his way past Nunor to follow Syrani. Alain was close behind Darmon, but she was more polite as she passed Nunor.

"Halfhelm," Alain said with a quick nod. Her tone was almost neutral, but not quite.

"Alain," Nunor returned.

Syrani walked towards the wall, then kept walking, softly falling sand all around her. She kept her head down, searching the temple floor, Darmon inches behind her.

"What am I seeing, Tiryn?" Nunor watched Syrani grow smaller as the distance between them surely grew larger, but he could not comprehend it clearly. "Magic?"

Tiryn put a hand on Nunor's shoulder and guided him forward. "No, just some skilled trickery. You'll see in a moment."

Nunor let Tiryn guide him forward, and after a moment he realized Tiryn had led him through a sandy doorway and into a long hall. Golden brown grains of desert earth rained down in a steady, rhythmic motion. All around him was sand, falling and blending seamlessly into more sand.

"Ah, clever." For the first time, Nunor lifted his gaze upward. He could not see the top of the temple, only an indistinct blackness. "How do the rooms not fill with all the earth? How are we not swimming in it?"

Or worse, he thought, *drowning?*

"We might be," Tiryn said cheerily. "The temple may be sinking back to where it was, only it's happening slowly enough to not notice." Nunor turned to yell at him, but Tiryn shrugged and added, "Or perhaps there's a system that just channels the sand back up to perpetually create this falling effect."

"Fucking elves."

A few moments later, after following Syrani diligently through another series of rooms, they felt the first tremble shake the temple.

"Feels like you might have been wrong about this place not sinking, Tiryn." Nunor chanced a look up again, but could still not see the ceiling of the temple.

Ahead of them, Syrani glanced over her shoulder at him, but said nothing.

"How long do you think we have to find Rushavi and leave before the entire structure collapses?"

"Not long, I'd say," Darmon answered for him. "Best pick up the pace, she-elf, or you'll kill us all."

"Ardu's tracks are difficult to see." Syrani knelt close to the ground. "They've all but disappeared. But I think we're entering the heart of the temple."

"What makes you so sure of that?" Darmon asked. "Besides that, we've been wandering through this elvish death trap for a mile or more."

"The sand sounds different."

Nunor waited for Syrani to explain further, but she didn't.

"She's not much for chatting, is she?" Nunor whispered to Tiryn.

"I hadn't noticed."

Soon, even Nunor could hear the difference the sound of the sand made as it fell. The cadence was different, almost like …

"It's falling onto hard ground," Nunor said. "There's solid ground up ahead, thank the Great Ones."

Tiryn snorted behind him. "Tired of the sand already?"

Nunor only mumbled a few choice curses under his breath.

The ground they found was indeed very solid. It was also the same reddish color as the stones at the Elori home. They entered a large chamber, this one very different from the entrance to the temple.

"Not so much sand here." Nunor turned, giving the room a cursory look. "Where to now?"

Syrani and Tiryn both examined the adjacent walls, but it was Tiryn who answered. "I don't know. I think we've reached a dead end."

Darmon grumbled. "Then where's the damned amulet, hm? Should it not be here?"

"And where is the child?" Alain added. "Are his tracks still present?"

Syrani shook her head. "No more tracks."

"So he disappeared?" Nunor snorted. "Right." He looked up, surprised to note that he could see a faint light.

"There's something not quite right about this room," Alain said softly.

Nunor could sense it as well. He nodded. "There's dwarfen magic in here."

"Why would there be dwarfen magic in a temple of the Great Ones?" Tiryn asked.

Nunor shrugged. "Dunno. But when I think of a room with no exit and dwarfen magic, I think—"

"Hidden doors," Alain finished.

Nunor gave her a wink. "Right." He pointed to the wall furthest from him. "You start there?"

Alain scoffed. "Do you know what you're looking for, Halfhelm?"

Nunor bit back the biting retort that first came to mind and instead just shrugged. "Let's find out, hm?"

Nunor searched for any sign of a hidden door or latch.

There were no cracks or hinges or anything else that might give away the presence of any such things. There were plenty of superficial scratches, but most were not deep enough for him to even get a fingernail wedged into for purchase. But he could still feel the magic in the room, he could even sense it beneath his palm as he brushed a hand along the surface of the walls.

He could hear Alain doing the same, even hear her cursing when a nick in the floor didn't reveal itself to be a hatch.

Another quake shook them, and Nunor had to steady himself on the wall. They were getting stronger.

"Nunor, tell us what to look for." Tiryn began feeling along the same wall Nunor had just finished examining, reaching higher than Nunor could on his own.

"Anything out of the ordinary," Nunor grumbled back.

Darmon was the only one that did not help in the search for the hidden door. He remained in the center of the room, watching the others as they worked.

"Darmon, you lazy fuck, get to looking!" Nunor shouted at his cousin. "The temple won't stand for long."

"I've got something." Alain stepped back, motioning for Nunor. "Here."

Nunor rushed over, his armor and axe clanking as he ran. Alain pointed out a thin crack, and Nunor traced it out with his fingers. It was shallow, barely deep enough for the pads of his fingers to feel, but it went in a full circle.

"That's it, alright."

"How do we open it?" Alain asked. "No handle, no lever. I already tried pushing it all over."

Nunor shook his head. "It needs pushing from the other side."

"And how are we meant to do that?"

Nunor thought for a moment. "Not enough of a gap to wedge a blade in. Which means there must be some mechanism on the other side." He held out a hand. "Your hammer, Alain."

She shook her head. "No."

Nunor sighed. "I just need the gem set into the cheek."

She snorted. "I'm not ruining my hammer for you."

"I'll fix it when we return to Doldural. Just give me the damn gem."

"You?" Alain laughed. "Fix my hammer? Do you have any idea how priceless this weapon is?"

Nunor rounded on her. "Yeah, I made the damned thing, so I've got a decent idea." He held out his hand again. "Gem. Now."

Alaine glared at him, but she took out her hammer and gently pried the large red gem from the cheek and passed it to him. "Why that gem?"

"It's imbued with a bit of magic." Nunor smeared the gem, a rose-cut ruby with a smooth back, against his arm. It came away with a thick layer of sand and cactus jelly from his skin. "It amplifies impacts." He looked over at Alain. "You never wondered why you could smack your practice dummies away like flies with that thing?"

Alaine's glare deepened into a scowl.

Nunor slapped the gem on the door. It stuck beautifully, the combination of the sticky cactus jelly and the fine grit that had stuck to his body making a rudimentary mortar. He motioned to the gem. "Right. It's ready for you."

Alain looked from him to the gem. "For me to do what, exactly?"

"For you to hit it, you—" Nunor stopped himself before he insulted her. It was never polite to insult a woman. He groaned. "Just hit the damned thing."

Alaine shoved him back. She was not gentle, either. She hefted her warhammer once before striking.

The ruby shattered, and there was a loud, reverberating gong long after Alain returned her weapon to her back.

The sound faded after a moment, but nothing further happened.

"Nunor, not to ruin that moment you were having, but I could have easily done that with my own magic," Tiryn said. "No need to deface the lady's property."

"Oh, fuck off, Tiryn. Your magic would have just splashed against the stone like Darmon's morning piss."

Darmon spat out a string of profanities, but Nunor didn't care to listen.

"I think he's right, Tiryn. This isn't elven magic." Syrani touched the door, which had still not opened. "It feels older."

"It's closer to dwarfen magic, but even that isn't right." Nunor inspected the door. "It should open. Why hasn't it—"

The door began to open.

It moved slowly, the sound of grinding stone deafening as they waited. Darmon crawled through the door as soon as it was wide enough for him to squeeze through.

"Dammit," Nunor grumbled. He followed after Darmon, stepping over the lip of the doorway and beyond. He had expected a separate room, but what lay beyond the hidden door was little more than a narrow tunnel.

Alain came up behind him, shoving him when Nunor stopped moving long enough to inspect his surroundings.

"Keep moving, Halfhelm," Alain said. "I've got an elf on my ass."

Darmon had also stopped, leaning against the wall of the tunnel and sitting with his knees almost in his chest. "What is this shit? I thought you said we were in the heart of the temple?"

Syrani followed behind Alain, who was scrambling over Nunor to be closer to Darmon. Syrani looked uncomfortable. The tunnel was narrow enough for her frame, but the height forced her to remain on all fours. "I believe I said we were close to the heart of the temple."

"Syrani, I need a little more room," Tiryn said. His voice was muffled. "I believe the door will be closing soon."

Nunor shifted a few feet further into the tunnel, then sat much like Darmon did, but with his back on the opposite side of the tunnel. Syrani and Tiryn both came into view, and the sound of grinding stone told them the door was shutting.

It closed much faster than it had opened, and within seconds they were cast into darkness.

"Everyone alright?" Nunor asked.

"I think there's something in the tunnel," Tiryn said. "Hold on."

A witch light flared to life, illuminating the door.

Beside the door was a body.

Alain screamed, and even Nunor jumped at the sight of the hollow skeletal head that faced them.

"Fucking shit," he said with a startled exhale. "What is that?"

"It's not human, or anything else I've ever seen," Syrani said. She touched the skull, which seemed strangely disfigured. "It's not bone."

"It's stone," Tiryn said. "It's a golem." He produced another witch light, and the pale yellow light drifted over to illuminate the entire creature. "He's dead. Poor thing must have used the last of his energy to open the door one last time."

There was a silence in the tunnel for a moment. Nunor contemplated what that meant for their eventual escape from the temple. He was sure the others were thinking the same or similar thoughts.

"No use sitting around and weeping about it." Syrani shoved at Nunor's thigh. "We should keep moving."

They crawled through the tunnel. Darmon and Alain took the lead, Nunor staying as close he could to Alain's heels. Syrani and Tiryn followed behind him. Tiryn was kind enough to send a few bobbing witch lights to the front of the line to light their way.

The quaking in the temple continued. There were now only a few moments between each shudder of the earth. Nunor could feel sweat dripping into his eyes, and his breathing was labored.

How long until we reach the end? Or will we run out of air first?

"Do you hear that?" Syrani asked.

Everyone paused. Nunor could only hear Alain's breathing. Hers sounded just as heavy as his.

"Sounds like crying," Tiryn answered. Nunor couldn't turn to see the expression on his friend's face, but Tiryn sounded worried.

"It's Rushavi," Syrani said. She shoved her way past Nunor, climbing under him. Nunor cursed when his head hit the roof of the tunnel. "Get out of the way, you three."

Alain pressed herself into the tunnel wall, and Syrani was able to move past her with less issue. Darmon complained, but there was no room for him to draw a blade and threaten Syrani, so he eventually relented when Syrani simply pushed him down and crawled over him.

Syrani moved through the tunnel much faster than Darmon, and she was out of sight after a moment.

"That was rude," Alain muttered.

"Better for someone to reach the boy sooner rather than later," Tiryn said. "Keep moving, if you don't mind."

They reached Syrani and Rushavi only a few minutes later. There was light at the end of the tunnel, and two figures were outlined against it. The light was broken, and as they drew closer, Nunor realized the brightness streamed through several cracks and gaps between fallen stones that blocked the exit of the tunnel.

"Syrani?" Tiryn asked. "How is he?"

"Hurt, but only a little. The tunnel collapsed during one of the quakes."

"Fresh air!" Nunor inhaled deeply. The air coming from beyond the tunnel's exit was not truly fresh, but it was not so stale as what he had been breathing for the last several minutes.

"You do poorly underground for a dwarf," Alain remarked. She sat down, wiping sweat from her brow.

"Halfhelms aren't allowed in families, Alain. You know that. I never spent time in the mining tunnels of Doldural."

"Where is the damned amulet?" Darmon asked. He began searching Rushavi, patting fiercely at his body. "Where have you hidden it, you little shit?"

"Keep your hands off him." Syrani shoved Darmon, sending him rolling back into both Nunor and Alain. "He doesn't have the amulet."

"How do you know he hasn't got it, hm? Did he already give it to you, she-elf?" Darmon roared, struggling back into an upright position. He lunged for Syrani, but Nunor grabbed his arm and held him back.

To Nunor's surprise, Alain also held Darmon's upper arm.

"Darmon, stop!" Alain pleaded. "We don't have the time to fight amongst ourselves."

"I won't need to fight if the bitch elf would tell me where the amulet is."

"It's through there." Syrani pointed through the gaps in the blockage. "Rushavi says the tunnel collapsed, and Ardu managed to squeeze his way between a couple of stones. But the rocks shifted, and now Rushavi can't get through."

"You understand the boy, too?" Darmon grumbled. "How is it that the elves are the only ones to speak to the boy?"

Rushavi was still crying, his small fists balled and his arms raised over his head.

"He doesn't speak in the normal sense," Tiryn said over

Nunor's shoulder. "Everything he communicates is done in images. Memories and the like. But it can be understood."

Syrani touched him briefly on the shoulder. "Rushavi, I'm going to try to move some of these rocks so we can get to Ardu, alright?"

Rushavi made no indication that he was listening.

Syrani started with a small stone, near the top of the blockage. When it was pulled out and did not cause an immediately cascade of stone, she continued.

Soon, a hole no larger than Nunor's head was unearthed.

Rushavi, who had stopped crying and was watching Syrani intently, immediately dove through the hole. Syrani grabbed his ankle, but the child slithered through her grip and disappeared into the unknown beyond.

"Rushavi, wait!" Syrani reached an arm through the hole, but her hand was empty when she withdrew it. "He's running after Ardu."

Syrani grabbed another stone and yanked it free. Smaller ones tumbled down around her, but she paid them no mind as she clambered through the enlarged hole. Her shoulders were too wide, but she managed it. Syrani was about halfway through the hole, only her hips left to shimmy through, when another quake shook the tunnel.

"Fuck," Nunor grumbled. "Shove her through."

Alain and Nunor both reached over Darmon and pushed against the soles of Syrani's boots and her calves. The she-elf slid through the hole and was gone from sight. The hole collapsed only a second later.

Nunor instinctively covered his head as rocks continued to fall.

He waited in the dark for the sound of stones falling to cease. Tiryn's witch lights had gone dark, and there was both someone on top of him and someone beneath him. Nunor could feel breath on his cheek.

"Is everyone alright?" It was Tiryn's mouth that was so

close to his ear, though how Tiryn had ended up shielding him, Nunor couldn't be sure.

"I'm fine," Nunor answered.

"Halfhelm is crushing me," Alain said in a pained voice. "I think your knee is in my side."

Nunor shifted, and Alain sighed.

"Thank you," she murmured.

"Darmon?" Nunor asked.

There was a groan from under Nunor's arm. "Here. Took a hit to my head from a rock. Maybe an elbow."

"Tiryn?" Nunor asked.

"I think my arm is broken," Tiryn answered. "It's pinned in the debris."

Alain and Nunor both cursed.

A pair of witch lights illuminated the tunnel once more.

Nunor briefly remembered pulling Alain down under him before the tunnel started to collapse, but Nunor had evidently tried to protect Darmon from the falling stones as well.

Or Darmon ducked under the first body he could cower beneath.

And Tiryn had squashed all three of them under his own body.

"You've got blood on your face, Tiryn," Nunor said.

"I'm far less concerned about my face at the moment, my friend." Tiryn winced. "Would you be able to get my arm free?"

There was a moment of disentangling bodies. Alain and Nunor worked in tandem to remove Tiryn from the pileup his arm was stuck in. It took only a moment.

Alain made a face when Tiryn was finally able to cradle his arm to his chest.

"I think it's broken, alright," Nunor said.

Tiryn's forearm was already swollen and bruised, and

there was a clear spot in the middle where the bone had been split.

"I don't believe it," Darmon grumbled. "The path back has been blocked as well."

"What do we do now?" Alain asked.

"I think all we can do is wait," Nunor answered.

JAIMES

J aimes did not sleep for more than a few restless hours. The bed felt empty without Eilonwy next to him. But he had wanted her out of Larten. Had orchestrated a trick to get her to Vyris. This was precisely what he wanted.

Yet it did not make her absence easier to bear.

He lay in bed, staring out of the open window. The sky was still dark, though not as dark as it had been when he had awoken from his light slumber to read her note again.

Even now, the small scrap of parchment she had left on his pillow was pressed against his chest.

She didn't suspect a thing. She told me that she would be back soon.

He felt faintly ill.

When she realizes I've deceived her, she'll be furious.

But the deception had likely already been found out. Eilonwy was well on her way to Vyris by now.

There were several sets of stomping boots in the hall outside, and Jaimes listened as they descended the stairs.

The King's Guards. Seems they are early to rise this morning.

Or perhaps they were always up before the sun? He didn't

know for sure; he was usually never awake so early himself. Only Mathius and Eilonwy …

Eilonwy. Great Ones, I will miss her while she's away. But it's only temporary. She will be back soon.

Jaimes rolled from the bed with a sigh, still holding Eilonwy's letter close to his chest. His knee twitched angrily, and he reached for the nondescript jar on the nearby table.

"I suppose, if others in the inn are rising, then I can too."

Mathius was sure to be awake and already working on breakfast.

Perhaps he could use some help, since Eilonwy is gone.

He took his time dressing, though. First rubbing cream on his knee and down his twisted shin. The muscle of his leg, he noticed, was not as atrophied and weak as it once was. It had only been a few months since he and Eilonwy had perfected the formula for his medicinal cream, but the physical change in his once nearly crippled leg was more than he had once thought possible.

Outside, he could hear men, presumably the King's Guards, shuffling about under his bedroom window. He heard the whinnying of horses and the clinking of armor.

Odd.

He slipped a pair of pants on and went to the window to investigate.

Below, in the middle of the lone street that ran through Larten, stood the King's Guard that Mathius often referred to as the captain. He waited atop a dark horse, a helmet balanced on the pommel, with three other horsed knights surrounding him. He held a torch in one hand, and the reins of his horse in the other.

A fourth knight, this one on foot, stepped into Jaimes's view from the direction of the inn's entrance.

"And?" the captain asked.

"A fire has been lit in the kitchen and by the garden exit. They are trapped inside."

Jaimes froze in place.

"Good." The King's Guard held the torch out, circling his horse slowly. The four knights with him each lit a bottle stuffed with rags against the torch. Jaimes did not have to guess what might be in them. He recognized the dark amber glass as the bottles smashed against the side of the inn and flames broke out across the outer wall.

"Wait!" Jaimes shouted through the window. "What are you doing?"

The King's Guards all looked up at the sound of his voice, but none answered. They rode off, and Jaimes turned from the window in a panic before they had disappeared from sight.

"Shit," he cursed. He grabbed his boots from the floor and bolted for the bedroom door.

Smoke was only just rising from the first floor, and the smell was not yet strong. He beat his fist against the closest door. "Fire!"

He moved to the next, and the next, hammering against each one.

"Fire, fire, get up! We have to get out of here."

He continued shouting, pausing long enough to slip his boots on. He still had no shirt, but there was no time to double back for one now.

He tried for the stairs, only to see that flames were already licking at the bottommost steps.

There was a scream from downstairs, a manly sort of startled cry, and Jaimes leaned over the railing to look below.

There was a fisherman, one he recognized as an on-and-off again regular, beating back the flames with some sort of cloth.

"Wake the others down there!" Jaimes called to him. "Get them out!"

The man looked up briefly, catching Jaimes's eyes. He ran off, but to where Jaimes could not tell.

There were more shouts, some of alarm and some of fear.

Someone was at Jaimes's elbow, looking down at the fire that slowly began to eat its way to the second floor. "We're trapped. What do we do?"

Jaimes was thinking. "We'll have to take a window. It's not a long drop."

There was the sound of splintering wood, and Jaimes looked towards the sound. Someone had already had his exact thought, and through an open bedroom door he could see the smashed shutters and a large bottom as someone clambered head first through the window.

"Come on! Follow me!" Jaimes shouted.

There were only four others besides himself, all of them male. He led them through the nearest room, lifting a chair to smash the shutters off the windowsill. Wood clattered to the ground below.

"This is the back of the inn. The ground is soft, and it should be furthest from the flames."

He hadn't even finished his words when the first man had already slipped a leg over the window frame to leap to the ground below.

"Go, all of you. I'll follow in a moment."

No one paid him any mind.

He ran back to his room. Flames from the thrown bottles had found their way to the window and were charring through the wood. It was unbearably hot and smoky.

He thought briefly of Vash.

Jaimes ran to the wardrobe, tossing things left and right. He pocketed the pouch containing the little black book and kept digging. Eilonwy's sword was missing, and he hoped she had taken it with her. But his own sword, untouched for years, still remained where he had left it after Roland presented it to him. Jaimes had never even used it.

He grabbed it, and a belt that he had tossed aside. As a quick afterthought, he grabbed what he hoped was one of his own shirts and held it over his mouth to stop the smoke from entering his lungs.

By the time he reached the nearby room where the others trapped on the first floor had gathered, they were all gone. Jaimes could still hear shouting, both from outside and from the floor below. He held the items in his grasp close to his chest and draped first one leg and then the other over the open window until only his rear balanced on the thin sill kept him from falling to the first floor.

It was not a long drop, but his damaged leg did not keep his weight. Jaimes fell to the ground, his knee flaring in pain, and he immediately buckled to a half roll, half stumbling collapse.

Jaimes heard a nearby scream, this one definitely of a woman. He rose unsteadily to his feet, limping around the corner of the building in the direction the cry had originated from.

A woman lay in the street near the garden entrance to the inn. She wore a thin nightgown, and there was a spilled bucket of water rolling to a stop not far from her outstretched hand. She was not moving, and a pool of red liquid seeped slowly from under her and spread across the stones.

Metal clinked behind him, and Jaimes instinctively ducked and turned.

A King's Guard stood where Jaimes had been only a second before, a bloodied sword in his grip. Jaimes dropped his belongings and quickly pulled his own sword from its leather sheath. The blade was heavier than the training swords he had used as a younger man, but he remembered easily enough how to plant his feet.

The knight laughed, taking a similar stance. "You think you can fight a King's Guard?"

"Why are you doing this? Why burn the inn?" Jaimes

motioned towards the prone woman. The puddle of blood around her continued to grow. "Why kill her?"

"It's time for us to return to Etritia. And we couldn't leave a traitor in Larten. So all of Larten must die."

There was another scream, and Jaimes turned instinctively to follow the sound. It came within the inn, beyond the inn's garden entrance. Jaimes rushed towards the door, coughing on the smoke that had begun to seep into the garden. A large cart had been pushed to block the garden door, making it impossible to open from within.

Jaimes rushed for the cart. "There are still people inside!"

The knight cut off Jaimes's path, putting himself between Jaimes and the blocked garden door. He raised his sword. "And they will stay inside until they burn."

Jaimes slid to a stop, one arm up to protect his face from the heat of the flames. The other held his sword, though he couldn't be sure he could actually use it.

I can't fight him.

Another thought chased quickly after the first.

Where is Mathius?

The knight made his attack. Jaimes sidestepped, nearly tripping over the dead woman in the alley.

What happened to the men that came through the window before me? Are they also dead?

Jaimes blocked the second attack, but did not push an attack of his own. The flames continued to grow, and the screams within the inn began to fade away even as the shouts and cries of those in the streets grew louder.

They must be killing people as they leave their homes to fight the flames.

Jaimes blocked another attack, then did a half turn and parried. It was caught on the flat of the knight's blade.

Where is Mathius? Was he inside? Is he still?

Jaimes charged, a guttural howl escaping his lips. The knight only blocked the first of his flurried attacks, then switched to dodging. Jaimes heard him curse from under his metal helm.

There were only a few places where a sword could pierce the knight's armor. There was a small gap between the chest and back pieces, and that was where Jaimes focused his attacks. If he could only wound him, the knight might flee, and Jaimes could turn his attention to dousing the inn.

But no matter how fast Jaimes moved, the knight was slightly faster. Jaimes blamed his leg. It slowed him down.

Jaimes hesitated for a brief moment, analyzing the knight. The knight charged, surprising Jaimes. Their blades met, and Jaimes felt his leg beginning to buckle under the knight's weight.

The King's Guard sensed it as well, and braced more of his weight against their crossed blades.

Jaimes gritted his teeth, cursing to himself.

He will kill me, and how furious will Eilonwy be with me then?

He removed one hand from the hilt of his sword, briefly balancing his weight with it against the slick ground. Then he rested the fingertips against the knight's chest. If the man noticed, he made no indication.

Jaimes closed his eyes and sent a wave of arcane energy from his palm into the knight's chest.

The pressure against his blade was suddenly gone, and Jaimes felt the shoulder that supported his weapon relax.

He opened his eyes. The knight was now slumped against the wall of the inn, and a large dent was in the chest of his armor. He did not move.

Jaimes took the bucket from the slain woman and ran to the street.

All was in chaos. The fire tinted the sky in a red-orange haze, and thick black smoke billowed up into the air. All around him were dead and dying, and a few knights hounded after the ones who ran.

"Mathius!" Jaimes called. He searched the faces of those who lay in the street closest to him, a sword in one hand and a wooden pail in the other. "Mathius, where are you?"

He got no answer.

Behind him, the inn's great timbers groaned and crashed suddenly, and sparks flew up into the air. Jaimes watched as the wind carried a few embers onto nearby shops, where they settled on roofs.

"Shit."

All of Larten will burn.

Where is Mathius?

A roar filled the night, mighty and terrible. Jaimes thought instantly of the great demon that had shaped itself into a dragon.

But Vash killed it.

The dragon that landed in Larten's small square with a thunderous crash was not the demon that the fire spirit Vash had destroyed.

It was Melonya.

Rain descended on the town, heavy and cold and with a suddenness that Jaimes could only attribute to the arcane.

The beams of the inn hissed and sizzled and spat, but the red flames began to dull and die.

Jaimes wiped wet hair from his eyes, searching the surrounding dead. "Mathius!"

Heavy metallic thuds, footsteps, paused his search, and Jaimes spun to block the incoming attack.

But the knight stopped suddenly, his breath escaping in a loud, shocked gasp. He fell forward, hitting the stones with a splashing crash. There was a charred mark on his back.

"Jaimes!"

He looked up.

Eilonwy was running through the thick rain towards him.

Her silver hair was wet and hung limply against her face. Her clothes were soaked through and sticking to her skin.

"Eilonwy, you came back?"

She pulled him into her arms, then released him and shook him. "Don't ever trick me like that again!"

"I-I'm sorry, I just wanted you to be safe."

The inn collapsed suddenly, and Jaimes ducked and covered his head with both forearms, though they still held his sword and the little bucket.

Eilonwy motioned to the fallen building. "And look what was going to happen to you." She wiped water from her eyes. The rain was slowing, but not altogether stopped. "Where is Mathius?"

Jaimes shook his head. "I don't know."

The rain stopped. It was gone nearly as quickly as it started.

"Was that you?" Jaimes asked.

Eilonwy nodded. "Melonya smelled the smoke before we reached the town. I had time to pull together enough energy for it."

Jaimes stared at the inn. It had been his home. And now it was gone. And his mother's things …

He shook his head.

"Help me find Mathius."

They did not leave each other's sight as they searched. They were not the only ones that called out for loved ones. More than one person found their friends and family members lying in gutters or in alleys, unresponsive.

The town was in shock, but it did not stop a few stares as Eilonwy was spotted.

Melonya, for her own safety, had left Larten shortly after descending into the town. According to Eilonwy, she had taken a fistful of King's Guards with her.

"We can't linger here. Not when you look like this," Jaimes said.

"We don't leave until we find Mathius."

Mathius was not among the dead that filled the streets.

"There were still people inside the inn. I … I heard them screaming."

Eilonwy's expression was pained. "If he isn't out here, then …"

"Then he's gone."

Something struck Eilonwy in the shoulder, and she cried out, startled.

"Leave, elf." A woman knelt in the street, cradling a young man with pale skin and lifeless limbs to her chest. "This is your doin'."

"What?" Jaimes stepped in front of Eilonwy. "No, this isn't her doing. She *saved* you."

Eilonwy touched her shoulder, where the cloth had torn and there was a small scrape. "I will leave, just please tell us if you have seen Mathius?"

"Mathius?" A man, bloodied and haggard, called from behind them. "And how is it that ya know the innkeeper?"

"She's the ale girl," another man called. It was Artur. He emerged from his wife's shop, mostly unscathed. His eyes were wide and fearful. "It is you, yes? Ya look different, but I can see it."

More people were gathering. Some were still in shock, their eyes glassy and their steps slow and unsteady. Others, like the woman cradling her son's body, were angry.

"Eilonwy, we need to leave," Jaimes said. He kept his voice low, but he pulled on Eilonwy's elbow, gently tugging her towards the nearest gate out of town.

"Not until we find Mathius," Eilonwy repeated.

"So it was Mathius, was it? He was the traitor." The first woman spat into the street, then grabbed a loose stone and flung it in Eilonwy's direction. It fell short, the aim not nearly as true as the first had been.

Another stone quickly followed, this one from a different direction.

Jaimes spotted it and reached out a hand. "Stop!"

He was speaking to the man that had thrown the stone, though his shout was too late. But the stone did stop. It hung in the air for a brief moment, then dropped unceremoniously to the ground.

The man who threw it took a step back, his mouth hanging open.

Jaimes stared at his outstretched hand for a moment, but he had felt no buzz of arcane energy.

He looked over his shoulder at Eilonwy. Her hand was also outstretched, the palm glowing a faint blue.

"Please, has anyone seen Mathius? I will leave as soon as I have an answer."

No one spoke. The street was quiet.

Eilonwy's hand fell. "Very well. I will leave. But *I* did not cause this fire." She swept her hair behind her ears, looking very vulnerable for a moment. "Please believe me. I was not here when the fire started, and I did all I could to stop it and keep it from spreading."

"Then who did this?" the woman called. She still held her son in her arms. "Who killed my boy?"

"It was the King's Guards," Jaimes said. "They were given orders to burn the town and kill everyone here."

"Lies." It was Artur again. "The King's Guard are supposed to protect us."

"The King's Guard are supposed to hunt down elves and elf supporters and kill them," Jaimes corrected. "They knew there was another elf supporter here in Larten. And when they could not find out who it was, they decided to destroy the entire town."

There was a sound like heavy wind on the air, and many of the villagers that were present screamed and fled. The woman, Jaimes noted, did not move.

Melonya landed in front of where the inn had been, though there was nothing more than wet and charred rubble.

"Come on, Jaimes. We have our answer." Eilonwy touched his shoulder and stepped away, heading for Melonya.

Jaimes stared at the remains of the inn.

It had been his home. His father and mother, both mothers, had died there. And it was gone.

And Mathius was gone.

"Jaimes," Eilonwy called. She was already seated in Melonya's saddle.

"Just a moment."

He retrieved the items he had dropped. The shirt he slipped over his head, tugging the wet fabric down. The sword he hastily sheathed and threaded onto the belt, which he passed up to Eilonwy before scrambling into the saddle himself.

Another rock sailed over, hitting Melonya square on the haunches. She did not flinch, but a deep growth rumbled through her chest. Her serpentine neck swiveled in the direction the stone had come from, and her teeth bared.

"You dare strike me?"

"Melonya, leave them," Eilonwy said. "They have lost too much. They are angry."

"They are angry with the wrong people."

"Maybe they'll realize that one day, but I don't think it will be today," Jaimes said. "Let's just go. There's nothing for us here."

"And Mathius?"

Jaimes took a deep breath, casting a final look back at the inn.

"Gone."

3 0

FERRAND

The knight was breathless and red-faced when he found Ferrand. "There is a woman to see you, Commander."

Ferrand sighed, but continued walking. The day was nice, and there were plenty of dead and dying to see as he walked the streets of Etritia. The dead hung from gallows, while the dying lay in the streets or cowered in alleys. Their stink was carried away on the breeze that blew in from the north. The streets were filthy, but the air was crisp and clean.

"She requests your immediate attention," the knight continued.

"Tell Madam Moira that she will get her twins back when I am done with them, and not a moment before." A rat scurried across the street some twenty feet in front of him and into a home. The rat had once been a clothier, if Ferrand recalled properly. But now he was just a rat, and soon he would likely be dead or dying.

"It's not Madam Moira. She's on the other side of the gate."

Ferrand stopped. "The other side of the gate?"

"Yes, Commander."

"Is it that bitch from the kitchens? I'll have her head if it is." *And perhaps a lot more of her before I take the head.*

"No, I've never seen her before. And she would be easily recognized after only a glance." The knight grimaced. "She's missing an arm."

Dix.

"What the fuck is she doing here?" Ferrand murmured.

"Sir?"

"Have her brought in. But keep her in the gatehouse. And search her for weapons, unless you want to end up dead."

The knight stammered out some inane pleasantries and ran off again. Ferrand followed at a more sedate pace.

Dix had followed him to Etritia. And how long had she been around, he wondered?

Long enough to survey the city. To decide how best to invade and slaughter everyone here, perhaps?

Ferrand stopped at the barracks before reaching the gate-house. It was empty; his best men had been sent south. Of the ones that were left, they were either patrolling the streets or guarding the Etritian gates.

Or dead, Ferrand thought grimly.

Most of his older King's Guards were gone, murdered by some unseen specter haunting the alleys and hunting knights in red and blue checked surcoats. The ones that were left were the younger men that had left their families to die in Etritian destitution. They were useless, good for only the simplest of tasks, and committed to Ferrand only in word. Not like Clay, who would be returning from the Southern Cities soon. Not like Dirk had been, before that kitchen bitch had killed him.

Ferrand poured a glass of wine, emptying the carafe that sat atop his favorite table. The heavy glass thudded hollowly against the thick wood of the tabletop. Ferrand did not sit. He did not savor the dryness or the deep red of the liquid, and instead drank the glass in one long pull until the wine was gone. A sweep of his hand sent the carafe to the adjacent wall, where it shattered, leaving a splash of residual liquid to run down to the floor.

"Fucking Dix."

She was in the gatehouse, just as he had instructed. Dix sat in one of the few chairs on the bottom floor of the gatehouse, though hers had been dragged against the wall across from the entrance. She leaned back until the front legs of the chair were no longer touching the floor and her head rested against the wall. Last time Ferrand had seen her, Dix's head had been badly shaved and scabbed. He could still see the old cuts on her scalp, but she now had a layer of thick and very short hair.

"Ah, Ferrand, there you are. I sent for you some time ago." Dix smiled at him. Ferrand was sure that more of her teeth had gone missing since he had last seen her. Her smile, more like a threatening smirk than anything friendly, was disgusting and unnerving to see. "Were you avoiding me"?

The four King's Guards that guarded Dix parted for Ferrand, and he stopped a few steps in front of her. "I am a busy man. And I do not come at your call, Dix." He addressed the knight closest to him, though he kept his eyes on Dix. "Did you take her weapons?"

"They're upstairs."

Good. They're not complete idiots.

"You know I don't need a blade to kill your men, Ferrand." Dix tilted her head. "You're just being rude."

"How long have you been in Azimar, Dix? Did you tail me after my last trip north?"

Dix laughed. "Tail you? No, Ferrand. I did not need to tail you." She spat at his feet. "You're easier to hunt than a fox. You've lost all your northerner talents." She paused, inspecting the fingernails on her only hand. They were filthy and black with dirt, and Ferrand could see calluses formed from years of handling weapons. His own hands had similar calluses. "I've only been in Azimar for a day, no more."

"And what do you want?"

"Jorvun has asked me to check on his new pet."

"Everyone out."

Silence from the four King's Guards.

"I said out!"

They shuffled out quickly, slamming the door to the gatehouse behind them.

Dix didn't move, and Ferrand never took his eye from her.

"I am not Jorvun's pet."

"But you are, Ferrand." Dix sneered at him. "Tell me, have you stopped bleeding when you shit? Can you still taste him on your tongue at night?"

Ferrand lunged at her. Dix made no attempt to evade him, even when his hand closed around her throat. Instead, she lifted a leg and wrapped it around his thigh.

"Squeeze harder. Maybe you'll make me feel something."

Ferrand put a hand on her thigh, and Dix smirked. The smirk faded when Ferrand pulled the concealed dagger from her torn pants. He inspected it briefly. Sharpened bone, likely from a large prey animal. A weapon meant for stabbing, not cutting. The hilt was wrapped in thin leather. Deer hide, if Ferrand had to guess. He tossed it across the room, and it bounced and skidded across the stones.

He let her go, slamming the front legs of her seat back onto the ground.

"I am not Jorvun's pet. I paid a price for a valuable item, no more."

Dix rolled her shoulders and stretched her neck. "Jorvun only wants to know how things go in Etritia. Rumors have reached us that the city is not faring well. That she may fall with nothing more than the passing of time."

"The rumors are false. Only the weak of Etritia will fall. The strong will survive and be better for their suffering."

Dix tilted her head, staring at him. Her eyes looked nearly lifeless. "That is the northerner way."

"Yes."

"These people are not northerners. They are Azimarian. Softer, weaker."

Ferrand shook his head. "Not all of them."

Dix narrowed her gaze. "Do you think there will be enough to defend your castle when we come for it?"

Ferrand leaned close, bracing himself on the arms of Dix's chair. He pinned her hand down beneath his for good measure. Dix let out a soft moan, punctuated with a throaty chuckle. "Tell Jorvun that the next time I see him, I will be the one making him into a pet."

"You'll be able to tell him yourself soon enough, Ferrand."

Ferrand flipped Dix's chair onto its side, sending her rolling to the floor. "Leave. Leave, before I kill you."

There was a small amount of blood in the corner of her mouth where her lip had been split or bitten. Dix wiped at it with the back of her hand, glaring at Ferrand. She stood. "My weapons."

Ferrand smiled, the scarred half of his mouth pulling unpleasantly. "You don't need them, remember?"

<hr />

Madam Moira was waiting outside his bedroom when he arrived. She was sitting on the floor, her scuffed and dirty shoes beside her. Madam Moira's hair, usually neat and styled in an array of softly curled locks that drew the eye to her attractive neck and shoulders, was limp and loose and looked like it had not been washed in some time.

"Commander." Moira stood as he approached. She stepped on the hem of her dress and nearly tripped, but caught herself on the wall before she fell. "I demand you return my girls to me at once."

Ferrand laughed. "You demand of me?"

"The payment you supplied only covered a fraction of the time they have spent with you. They should be sent home immediately." Madam Moira pushed her hair away from her face, but it did nothing to make her appearance more attractive. "You cannot keep them, Commander."

"Oh, can't I?" Ferrand stepped closer, kicking Moira's shoes out of his way. Madam Moira hesitated before pressing her back into the wall and shying away from him. "Moira, I have made you the richest woman in all Etritia. You *owe* me."

Moira shook her head. "No. You can return them to me." Her lower lip trembled as she spoke. "I owe you nothing."

Ferrand sighed. "How much gold would it take to have you leave my sight?"

"I don't want gold," Moira said. Her voice was hardly above a whisper. "I want to make sure my girls are alive and safe."

"Oh, is that all?" Ferrand grabbed Madam Moira by her hair, yanking her head back. Moira's pained scream was cut short by the curved blade that cut across her throat.

Blood sprayed across the door to his small quarters. By the time Ferrand returned his blade to its place on his belt and fished the key to his room out of his vest, blood had covered Moira's exposed collarbones and the first several inches of her dress.

Ferrand pushed open the door, holding Moira just outside the doorway. The two naked women in his bed sat up, but the chains around their necks that fastened them to the wall prevented them from approaching.

"There you are, Madam Moira. They are alive. Are you satisfied?"

Blood burbled from Moira's mouth and neck as she tried to speak.

"Don't worry." Ferrand released Moira, letting her fall to the stone floor in the hall. "I'll take care of your twins for you."

Moira reached for Ferrand's boots as he stepped over her and into the bedroom. Ferrand kicked her hand away and shut the door behind him.

The twins stared at him, their eyes dull and empty. He wasn't sure they even realized what they had just witnessed.

"That bitch got blood on my boots." Ferrand sat at the foot of his bed and removed his shoes. One of the twins began pulling his tunic off while the other touched his back and sides with delicate hands.

A scream from the hall interrupted Ferrand before he could remove his trousers. He stood and returned to the door.

Just beyond, her hands covering her mouth as she stared at Moira's body, was the kitchen wench, Illa.

"Oh, good. I won't need to find you later." Ferrand pointed at the mess before him. "Clean this up. And be quick about it."

"Y-you killed her?" Illa asked.

Ferrand shrugged.

"Why?"

"Don't ask questions. Just clean this filth up. Or would you prefer to join her?" Ferrand glared at her. "No one would miss you if something were to happen. You would just be another woman tossed into the Knife to decompose on your way to the sea."

Illa began to weep. There was no sound to it, only the streaming of tears and the shaking of her hands as she continued to stare at the body between them.

Ferrand turned around and shut the door behind him once more. His twins were still sitting up in the bed, waiting for him. "Where were we, ladies?"

THE CHILD

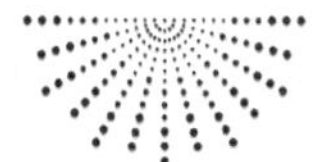

Once the wind came, it was easy to slip from his mother's grasp.

It was Ardu's idea.

Ardu had the best ideas.

Rushavi had felt something pulling him as they traveled. He had ignored it at first. There were far too many other things for him to be concerned with. His clothes never fit, his feet burned and his skin itched.

And he was hungry. Always hungry.

But as they traveled, the gnawing sensation of something calling to him grew stronger. Stronger than the itching, the burning, and the hunger.

Ardu said it was something special. Something that had once belonged to their creators. And that it was up to Rushavi and Ardu to find it once more.

Ardu was smart, and he had never lied to Rushavi.

When the winds came, Ardu's sister was sleeping. Sleeping, and dreaming.

She was the one who had summoned the temple, and Ardu suggested he and Rushavi take the chance to find the amulet.

Rushavi was unsure at first, but Ardu was quicker to decide. He could only follow his companion after Ardu ran into the center of the storm.

Ardu only stopped running when they entered the temple.

Rushavi shook himself. He hated the way the sand stuck to his skin and in the folds of his clothes.

"We don't have time to waste, Rushavi. The others are following us, and we have to find the amulet before they make us leave the temple." Ardu was staring up at him, his short tail with its large bulbous tip swishing along the floor and leaving dragging marks in its wake. *"Do you understand?"*

Rushavi nodded.

He had seen how the others argued about him. And about Ardu. They never stopped watching him.

"Are you ready?"

Rushavi nodded again.

Ardu led him through a maze of rooms and hallways, never pausing to consider what direction to go first.

Rushavi wondered how his companion knew where to go.

"I'm listening to what my instincts tell me. We'll find the amulet."

Rushavi wasn't sure what that meant, but he trusted Ardu.

Their first real struggle came when the maze of halls ended. The room they were in was made of stone, not sand. Rushavi was grateful that he no longer had to run barefoot across sand, but he could see no exit.

Ardu hesitated, pacing along the walls.

"There is a secret door ... somewhere ..." Ardu stopped. *"I think it's there."*

Rushavi saw nothing.

"It's hidden, Rushavi," Ardu said. He seemed mildly annoyed.

Everyone was always annoyed with Rushavi. Even the long-eared ones that spoke to him, though they were the best at hiding it.

"I'm sorry," Ardu said. *"I don't mean to be harsh with you."*

It was fine. Rushavi knew Ardu would never stay upset with him.

"That's right. Because I'm your closest friend. I am your oldest companion."

And they had saved each other's lives. They would not be where they were now without the other.

"Exactly." Ardu spun in a circle. *"Can you lift me up?"*

Rushavi picked Ardu up. He was heavier than he looked, and was too large to hold comfortably, but Rushavi managed. Ardu gave him instructions—a little to one side, a step closer to the wall, hold steady—and with a thunderous sound, Ardu struck the wall with the end of his tail.

The whole temple shook.

Rushavi lost his footing, dropping Ardu and falling himself. They both remained on the floor until the shaking subsided a few seconds later.

"Are you alright?"

Rushavi nodded, then noticed the red water on his shins where he had scraped them on the stones. He screamed once, pointing at the marks.

"It's alright!" Ardu crawled his way into Rushavi's lap. *"It's just blood. Just a little scrape. The bleeding will stop, and you'll be fine."*

Rushavi had never seen blood before. The marks on his legs hurt, but only a little.

"Trust me, Rushavi. You'll be just fine in a few minutes. Just take a deep breath."

Rushavi took a breath. Then another, this one deeper. The pain began to fade.

"Better?"

Rushavi nodded.

"Then let's keep going. The amulet is close, I can feel it."

Rushavi could feel it, too. That tugging feeling in the pit of his stomach was stronger than ever.

Both Rushavi and Ardu climbed into the newly formed door. On the other side, there was a small creature, no bigger than Rushavi himself, that held a pair of ropes in his thick stone fingers.

"A golem. He must be the one that opened the door for us."

Rushavi patted the golem on the head.

"He doesn't have much life left. He's been here for so long, waiting for someone to come and open this door. Once he dies, the temple will die with him."

Rushavi gave the golem another pat on the head.

They continued. The tunnel was small enough that Rushavi had to duck and walk with a slight bend in his knees. Ardu crawled along on his belly, keeping his wings tucked close to his body. He led the way through the darkness, his tail raised so Rushavi could keep a hand on the bulbous end.

Another tremble shook the temple, and Rushavi heard the sound of falling rocks.

"Syrani was upset with me for freezing my growth. But can you imagine me trying to fit through this place if I hadn't?" Ardu made a burbling sound that Rushavi had learned to accept as a kind of laugh from his companion. *"And how would you, a tiny little infant, manage to find your way through this temple to the amulet?"*

It wasn't possible, that much was obvious.

Ardu seemed surprised when they reached the end of the tunnel.

"It's blocked."

Rushavi was less surprised. He had heard rocks falling earlier, and there had been a few quakes since they had scrambled into the tunnel. If some had blocked their exit, then perhaps they would be better off waiting for the others to catch up and help them.

"Don't be silly, Rushavi." Ardu turned, giving Rushavi's head a gentle bump with his own. It was an affectionate gesture that Ardu had done for as long as Rushavi could remember.

Which, to be fair, was not all that long.

"I can break through this blockade in no time."

Ardu broke through about half of the blockade with a well-aimed strike from his tail. But more rocks immediately fell to fill the hole he had created.

"Oh. Perhaps this will not be as easy as I thought."

Rushavi sat, staring at the wall of stones that blocked their path. For a moment, he had seen light on the other side.

If Ardu struck the wall again, he might be able to slip through before the hole filled. After all, Ardu's scales were thick and tough. He could handle a bit of debris. But Rushavi would not be able to follow.

"I don't want to leave you behind!" Ardu cried. *"We'll find a way for both of us to through. Why don't you see if you can lift some of these rocks yourself? Maybe we can make a hole big enough for both of us."*

Rushavi tried to lift one of the larger stones, but it wouldn't budge. His arms were too weak, and even his fingers had trouble gripping the small deformities in the rock.

It was no use. He didn't have the strength.

Ardu would just need to go on without him.

Another tremble shook the temple. They were becoming stronger. The temple would fall soon.

Ardu argued with him, but Rushavi ignored him. If this amulet was as important as Ardu made it seem, then there was little point in wasting time arguing.

"Fine. Then you can sit here in the dark while I find the amulet."

Ardu seemed annoyed again, but no sooner had Rushavi made the observation than Ardu continued. *"I'll try to be quick about it, Rushavi. I'm sorry. I'm not angry. I just don't want to leave you here."*

Eventually, Ardu did leave the tunnel and continued.

So Rushavi waited in the dark for his companion to return. Or for the ones that had followed them into the temple to catch up, whichever came first.

He began to sob.

Light shone from the back of the tunnel after some time, and Rushavi thought he could hear voices. But the tunnel was dark, and the light was little more than a pinprick in the distance, so he paid it no mind at first.

He continued to sob, occasionally looking up to see that the light had grown larger. The voices grew more distinct, though he could not understand the words.

Finally, from the darkness, someone found him.

She spoke softly to him, but Rushavi still hadn't learned the language of his mother's friends. She wiped at his face and fussed over the scrapes on his leg. A small light floated around her head, and Rushavi watched it for a moment, his tears fading.

"Rushavi ... Ardu ..." the woman said to him. Her lips did not move, and Rushavi was sure there were many words he could not understand. But there was a sense of urgency, and Rushavi felt a wash of fear from her.

Rushavi pointed at the collapsed tunnel. The hole Ardu had made was long gone, but there were still hints of light through the gaps in the rock.

The woman said something aloud. Rushavi tilted his head.

"I understand," she said. She asked a question, but all Rushavi caught was *"... amulet?"*

Again, Rushavi pointed at the wall of stones. If Ardu had found the amulet, surely he would have returned by now …

The woman's companions joined after a few minutes. He recognized them, of course. The woman was the companion to Ardu's sister. The long-eared male that had learned how to speak to him was there. It was not as easy to understand him as it was to understand Ardu, but Rushavi was still able to have short and simple conversations with the male. And the three others that were only a little bigger than him were also present. They dressed like the adults and spoke in gruff voices that startled him, but their size made Rushavi wonder if they were still young like himself.

They argued, and one of the smaller ones grabbed Rushavi and shook him until the woman separated them. The shouts were loud, and even covering his ears did nothing to drown the noises out.

Someone touched Rushavi. Even though it was a gentle touch, he jerked away. Why did others insist on touching him? It was unpleasant.

The woman began moving stones. She was much stronger than Rushavi, and she carefully chose the stones to move before touching them. Rushavi watched as the hole she made began to grow.

When it was big enough, Rushavi dove through the hole after Ardu. He heard shouting, and the woman tried to grab his legs. But he kicked her hands off and continued.

He hit the ground palms first and managed a half roll, landing on his back. The room was much brighter than any of the others he had been in. Looking up at the ceiling, he could see why.

The ceiling was made from something hard and clear that did not block any of the sunlight. He could feel the heat of the outdoors on his skin and see clouds through the transparent roof.

Rushavi sat up. There were strange stones and columns in

the room. They weren't the red color of the stones he sat on, nor were they the golden brown of the sand much of the temple had been made from. The stones were a bright white, and many appeared to be broken.

But where was Ardu?

"I'm here, Rushavi!"

Rushavi turned in the direction Ardu's voice pulled him. Ardu was crouched behind a large column that had been overturned.

Rushavi wondered why his companion looked to have been hiding.

"There were people here. They were searching for something, so I hid from them."

Men, here? Looking for the amulet?

"Not the amulet. I found the amulet, though I haven't retrieved it yet." Ardu came closer, his tail dragging along the floor. *"They were looking for something else. They didn't see me, though."*

What else could have been here worth looking for? And how would someone else have found this room?

The floor shook again, the strongest tremor yet, and Rushavi lost his balance. Ardu scrambled towards him and curled into his lap until the shaking subsided.

"Are you alright?"

Rushavi nodded.

There was a sound behind him, and Rushavi turned to see the woman rising to her feet.

"What are you doing here?" Ardu asked.

Rushavi didn't understand her reply, but he could clearly sense her agitation.

Ardu turned and walked away before the woman even finished speaking. She raised her voice and followed him but stopped when she reached Rushavi's side.

She looked down at him and sighed. There was dirt on her face. She offered Rushavi a hand and helped him to his feet.

"... *amulet?*" she asked him.

Rushavi shrugged. He had no idea what she was trying to ask.

"*The amulet is over here, she-elf. But we don't need your help to get it. Rushavi and I are perfectly capable on our own.*"

Whatever the she-elf said to Ardu in reply was short and harsh. And Ardu did not answer.

Rushavi followed Ardu. The dragon led Rushavi towards a very strangely shaped rock with several gaps and jagged points. Rushavi stared at it for a moment.

"*You do realize what this is, don't you?*"

Rushavi did not.

"*This is a dragon's skull.*" Ardu stood up on his rear feet and pressed his front claws against the stone. "*And the amulet is inside the skull's mouth.*"

Rushavi looked from the skull to the surrounding skeleton, now understanding what he had been looking at. These were not stones, but bones. And the size of them suggested the creature had once been enormous. Larger than Ardu's sisters combined. Large enough that Rushavi struggled to comprehend the size it must have been while alive.

"*Do you see the amulet?*"

Rushavi looked between the teeth of the skull. There was a glimmer of amber amidst the white bone. He stood on his tiptoes, bracing his weight against a fang that was almost as wide as Rushavi was tall.

He could see the amulet.

Rushavi climbed over the lower jawbone, slipping between two teeth, and slid down into the mouth of the long-gone dragon. Ardu scrambled after him, his sharp claws finding purchase where Rushavi's fingertips could not.

Rushavi lifted the amulet to eye level, examining the stone. It was not the single color of amber, but flecked with greens and browns as well. And it was warm.

The temple shook again.

Rushavi fell to his buttocks, hitting his shoulder against some part of the skull. The pain made him cry out in surprise and shock and clutch at the spot that had been injured. He did not drop the amulet, though.

Ardu climbed into his lap again, and Rushavi instinctively wrapped both arms around Ardu as crashing sounds echoed around them.

He heard the woman shouting, but he still could not understand her.

A tooth dislodged from the jaw of the dragon's skull, and Rushavi screamed as it fell towards him.

HALCIA

Halcia had long grown tired of waiting for her companion to return. She was not the only one, judging by the way Suvusa paced and Grinor stared at the temple.

There was no door. Elori and dwarfs alike had searched for one, and all had returned with no luck.

"Syrani? Please answer."

There was a long pause before Syrani replied.

"We are fine, Halcia. Rushavi and Ardu elude us. We will find them."

"How long until you return?"

There was no answer.

"Syrani?"

Still no answer.

Suvusa stopped her pacing and knelt in the sand, sitting back on her heels to glare at the temple. "Here is Farnir's temple, after all these years, and my son is trapped within."

"He is not alone. He will be returned to you." Halcia sat as well, settling herself deep into the sand. The warmth of it was relaxing, and her claws sank nicely into the golden brown silt.

"Are you not angry that we are out here, away from our loved ones?" Suvusa asked.

Halcia huffed. *I am very angry. But what has been done cannot be undone. We must simply wait.*

They stared at the temple together. Grinor came to join them, his stout figure comically small next to Halcia. His head barely reached her shoulder as she stretched on the desert floor.

"Shame we can't find the entrance," Grinor said. His voice was thin and a bit shaky. Halcia wasn't sure if it was due to age or his fear of her.

They stared for a moment. The temple was grand in its own odd way. The constant movement of sand was mesmerizing, though Halcia found it difficult not to picture Syrani and her allies being slowly buried. The glass edges were brilliant in the high sun, and though the glass itself was dull and clouded, it reflected light wonderfully. The whole structure had an eerie way of tricking the eye into thinking it was alive.

Impossible.

"Did you say something?"

Halcia started, surprised Grinor had heard her thoughts.

But Suvusa answered his question instead. "Is there no other way inside?" Suvusa asked. "Surely such a large temple has another door?"

Grinor shook his head. "I've sent dwarfs searching, but they have yet to find anything."

"Anything?" Suvusa asked.

"There is too much sand. They've tried fighting through it, but it seems to continue endlessly."

"What about an entrance from above?" Suvusa asked. She looked pointedly at Halcia. "From the sky?"

Halcia rolled her eyes. *I searched, but I saw nothing.*

"Whatever entrance Rushavi and our allies used has vanished behind them, my lady," Grinor said.

"There is nothing to do but wait," Halcia repeated.

"My son is in there," Suvusa snapped. "And I do not trust Darmon with his safety."

"I doubt Darmon would harm the child." Halcia stood, stretching her hind legs. She was quickly growing tired of the conversation.

"Have you paid no attention to the way he stares at Rushavi?" Suvusa asked.

"No," Halcia snapped. She bared her teeth. "I've been too busy accepting silly gifts from your people to do much sightseeing."

Suvusa also stood, her hands planted firmly on her hips. "We have treated you as one of the Old Gods. You've been revered and loved!"

"I am not one of the Old Gods," Halcia growled, the sound low enough to make her chest hum. "I only want to be left alone."

A crowd was gathering. Halcia spotted Hiruscu amidst several dwarfs and Elori. He approached slowly, and Halcia noted many of the onlookers had a frightened look to their eyes.

Good, let them fear me. Perhaps I can finally get the peace I wish for.

Suvusa lifted her chin. "I am sorry we have angered you. No one will approach you again."

"Good."

"Ladies, please." Grinor raised placating hands. It looked ridiculous. "Suvusa, while Halcia may have not noticed the stares from Darmon, I assure you that others have. Darmon cares only for the amulet. No harm will come to Rushavi. Nunor and Alain will see to it. And the elves with him will protect Rushavi as well."

"Suvusa." Hiruscu put an arm around his wife and spoke to her in rapid Elori.

"Halcia insists that nothing can be done but to wait," Suvusa answered in Azimarian. She was glaring at Halcia.

Halcia glared back, narrowing her eyes.

"Wait?" Hiruscu asked. "For what?"

"For the door to reopen, if I had to guess." Tathiel wove his way through the gathered Elori and dwarfs. "I've found where the door *should* be, but it's closed."

Suvusa turned to Tathiel, though she did not leave her husband's embrace. "Can we open it?" Suvusa asked. "Please, I can't leave Rushavi in there."

Tathiel shook his head. "I don't see how."

Suvusa addressed Halcia again. "You said before that you asked the temple to open, and it did. You may not think you are an Old God, but the Old Gods listen to you."

Halcia snorted. Suvusa blinked at the blast of warm air that hit her in the face.

Suvusa continued. "Can you ask for it to be opened again?"

Halcia once more sat back on her haunches. *"I have tried."*

Suvusa's shoulders slumped. "Then there really is nothing to be done. We must simply wait."

Halcia fought the urge to tell Suvusa that it was just as she had already said many times. Instead she dipped her head apologetically. *"Rushavi will be alright. Syrani will see to it."*

"You are right, of course." Suvusa nodded. "I must be content that I have seen Farnir's temple. After all these years—"

The ground shook suddenly. Dwarfs and Elori alike lost their balance. Halcia managed to maintain her balance, but she was one of only a few that did.

"What was that?" Grinor asked, taking Tathiel's hand and letting him pull him to his feet.

"Halcia?" Tathiel was looking at the temple, though Grinor's forearm was clasped in his hand. "Do you feel that?"

There was a deep ache in the pit of her stomach, and a gentle tugging pulled her towards the temple. Emotions that were not her own surged through her. Some were fleeting, such as fear and anger. Others lasted the length of Halcia's panicked heartbeat. The most lingering was that of bitter-sweet regret. *"Yes, I feel it."*

I feel it all, Farnir. And I am so sorry for you.

"What, what is it?" Suvusa asked. She had landed entangled with Hiruscu, and both had managed to find their knees. Hiruscu was getting to his feet, his hands cupping Suvusa's elbows.

"It's going to collapse," Tathiel said. "Farnir's temple has served its purpose, and the magic holding it together is unwinding."

"No, that can't happen," Suvusa said. "Not while Rushavi is still inside!" Suvusa grabbed a dwarf by the shoulder and pointed at the temple. "Dig! Dig it out!"

The dwarf looked to Grinor, who seemed too bewildered to speak.

Suvusa spoke in the Elori tongue, gesturing to the temple. She pushed Hiruscu forward, then pulled herself to her feet. "Go, get Rushavi."

Hiruscu and several of the Elori ran towards the temple. They fell to their knees and began to claw at the sand with their bare hands.

"Suvusa, stop," Tathiel said. "You won't be able to do anything to help."

A dwarf stomped his way past Tathiel and began to dig as well.

Grinor called after the dwarf. "Stop, you shouldn't do that. It might make the temple fall faster."

"We were ordered to make sure Darmon leaves the temple alive if at all possible," a second dwarf said. He joined the first, as did several others.

"*This is ridiculous,*" Halcia said. "*Grinor is right. You'll just make things worse.*"

"How can it be worse?" Suvusa asked. "My son and your companion are trapped in a sinking tower built of sand."

"Suvusa, please," Tathiel pleaded. "Tell them to stop. We can find another way to get them out."

The ground shook again, and the sinking sensation in Halcia's stomach doubled.

"*There's no point in trying to reason with them, Tathiel. They are too afraid.*"

Halcia took in a deep breath and released it in a roar. She had never before made such a sound, and it shook her entire chest and burned her throat nearly as much as her fire did.

Several of the Elori screamed. Many more of the dwarfs drew weapons and faced her.

"*You would dare face me?*" Halcia laughed. "*The whole lot of you could fit in my stomach, armor and all, and I would have room for dessert.*"

"Suvusa, tell the Elori to step away," Tathiel said. He stood between her and Halcia, his arms opened wide. "They will do more harm than good."

Suvusa shook her head. "No."

"Hiruscu," Tathiel glanced over his shoulder at the dark-skinned Elori. "Tell them to back off."

Hiruscu spoke to the Elori in front of the temple, and they all began to slowly step away from the structure.

The ground shook again.

Halcia addressed the dwarfs. "*The temple will fall soon. There is nothing that can be done to stop it. Anything you do now will only make it worse. But those trapped within will need your help to unbury themselves once the sand has fallen.*" Halcia widened the snarl that bared her teeth. "*Would you prefer to be out here, ready to help them? Or would you like to take your chances against my teeth?*"

The dwarfs slowly sheathed weapons and backed away.

Syrani's voice suddenly came to Halcia. *"I found Rushavi and Ardu. The temple is crumbling."*

Halcia did not answer Syrani.

Instead, she turned to Suvusa. *"Now. As I said before. We must wait."*

33

TIRYN

Tiryn's arm did not hurt. Not enough to bother him, anyway.

No, what bothered him far more than his broken arm was the constant bickering between Nunor and Darmon. Dwarfen tempers were notorious for being short and mighty, much like the dwarfs themselves, but Darmon's anger was like none that Tiryn had ever seen before.

"I can't believe you got us into this mess, you nameless ass."

Nunor rounded on his cousin, leaning over Alain to shout back, "And how did I cause this, you fuckwit?"

Darmon also leaned over Alain, pinning the poor woman against the tunnel wall to scream at Nunor. "*You* joined this elven bastard on his insane quest. *You* convinced my father to hole our people up in Doldural like pigs in a pen awaiting slaughter. *You* insisted on finding the boy, rather than hunt for the amulet without him. And *you* have refused my aid on every step of this journey." Darmon pushed Nunor squarely in the chest. Nunor hardly budged. "And when we die in this dark pit, it will be *your* fault."

Nunor pushed Darmon, offsetting his balance but not

329

quite knocking him over. "If you hadn't been such an insufferable monster and actually tried helping, maybe Rushavi would have trusted us all enough not to go running off on his own, and we'd have the amulet already."

"Fuck off, Halfhelm!" Darmon dove over Alain, tackling Nunor.

"Gentlemen, please," Tiryn said. "Not while we're stuck in such a small space."

The two dwarfs ignored him, choosing violence over diplomacy. Tiryn could hear fists striking flesh as the two rolled around in the cramped quarters the tunnel afforded them.

Alain growled and grabbed whichever of the two dwarfs happened to be on top and tore him off his cousin. She managed to not only pull the two apart, but gave Tiryn enough room to put a barrier up between Darmon and the others.

"Are you two quite finished being a pair of utter jackasses?" Alain asked. "I am sick and tired of watching you act like a couple of idiots."

"We're stuck here, whether we like it or not, until either Syrani returns and can help us dig our way out of this tunnel, or until the whole temple falls around our ears and crushes us to death." Tiryn stared at a long crack that his witch light illuminated. It was wider than it had been a moment ago. He doubted the dwarfs noticed it at all. Tiryn tried to keep his voice calm and level, but he wasn't sure any of the others cared much. "I would prefer if we spent that time remaining civil and clearheaded."

Darmon had his back to the blocked tunnel exit. He punched the arcane barrier, and it reverberated with a hollow sound. "Let me out, you long-eared fuck."

Tiryn shook his head. "No."

"Alain, make this cunt drop this damned barrier."

Alain hesitated before answering. "I'm sorry, but I won't do anything of the sort."

Darmon sneered at her. "So you'd let my nameless cousin steal the amulet from us and con my father into giving him the crown?"

"I don't want the damned crown, Darmon!" Nunor shouted. He took a breath, then continued. "I just want a better name. I want to save my people from needless war. And if I have to take the crown to stop our people from spilling their blood for no reason, then so be it."

"So you admit that you would take the crown?" Darmon asked.

Nunor sighed. "Damn you, Darmon. I meant—"

"Fine." Darmon balled both fists together and brought them down on the tunnel's blockade. The tunnel shuddered, and small pebbles rained onto Tiryn's head. "You can take the crown when I'm dead."

"Darmon, stop!"

Tiryn wasn't sure who had shouted, him or Nunor.

Darmon brought his fist down again, and a couple of large rocks tumbled to his feet.

"When they find the amulet, perhaps they'll find our bodies as well." Darmon struck again.

Tiryn dropped the arcane barrier, and Nunor grabbed his cousin and pinned his arms behind his back. Alain was frozen where she sat, staring at Darmon.

Darmon shook Nunor off him. "Perhaps then my father will realize he should have listened to me."

Darmon struck the blockade once more, but it wasn't truly necessary. The sound of grinding stone drowned out any curses or shouts they may have made amongst themselves. The tunnel was collapsing, and Tiryn hardly had enough time to cast another barrier before everything went dark around them.

For the second time in only a few minutes, Tiryn was very pleased to realize that he was not dead.

There was brightness all around him, and he could hear shouting and some wailing cries.

It wasn't until he cautiously lifted his head and the sun immediately warmed his slightly burned skin that Tiryn realized they were no longer inside the temple. Sand and small rocks rolled down his back as he slowly surveyed their surroundings.

The temple was gone. The only sign it had been there at all was the large depression in the desert sand that he and his dwarfen companions were huddled in.

"Nunor?" Tiryn asked. "Are you alright?"

"You've done it again, you crazy elf." Nunor grumbled from somewhere under Tiryn's chest. "Please get off me, I think I'm crushing Alain again."

Darmon, unlike Alain and Nunor, was not pinned beneath Tiryn's body. Darmon had been too far away for Tiryn to pull him to safety, and Tiryn had been unsure if he could make a barrier large enough to enclose them all.

Miraculously, Tiryn's barrier had stretched enough to keep Darmon from harm.

Darmon seemed more surprised by it than Tiryn was.

"You saved me. Again." Darmon shook sand from his beard and rose to his feet. "Fucking elves."

Syrani.

Tiryn stood, using his good arm for leverage as he got to his feet. "Syrani?"

He spotted her location in an instant. There were perhaps half a dozen Elori around them, and they worked together to lift large white bones that looked startlingly like giant dragon's teeth off their bodies. Tathiel and Halcia were nearby. Halcia seemed unsure if she should approach, and Tathiel stood aside to let Elori and dwarfs alike rush to assist those buried in debris.

"Nunor, come help." Tiryn ran to where the Elori were shouting and pointing and dragging stones and bones away. He shoved aside a man who was struggling to lift a splintered jawbone. He lifted it with one hand and dragged it away several feet.

Beneath it, covered in a layer of dust, Syrani was curled around Rushavi. Her arms were covering the boy's head and one leg was draped over his side to protect his internal organs. She was bleeding from cuts on her arms and legs and her head.

"Syrani?"

Syrani stirred, lifting an arm so Rushavi could sit up. "We're fine, Tiryn."

When Rushavi sat up, his eyes blinking, he was holding Ardu tightly to his chest.

"Oh, thank the Great Ones." Rushavi's mother, Suvusa, pushed her way past several Elori and fell to her knees in front of Rushavi. "My little boy …"

Suvusa continued in the rapid tongue of the Elori, eventually lifting Rushavi into her arms and cradling both him and Ardu. She grabbed Syrani's arm. "Thank you. Thank you for keeping my boy safe."

Syrani muttered a reply.

Tiryn's arm ached. He held it close to his body. "Dare I ask about the amulet?"

At his question, Rushavi looked up at Tiryn. He held out a fist, palm up. When he opened it, there was a small yellow-brown stone in his hand.

Tiryn nodded, then squatted until he was eye level with Rushavi. He closed Rushavi's hand back around the amulet.

"Can you hold on to that? Can you keep it safe?"

Rushavi nodded.

34
ARELLA

"Please just stay in there a little longer. I know you want to come out, but we can't leave yet. We're still waiting on people to come help us."

"Arella, please," her grandmother called from the kitchen table. "It's too early in the morning for you to be whispering to that egg."

Arella returned the white dragon's egg to its spot on the mantle, and it twitched dangerously before stilling.

"Come on, have some breakfast with us." Ishta motioned towards the empty spot on the bench beside her. "I don't smell that bad, do I?"

Arella wrinkled her nose. "You could use a bath."

Ishta laughed, but her grandmother chastised her. "Arella, don't be rude. Now come and eat."

"It's too early for breakfast. The sun won't wake for hours." She sat begrudgingly, took a bit of cold sausage from the table and bit it in half. "Why are we up this early, anyway?"

"Don't speak when you have food in your mouth. It's impolite."

Arella swallowed. "It's impolite to keep me from my bed without telling me why."

"My nephew will be coming soon. He sent a messenger to tell us they were only a few miles away." Roland bit into a boiled egg, giving Layle an apologetic look when the soft yolk dribbled onto the table.

Arella suckled on the other half of her sausage. "Is the messenger already gone?"

"No, it's right up there." Ishta pointed up into the rafters of the kitchen.

Arella followed where she indicated, but there was only a very large crow standing silently atop a beam.

"A bird?" Arella looked from the crow to Roland. "Are you sure that your nephew sent a bird?"

"Quite sure. Alastor is fond of his little messengers."

Arella stood, walking to stand where she could see the crow better. It followed her as she moved, its head tilting this way and that. "Did he train it or something?"

"No, he *makes* them," Ishta said. "And then, when the magic keeping them together fades, they just turn into dust. I've seen it."

Arella gave the bird a hard look. "But it looks so real."

"It is real. Until it's not," her grandmother said. "Magic is very strange."

"Do you think he would teach me how to make birds from magic?" Arella asked, turning to Roland.

Roland looked to Arella's grandmother before answering. "I'm not sure. It would take time to learn how to do it. And I'm not sure how Layle would feel about you learning arcane arts."

Arella pouted. Her grandmother would never let her learn magic. "Just because grandmother can't do magic doesn't mean I'm not permitted to, either!"

"Arella!" her grandmother snapped. "Keep your tone in check, young lady."

Arella crossed her arms over her chest. She was so tired, and her face was hot and her eyes stung with the threat of tears.

"Hey, there, princess." Ishta stood, pushing Roland slightly as she came around the table towards her. "How about you and I go outside and see if we can catch some fireflies before the sun comes up, hm?"

"I don't want to," Arella said softly. She liked the way Ishta had called her princess, though she suspected it was out of habit. "I don't like fireflies."

"Oh, that's a shame. Because I love fireflies." Ishta opened the door, letting in fresh air from the outdoors. "And we don't have them any more in Etritia." She held the door open. Arella could already see small winking yellow-green lights. "Are you sure you won't come with me?"

Arella followed Ishta out of the house, shutting the door behind her. But she sat at the edge of the garden, watching as Ishta chased the twinkling lights and tried to catch them.

Ishta was not doing well, and with every failed attempt to cup the small insects in her palms, Arella had to stifle a snort.

"I hear you giggling back there," Ishta called over her shoulder. "If you think you can do better, then come show me."

Arella stood and joined Ishta. "You have to be slower, or they just fly away."

"Ah, of course." Ishta pointed at a light that blinked a few feet away. "There's one!"

Arella tracked the small black insect, holding her hands open and ready. "I can get it."

"Don't let him get away, now."

"I won't." Arella stepped slowly towards it, waiting patiently as it floated slightly out of her reach. "Come back down, I won't hurt you."

The insect blinked again, as if responding to her request, then drifted further away. Arella followed, reaching her cupped hands up. This continued for a few moments, with Ishta shouting words of encouragement after her. Finally, the firefly dropped low enough that Arella could bring her hands together to enclose it.

"I got it!" Arella turned and hurried back to Ishta. Almost immediately, she felt the tiny legs of the bug touching her skin and its wings beating against her fingers. "Ew, it's touching me." Arella opened her hands and let the firefly escape.

Ishta held out her own hands, which were also cupped together. "Come look, Arella."

"Oh, did you catch one too?"

"I did." Ishta bent over so Arella could look through a small gap in her thumbs. "Take a look."

Arella did and counted more than five little glowing lamps in her hands. She gasped and gave Ishta a glare. "You can catch them just fine without me."

"Yes, but you feel better now, don't you?"

Arella groaned and flopped onto the grass. "No. I'm still mad." She yawned. "And tired."

"Come on, now." Ishta opened her hands and shook the fireflies free. "You've been waiting for this morning for weeks. Try to be a little excited."

Arella frowned. "I am excited. But ..."

Ishta sat beside her on the grass. "Yes?"

Arella lay back, staring up at the night sky. There were so many tiny pinpricks of white across the inky blackness, and she wondered if she could count all of the stars that hung above her. "I'm scared, Ishta."

"So am I." Ishta lay beside her, and she briefly touched her forehead to Arella's temple. "But we have to hope that everything will be alright."

Arella thought of the visions of snow-covered lands she did not recognize, and of the body lying in a pool of red. "What if it isn't?"

"Then we continue anyway. Because we're doing this for the whole world. Not for ourselves."

"And if someone we care about dies?"

Ishta turned onto her side, propping her head up on her hand. "People die every day under Mothlenor's rule. Needless deaths, painful deaths. People that I care about have suffered and died." She lay back down with a sigh. "The world is bigger than one person, Arella. Even if it's someone you care about. You have to keep going."

"It sounds … sad."

"It is. It's sad, and painful, and it feels like every day you're being stabbed right in the chest. But you have to keep going. Because there are others that you care about, and they are still suffering and dying. And because you can put a stop to it."

Arella chewed her lip. "Would you feel the same way if it was the queen that died?"

Ishta was silent for a long moment. "Yes."

Arella suspected she was lying, but said nothing.

Ishta pointed above them. "Do you see that bright star up there?"

Arella searched for the brightest star she could. It was easy to find and was twice as large and as bright as its neighbors. "Mm hm."

"Do you see how the surrounding ones make a kind of pattern around it? Like an inverted triangle?"

Arella squinted. "It's not a very good triangle."

Ishta snorted. "No, I suppose it's not." Ishta tucked her hands behind her head. Arella did the same. It stretched her back and shoulders nicely.

Ishta continued. "That's the Shield of Azimar. My mother told me about it when I was a child. If you make a wish on it every night, it's supposed to bring you good luck."

"What's the bright star supposed to be? It's not a part of the Shield."

"It's just the marker for it. An easy way to find the Shield of Azimar."

"Oh."

Ishta rolled over again, smiling. "You want to try it?"

"Wishing on the Shield?"

"Why not?"

Arella nodded. "Alright."

Ishta nodded and rolled onto her back once more. "Alright, close your eyes and make a wish."

Arella closed her eyes. "I wish—"

"No, not out loud!" Ishta interrupted. "You have to keep the wish to yourself."

Arella started again.

I wish that everyone searching for the amulets lives, and that the vision I saw never happens.

Arella opened her eyes, realizing she could hear horse hooves on the path up to the house.

"They're finally here," Ishta said, sitting up. "Did you make your wish?"

Arella sat up as well. "I did."

Two figures on horseback approached up the hill. Ishta stood and helped Arella to her feet.

"Good morning!" one of the horse riders called. "We're looking for the local healer woman. Is this her home?"

"It depends," Ishta answered. "Who has come calling at such a ridiculous hour?"

"The hour is ridiculous, but my presence is expected."

"Alastor, then, I presume?" Ishta asked.

The rider dismounted from his horse. "Ah, so Layle sent a couple of young ladies to greet us!"

Ishta put a hand on Arella's shoulder. It was warm and weighty and comforting. "This is Layle's granddaughter."

"And you are?"

"Not interested." Ishta snorted. "Your uncle already

warned me about you, so I thought I'd save you the effort and let you know I prefer women over men."

The other rider laughed, and Arella realized the figure under the hooded cloak was female. She also jumped down from her horse's saddle and led it closer. "Stopped before you could even get started, Alastor."

"You're the woman in the message Roland received," Ishta said.

The woman pulled her hood back, and Arella gasped in surprise. The female rider lifted an angular brow. "Never seen someone like me before, child?"

Arella could only shake her head.

The woman shrugged. "I am not surprised." To Ishta she said, "My name is Nieve. Would you let us enter, before we are seen?"

Ishta motioned towards the house. "Of course. You are expected, after all. Arella, would you mind following them while I take their horses to the stable?"

Arella nodded, then tilted her head. "Sir Plow won't want to share her stall."

Alastor laughed. "Sir Plow? That's a very good name for a farm horse. Did you come up with it?"

Arella nodded again. "I did. But she's not a horse. She's a donkey." She turned to Ishta again. "And she hates sharing her stall. Roland's horse is in the other stall."

"It'll be fine, Arella. Sir Plow can spend the rest of the night in her paddock." Ishta scratched each of the horses under the chin, and one nickered quietly. "Come on, sweet things. I bet you could use some rest."

"The horses have been on the road together for a few weeks now. A few nights in a stall together won't bother them," Nieve said. She passed the reins of her horse to Ishta, and Alastor did the same. "Now, I would love to hear the story of how you came up with the name Sir Plow for a female donkey. Will you tell me?"

"Yes," Arella said slowly, staring at Nieve and her long ears. "But grandmother says it is rude to leave guests outside. So we have to go inside first."

"Of course. Would you lead the way?"

Arella lifted her chin and turned on her heel. "Follow me!" She made her steps long and purposeful, and she could hear the crunch of grass and leaves as both Alastor and Nieve followed her. There were still fireflies out, but the sky was not quite as dark as it had been when Arella was first awoken, and the path to the house was short and easy.

But she was not recalling the story of how Sir Plow got her name. Arella was instead recalling the dreams that had woken her almost every night for several days now. And of the body that lay in the snow, covered in blood. The body that had long ears like the elf Nieve.

Roland and her grandmother were deep in conversation when Arella opened the door to the house. Their heads both snapped up at the sound, and Roland stood as the three of them entered.

"I found our guests, grandmother. May I go back to bed now?"

"You don't want to stay awake and hear about their journey to us?" Roland asked.

Alastor shook his head. "It's probably best she doesn't, actually."

Arella's grandmother was staring at Nieve, who stood with her head slightly down. "You didn't tell me there would be an elf with your nephew, Roland."

"Alastor was coming from an elven village. And was bringing someone." Roland snorted. "I thought it would be clear he would be traveling with an elf."

"Foolish of me to think that you would not bring more danger to my doorstep."

"Grandmother," Arella snapped. Layle finally looked at

her, and Arella was surprised to see anger in her eyes. It faded quickly. "May I go back to bed?"

"Yes, if you want. I'll prepare a proper breakfast in a few hours. Something with eggs, since you and Ishta have been working so hard lately. I'll come wake you."

Arella murmured her thanks and made for the bedroom. She hesitated as she passed the mantle and turned back. Roland and her grandmother were arguing in low voices, and Nieve replaced the hood on her cloak and stood close to the door. Alastor was the only one who seemed comfortable at all, and he grabbed two links of sausage from the platter still on the table and bit both clean in half before helping himself to a seat and a bit of bread.

Nieve turned her back on Roland and Layle, her eyes catching sight of Arella right away. Arella smiled. Nieve returned the smile, though her face was faintly red.

Then Arella stood on her tiptoes, grabbed the dragon's egg from the mantle, and fled for the bedroom.

She carried the egg against her chest, both arms wrapped tightly around it. It was difficult to get into the bed she and her grandmother shared without using her hands, but she managed it. Once she was seated comfortably, with the egg in her lap and the covers over her head and draped down her back, she spoke to the egg again.

"Now. Now you can come out. I need your help."

There was a faint cracking sound and the softest burbling trill from the egg.

"Finally. I thought you would never let me hatch."

35

JASK

J ask tightened the drawstring on his bag, leaving it on the bed he had slept in for some ten years. He'd shared a room with two other brothers before that, but this had been his room, his bed, ever since he had been chosen to serve as the Archivist's personal aid.

And now I plan to leave, he thought.

Not for long. Just a year, perhaps two.

I'll return.

He left his packed belongings and went to meet the Archivist.

She was sitting where she always did, on a wide plush chair stacked with pillows behind a grand and very empty desk.

When he was younger, Jask would often see pages upon pages on the desk. There had been star charts and maps and even a handheld telescope. Now there was only ever one book and a constantly moving pen.

"You're late. I sent for you some time ago."

"I'm sorry. I was arranging the items we collected from the temple," Jask said.

The Archivist looked at him with steady eyes. One was a

345

pleasant hazel. The other was white with flecks of countless other colors.

He had read descriptions of the man called Ferrand and his empty eye socket and the black, dead void within.

The Archivist's Seeing eye was the opposite—alive and bright and sparkling.

And it unnerved him just the same.

"I know what you were doing," the Archivist said.

Jask did not answer.

"Why did you not leave that task to your brothers?" she asked.

"It seemed too important."

The Archivist smiled. "I love that about you, very much. You can't leave others to do the important work alone."

Jask shifted his weight. "Did you want to see them?"

The Archivist scoffed. "After all these years? Of course I do. But first …"

"Yes?" Jask asked.

"You were seen, Jask."

Jask shook his head. "I looked. There was no one in that part of the temple."

"You were seen by the hatchling." The Archivist pointed at the opened book on her desk. "Ardu."

Jask sighed. "I'm sorry."

The Archivist shrugged. "No matter. I doubt he will mention it to anyone other than his companion, and Rushavi will say nothing." She stood, holding out a hand for him to take. "Now, show me."

Jask took her hand, wrapping their arms together. They left the Archivist's quarters and continued through the keep. "Do you think they will be safe here?"

She shrugged again. "Not as safe as they were in Farnir's temple, but safe all the same." She patted Jask on the arm. "Speaking of which, did you return my gem?"

"I did," Jask lied. "It's right where you said to leave it."

"Good." The Archivist nodded. "None can enter or leave the Archives without Onia's Heart."

"I know," Jask said. He pointed at a nearby door. "I put them in here. Close enough that you can come see them without my aid."

"How thoughtful," the Archivist said with a chuckle. "Do you anticipate me visiting them at all hours of the day and night?"

Jask laughed. "I wanted to leave you with the option."

Jask opened the door and was pleased by the gasp from the Archivist.

The room had been furnished with every shelf, table, and bookcase that could be spared. Plus many that had been in good use before being moved. Every surface had been covered by blankets or spare shirts and pillows. Jask had even donated his own bedding, since he would not be using it for some time.

And adorning every surface, nestled on pillows and swaddled in linens, were innumerable dragon eggs.

They were in more colors and shades than Jask had thought possible. He had attempted to sort them by color as they were brought in from Farnir's temple, but he had abandoned the idea quickly. Even the shapes and sizes were not uniform. Some were longer than they were wide, others squat and fat with an oblong top.

The Archivist lifted a perfectly round egg about the size of an orange and the shade of hyacinth blooms. "They're all here."

"Are you pleased, Archivist?"

The Archivist smiled. "Here, in this room, with these young ones, I am not the Archivist." She returned the egg to its place, but her fingers remained on its surface. "I am the mother, and these are my children. You all are."

"Of course, Onia."

3 6

MOTHLENOR

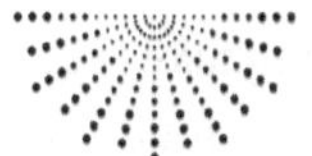

No more than an hour had passed since Mothlenor had sent Trissa to bed. Anna had even retired for the evening after joining him in the bedroom. His tower was quiet, the only sounds the scratching of his pen across parchment and the occasional sound from outside his broken window.

Mothlenor's strength had begun to return. He could feel the power of the arcane energy that flowed through him. It was not enough to summon Nevina's soul once more, but it was enough to perform the smaller talents he had grown to rely on.

Soon enough, he could send his wraiths out into Azimar to search for Ajax and his companions. He could finally cripple his brother's plans to collect the amulets. How many had Ajax found now? One, at least. In Vyris, at the top of that mountain. A second, maybe, a few years before. Ferrand had lost several men aboard a merchant ship. There had been two dragons there, much like there had been two dragons at the mountaintop.

Had more amulets been found that he did not know about? Were all four already collected?

349

No. Mothlenor dropped his pen. *There are still amulets out there to be found. I can feel it.*

On the tabletop, only inches from where his pen had rolled, sat the silver stand he had fashioned to hold his new dragon's eye. He had attached a small magnifying glass to it, so that he could see into the depths of the eye without straining his eyesight. It had been Trissa's idea, though she had actually suggested he make the dragon's eye larger, so she didn't have to squint so much while staring at it.

Trissa could be very bright, even without a tutor to guide her yet.

He pulled the stand closer and concentrated on the small gem it held. With only a small amount of effort, the stone lit up in an array of colors. He watched through the magnifying glass as the colors swirled for a moment before settling into muted tones of brown and cream and finally solidified into an image of Ajax.

He still looked as he had when Mothlenor last saw him in person. His red hair had not faded or become streaked with grey. There were no wrinkles in the corners of his eyes or around his mouth. None that he could see through the small stone, anyway.

He appeared to be talking to someone, and Mothlenor was surprised when the familiar form of Anna's lover appeared over Ajax's shoulder.

Mothlenor squinted, making sure the woman he saw was indeed Ishta. "What is she doing there?"

Already found allies, I see. I should have killed you when I had the chance.

She hadn't been outside the castle for very long, and yet she was already elbow to elbow with Areanath's conspirators.

Mothlenor raised an eyebrow, thinking.

How far could Ishta have gone in such a short time?

Not far, unless she happened to find a horse. And that

was unlikely so close to Etritia. All the horses had been taken from the surrounding farms years ago. Those that still owned horses were not likely to part with them for what little coin she may have saved while in the castle.

She could have gone to Vyris, perhaps. Or chanced upon someone desperate enough for money that they would sell her a steed. But Mothlenor did not think either possibility was likely.

Which means that Ajax and his companions might be closer than I thought.

A rough knock at the door pulled his thoughts away from the dragon's eye, which went dark before his eyes even left it.

"Enter."

Ferrand opened the door but did not come inside. "I thought you might like to hear some good news, my lord."

Mothlenor scrutinized Ferrand. There was something different about him. He had not been the same since his last trip north, though it had taken Mothlenor time to realize it. Ferrand's temper seemed shorter than ever, and rumors that he had murdered someone for minor offenses had reached his ears more than once.

"Yes? What is it?"

"We've captured one of Ajax's companions."

"Where are they now?" Mothlenor stood, pocketing the dragon's eye.

"In the dungeons." Ferrand smiled. The movement tugged grotesquely at the burned half of his face. "Shall I lead you to him?"

Mothlenor followed Ferrand down the curved stairs of the dungeons. They did not descend to the bottom level, but stopped at the second landing and entered the middle section of the castle's jails. Before they had been sealed off, this had been where thieves and rapists had been held, while the upper section mostly held drunks and brawlers for a few days at a time before they were released. The deepest section, where no light could be seen and where the rats had claimed most of the cells for their own, was where the murderers and other such dangerous men were kept until their death.

Now only Ferrand knew what system, if any, was used to sort those kept in the dungeon.

Ferrand guided him through the long halls of the dungeon. They did not carry a torch, and their eyes adjusted quickly to the dimness. There was light from oil lanterns hung on the walls every dozen or so steps. It was not near enough to see the far corners of the cells they passed, but he could see the faces of the men that pressed their cheeks to the bars and begged for freedom.

There were so many men. He did not recognize most of them.

"Where are all of these people from?"

"The Southern Cities, mostly. A few from places closer to Etritia. All captured for committing various crimes against the crown, my lord."

"Such as?" Mothlenor passed a cell that held a man and two children. They huddled together under a ragged blanket, and the father's eyes followed Mothlenor as he passed.

"Aiding elves or dwarfs, speaking out against your laws regarding non-humans …" Ferrand gestured towards the family of three. "Raiding Etritian supply caravans."

"They raided a caravan?" Mothlenor asked, surprised.

Ferrand nodded. "Used the boy to distract the guards while the girl and father tried to make off with a couple bags of apples."

"Apples?"

"They said they had been harvested from an orchard in their village, and we had no right to pick the trees clean. And that they would make sure everyone in the village got a share." Ferrand spat through the bars of the cell. "But theft is theft, and theft from the king's mouth is worse."

Ferrand continued walking. Mothlenor followed at a more sedate pace, scrutinizing the cells more carefully.

"And here, my lord, is one of Ajax's companions."

Mothlenor stopped in front of the cell and stared at the man within. He did not recognize him at first, but he looked familiar enough to give Mothlenor reason to pause.

"What is your name?" Mothlenor asked.

"Why don't you have your little fuck boy here tell you? He seems to know enough about me."

Mothlenor turned to Ferrand, who stared angrily at the man on the other side of the metal bars. "Ferrand? Where did you find this one?"

"Larten. He was the innkeeper there, before we burned the whole building to the ground. Goes by the name Mathius, but not too long ago he was the captain of the *Kingfisher*."

Mothlenor raised an eyebrow. "Interesting."

NUNOR

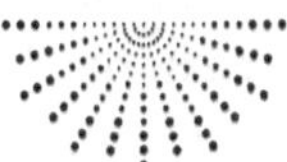

"So that is how the amulet was found?" Darlyth asked.

Nunor nodded. Across from him, Tiryn also nodded his agreement. Beside him, Alain was silent and did not move.

Darmon drew in a breath. "That … is not quite the whole story."

Nunor closed his eyes briefly.

Fuck you, Darmon, you slimy bastard.

Darlyth raised an eyebrow. "And what is the whole story?"

Darmon cleared his throat and leaned his forearms on the table of the king's council room. "Tiryn got just about all of it right, my king. Except …"

Darlyth's eyes narrowed onto Nunor. "Except?"

Nunor would have smashed his cousin's head right into the table if Darlyth weren't present.

"Except Tiryn made it sound as though the tunnel we were trapped in, and the whole temple structure, very conveniently collapsed while we were arguing." Darmon cleared his throat again. "What Tiryn failed to mention is that I happened to be punching the shit out of the tunnel at that moment, and that we're all pretty certain I caused the final collapse."

Tiryn gave Nunor a surprised look.

You and me both, friend.

Darlyth sat back in his chair. "I was aware of that already."

Darmon's shoulders relaxed. "You were?"

"Alain did not want to wait until the appointed time to discuss what had transpired in the desert. I was …" Darlyth paused, then let out a sigh. "I was about to say that I was unavailable to hear her interpretation of events, but I'll just come right out and say that I was very ill and couldn't see anyone. Not even my son, my favorite nephew, or even the spy I had sent to keep an eye on you, Darmon."

Alain's face went pale, and Nunor laughed.

"You send her to spy on me?" Darmon yelled. Then, surprisingly, he nodded. "I probably needed it, to be honest. I've been a prick."

"The biggest prick," Alain corrected. Her voice was a little shaky. "An absolutely massive prick, and I am so glad to be able to say so now, Darmon."

Darlyth laughed, and the sound was still strong enough to make the room echo. "Yes, I sent her with you to keep an eye on your actions and report them back to me. I thought you might do something stupid enough to get yourself killed, and when Grinor relayed what she had told him about your journey through the temple, I knew I'd made the right call."

"I'm sorry, Father. I just felt …"

"Lost?" Darlyth supplied. "Confused? Cheated?"

Darmon nodded. "All of that. And I got so angry that I almost killed us all."

"And an innocent child," Tiryn added.

"And a young dragon," Nunor said.

"And a very nice she-elf," Alain said, crossing her arms over her chest. "I happen to like Syrani."

"Alright, yes, I almost killed a bunch of innocent people

because I'm a massive prick." Darmon looked pained. "And I'm sorry."

Darlyth leaned forward, resting against his forearms in much the same way his son did. "Darmon, you're my son. But you are a damned hot-headed mess. You are not meant for diplomacy. You're meant for fighting." Darlyth balled his hands into fists and pounded them on the table. "For battle, for war!" His hands eased open, and he shrugged. "And I hope against hope that you are unneeded."

Darmon nodded. "So you'll make Nunor king." He turned to Nunor, and Nunor wasn't sure if he should prepare for an embrace or a punch to the jaw. "Cousin, all I ask is that you keep me here, where I can be used if I am needed."

"I'm not dead yet, Darmon." Darlyth laughed, but the laugh turned into a hacking cough. Darlyth chugged from a mug of ale and waited for the fit to subside. "As I was saying, I'm not dead yet. But Nunor has earned a new name. One that is unstained by the deeds of his forefathers and will allow him to be named king if I so choose." Darlyth held out his hand. "Now, the amulet, please."

Nunor's breath caught. "Ah, well—"

"You left it in the desert, didn't you?" Darlyth asked.

"We thought it best if it remained with the young child that found it. For the time being," Tiryn said.

"And the elf Syrani? Her dragon? They returned home?"

Tiryn cleared his throat and answered for Nunor. "Actually, they have decided to remain in Cai Myrh for the moment. To be close to both Rushavi and Ardu. And the amulet, of course."

Darlyth shrugged. "Fair enough. So long as we know the amulet is safe. And the child, of course. I don't need a pretty rock to change a name."

Nunor let out his breath.

"So, Nunor. Have you chosen a new name?"

"I think I have." Nunor nodded, rising to his feet. "I

choose the name Stormforged because it was through a sandstorm that my destiny was finally changed."

Darlyth laughed. "I like it."

He also stood and embraced Nunor. "I welcome you to my family, Nunor Stormforged."

THANK YOU FOR READING!

I hope you enjoyed *The Book of Earth*.
Please feel free to leave a review on your preferred
storefront.

Reviews help other readers like you find my work, and your
support means I can continue doing what I love: Writing.

As always, you can stay up to date on publishing news and
special offers by joining my newsletter at
JacklynHennionAuthor.com.

Thank you!
Jacklyn Hennion

ABOUT THE AUTHOR

Jacklyn Hennion is an avid lover of sweets and wine. She enjoys Netflix and video games, and often spends the evenings winding down with a bit of crochet work. She and her husband currently live in Oklahoma. *The Book of Death* is Jacklyn's first published novel.